the Maid of the White Hands

nonfiction

The Fiction of Sex

The Problem of Measure for Measure

Danger! Men at Work

Modest Proposals

Women and Power

The Female Form

The Women's History of the World

The Rites of Man

The Children We Deserve

Ben Jonson: His Life and Work

Ben Jonson: His Craft and Art

the Maid of the White Hands

The Second of the
Tristan and Isolde Novels

ROSALIND MILES

CROWN PUBLISHERS
NEW YORK

Published by Crown Publishers, New York, New York.
Member of the Crown Publishing Group, a division of Random House, Inc.
www.randomhouse.com

CROWN is a trademark and the Crown colophon is a registered trademark
of Random House, Inc.

Originally published in Great Britain by Simon & Schuster, London.

Printed in the United States of America

Map copyright © 2002 by Rodica Prato

Design by Lauren Dong

Library of Congress Cataloging-in-Publication Data
Miles, Rosalind.
The maid of the white hands : the second of the Tristan and Isolde novels /
Rosalind Miles.—1st ed.
1. Isolde (Legendary character)—Fiction. 2. Tristan (Legendary character)—Fiction.
3. Cornwall (England : County)—Fiction. 4. Knights and knighthood—Fiction.
5. Arthurian romances—Adaptations. 6. Adultery—Fiction. 7. Ireland—Fiction.
8. Queens—Fiction. I. Title.
PR6063.I319M35 2003
823'.914—dc21   2003003728

ISBN 0-609-60961-0

10 9 8 7 6 5 4 3 2 1

First American Edition

For the one walking in the Beyond,

Unforgettable,

A true Irish Queen

the family trees of cornwall, lyonesse, and pendragon

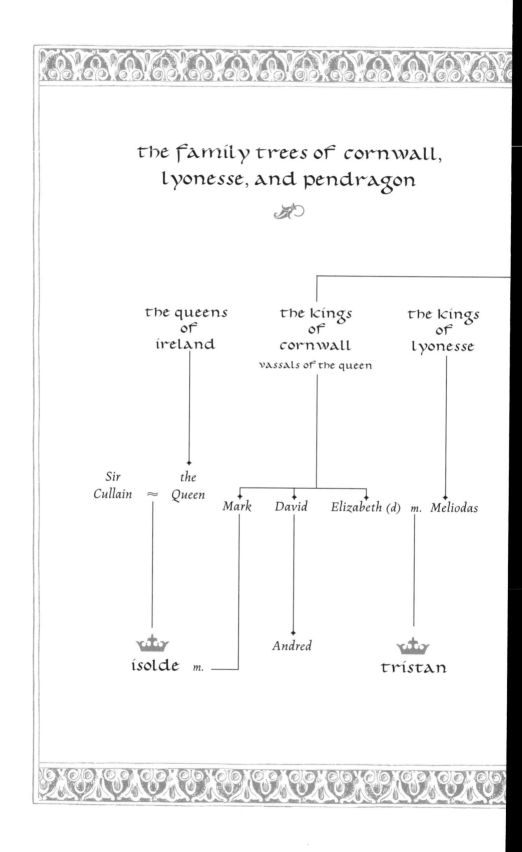

the queens
of
ireland

the kings
of
cornwall

vassals of the queen

the kings
of
lyonesse

Sir
Cullain ≈ the
Queen

Mark   David   Elizabeth (d)   m.   Meliodas

Andred

isolde   m.

tristan

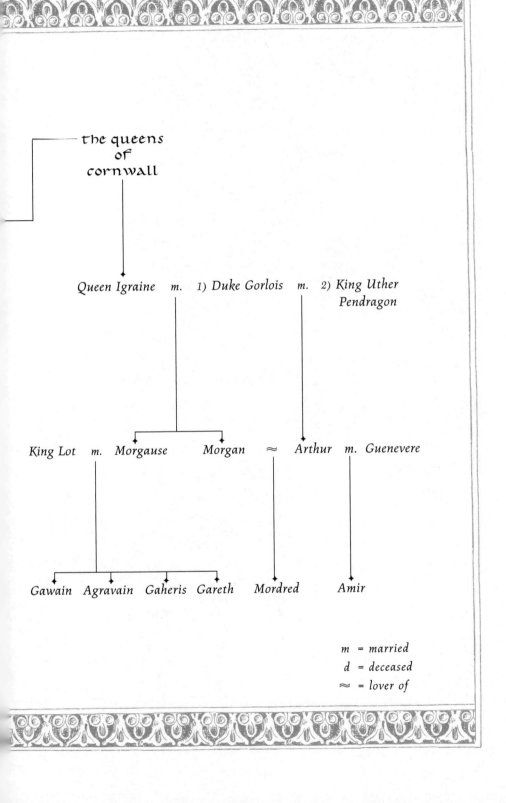

the queens
of
cornwall

Queen Igraine   m.   1) Duke Gorlois   m.   2) King Uther
Pendragon

King Lot   m.   Morgause   Morgan   ≈   Arthur   m.   Guenevere

Gawain   Agravain   Gaheris   Gareth   Mordred   Amir

m = married
d = deceased
≈ = lover of

Pictland

Lothian
Roman Wall

Terre
Foraine

Emain Macha

Listinoise

Druid's
Sacred
Grove

Dubh Lein

Gore

The Humberlands

Merlin's
Cave

Lindsay

The Island
of the West

Mercia

The Welshlands

The Middle
Kingdom

Caerleon

London

The Summer
Country

Avalon

Camelot

Tintagel

Castle
Pleure

Cornwall

Lyonesse

The Narrow Sea

Castle Dore

Forest
of Broceliande

Little Britain

the Maid
of the
White Hands

At the time of King Arthur and Queen Guenevere, there was a king called Meliodas, lord of the country of Lyonesse. He wedded the sister of King Mark of Cornwall, and thereafter he was unjustly cast into prison when his wife was great with child. Then the young Queen ran mad with grief into the wood and fell into her travail betimes. She bore a son after many grimly throes, and she called the boy's name Tristan, for her sorrows, and so she died.

Then Merlin brought Meliodas out of his prison, and the King married another queen, who ordained to poison Tristan so that her children should enjoy the land. But it happened that the Queen's own son drank the poison and fell down dead. Then the King drew his sword and said, "Tell me what drink this is, or I shall slay thee." And she fell to her knees and told him she would have slain Tristan.

So she was damned by the assent of the barons to be burned. And as she was brought to the fire, young Tristan knelt to his father and begged a boon.

"You shall have it," said the King.

"Give me the life of my stepmother," said Tristan.

"Take her, then," said the King, "and may God forgive her, if you can."

So Tristan went to the fire and saved her from her death. And thereafter the young Tristan went into France and became a knight great in all chivalry for his bigness and grace.

Then the Queen of Ireland made war on King Mark of Cornwall, and Sir Tristan rode to his uncle the King and took the battle on. And the Queen of Ireland had a daughter who was known for her beauty through all the world as La Belle Isolde. She was the most noted healer of all the isles, and despite the enmity between Ireland and Cornwall, she saved Sir Tristan when he suffered a deadly hurt.

So King Mark devised to wed a maiden of such praise, and swore his nephew Sir Tristan to win Isolde for him. And the Queen of Ireland ordained a drink of such virtue that the day La Belle Isolde should wed, she should drink it with King Mark and either should love the other all the days of their life. But on the sea voyage to Cornwall it chanced that Isolde drank from the flasket with Tristan, and thus happed the love which never departed them, neither for weal nor for woe...

—Morte D'Arthur

chapter 1

The worst of the winter storms lashed the Western Isle. Raging seas beat on the ancient citadel of Dubh Lein and the night-riding demons howled through the sky overhead. But in the Queen's Chamber the air was hushed and still.

One tall candle lit the figure on the bed. Her white silk shift gleamed in the torchlight shining from the walls, and on her hand she wore the ancient ring of Queens. Beneath the billowing blood-red canopy, the long elegant body and strong face were as beautiful as ever they had been in her life. But the skin had the pallor of oncoming death, and the long henna-colored hair streamed out on the pillows as if the sleeper had already been laid to rest in the quiet earth.

A low fire burned sadly on the hearth, and standing braziers warmed the far corners of the room. Moving to and fro on silent feet, the Queen's women fed the glowing coals with sweet herbs, rosemary, thyme, and rue. They took care not to disturb the tall, hawk-faced old man watching by the bed. Imposing as he was, after so many long hours and days he was part of the sickroom now.

Hovering by the door, the youngest of the maids wept and wrung her hands. "She should be in the infirmary. That's the place to die."

"Hush, child."

The chief attendant placed a comforting finger on the girl's trembling lips. "All the Queens of Ireland die in this bed. Her mother and her mother's mother went from here to the Otherworld. As Queen Isolde will, when her time comes."

Isolde . . .

A sudden gust of wind stirred the shadows in the room. Clustered around the walls, countless swan lamps flickered and danced, each tiny flame sheltered by upreared wings. The warm light played over the crimson hangings of the bed, the low gnarled ceiling, and the cream-washed walls, and lingered lovingly on the still watcher keeping his solitary vigil in the shining gloom.

"Young Queen Isolde?" The little maid's tearstained face lit with the memory of a merry laugh and a cloud of glowing hair. "She'll be coming back now, won't she? She'll be our next Queen?" Her eyes moved uncertainly to the still figure in the bed. "If...?"

"When the Queen dies, yes," said the older woman with soft certainty. "Ireland has always obeyed the Mother-right. The throne has passed from mother to daughter since time was born. Isolde will be Queen."

Fools! How could they be so sure?

The hooded figure standing beside the bed wrinkled his lips in a savage snarl. Didn't they hear the booted feet below, the clink of spurs, the rattling of swords? Didn't they know that the wolves were already gathering, drawn by the scent of blood? He looked down. Why, even the unconscious woman lying here knew that her knights and lords had come to carve up her kingdom before she had breathed her last.

And before her rightful heir could return to claim her throne. The old man gave another silent snarl. How many ages had the throne of the Western Isle passed down from mother to daughter in the line of Queens? Yet every rising generation was at the mercy of rapacious men. He raised his eyes to the ceiling in a furious prayer. *Hurry, Isolde, hurry, or you will come too late!*

IN THE CHAMBER BELOW, the young knight leaned back and looked around with a challenging stare.

"She's our next Queen, you say. Tell us then, Gilhan, why isn't she here?"

The knight at the head of the table smiled thinly and eyed the speaker as coldly as he dared. So Breccan was already questioning Isolde's right to the throne? This was going to be worse than he thought.

"Rest assured, Sir Breccan," he said with elaborate courtesy, "Queen Isolde will be with us soon."

"She's still in Camelot with the High King and Queen?"

Gilhan nodded. "Visiting on behalf of her husband, King Mark."

"But has she been sent for?" Breccan's hard gaze fastened on Gilhan. "Does she know that the old Queen's dying—that you're ready to make her our Queen?"

Gilhan felt a strong tremor of unease.

"Not yet," he replied calmly, schooling himself to ignore Breccan's predatory air and the equally hard-faced men seated on either side. Breccan's knights were already feared throughout Dubh Lein. No one would be surprised if their master seized the chance to advance himself and them.

"I'll send to her now." Breccan nodded to the tallest of his knights. "You'll go, Ravigel." He turned back to Gilhan. "He's the best man I've got."

"Not so, Sir Breccan," said Gilhan silkily. "I am Lord of the Council. I shall send word." Swiftly he reviewed the assembled company with growing doubt. Who could he count on? Who would support him here?

He did not need to look at the dark, brooding figure on his left, staring at Breccan as if he were a scorpion, to know that this man at least was loyal to the rule of Queens. Ireland had been the Sacred Island of the Druids as far back as any man could count. As Chief of the Druids in the Western Isle, Cormac would defend the Mother-right to the death.

But the Queen had rarely summoned Cormac to court. When she sought his mystical wisdom, she traveled to the Druids' secret grove, a world away. Gilhan suppressed a sigh. Cormac's life in the green heart of the forest, a living world of sweetness, faith, and trust, was a poor preparation for the false smiles and hidden knives at court.

Who else was there? Gilhan glanced around the long table with a sinking heart. The dying Queen had been a creature of fierce and fleeting passions, governed by her body's every whim. Too many of these men had been her lover, some for one night alone, and all of them discarded sooner or later for another man. Hardly the way, Gilhan reflected grimly, to secure their loyalty now.

And others, however faithful in the past, would run with the pack to greet the rising sun. Take Vaindor, thought Gilhan with dry disdain, watching an imposing older knight smiling with approval on Breccan and his band. It was a long time since Vaindor, one of the Queen's former champions, had played any significant role at the court of Dubh Lein. Breccan had only to flatter Vaindor's arrogance and the knight would be his for life. Others too could be easily influenced. Take old Doneal there, restlessly drumming his battle-scarred fingers on the table: if Breccan offered him the smell of blood and the excitement of a raid, he'd leap at the chance to swing a sword again.

Indeed, after the long, dull years of the Queen's decline, most of them would rally behind a leader who offered them war, when all the country wanted was peace. Gods above, Gilhan lamented inwardly, where are the men of strength and honor we used to have? Where are the older knights whom the Queen in her excesses drove away? Even one of them now would be worth his weight in gold—old Fideal, say, or any of her former champions, who in her younger days had loved her more than the world. But Fideal was one of many who had gone away from court, determined to seek a simpler way of life. Who was left? Gilhan forced himself to stifle his concern. Cormac the Druid might prove to be the only ally he had.

He turned on Breccan. "Why the unseemly haste?" he said sternly. "The Queen's soul is passing into the Beyond. We are here to honor the Mother-right and prepare for Isolde's return."

Breccan smiled at him, a white show of handsome teeth. "Are we so?"

Gilhan made his voice soft and dangerous. "Do you question that?"

"Never!" Breccan widened his eyes in an innocent stare. "But some think the Mother-right is a thing of the past. They say the Romans brought in the rightful rule of men when they tossed their troublesome women off the nearest rock."

Sir Doneal's old eyes lit with reminiscent fire. "Still, our warrior queens showed the Romans a thing or two. Great battles, eh?" He chuckled. "And thousands of dead Romans piled in heaps for the crows!"

"Old days, old ways," said Gilhan forcefully. "The Romans are long gone."

Breccan hid a teasing grin. Oh, how he loved tormenting these old fools! "But the Christians are here. And where Christians rule, the days of the Queens are done."

Gilhan's face darkened. "Is this the fate you foresee for our Queens?" He paused, weighing his words. "Where's your loyalty, sir?"

"What?" Breccan's hand flew to his sword. "You dare to question my loyalty, Gilhan? When my kin have been champions of the Throne since time began?" He gestured to the knight seated on his left. "When my own brother was the Queen's last chosen one?"

"Sir Tolen, yes."

Gilhan treated the slumped figure beside Breccan to a pitiless stare. Yes, Breccan came from the island's leading clan, a long line of men chosen to be royal champions and companions of the couch, all loyal, brave, and born with a flashing charm. As the last of many men favored by Ireland's Queens, Tolen had been an inevitable choice ten years ago, almost too handsome to be borne, gifted with raw sensuality and feral grace.

But the horizontal hours and self-indulgent years had taken their toll. How had this bloated, red-faced ruin of a man ever graced the Queen's bed? And how must Breccan resent his older brother's favored place with the Queen, when he, younger, fitter, faster, bolder, and hungrier, was forced to prowl the wilderness beyond the gates, barred from the enchanted place of love and power?

Tolen felt their gaze and stirred. "What?"

"It's nothing, Tolen. Nothing to do with you," snapped Breccan. "Now Gilhan, about the Queen . . ."

Gilhan sat very still. A fearful vision of the future unfolded before his eyes. He saw a world without the rule of Queens, where chosen ones like Tolen could be treated with contempt. Where Breccan and his kind showed that might was right, and lesser creatures struggled to survive. But what would he do with Isolde? Could Breccan be thinking of making himself the new Queen's champion and chosen one, her companion of bed and sword? By force if need be, if Isolde would not consent? And if she disdained his advances, could her days be numbered too?

Gilhan watched Breccan's brutal features rearrange themselves in a wide, honest smile.

"Come now, let's pull together," said Breccan easily. "No more hard words. You know you can trust me, Gilhan."

Gilhan nodded and returned the smile. On the contrary, sir, you've just told me why I can't.

THE WIND SWEPT around the castle and knocked on its windows and walls. On the shore below, the ebbing sea sang with a soft, withdrawing roar. Waiting in the shadow of the great bed, one of the Queen's women began a low lament.

At the still center of the chamber the long white figure on the bed stirred and opened her eyes. "Merlin?"

"Yes?"

"You hear the wind and the sea?"

Merlin leaned forward. "What else?"

"The Lady has sent her messengers to take me home. I shall leave on this tide."

The old enchanter felt his flesh stirring as it always did to the sound of her rich, husky voice.

"All life returns to the sea, where it began," he said somberly. "Your chosen one, Sir Tolen, is keeping a vigil below. He prays to see you once to kiss your hand."

She gave a soft laugh like an otter's bark. "My chosen one now is the Dark Lord, Penn Annwyn."

"You will not admit Sir Tolen?"

"Tell him I blessed him with my dying breath." The lovely head on the pillow moved to and fro. "Is Isolde here?"

"Not yet."

She shifted fretfully. "She cannot come in time."

"In time for what?"

A low, throaty chuckle came from the bed. "Don't play with me, old fox. You yourself could not get here from Cornwall before I go to join the Old Ones on their shining thrones."

Only the highest place for her in the world beyond the worlds, Merlin noted: always a queen. He suppressed a smile. "What is your word for Isolde when she comes?"

Darkness clouded her face. "Did I wrong her, Merlin? Should I have given up the throne and made her Queen?"

The old enchanter considered. "No," he said softly at last. "She never wanted to be Queen before you died."

The Queen's long white fingers fretted at the cover of the bed. "But I told her I would hand over the kingdom, years ago—give over the rule to her and withdraw—"

Merlin shook his head. "You are the Sovereignty, the spirit of the land. She knew it was not in your power to divorce yourself from that."

"My power, yesss—"

He felt the force of the Queen's burning stare.

"—which Isolde must have after me," she hissed, her eyes never leaving his face. "Swear to me, Merlin, you will—" She broke off and gasped for breath.

"I know what you would say," he said gently. "And I swear."

The Queen's fingers wandered over the coverlet to the ring on her left hand and drew it off.

"For Isolde," she commanded with a joyful smile. "And only for her."

Merlin took the great circle of emeralds and turned it in the light. Watching him, she saw its green flames dancing in his golden eyes, and seized his wrist.

"Swear you'll give it to her!" she rasped.

He threw her off. "I have sworn."

She gave a disbelieving laugh. "I know you, Merlin. Your only concern is to keep Pendragon safe. As long as your boy Arthur is High King, you'd be willing to keep Isolde out of her rightful place."

"I would indeed, when the stakes are as high as that," he agreed, glimmering. "Just as you would, my dear, if you were playing the same game."

"Ah, Merlin . . ."

She would try to win him over, he knew, and her powers of seduction were beyond compare. Already he felt his pulse quicken under her dark, lustrous stare.

"You were the best of my lovers," she said huskily. "But you know that."

Merlin laughed. "I know no such thing, only that you must have told all of them the same tale. Have no fear for Isolde, I shall not bar her way. My only desire is to keep these islands safe."

The Queen split the chamber with a raucous laugh. "You're lying already, old man." She chuckled, fighting for breath. "Well, what else did I expect?"

Merlin's eyes flared. "Lying?"

"You love Arthur, not some dream of peace. And Tristan, too, whether you admit it or not. All the world knows you see yourself in them. You've never forgotten what it was to be like them, fatherless and disowned. So you cherish them both, and watch over them to save them from suffering as you did. Lost boys, wounded men, all of you, all fatherless and disowned, all born to fight and struggle for your own."

She lay back exhausted. Merlin's smile emitted a sulfurous fire. "What of it?"

"Isolde was the greatest blessing of my clouded life. To me, she's been the living light in an unsteady world and the beautiful daughter I never dared dream I would have. But she's nothing to you. You'd sacrifice her in a second to save Arthur or Tristan."

Merlin watched the light fading in her eyes. "Then you must trust to the Great Ones that her fate lies with one of theirs."

Far off, the slow sad music of humanity began a dying fall. Merlin closed the heavy eyelids with a practiced hand. "And you will have to trust me, too, my dear."

chapter 2

"The Queen of Ireland's dying?"

"Maybe gone already, sir. She was sinking as I sailed, beyond recall."

"And no one there saw you come or go?"

There was a quiet laugh. "You know me, sir. You pay me to see and not be seen. Even the King doesn't know my face."

The knight tensed. "My uncle sees more than you think."

"Then Cornwall is blessed in you both, Sir Andred." The gray figure made an obsequious bow. "King Mark to hold a watch over state affairs, and yourself to be His Majesty's eyes and ears."

Had he offended the young knight? The speaker gave an inward shrug. All the world knew that the King lived to hunt, and left everything else in his clever nephew's hands. But no one would argue with that black-eyed stare.

Andred turned away. "You have done well. And you will be well paid. Stay near at hand, I shall need you again."

With a flick of his head, he dismissed the shadowy messenger, his mind aflame. The old Queen dying? Then Isolde would be Queen. That meant ruler of the Western Isle in her own right, as well as Queen of Cornwall as wife of King Mark. Queen twice over, then? He gave an angry laugh. That was too much. What would she do now?

He moved into the window and gazed out over the castle walls. Autumn was dying and winter was hard on its heels. The last yellow leaves haunted the woodland like ghosts, and the dark months ahead were massing on the horizon like storm clouds at sea. From its hilltop by the shore, Castle Dore commanded scenes of melancholy beauty all around. But Andred never let such thoughts cloud his mind. Let Druids and dream-weavers worship this rocky land with its wild coasts, deep forests, and sunlit meadows carpeted with flowers. Any fool knew that land was only power, if a man held it right.

But first he had to call the land his own. Mine. When will it be mine? Andred clenched his fists. Would he ever forgive the Gods for making him the King's nephew, not his son? And the son of a son too, so that Tristan as the son of a daughter stood before him in the Mother-right? Well, the Old Ones liked to joke. But the true man of destiny made sure that the laughter stuck in their throats.

As I shall, never fear.

With Elva.

With her love.

He scanned the sky for a sight of the watery sun. Noon: soon she would be here, and the chamber would be filled with courtiers gathering to welcome the King back from the hunt. Andred glanced around, intent as always on his uncle's good cheer. At either end of the long, low, white-washed hall, great fires leaped up the chimneys, scenting the air with apple, holly, and oak. The floors were bright with beeswax, and the blue and white banners of Cornwall hung from the walls. A flicker of comfort warmed Andred's cold heart. One day all this would be his.

And hers.

He turned his eyes to the door. She was coming, he could feel it, she was here. Attuned as they were to each other after so many years, he was not surprised to see the heavy black oak swing back as a woman surged into the room like a forest fire. Clad from head to foot in hissing silks, she burned with a hot, green flame, and his soul leaped to greet her across the echoing void: Elva, Elva, here I am, come to me . . .

Yet he could not look at her without pain. He knew she was his, this tall, glorious, mad-eyed woman, all sinew, skin, and bone. Forget her fool of a husband, as they had for years. From her lofty headdress with its billowing veils to her long white feet, she had thrown in her lot with his and given him her life and soul to command. He laughed inwardly. Let all the jealous ladies of the court condemn her for her never-varying green gowns. He loved to see her dressed in this scaly viridian, her long, lean body shimmering like a snake.

And with all this in his grasp, he had thrown it away? He bit back a furious groan. Whatever had possessed him, a few years back, to persuade Elva to make love to the King? He had seen himself leading her as she led the King by the nose, and the pair of them ruling Cornwall through Mark. It had never occurred to him that his uncle might turn to Elva and return her show of affection with all the ferocity of a stunted heart. Still less had he dreamed that she might love Mark, too.

And Mark above all men—that idle, selfish apology for a king...

Gods above, what a fool I was—what a fool...

He felt her long white arms winding around his neck, and turned to her blindly, hungry for her touch. They came together without words, as they always did, and he slaked his thirst on her mulberry mouth.

She pushed him away and tried to read his face. "What is it?"

He gripped her wrist. "Where's the King?"

"Back from the hunt. I heard the horns, and saw them all ride in." She stared at him. "What's happened?"

"Isolde is to be Queen of the Western Isle."

She caught her breath. "The old Queen's gone?"

"Dying, or dead. Isolde will succeed. Then she'll have all the power she wants."

He could see Elva's mind casting to and fro. "And the freedom to travel as she pleases—to stay in Ireland and forget Cornwall and Mark—"

"With her knight, of course," he said venomously. "Sir Tristan must go with her wherever she goes."

"Darkness and devils!" she swore. "We'll never catch them now."

"Never is too long a word to say."

Elva gave a bark of impatience. "We've been after them for years," she said furiously. "And all this time, they've been too much for us."

He shook his head. "Sooner or later they must betray themselves. With every day that passes, their luck runs out."

She looked at him askance. "Some would say the same of us."

He took her in his arms and stroked her cheek. "You are not the unfaithful wife of a king. And you've never been expected to provide an heir."

"Whoever thinks Isolde will do that?" She laughed sarcastically. "All the world knows it's a marriage only in name. No one believes that Mark will bed her now."

"No," Andred said slowly, his dark eyes aglow. "But Mark might be made to believe it—and if he did..."

She gave him the cunning look he could not resist. "You mean . . . ?"

"Work on Mark," he said softly, "feed his vanity. Wake up his jealousy of Isolde, now that she's Queen in her own right and not merely as she was before." He gave a cruel laugh. "Remind him how he hates being a vassal king through marriage to him holding Cornwall under Queen Igraine. How he loathes being male in a world where women are born to rule."

She caught his mood. "Unsettle him? Tell him it's time the marriage vows were fulfilled? Make him feel that Isolde is insulting him?"

"Whatever she does." He laughed. "And however hard she tries."

"Tristan, too." Elva's eyes were bright with invention. "Isolde will surely take him with her to Ireland to establish her rule. It shouldn't be hard to make Mark suspicious of that."

Andred paused. Yes, the merest suggestion of Tristan as Isolde's King in Ireland would awaken Mark's fears. But how would this bring about the rule of the kingdom he craved? They both knew how far he was from this lifelong goal.

No matter. Anything that discredited Isolde or Tristan would take him a step or two further along the road. If they could widen the breach between Mark and Isolde, that could lead to all sorts of interesting things. Better still, if they could drive a wedge between Tristan and Mark, then Tristan would no longer be the favored heir. And there was the added pleasure of paying Tristan back, because Mark made no secret of his preference for Tristan, as his sister's son. How much of all this was pure malice and the instinct to torment? Andred grinned to himself. He didn't know. Enough to say that it gave him the purest delight.

He gave a decisive nod. "We make Mark think that the two of them are against him, whether or not we can prove it."

She showed her sharp white teeth. "And then strike?"

Oh, how he loved her when she followed his very thought. "Now is the hour."

There was a noise in the corridor. Instinct born of long experience drove them apart.

"It's the King!" Andred muttered.

The door opened and an ungainly figure strode in, slapping his riding whip against his boot. The smell of horses and dogs came in with him, the foam of his stallion's sweat staining his thighs and a pack of wolfhounds slavering round his heels. His well-cut leather riding habit and fine breeches covered a long, badly made body, and his undersized head poked with an awkwardness that his feathered cap did nothing to conceal. Beneath it his thin, straggling locks of sandy hair were streaked with gray, and his small, stone-colored eyes looked irritably about.

"Andred!" he cried.

"At your service, sire!"

Andred hastened forward with a fulsome bow. Behind Mark, he noted with contempt, swirled the familiar crowd of toadies and parasites, all hoping for the King's favor and largesse. In the midst of the colorful throng was the squat black shape of the King's Father confessor, the priest Dominian. Andred knew that the holy father would never see himself as one of Mark's hangers-on, but he shadowed the King just as devoutly in the name of his God.

So be it: Andred paused. He did not disdain the fervent little priest, and a wise man made an ally where he could. But no, he must never allow himself to think that he and Dominian were playing the same game.

Andred bowed again. "News from Ireland, sire. The old Queen is passing into the Beyond."

"What?" Mark's mouth fell open in alarm. "But she's only—" About my age was written on his face.

Andred bit back a cruel grin. Locked in his stunted boyhood, Mark would never come to terms with middle age. "So our Lady Isolde will be Ireland's new Queen," he said in solemn tones.

"Of course!" New vistas were dawning in Mark's fragile brain. When Isolde was Queen of Ireland, he would be King. Cornwall's power would extend over all the Western Isle. He rubbed his hands excitedly. "Well, she must go there at once."

Andred looked doubtful. "But surely she'll have to come back to Cornwall first?"

"Will she?" The words fell out of Mark's mouth before he was aware of it. Gods above, he'd only just gotten rid of her! Did she have to come back? With Isolde away, he could hunt every day and, when darkness drove him indoors, eat and drink his fill. With his Queen at his side, all such joys were curtailed. But that was not the worst he had to fear. There were too many other sour reminders when Isolde was there.

Women, his shrunken soul bleated, what were they for? Isolde now, why had he married her? Dimly he knew that others, men and women too, felt the sense of a rare, flower-like creature at the sound of her name. They saw a beguiling wisp of a woman in springtime green and gold, mantled in a cloud of shining hair. He watched her smallest smile gladden their hearts, and had no idea why. He only knew that everything she did belittled him. And because she did not know she was doing it, that made it worse.

"—if Queen Isolde doesn't come straight back here, some will say that she stayed away too long from Castle Dore."

Not too long for me, Mark wanted to say. Gods above, was Andred still droning on? "Why should they say that?"

"The people miss her, sire, and her healing skills. When she's away, they complain that old men die and women miscarry for the lack of the touch of her hand."

"Old men die anyway, and babes are cast!" Mark burst out. "It's lies, all lies. There's nothing magic in Isolde's hands. She knows a few herbs, that's all."

Elva swung around to support him, her long train swishing behind her like a tail. "Hovel-dwellers such as those the Queen cherishes will always complain. A king should take no heed of wretches like them."

"And you can tell her all this, my lord, when she returns." Andred paused for emphasis. "If she sees fit to come back . . ."

Mark glared at him, baffled. "You just said she must!"

"She must indeed, sire, if she wishes to pay you due respect. But if she decides that she needs not . . ." Andred arranged his features in a troubled stare.

Elva hastened to second him. "And perhaps her knight will insist that they make straight for the Western Isle—"

"Tristan?" Mark glanced wildly around. "Why would he do that? He should respect me too, shouldn't he?"

"You are his lord, his king, his kin," Dominian chimed in. "He owes you everything. Of course he must."

"Oh, Sir Tristan does respect you, sire, I'm sure," Andred insisted. "But you know how much his advice weighs with the Queen."

Mark's pebble eyes hardened. "More than mine?"

"I would hate to believe so, my lord."

"Well, now we'll find out, eh?" snarled Mark. "Isn't that what you mean?"

"Sire, you may easily set your soul at rest," said Andred earnestly. "Why not send them a summons that they must return?"

"I'll do it!" Mark cried. "Then if she comes here first, she'll prove she cares for me. And if she doesn't—" He paused and gnawed his underlip. "—then I'll know what to think."

If she does, if she doesn't, she will pay for it, Andred's heart sang. We have sown the seed of doubt and distrust, and it must grow. He did not need to look at Elva as she took the King's arm and led him away, murmuring into his ear. She knew what had to be done, and she'd do it too.

Dark waves of triumph surged up in his soul. I shall have you, Isolde, and Tristan too. You are mine. And not all the devils in hell can save you in the end.

chapter 3

*a*ll day long the sun hung low in the sky, covering the forest roof with golden fire. The holm oaks lifted their mossy heads to its glow, and the pink-and-cream honeysuckle reveled in its warmth, along with the ivy mantling every branch with a glossy sheen. Overhead, the last of the summer doves called through the trees, unmindful of the winter storms to come.

On the far horizon two riders appeared, racing out of the eye of the setting sun. Side by side they galloped across the plain toward the wood. As they gained the shelter of the trees, the first boldly overtook her companion and hurtled headlong down the leafy path. Breathlessly, she pulled up her horse in a clearing and came to a laughing halt.

"Tristan?" she called.

"Lady, here."

He was at her side, reining back his horse, and his beauty stabbed at her heart. That wondrous face with its shadowed gaze, the deep slate-blue eyes. *Almost ten years,* she marveled, *of knowing and loving this man, and still the lift of his head, the thrust of his jaw, makes me catch my breath.*

She did not know that he was looking at her with the same wondering love: Isolde my lady, Isolde my Queen.

Briskly, he vaulted from the saddle, making the sudden activity a cover for feelings that lay beyond words. How had he, a landless, wandering young knight, ever won this glorious woman as his love? Tall as he was, her long, slender body was a perfect companion to his. Her skin had the petal softness of wild rose, and a world of delight shone in her smiling eyes. She bloomed today like a flower in green and gold, with thick ropes of amber around her neck and waist, echoing the red-gold of her tumbling hair.

My lady—oh, my love . . .

He could still remember when he first saw her face, and could not remember how he had lived before. Alone, his only solace was to ride the roads at night, hearing the stars as they danced and called out to him, watching the twinkling, glimmering points of light. As the darkness deepened then paled toward the dawn, he would join his voice to the star-sounds overhead. Sometimes he sang his fears, sometimes his hopes, but over and over he sang his inner dream—Isolde my lady, Isolde my only love.

"Tristan? Where are you?" she called again with her teasing laugh.

"Here, madam, here." Securing his horse, he swung her down from the saddle, circling her waist with his powerful hands.

Tristan—

Her pulse quickened at the hard bite of his grip: *Goddess, Mother, how I love this man.* As her feet sank into the soft, loamy earth, she reached up and took him in her arms. He smelled of the woodland, strong and rich and clean, and the musky scent of his manhood teased her every sense. These days, she could trace the outline of his mouth in her sleep. But nothing would ever take away the glory of his kiss.

They stood together in the sun-dappled shade, sheltering for a while in their secret world. Far away they heard the faint echo of horses and hounds like a fairy hunt, dogs baying, horns calling thin and wild, and voices crying through the woodland deeps of long ago.

Tristan cradled her in his arms and looked up. "Is the whole court hunting with Arthur today?"

"It sounds like that. Everyone but us." She turned her head and a shadow crossed her face.

"Lady—" He knew at once what was troubling her. "No one will notice that we've turned aside. Everyone straggles as the hunt spreads out, and no one cares when the others get back."

"I know. And I wanted to be with you so much." She smiled into his eyes. "We haven't been alone since we arrived."

Tristan shook his head. "Queen Guenevere has been enjoying your company."

"And yet I've been so sad these last few days." She gave an uncertain laugh. "I don't know why. There's something coming. Something in the stars. . . ." She fixed him with her large-eyed, luminous stare.

Tristan knew her too well to brush her fears aside. "Then let us make the most of our time while we're here."

"Away from Mark, you mean?"

Her voice was unnaturally sharp. Tristan caught his breath and drew her to his chest. "Lady, I—"

She pushed him off and paced wildly away. "Gods above, Tristan, why did I marry him?"

He looked away. "Because I betrayed you. Because I was a fool."

She turned on him. "I wouldn't let your worst enemy say that!"

"When he sent me to woo you, I should not have gone."

"I could have refused him." Her lips tightened. "I was angry with you, and I threw my life away."

"Lady, lady—" He gathered her into his arms. "You married for your country. You wanted to keep Ireland safe."

She wrapped her arms around his waist and clung fiercely to the great body sheltering hers. "I feared Cornwall would make war on the Western Isle." She gave a twisted smile. "Well, I was wrong about that too."

The unspoken thought came between them like a curse.

Because the King is a coward. And even worse, a fool.

"Lady, lady," he sighed, "how were you to know that Mark wouldn't go to war? Even a coward can turn vicious if provoked."

She nodded. "And he still could." She gave a bitter laugh. "So I tied myself to him for life, as a woman and a queen."

He paused. "Yet the Great Ones have smiled on us too."

"Yes."

Isolde fell silent. They both knew how different it might have been. *If Mark had insisted on his marriage rights, when his barons were clamoring for an heir—if he had not been happy to leave her alone and spend his time with his mistress, his horse, and his hounds—if he had been jealous of Tristan . . .*

Tristan sighed. "The Gods weave both joy and sorrow into human lives. We have been blessed with a love beyond earthly dreams."

She gave a watery smile. "You're right." She leaned back into the safety of his arms. As she did, a cloud veiled the face of the sun and a shadow fell across the woodland like a great hand. She turned in fear. "What's that?"

Tristan stiffened. Born in a hollow tree, he was a creature of the woodland, and had ears like a faun. He cast about, scenting the air like a bloodhound, then pointed ahead. "Over there."

Hurriedly, he assisted her to mount, and together they rode forward through the trees. The light was fading and a sweet mist was rising from the earth, fragrant with leaf-mold and golden days on the wane. Tristan pressed forward unerringly, a hunter on the scent.

"There, madam."

Standing on the edge of the forest was a still, strange figure clad in lichen-green.

Tristan spurred toward him without fear. "Sir, what's your purpose? Do you seek the Queen?"

The stranger turned toward them as Isolde drew up. A lean, boyish figure, he had the eyes of one who slept too little and saw too much. With a brief bow to Tristan, he fell to one knee and offered Isolde a ring. "Your Majesty."

Emeralds and gold, winking in the sun—the ancient ring of Queens. The scent of bergamot came drifting down the wind, her mother's musky fragrance from the east. Now she knew the sadness that had been haunting her for days. "My mother . . . ?"

"Alas, lady . . ."

Tristan read her face. "Speak, man!" he cried.

The messenger bowed his head. "The Old Ones have called the Queen to the Otherworld. She was not sick, and she suffered no pain. But her fiery spirit wore out her mortal shell and she slipped the coils of earth for the Beyond."

Isolde nodded, white to the lips. Her mother had lived and loved, laughed and wept at twice the pace of a normal soul. She reveled longer, drank deeper, and suffered more than any mortal frame could hope to withstand. She had never been destined for the drowsy peace of the fireside, the soft sinking into widow's cap and shawl. Small wonder that the Dark Lord had called her to his side.

Isolde raised her head. "How did she die?"

He gave a sorrowful smile. "Blessing your name. And she did not die alone. My master traveled with her to the edge of the void."

"Your master?" She looked at him through a mist of tears. Golden eyes, woodland ways, green gown—*Merlin, of course.* "Thank you, sir." Covering her eyes, she turned away.

Tristan frowned. "Madam, there must be more."

The strange youth nodded. "My master bids you return without delay."

Isolde tensed. "Why?"

"The hungry sea, he says, howls 'round your isle. There are land rats and water rats, gnawing night and day. Moths lay their eggs in the fabric of what is rightly yours. Hungry mouths, hungry seas, hungry men."

Isolde stared at him, distracted. "Hungry men?"

Tristan nodded bleakly. "And one above all?"

"Yes, sir." The messenger held his gaze. "One indeed."

"Thank you." Tristan dismissed the young man with a bow. Together they watched him fade into the dusk.

Oh Mother, Mother . . . Isolde fought back her tears. "What does he mean?"

Tristan's eyes followed the green-clad messenger, then he turned back to her. "Remember, lady, at Pentecost last year, when your mother the Queen was making much of her knight?"

"Sir Tolen, you mean? When she pledged him her undying love before all the court, and told him he would be the last of her chosen ones?"

"That very night. And remember his brother Breccan?"

"How angry he was? Yes, of course. But he was only a boy."

Tristan smiled sourly. "Boys in Ireland soon become men. Then later he challenged Tolen—"

Her mind raced away. "You mean he's jealous of his brother? He thought he should be the next chosen one?"

"Beyond that," he said somberly. "With your mother gone and yourself out of the country, as you are . . ." He paused for emphasis. "Breccan may decide that Ireland has no need of queens."

"What are you saying?"

He raised his head, looking out on the falling night. "Breccan would not be the first to dream of making himself King." He raised his head, looking out on the falling night. "We must get to Ireland as fast as we can. If we make for the Severn Water, we'll find a ship there."

"But I have to go back to Cornwall to tell Mark."

"Don't you think he knows?" He gave an angry laugh. "Andred's men are everywhere."

Isolde shook her head. "I have to show him courtesy."

"Lady, send a messenger. We have a hundred trusty gallopers."

"He is still my husband," she said stubbornly.

"Yes indeed." Tristan nodded bleakly. *If only you did not* lay between them like a sword. He made a formal bow. "Go via Cornwall then, lady, if you choose. But you heard Merlin's warning. If you value your throne, you will not linger here."

She reached out and pressed his hand. Sadly, they rode together out of the wood. The last rays of the sun lay across the plain, lighting the way back to Camelot. Ahead of them the great castle glimmered in its green hollow, the mists of evening wreathing its white battlements and the bright banners flying from its gilded towers.

Afterward they knew they had had the last golden day of the season, a living reminder of how the Summer Country got its name. Even late in the year like this when the rest of the world shivered and grew cold, long hours of sunlight still blessed this enchanted land. Of all the kingdoms in the islands, summers were longest there. For the two of them, it was the summer of their love. But even then, they knew that winter must come.

chapter 4

night falling on a day of cruel cold, sleet in the air, and a wild wind on the mountains to blow them all away—Gods above, winter had roared in with a vengeance before a man could beware. And what mad-heads would hunt in this weather, when the whole of the island was wracked by these terrible storms?

Fearfully, the old woodman raised his eyes from his bundles of sticks and watched the cloaked riders streaming across the horizon, dark figures outlined against the setting sun. The black horsemen and hounds were hunting human prey, not boar or deer, he was sure. Well, the world was a sadder place since the old Queen died.

And no sign of Princess Isolde to take her place. The old man sucked on his teeth and chewed over the troubling thought. Well, Princess no longer—she'd been Queen Isolde ever since she wed the Cornish King, and now she was Queen of the island in her own right. Still, she'd been Princess long enough to wind herself around all their hearts.

Mistily, he recalled a lithe, laughing child as playful as a wave of the sea. He saw her again riding the surge like a mermaid, the only daughter of a doting mother, born in delight to rule the land with love. But now even the far-flung crannogs were murmuring that it would not be so—that the great lords meant to dispossess her and take her throne.

Yet could the Old Ones stand back and let that be? And the Great One Herself must resist it, She'd strike them down in the end. The old man shuddered. But evil men always followed their own will, and only a fool ever stood in their way. The wise man kept his head down, and made for home.

Home, yes, while these wild ones were about. Ye Gods, his aching back! Straightening up, he whistled for his dog, and turned his back on his bundles for the day. Time enough to gather sticks tomorrow, when the black riders were no more. Whoever they were hunting, it need not be him. Muffling his head in his wrap, with his dog slinking low at his heels, he melted into the woodland and was gone.

THE BAND OF RIDERS thundered along the ridge. On the side of the track the hillside fell away sharply to a mist-shrouded valley below. Ahead of them a dense stand of pines crowned the mountaintop, sheltering a natural fortress among the crags.

At the head of the pack one rider let out a shout and dragged his horse to a halt.

"What's the matter, Tolen?" cried Breccan, reining in behind.

"What are we doing here?" Tolen panted, pulling off his cap and knocking off the sleet. The raw tang of the frozen forest caught at his throat. "We've lost the light, we've seen no sight of game, and this wind'll skin us alive if we go on."

"Patience, brother," Breccan called, glancing around at his knights as they drew up. At his side rode Ravigel and young Tiercel, Ravigel's kinsman, with twenty or so young knights behind. Breccan's followers increased every day, Tolen noted uneasily, as more and more of the Queen's men turned to him. Well, they had no one else to command their allegiance and take up the service of their swords. Where was Isolde? When would she be here?

Breccan calmed his snorting horse and nodded ahead. "That's Odent's castle up there, beyond the pines. I thought we'd call on him."

"Odent?"

Dimly, Tolen pieced together a memory of a squat, pugnacious man, a former champion of the Queen and briefly among those who had shared her couch. But as the Queen's passion for younger knights increased and her interest in ruling grew less, Odent had given up in disgust and gone to live on his estate. Tolen squinted at Breccan. "He left court long ago. Why d'you want to see him now?"

"Look around you, brother." Breccan gestured to the wide sweep of the mountains and the valleys beyond. "From this crow's nest, he controls all the land around. I want to know who he will support."

"Support?" Tolen kneaded his temples to try to clear his head. Darkness and devils, why did he drink so much?

"What does it matter to you? That's for Queen Isolde to find out when she comes."

Breccan pursed his lips. "She won't be here for a while."

Tolen stared at him. "Why not?"

"She probably doesn't know the Queen is dead."

"But Gilhan was sending word—"

Breccan looked out thoughtfully into the dusk. "Well, you know he sent one of the young squires of his household, because he didn't trust any of us. With so many outlaws and ruffians on the roads, a messenger like that could easily come to harm."

Ravigel coughed, his pale eyes like stone. "Perhaps he already has."

Breccan looked at Ravigel and grinned, then turned back to Tolen again with a knowing wink. "Gilhan should have sent Ravigel. But he would insist on sending his own man."

Tiercel's answering smile gleamed white in the dusk. "A good galloper, but no fighter, so I hear. I doubt he'd get as far as the coast alive, let alone all the way to Camelot."

Tolen's bewildered gaze roved over the three knights. His brain felt like wool. "You've killed Gilhan's messenger? Why?"

Breccan looked at his brother with open contempt. "Don't concern yourself."

What were they doing? Stumblingly, Tolen pieced it together in his mind. So Breccan wanted to keep Isolde out of Ireland now that she was Queen? He'd only do that if he wanted to get the throne, in order to make himself King. And that meant he'd have to face up to any opposition and get as many of the Queen's knights as possible on his side.

Men like Odent.

Tolen nodded to himself. So that's why we are here.

But sooner or later Isolde must return.

"What about Isolde?" he said harshly. "You want to outwit her—usurp her—what?"

"I told you, Tolen." Breccan's eyes grew hard. "Leave all this to me."

"Sir!" There was a cry from one of the knights. "Riders ahead."

Coming down through the dripping pines was a strongly built older knight on a great bay horse, with three or four knights in attendance riding behind. He was heavily muffled against the biting cold in a hooded cloak and thick woollen leggings such as woodmen wore. A broad leather belt held his wraps in place, but he wore no dagger and no sword swung by his side.

"It's Odent!" said Breccan. "And he's unarmed." His eyes gleamed.

The older knight drew near and reined in his horse. "Breccan! And Tolen, too. What brings you here?"

Breccan produced one of his best smiles. "Oh, the hunt, the hunt, and we've strayed out of our way. So we thought we'd pay you our compliments as we passed."

"Very gracious." Odent peered at them from a pair of small, suspicious eyes.

"And how is your dear wife?"

"Dead, thank the Gods," said Odent with relish. "Carried off by an apoplexy not long ago. And not dear to me for many a long year, the old shrew."

"Your fair daughter, then?" Breccan persisted, with clear memories of a short, blinking girl as ugly as her father, but his only heir.

Odent snorted with cold mirth. "Fair enough to attract many like you. But she'll be mistress of her own inheritance, that's the way I've brought her up. She'll never have to put her life in the hands of a man. But why all this talk? What's the news with you?"

"You've heard the Queen is dead?"

Odent rolled his eyes. "Every crannog and hamlet has heard that by now. You'll be telling me next that you've come to commiserate with me on her loss."

"The Queen?"

Breccan shook his handsome head. He should have known better than to try to win Odent with words. Time to show his hand. "You hated the Queen. She kicked you out of her bed."

Odent's small eyes festered. "What's that to you?"

Breccan smiled expansively. "A new life, my friend. A new world, new hopes, new ways. You've heard what the Christians say. A world without women at the helm. No more rule of Queens."

"Never." Odent shook his head. "I lost my faith in this one, but that doesn't mean we should get rid of them all. I've been watching Isolde for years. When she takes the throne, she'll do very well."

"But the rule of men—"

"Never, I said!" For a moment the old authority flared in Odent's eyes. "Women are bad enough, but men are worse." He cocked a sardonic eye. "As you well know."

Breccan breathed heavily. "Think of this, then. On all sides now they clamor for the rule of men. The Christians—"

"The Christians?" Odent spat. "Would you honor that ignorant rabble above your own kind? Blood and bones, man, you're one of the Queen's sworn knights! And I'm not the only one who will stand in your way. Remember Fideal of the Glen? He'll fight to the death to protect the Mother-right."

"Fideal?" Breccan sneered. "You think I fear him?"

"Better men than you feared him in his day." Odent's face set. "Say what you like, he'll oppose you, and so will I."

Breccan conjured up a pleasant smile and reached out a hand in farewell. "So you won't give me your support? Well, let us part as friends."

Odent shrugged. "As you wish."

He leaned forward to clasp Breccan's gauntleted fist, his mind already turning to a cup of mulled wine back at the castle and a hot roast to come. He did not see the blade concealed in Breccan's left hand as the young knight made to clap him on the back, and he hardly felt the thin steel enter his neck. But his last word was drowned in a torrent of bright blood. "Fare—"

"And farewell to you."

With deep satisfaction Breccan watched the older knight's pupils contract to pinpoints of light, then he let go his hold on Odent as the light went out. With a last whisper of departing breath, Odent's heavy body slid from the saddle to the ground.

"Gods above, what—"

"My lord, my lord!"

Trembling with shock, Odent's knights spurred forward, only to find themselves surrounded by Breccan's men. Ravigel rode up to take charge, peering with interest at the lifeless hulk.

"Your lord is no more," he called out. "My lord is your lord now. He claims this fortress by the rules of war, and all those who will not serve him must leave at once. Ride back to the castle and tell all your fellows the same."

In silence they watched Odent's knights ride away.

"Breccan—" Tolen began hoarsely, his fingers unconsciously feeling for his neck.

But Breccan's attention was focused ahead. "Follow them, Ravigel. Don't let them raise the castle and bar the gates against us before we get in."

"Yes, my lord." Ravigel was already moving away. "Then we ride after Sir Fideal?"

Breccan tore his gaze away from the mountaintop. "Fideal?"

Ravigel nodded meaningfully. "If he's going to oppose you, better take care of him first."

Breccan gave a scornful laugh. "What, kill that old fool?"

"Not so old, sir. And a doughty fighter in his day."

"His day is done," said Breccan dismissively. "He won't trouble us."

"It's the work of a moment, my lord." Ravigel tenderly fingered the glistening edge of his blade. "Why not make sure?"

"Fideal is nothing." Breccan waved a contemptuous hand. He frowned. "Now the Christians, they're a different thing. If they're against me, you can have free rein."

"Gods above, Breccan, there are hundreds of them, maybe thousands now!" Tolen recoiled, aghast. "You can't kill every man who stands in your way."

Breccan stared into his brother's face with the eyes of death. "There'll be no trouble if they do what I say. The only question is, who else wants to die?"

chapter 5

Long hours in the saddle, driving forward into the night. A brief stop while she rested, stretched out on Tristan's shield, and he threw himself down on the ground among the men. Then on, and on, till day and night became one, and all she saw was the sorrowful face of the moon. She was aching in every limb, trembling with fatigue.

Or with fear? Do you dread to see your husband again?

Enough!

Ruthlessly Isolde silenced the troublesome voice in her head. Right or wrong, she had to go back to Castle Dore, and the going would always be hard at this time of the year. They'd had the last warm days of the season in Camelot and were riding now into the driving cold. A wind as sharp as elf-arrows sliced their flesh, and the first snows of winter were gathering overhead in the ominous bellies of the fat purple clouds.

"Not far now, madam," came a sharp Welsh voice at her side.

"Thank you, Brangwain." She gave the maid a smile. *But still too far for my peace of mind,* came the next thought. *Far from joy or the hope of joy whenever I see Mark.*

Mark . . .

Unbidden, a vision rose before her of a tall, ungainly figure striding in from the hunt, angry eyes peering suspiciously around, lank sandy hair falling over a long, heavy face. She gripped her reins in a spasm of self-disgust. Why did she marry this man? A king, yes, but born without the natural dignity of the humblest serf. A knight, but with less notion of chivalry than one of his own horses charging into the joust. A man who had lived to middle years without shedding the foolish boyhood habits learned long ago. A husband who had never shared her bed.

Enough, enough.

Nothing will change Mark now.

How different it had been ten years ago. Arriving at Castle Dore for the first time, she had seen a great palace newly built on the foundations of ancient kings, with a little town winding crinkle-crankle around its walls, a snug harbor and a quay below, and all had welcomed her with open arms. Even Mark himself, her bridegroom-to-be, had looked fine enough that day in royal red.

But had any young bride ever made such a willful choice? Dug a grave for her heart and leapt so blindly in? Isolde raised her face to the heavens, dry-eyed. Ten years ago she had wept all the tears she had to shed.

Too late now to lament the misunderstandings that had driven her and Tristan apart, and encouraged her to tie herself to Mark. Too far down the road to regret the rift with her mother that had made her want to seek another country, another world, another life.

Mother . . .

Gone away now into the silent land.

Lost and gone.

There it was again, the pain that would be with her till she died. The hot musky scent of the Queen's Chamber flooded her memory as the voice of her childhood echoed in her ears.

Why don't you love me, Mawther?

I always love you, little one.

Why do you leave me, then, to be with those men?

There was never an answer, and never would be now. The Queen had been in thrall to her own beauty all her life, and too many around her had been moths to that fast-burning flame. Born to love and be loved, she had lived for love alone and lost herself along the way. No wonder then that she had lost her hold on the land and also her place in her only daughter's heart.

Lost . . .

Lost and gone . . .

Tears stung the back of her throat and filled her eyes. *You are not lost to me, Mother,* she swore in her soul. *The Otherworld is only a step away. At the dawning of the day and at every moon's midnight, I shall remember you.*

A raw drizzle began, driving needles of cold rain into her skin.

"Lady?" came a concerned voice from behind. Riding at the head of the troop bringing up the rear, Tristan had read her drooping spirits from the set of her shoulders and the sad incline of her head. She turned and put her heart into her eyes: *all the better for your love.*

"Journey's end!" came the cry from the head of the troop. One by one the weary horses plodded to the edge of the ridge, and Castle Dore lay below them in the mist. Isolde shivered. *Far from joy and hope of joy when we enter there.*

Tristan urged his horse alongside hers. "The lookouts at the castle won't have seen us yet," he said quietly. "We could still make straight for the port and bypass Castle Dore."

She shook her head. They had had this discussion so many times. "No. I must see Mark."

"As you will, madam." Bowing curtly, he spurred to the head of the ride. "D'you hear me, Captain?" he shouted. "The Queen's orders are onward to Castle Dore!"

<hr>

THOUGHTFULLY STROKING his mustache, Andred hurried into the King's Chamber with his mind on fire. Only Elva and those with Druid sight knew that he had been elf-shotten in the womb, and the thick growth concealed a harelip, but Andred felt the silvery scar at times like this.

"The Queen here?" he greeted King Mark with well-feigned surprise. But he had known the very moment Isolde and Tristan crested the mountain ridge and started down to Castle Dore. Whatever happened, he was not going to be taken by surprise.

The Mother-right! he yelped in his hungry heart. Why did women rule, when men should have control? Why was Mark no more than a vassal of the old Queen Igraine, and not a man of power in his own right? When these Queens like Igraine and Isolde traced their rights from the Great Mother, then the sooner the Old Faith was destroyed, the better it would be. Why, even King Arthur, High King of all the land, still deferred to his mother as Cornwall's overlord. So Queen Igraine's hold over Mark was absolute. Darkness and devils, he prayed to his Gods of blood and bone, bring the Christians to power as soon as may be!

The Christians—they knew that God had granted women to be subject to men. The King's confessor, Father Dominian, had been cursed by his Maker with a poor, twisted frame, but his sharp mind held that idea above all. Moreover, he was determined that this truth would be known throughout the islands, come what may. Looking at the black-clad priest, Andred's spirits rose. Between them, they would surely win the day.

"Yes, the Queen's back, nephew, what do you think of that?" cried Mark in boisterous tones.

Smiling, Andred eased himself into the task of dispelling his uncle's good humor with seeds of doubt.

"Then let me assist you to make ready for Ireland without delay," he said encouragingly.

Mark stared. "What?"

"And Sir Tristan will remain behind, of course."

Mark shook his head. What in the name of God was Andred trying to say? "What d'you mean, nephew?"

"Sire . . ." Andred treated him to another smile. "Surely Sir Tristan should stay here in your place. Your Majesty will want to accompany the Queen yourself."

"To Ireland?" Mark started. "Why, in heaven's name?"

To assert your sovereignty, fool! Andred wanted to shrill in the King's ear. To be there as Isolde's King when she claims the throne, and so advance your own right to rule! Carefully, he veiled his gaze and pressed on.

"Her Majesty is recently bereaved," he said unctuously. "She must welcome your support."

Mark threw an uneasy glance his way. "Surely Isolde can handle this alone?"

He is afraid, thought Andred pitilessly. He fears to lift a sword in his wife's behalf. Gods above, a king and afraid? The old cry of anguish ran through his veins again: if I were King . . .

Dominian thrust forward his head on its twisted neck. "But the Queen is not alone. You are her husband, sire, and she must welcome your support. Indeed, perhaps if you and the Queen were together in Ireland as man and wife—"

"No!" Mark leapt up, twitching in every limb. After ten years, he knew that the secret of Isolde's childlessness was known to every soul in Castle Dore, but he was damned if he'd have it noised about like this! And he was double-damned if he'd let some eunuch of a priest lecture him on the duties of the marriage-bed.

He folded his arms and struck a commanding pose. "I shall not go to

Ireland. I am needed here. I'll send a troop of men along with the Queen, an army if she wants. But she must be in command."

Andred nodded toward the door. His ears had picked up sounds that others had missed, the jingle of approaching spurs and the swish of a gown. "Then you may tell her so yourself, Uncle, for here she is."

The King's Chamber was sour with the smell of dogs and the stale overlay of last night's drink. A tangle of wolfhounds sprawled on the floor and an overturned goblet lay at the side of Mark's throne, unheeded by all. Isolde caught her breath. *Goddess, Mother, the foul smell in here!* Well, Mark always passed his time like this when she was away. So be it.

She moved forward, feeling for whatever comfort she could find. "Your Majesty." She curtsied to Mark and bowed greetings to Andred and the priest.

"No, no, I must say Your Majesty to you!" Mark caroled fatuously, with an ungainly bow. "We meet as monarch to monarch now, not husband and wife."

Isolde held back a sigh. "I have to go to Ireland, sir," she said.

"But of course. Your kingdom awaits you, and you must claim your throne." Mark stepped toward Tristan and gave him a clumsy hug. "And while you're away, Tristan and I will hunt!"

She did not look at Tristan. "Alas, I fear Sir Tristan must go with me."

"What?" Mark scowled like a schoolboy deprived of a treat. "But you'll have plenty of knights in Ireland—all the Queen's men."

"Not so, sir . . ." She shook her head. "I don't know who to trust. But Tristan is your kinsman, so his loyalty is beyond reproach."

"My kin, eh? The only man you can trust?" Mark swelled with vanity. "Well, honor is the watchword of our house. Take him, then. I can see why you want him there."

Fool again, *fool!* chimed through Andred's brain. You are giving your wife into the arms of her paramour. Coward that you are, you are even glad that Tristan will face the dangers that are rightly yours, and make himself King of Ireland in your place. Who can wonder that he usurps you in your wife's bed!

But how to prove it? He stared at Isolde, then switched his gaze to Tristan. He felt it in the marrow of his bones that these two were lovers. It breathed from them, shone out in their every move. Look at them now, their eyes fixed firmly ahead, both knowing of old not even to share a glance. But he ground his teeth in vain. He needed proof, hard proof, before he could go to the King.

As I shall, he vowed, *before too long* . . .

Dominian stepped forward. "Queen Isolde?"

"Yes?"

Middle age had not improved the little priest, Isolde saw, feeling her compassion stir. His misshapen body grew more crooked every day, and his skin, like an old, well-oiled parchment, was yellow and translucent with pain. But nothing had extinguished the black fire in his eyes, burning with the fervent light of faith.

Dominian folded his hands firmly inside his sleeves. "We all need guidance, my lady, in the ways of God. As you go to Ireland, you will take one of our holy fathers with you to begin your reign?"

You will . . .

It was hardly a question. *Oh, the impudence of this ranting priest!*

"Thank you, Father, no," Isolde replied with strained courtesy. "Ireland has many holy men of its own. And my foremothers have governed Ireland since time began. I need no priest to inaugurate my rule."

Was she dreaming, or did Dominian flash her a mad glance of triumph: *oh, you will, madam, you will!* Suddenly the chamber was thick with dread.

Goddess, Mother, help me, for I am encircled by my foes!

chapter 6

The Queen gone? That bright spirit wandering in the void, lost forever in the astral plain?

The bowed figure on the throne set aside the letter and gave himself over to grief. Outside the window a steady rain wept with him, and he felt the cold in the depths of his heart. How like her to go out on a full, roaring tide, with the worst storm of winter raging overhead. Why had he never thought that she could die?

A sad smile lit his lips. All over the world, men would be asking themselves the same thing. Even here in France he was not the only one. Why, his old friend Ubert, King of the neighboring country, had spent a year in Ireland courting her in vain when they were both young and foolish enough for such things. Kings and princes, knights young and old, perhaps even the odd holy man or priest of the Christians, would be mourning her passage now.

His mind roamed on while the torches in the chamber burned low on the walls and the dogs shrank away from his sorrow, growling on the hearth. How had she met her death? She had lived for love: had she died for it too? Had her fierce passions shortened her crowded life? He nodded. It must have been so.

And now she was dead?

No, no, it was impossible, she was always so alive. He could see her still, flashing past in her favorite red and black, her beloved ropes of jet rattling at her neck and waist. She was with him now, he felt it, filling the quiet chamber at this moment as she had everywhere. He could hear her throaty chuckle, feel her teasing touch, and her fragrance came back to him with a pang as fresh as dawn.

Oh . . . oh . . . He could not hold back the tears. It seemed only yesterday that he had lain with her, skin to skin, held her beautiful long naked body against his heart, and begged her to marry him, to be his queen.

"I am already a queen," she had said with her velvety, mocking laugh.

"And I am a king," he protested hotly, "and worthy of your hand. I can lay a mighty kingdom at your feet." But even then he had known that the whole of France would not buy her love.

"Ask me again, Hoel," she had pouted, stroking his flank. "Love me now?"

So time went on, and how often had he asked her again, as the shadows lengthened over their youth and the golden days passed that would not come again?

So many unanswered questions, and now she was gone. He picked up the letter and began to read it again.

> "from the queen's lords of ireland to king hoel of Little britain in the kingdom of france, know that we have sustained a great sadness and loss . . ."

A heavy silence fell. The young man standing quietly in the window looked on with the curiosity of youth, for loss and death had not touched him yet. But his father was suffering, he could see that, and his own task was to help him now.

"Sir," he began as tactfully as he could, "you need a restorative? Let me order a glass of wine."

"No, no," muttered Hoel, covering his eyes with his hand. He could not look at his son. Clad in royal-red silk and velvet, with his sloe-black hair and eyes, Kedrin was a handsome young man, to be sure. But if the dead Queen had loved him and favored his suit, what fine-favored children would he have had with her.

The young knight watched his father closely and tried a new tack. "Sir, we must talk about Blanche. She was pressing me again this morning to know what you think."

But Hoel was not listening. "You know I named her Isolde, after the Queen's daughter?"

"Blanche? Yes, yes, you told us," put in Kedrin hastily, who had heard the story a thousand times. "You wanted her to be a healer like the Queen's daughter, too."

He shook his head. No wonder Blanche had rebelled in childhood and given herself a new and different name. What girl would want to grow up under the shadow of her father's great, lost love?

Hoel's mood lifted. "Well, she's done that, at least. She's not as famed for her skill as young Isolde was at her age, but she's only beginning as a healer, she's still young. And the people swear by her hospital—"

Kedrin shook his head. "Father, Blanche wants more than that. She wants a knight, a lover, a husband, like any girl."

"Not just a knight, Kedrin!" Hoel surged to his feet with a groan. "Gods above, ever since she saw him at that tournament when she was still a child, she wants the only man in the world that she can't have!"

There was a cry from the guard in the corridor outside. "The Princess Blanche!"

Kedrin gestured toward the door with a rueful smile. "Tell her then, Father. She's here."

"Goddess, Mother, help me!" Hoel turned away.

"Sister!"

Kedrin stepped forward appreciatively to greet the lovely, willowy girl coming into the room. With her delicate white hands and her interest in healing even as a child, it was easy to see why the people had nicknamed her "Blanche Mains." Blanche herself had always loved being the "Maid with the White Hands," and knew that her blond hair, as light as a baby's, and her translucent skin, marked her out as one of a special race.

Once, long ago at the time of their ancestor Lir, three children of the family had been turned into swans. Kedrin sometimes looked at Blanche's long, swan-like neck and her pale feathery hair and thought that she showed her descent from that cold kin. But Blanche herself could never be a swan. Swans paired forever, and each loved its mate like itself, while she cared only for herself. Even now he dared swear she felt nothing for her father's grief. She would only be thinking that the death of the Irish Queen would make it easier for her to get her own way.

"My lord and father."

Blanche entered in a breath of delicate air, curtsied to her father, and kissed his hand. Her tall white headdress nodded like a flower, and her pearly satin gown settled around her with a sigh.

"Sir, I have heard of your sorrow with a heavy heart," she said in a light, husky voice. She pressed a small vial into his hand. "Heart's-ease for your grief."

"One of your remedies?" Hoel took the vial and raised her to her feet. "Why, there's my girl," he said tenderly.

Blanche preened herself lightly. "Thank you, sir."

Kedrin hid a smile. As her brother, he often thought he was the only man in the kingdom proof against Blanche's fluttering, upward glance and winning smile. She had always been able to twist their father around her little finger and she was doing it now. He was aware of a growing unease. What was she up to?

Hoel smiled fondly. "Now what can I do for you?"

Blanche gave him the full force of her pale blue eyes. "You know, Father."

Hoel looked at Kedrin for support. "Your brother and I think that you're too young."

"I'm twenty, Father. Many girls of my age have three or four children by now."

"Not my daughter," said Hoel firmly. "Not a princess of France."

There was a pause. "You won't allow me then to have a knight?"

Hoel attempted a smile. "Don't forget, my dear, I was a knight myself. I loved the finest lady in the world and served her in chivalry all my days. Would I deny that joy and pride to you?"

The finest lady...? Blanche stiffened and her heart grew cold. Oh, you mean the Irish Queen, of course, Father dear. Not your wife, our poor mother, just as well she died when I was born and did not have to spend her life in the shadow of this love.

"Deny me?" Blanche's look was as chilly as rain on glass. "I hope not, sir."

"But if you must have a knight, look at one of your own kind!" Hoel protested. "Hundreds of French men would lay down their lives for you." And for the chance of marrying into royalty, he did not say. But Blanche knew that too.

Blanche tossed her head. "Sir Tristan is known as the most peerless knight."

Kedrin grinned. "Many people would say that's Sir Lancelot of the Lake."

"Tristan's bigger and stronger, and he's had harder battles too," said Blanche crushingly, "He saved Cornwall when the Irish attacked, and if he hadn't killed their champion, they'd be vassals now. And the Old

Ones had singled him out long before that. He was given his sword by the Lady of the Sea, just as Arthur was favored with Excalibur." She turned back to her father. "Wouldn't you want a man like that as your son-in-law?"

Son-in-law now, Hoel noted, not merely knight. He glanced at his son.

"Sir Tristan serves Isolde, the Cornish Queen," Kedrin said gently. "He's been her knight for years."

A look of triumph swept over Blanche's face. "But he can't marry her! She's the wife of King Mark."

"I know, I know." Hoel waved an impatient hand. "But he's sworn to follow her. And now that she's Queen of Ireland, he'll go there too. Do you want to live like that, moving from country to country and court to court?"

"When he marries me," Blanche pronounced with certainty, "he won't follow her. He'll stay with me."

Worse and worse, thought Hoel, defeated. He made a final throw. "He's a man of sorrows, girl," he said roughly, "born of sorrowful kin. His mother lost his father and ran mad with grief, then died giving birth to him in the depth of the wood. Then his stepmother tried to poison him and his father sent him away, though he'd saved the woman's life."

Blanche played with the fronds of her hair. "And now they're all dead," she said sweetly, "and he's King of Lyonesse."

Kedrin laughed. "If you must have a king, dear sister, there are plenty 'round here."

Blanche set her chin and ignored him. Her voice rang like icicles in the wind.

"Sir, I shall have him, whether you want it or not. I shall invite him to a tournament, then at the right time, you can treat with him for my hand." She curtsied and moved to the door. "I think you'll both agree that I am right."

The two men watched her go. Kedrin stepped up close to his father so that none could overhear. "You can't permit this, sir. You've heard the talk about Sir Tristan and Queen Isolde."

"Yes, and it may mean nothing," Hoel said stubbornly. "Every queen has her knights. But still..." He heaved a sigh, with the memory of his own loveless marriage unhappily keen and fresh. "Whatever there is, it bodes ill for another love. A knight may worship his lady in all purity from afar. As long as he serves Isolde, Tristan can never love Blanche as she deserves."

"And as she wants!" Kedrin cut in. "Any man who loves Blanche will have to yield to her every whim. And that's not Sir Tristan, from all I've heard."

"You're right," agreed Hoel grimly, pacing around. "He's not the man for her. And for the sake of the kingdom, surely we can find her a nearer alliance than Lyonesse."

He snapped his fingers at his son. "Ride tonight to Amaury of Rien Place. If she wants a handsome young knight, he's dashing enough."

"And near enough, too. We might even join the two kingdoms together in time."

"In your time, maybe," grunted Hoel, "not in mine. For now, let's keep Sir Tristan out of France."

The two men locked eyes. One thought hung in the air between them. *And if we can do that, Goddess, Mother, then we'll bless Your sacred name all our lives!*

chapter 7

*G*ods above, was there a better season than winter, when the cold sent the blood singing through your veins and bit into your lungs? Breccan released his breath in a sigh of contentment and watched the misty plume fade into the air. And what could be finer on a bitter day like this than a brisk gallop into the hills? With a short visit, say, to a handful of pitiful monks, a show of swords to stiffen their resolve, and then back for an evening's carousing in the Knights' Hall?

He stamped his feet for warmth and looked about. All around him the frozen stable yard rang with the dawn clatter of hooves as the riders made ready to go out. To his left, Ravigel was ordering the knights with his habitual stone-faced command, while his nephew Tiercel listened attentively at his uncle's side. Breccan nodded. Yes, Tiercel would do well. The young knight was bold and sharp, and he knew how to go with the current when the tide of affairs was running fast and free.

As it was now.

Unlike Tolen, alas. His dissolute brother knew nothing except his own low lusts and desires. Breccan watched the bloated figure weaving its way into the yard and felt his good humor draining away. He could smell the stale reek of wine as his brother approached. Gods above, it was one thing to get drunk every night as every knight did, but since when had Tolen breakfasted on wine as well?

Breccan paused. Since the Queen died, Tolen had been red-eyed and weeping every morning, and reeling drunk by noon. Could he have loved her? Snorting, Breccan put the thought away. A true knight never felt such weakness, whatever nonsense the poets and dream-weavers put about. Still, was Tolen any longer a knight at all?

"So, brother," he greeted him sourly, "ready to ride?"

"Ready for anything!" said Tolen thickly, with the remains of a tattered bravado in his air. "Where do we go?"

"On a spiritual journey, brother." Breccan gave a cynical laugh. "To call on our brothers in Christ."

Tolen gaped. "The Christians? What for?"

"For the same reason that we went to see Odent. We need their support for what we're going to do."

"What you're going to do, brother, not I," Tolen said rudely. "Our kin are prominent enough for me. If you go any further, you're going to unseat the Queen." He belched and tenderly rubbed his groaning gut. "And that I'll never do."

"Never, brother?" Breccan's face closed like a fist.

But Tolen did not notice his brother's gathering rage. "Oh, I won't oppose your trying to win favor with the lords and Druids, that's fair enough. But the Christians? Why bother with them? They're nothing but a handful of hermits and fanatics starving in cells."

Why bother? Breccan wanted to strike Tolen to the ground. He forced himself to stay calm. "Wrong again, brother. They're the coming men. See what gains they've made in these islands since they arrived. They were just a handful of men in a rowing boat, and now they have churches and communities everywhere."

"Yes, but—"

"And it will go on. They're men with a mission, brother. They mean to take over the world."

"Gods above!" Tolen thought of the grim, chanting monks and their mad-eyed leaders, and gave up. "How can you deal with them?"

"As I deal with all men, by joining their interests to mine. They want the freedom to pursue their faith. When I have power in the land, I can give it to them."

"But surely—" Tolen gave a blustering laugh. "That tale of theirs about the man-god who hung on a tree—it'll never challenge the Mother faith. The Great One has seen many such come and go."

Breccan stared at him. How could this fool be his own flesh and blood? He looked around the yard. The horses were dancing about, on fire to be gone, the men mounted and awaiting his command, and he was wasting his breath.

"Mount up," he said curtly. "We're going to see Brother Eustan and his men."

"Men, yes." A spark of understanding lit Tolen's fuddled brain. "That's it, isn't it? You need the Christians because their God demands the rule of men."

"Praise the Lord!" Breccan rolled his eyes. "Yes, the Christians refuse to recognize women in authority. Under them, the rule of Queens is dead."

A primal jealousy stirred in Tolen's depths. "King Breccan, then?"

Breccan winked and flashed him a smile as white as a pike's. "Mount up, brother" was his only response. "It's a long ride up into the mountains, and we're burning good daylight here!"

FOR THE BEAUTY of the earth and the glory of the skies . . .

For all Thy creation that swims, crawls, or flies, we praise Thy name, O Lord.

Offering prayers and thanks, at peace with the world, Father Eustan crossed the rough green between his cell and the low wooden chapel, where a handful of black-clad brothers were already pressing in. The grass underfoot was spangled with hoarfrost, each blade of grass glinting with its own light. When they sang the first office at prime, a rosy dawn had been fingering the small community of cells with a cold, fiery light. Now the sun was up, but there was still no warmth in the sky.

But Eustan did not see the poor dwellings or feel the frost tormenting his raw, sandaled feet. His eye fell on a blackbird, pecking its carefree way around the green. He drank in the boundless perfection of the sunlit morning and his heart rejoiced. How beautiful are Thy works, O Lord our God . . .

It was colder inside the chapel than out, and he shivered as he passed under the rough wooden cross above the door. But soldiers of Christ vanquished the frail flesh, and those who could not, Eustan sadly but sternly sent away. God demanded men who could bear the cruel itching of the monkish habit, the poor diet, the rules of silence and the ever-broken sleep, and still rise up smiling to chant the hours and praise His holy name.

And here they were, his followers, a dozen of God's finest, bright-eyed and bold, standing shoulder-to-shoulder in the humble space, heads bowed in prayer. He moved through them to the low altar, rejoicing in his soul, and turned to face his flock. "Brothers in Christ..." he began.

AND THEY CALL this a holy place? Grinning like a wolf, Breccan did not try to hide his contempt. When he was King, nothing would be too fine for him. And these people who preached the coming of the King of Heaven contented themselves with living in ruins like these?

All around him he could hear Tolen, Ravigel, Tiercel, and the rest of the knights thinking the same thing. The ride here had been hard, picking their way along narrow mountain paths to a ring of standing stones where the Christians had settled in the remains of the old stone circle and built their huts. No wonder their wretched hovels looked ready to fall down, fashioned as they were out of broken rocks.

Clever, though. Breccan chuckled to himself. Living so humbly, they'd never be the envy of the folk who lived around here, or arouse their mistrust. They had won the people's hearts in other ways too. They lived cleanly, devoted themselves to their God, and shared all they had. Those who fell sick were more than glad of their simple ministrations and wholesome care. Yes, they were good men. Breccan sucked his teeth. This could prove harder than he had thought.

He nodded curtly to Ravigel. "Ride on and give them warning of our approach."

Ravigel bowed.

Breccan watched the knight spurring away, and the worm of resentment turned again in his heart. Why couldn't he count on his brother Tolen like this? Breccan's lip curled. Brother...? Suddenly he knew he no longer held any kinship with the dull-eyed thing sweating and swaying vacantly on his horse, reeking of wine and, he dared swear, fear.

Fear? Oh, Tolen! A dull rage swept him. Time was, big brother, when you yielded to no man, beat down any knight at arms and royally sated the Queen in her own bed. And now—he felt the cold wind of fate brushing his cheek—now you are nothing. And a danger to me, even worse.

"Sir?" Ravigel was cantering down the track. "Father Eustan says he will see you now."

"He will see me?" muttered Breccan. What, a religious fool dictating terms to him? He reminded himself that he needed Eustan's support.

And when the monk knew what they'd come for, things would soon change.

"On, then!" Breccan cried.

Keenly, he pressed forward up the mountain path. But one glance as they drew near made him think again. Father Eustan was surging out of the chapel with his monks at his back and drawing himself up on the green as if to repel an attack.

"Greetings, lords," he called dourly. "Welcome to our humble house of God."

"And greetings to you."

Smiling, Breccan swung down from the saddle and threw his reins to Ravigel. Carefully, he studied the man facing him. Tall, lean, and impassive, Father Eustan gave little away. Like all his kind, he wore a long black habit of the coarsest wool, belted at the waist with a length of rope. A raw tonsure disfigured his shaven head, and his feet were cracked and bleeding from the cold. But the large, lustrous eyes burning deep in their sockets showed no concern with this. Here was a man who cared only for his God.

"So, sir," he challenged with a unfriendly stare. "What can a handful of Christ's messengers do for you?"

Breccan paused. Where was the gentle, timid Christian he'd imagined?

"I am Breccan, a knight of the Queen," he struck back as suavely as he could. He gestured toward Tolen. "And brother to the late Queen's chosen one."

Too late he realized that the half-glazed creature at his side did nothing to enhance his claim. Gritting his teeth, he pressed on. "We are here to help you. We have come to offer you our protection in these troubled times."

"Troubled? How so?" The monk's large brown eyes held Breccan in a disbelieving gaze. "And why should we need protection from you?"

He gestured behind him to a thickset monk brandishing a stave. Next to him stood another burly form armed with a pitchfork, and another with a battling gleam in his eye. Next to him a young monk clutched a sickle, and next—Gods above! Breccan's brain reeled. Were they all fighting mad, these servants of the meek and mild Jesus who preached love for all?

"Troubled, Father," he resumed angrily, "because the old Queen has died. And who knows what will follow in her wake?"

"On the contrary," said Eustan sharply, "we know very well. Isolde will succeed. She is the rightful heir and she is our Queen."

"But your own faith—your own sacred texts—" Breccan heard himself stuttering and ground his teeth in rage. How could he be losing this battle of wits? "Your Holy Writ," he resumed, breathing heavily, "tells us that man is made in God's image and woman was formed for sin. Therefore your own Saint Paul instructed the world that no woman may hold power over men."

A smile of amusement kindled the monk's dark eyes. "But our Lord Jesus Christ was born of woman, as you may have heard."

"But she didn't rule over him," insisted Breccan. "She was not his Queen. Your God has come to sweep all that away. We need a man of power to govern the land." He remembered in time to put on a kingly smile. "And I am here to take that burden on."

"Are you so?" Father Eustan pretended to think. "Well then . . ."

Darkness and devils! Breccan could have sworn the monk was laughing at him. Recklessly he pushed on.

"Either you're with me or against me, monk. Support me now, preach me to your people, and I'll build churches for you throughout the land. You and I together can do God's will!"

"Ah, sir, there we differ in our theology." Eustan was smiling broadly now and stroking his chin. "You believe that you are called to do the work of God. We believe our Lord can do His own."

Breccan stiffened. "What do you mean?"

"If God wills the destruction of the Queens, He will bring it about," Eustan said harshly. "He does not require His servants to join in squalid plots to overthrow the rulers of the land. We are here to glorify His name, to help His people and to live holy lives. Tell me how any of those are served by helping you."

Squalid plots . . .

Breccan was aware of Ravigel's cold breath in his ear. "Cut them down, lord. You'll get nothing here."

Yes! Cut them down, make this arrogant priest eat his words and choke on his own blood. A red mist gathered behind Breccan's eyes. He saw Tiercel's hand on his sword and heard Ravigel's heavy breathing as he scented a kill, and trembled with delight. Then Tolen's warning came ringing in his ears. You can't kill every man who stands in your way. You'll never make yourself King if you do that.

Killing Odent was one thing, a cruel husband and a brutal lord who'd be mourned by none. But to kill a dozen unarmed holy men—for so the story would be told, despite the welter of clubs and sticks and scythes—no, that would damn his name forever in the land. No matter that most of the folk did not follow the Christian faith or give a fig for the Christian's God. In Ireland, the freedom to live was a sacred thing.

He gave a ghastly smile and a slight shake of his head, telling Ravigel, no.

"Well, sir?" came the monk's uncompromising voice. "We say God will decide, not human ambition and greed. Do you disagree?"

There was nothing to say.

AFTERWARD, RIDING BACK down the mountain, Breccan's fury grew. Defeated, humiliated in front of his men and sent packing with a holy flea in his ear—with every step of his horse, another sharp insult clouded Breccan's brain.

"I told you so, Breccan." Riding beside him on the narrow track, Tolen reached for his water-bottle and brought it to his lips. Only when a ruby trickle ran down his brother's chin did Breccan realize what was happening.

Tolen drinking again? When he was drunk already, in a place like this? Didn't he see the sheer drop at the side of the track? Breccan's fury peaked. Gods above, if his horse shied, he could kill them all!

Tolen released a fat belch of contentment. "Listen to me, little brother," he began expansively. He laid down his reins on the patient horse's neck and took another deep pull on his wine. "You need to learn a thing or two from me—"

Breccan looked into the chasm at the edge of the path. "Tolen, take care. One slip and—"

"Don't tell me what to do!" Tolen laughed nastily. "You're not King yet." He poured a steady stream of wine straight down his throat. "And you're not going to be if you keep on like this."

"How so?" Only Tolen's guardian angel would have recognized the shadow of gathering menace in Breccan's voice. But any hope of protection was far away.

Tolen's face flushed. "You won't do it, brother," he said thickly, "because you don't understand the game. The Christians don't care about you, you're nothing but a petty warlord to them. And you think you can make yourself Isolde's chosen one? She won't look at you, she's already married to a king. If you take her by force, you'll have all Ireland on your back. But you don't see any of that. You're a fool, little brother, and you always were."

With the sense of a speech well made, Tolen fumbled for his bottle again.

Oh, the comfort of cold steel. Breccan curled his fingers back into his sleeve and coaxed his hidden blade down into his hand. Come, my little love, time to go to work. Easy now, that's right. Then as I laugh and clap Tolen's horse on the rump—*go!*

There was a terrible scream. Recoiling from the dagger in its flank, Tolen's horse leapt sideways, lost its footing, and fell from the narrow path. For the rest of his life Breccan would remember his brother's vacant look as he groped for his reins while the earth fell away. For a second, horse and rider hung suspended over the void. Then dropping into the silence of eternity, they were gone.

The ride came to a halt. Ravigel rode back up the line and peered over the edge. Far below lay two small remote figures, pale and still.

Ravigel blew out his cheeks. "Terrible thing, sir, to lose a brother like that." He looked Breccan hard in the eye. "But a riding accident can happen to any man."

"Yes," agreed Breccan, his eyes moist with grief.

"And Sir Tolen had been drinking since we set out. All the men will say that."

"Yes. Thank you, Ravigel."

Breccan arranged his face in an attitude of loss as the knights crowded around to mutter and bow their heads. Bereavement would suit him, he knew. Tears were easy, he should shed a few now.

As he did, Tolen's words came back to him, and he crowed with inward delight. You were right, dear brother, I couldn't kill every man standing in my way—but I could kill you!

chapter 8

throughout the winter forest no birds sang. Damp glistened on the leaves of every tree, and all the woodland shrank back to its frozen roots. Untamed from primeval times, the forest rolled on for mile after shadowed mile, roofed by the matted branches of old oaks, walled in by thickets of elder and tangled briar. The only ways through the wood were narrow, hidden tracks. Cornwall's last wilderness guarded its secrets well.

A dank chill stirred the air as they approached. A shiver ran through the underwood, and the track narrowed till they had to travel in single file, Tristan and the strongest of the troop in front, then Isolde and Brangwain in the middle with the rest of the guard behind. The horses were uneasy as they went in, rolling their eyes and flattening their ears to their heads. Nervously, they trod forward over the rotting leaves. Isolde leaned forward and patted her mare's soft neck. *Yes, it's a dark, strange place, but take heart, my dear.*

She gave a sigh of relief. It was worth any trial to be away from court. *This forest could be the worst place in the world, but we are together, I am with my love.* Joyfully, she drew the living air of the forest into her lungs, the moist, clean smell of the leaf-mold, the pure breath of the trees. There was no evil in nature, she was sure of that. If any darkness lay hidden in this forest, it came from the heart of man.

Man...

She felt the faintest prompting of unease. "Sir..." She called up to Tristan riding ahead. "Who owns this land?"

"The forest, my lady?" Tristan frowned and reined back. "No knight that I know of."

He paused as half-remembered rumors nagged at his mind. What was it he'd heard, a rogue knight who lived here unseen, lord of a disappearing castle that no man could find again? He suppressed a snort of disgust. Nonsense, every word, like the tales of the Fair Ones coming out of their green hills and hollows to steal mortals away. They were all armed, including the women, Isolde riding with her mother's broadsword at her side and Brangwain ringed with steel. And escorted by Castle Dore's best troops, they had nothing to fear. No, there was no need to trouble the Queen with this.

But Isolde knew him too well. "What is it? We don't have to go this way, after all. We could miss out the forest and go by the high road."

"Madam, we must get to Ireland by the shortest route," Tristan said brusquely.

Isolde sighed. "I know. I fear we have wasted too much time as it is. Merlin never in his life sent a warning in vain."

Tristan nodded. "Onward, lady!" he said crisply, and on they went.

Slow as a slug, the winter sun crawled up the sky. But little of its warmth reached the earth below. Underneath the trees lay a dimly lit, cold, green world, and the deeper they went into the forest, the darker it became.

Now the undergrowth itself looked pale and sick, as if tainted by some evil in the heart of the wood. But Isolde saw glossy ivy and sturdy honeysuckle on every tree, and had to smile. Years ago she and Tristan had vowed to be just as faithfully entwined, two living creatures growing together as one. She greeted them now like old friends: *how are you, my dears? I am glad to see you here.*

At the head of the troop she saw Tristan lift his head sharply and read his face at once. He could hear the glowworm polishing his lamp in the grass or the smallest ladybird calling her children home. "What's amiss?" she called.

He shook his head. "Nothing I can see."

Brangwain stirred uneasily. "My lady—"

She could see the warning in the maid's clever dark eyes. Like all those from the Welshlands, Brangwain was Merlin's kin and saw more than mortal sight. She turned to Tristan again. "Should we turn back?"

He shook his head. "Anyone in the forest knows that we're here. If they want to take us, they could ambush us any time. But they'll probably leave us alone. No ruffians will attack a mounted troop, and outlaws have every reason to lie low."

"So we press on?"

With an effort, she resisted the urge to smile into his eyes. Even here among a handful of trusted men, she had to be careful not to betray their love. *But in Ireland, in my own land, surely we'll be free?* Her heart lurched. *No, not even there, as long as there are prying eyes and tattling mouths, burning to carry bad words back to Mark.* Suppressing the ache in her heart, she drove her horse on.

The short day was ending and it was darker now. The path had dwindled to a winding trail, and the raw cold and damp were settling into their bones. Yet Isolde's spirits were growing lighter with every step. Surely Tristan was right. If any villains were sheltering in the wood, they must have decided by now to leave them alone.

Ahead of them the path widened into a clearing closely walled by trees. Here, great clusters of ivy rioted with the faithful honeysuckle, hand in hand amid banks of bracken and furze. The peace of a thousand years hung over the dim green space, and pale fingers of light brushed the forest floor. Isolde's heart lifted. They could camp here—even make a fire.

Not for the first time, Tristan read her thought. "So, lady, what's your will? Rest here, or go farther before the light fails?"

Isolde laughed. "Rest a moment, at least. How much longer will the daylight last?"

She did not hear the rustle in the undergrowth, as soft and stealthy as a snake in the grass.

"Lady—" Tristan froze, pointing like a dog.

Stepping through the trees at the head of the clearing came a blood-red figure on horseback, with a lady at his side. Behind them were a pair of mounted men. The knight's fearsome armor covered a fighter's hard, well-knit body, with powerful shoulders and strong quarters below. He wore his visor up, revealing his face. There was something unspeakably dreadful about the jutting forehead, the hollow cheeks, and square, lipless mouth, grinning like the last smile on a skull. But all that was nothing to the lady at his side. She was sitting on her horse with a noose around her neck.

"Madam, look!" cried Brangwain, her hand flying to her mouth.

Isolde stared in horror. But for the rope, the lady was finely dressed in a rich cloak of fur trimmed with ermine and a riding habit of gleaming chestnut kidskin beaded with gold. Her headdress and veil were of tawny satin and lace, and her leather gauntlets were studded with jewels and pearls. But the hands that held the reins were roped like her neck, and her eyes were set in a wide, glassy stare. Her still, white face looked only half alive, dusted with the livid sheen of death.

The strange couple drew up facing them. Isolde could not take her eyes off the hideous rope. She glared at the knight. "Explain yourself, sir!"

The knight gave a smile as white as polished bone. "This is the Lady La Pauvre, widow of a noble knight. She is my captive by the rules of war."

His voice, both rasping and sharp, pierced Isolde's ear. "A poor lady indeed to find herself in your hands! And who are you?"

"The people around here call me Sir Greuze."

Isolde's eyes widened. "I know your name! You were refused admittance to the Round Table for the cruel habits you learned in the East."

"And banished by the King, I believe," Tristan cut in, "after your wife died by violence at your hands." He stared at the knight in scorn. "Let us give you your full title, sir. You are known as Sir Greuze Sans Pitie—the knight without pity for a single soul."

"True, every word." A slow chuckle escaped the knight's bloodless lips. "Pity, you say? When I was banished, no man pitied me. I suffered for ten years and more before I could slip back into this forest and start life again."

"But the lady—look at her, man!" Isolde spat. "She is ill! She needs comfort and care, not treatment like this."

Sir Greuze tugged on the rope and drew the lady to his side, poking and prodding her like a side of meat. "This one has disappointed me, I must confess. She was a beauty when I took her from her lord. But she lost her mind when I cut off his head."

Tristan's hand was already on the hilt of his sword. "You killed her lord?"

"I did indeed, though he fought like a Trojan to save her life. After that, she ran mad. Since then, she has never said a word. That was her revenge, the only way to thwart me of my prize." He gave a hideous laugh. "I bedded her anyway, she was mine to use. But no amount of bedding or beating has brought her to herself."

"Goddess, Mother!" Isolde could not contain herself. "How did she or her lord deserve this at your hands?"

Greuze leaned forward. "My fortress, Castle Pleure, lies a step from here. When a knight and his lady enter my domain, if the new lady is more beautiful than mine, I kill the one I have and take her instead."

Tristan laughed in scorn. "And her knight stands by and lets you do this?"

"Oh, the knight usually challenges me." He grinned. "And I always win."

"Not today, sir."

Greuze widened his eyes and smiled his bony smile. His sword lay in his hand, the sun glinting on its slender, cruel edge. "We shall see. But your lady is clearly more beautiful than mine, so you'll agree that mine must die."

He raised his sword and whirled it around his head. The blade hissed through the air, there was a sudden spout of red, then the lady's head toppled onto her shoulder and bounced to the ground. Her headless trunk sat for one endless moment on her horse before crumpling in the saddle and following it down.

"Goddess, Mother!" cried Tristan hoarsely. "I'll have your life for this!"

"The Great Ones will punish you, never fear!" Isolde shouted, beside herself. "Women are sacred wherever the Mother-right rules."

"Sacred—" Greuze stared at her unmoved. "When you're mine, I'll have your tongue cut out."

"Yours?" Isolde stared at him, trembling in every limb. "You're mad."

"Do you know who you insult?" cried Tristan. "This is Queen Isolde, and I am her knight—"

Greuze winked at him. "I know who you are."

"Then you know that I never yielded to any man. And I give no quarter to a monster like you. I challenge you to the death, here in this grove. Make ready to die like the lady, without mercy or grace."

Greuze opened his slit of a mouth to cackle like death. "You think so, sir?"

He nodded toward the edge of the wood. Emerging one by one from the undergrowth were a dozen knights, then fifteen, twenty, and more. Behind them came a rank of archers, bows drawn and arrows set to fly.

Silently they surrounded the travelers, and every glinting point was aimed at Tristan's heart.

Greuze watched them take their places, murmuring with delight. Then he turned to Tristan with a ravening smile. "So, sir, your Queen is mine, I think."

think again, devil!"

Bursting like a boar from a brake, Tristan hurled himself violently from his saddle and seized Greuze by the neck. Locked together, the two men fell heavily to the ground as their panicking horses shied and scrambled away, scattering the men at arms as they went.

"Brangwain!" Isolde cried, reaching for her sword. Her mother's great battle companion came singing from its scabbard, the cabochons on the hilt firm and fast in her hand. But the maid had already drawn her own weapon and advanced on Greuze's men.

"Get back, all of you!" Brangwain shouted.

"Halt!" With an answering shout of defiance, Isolde took up a position across the clearing, defending the space where Tristan and Greuze were struggling on the grass.

Her mother's battle-cry joyfully filled her throat as she pointed her sword at the figures fighting on the ground. "One step farther and your lord dies!"

"She's a banshee!"

"No, they're witches both!" Baffled and cursing, the knights fell back.

Tristan leapt to his feet and tore his blade from its sheath. Greuze was only a moment behind, snatching up his own sword from the ground.

"So, sir, we fight," Tristan panted. "To the death, I think?"

"Your death, slave!" Greuze forced out through gritted teeth. "And I'll make it a slow one, when I have you down."

The leader of the knights leaned forward urgently. "What's your will, my lord?"

Greuze gave a scornful laugh. "Watch and learn!" he shouted back.

"I'll deal with this knight, then you can do with these women whatever you like."

"Set on, then!" Tristan cried. He advanced on Greuze, his great sword Glaeve flickering like a dragon's tongue. But Greuze leapt on to the attack with a stroke so violent that it almost knocked Tristan down. Isolde's stomach clenched. Greuze's claim to be a deadly warrior was no idle boast.

She could see from the set of Tristan's shoulders that he knew it too. Rallying, he set about Greuze with a flurry of long, sweeping strokes, varied with unexpected, jabbing moves. Before long Greuze's blood-colored armor had a sickly sheen as a show of red seeped from a shoulder-joint.

The dying sun slipped slowly down the sky. High overhead the roosting birds rose chattering from the trees, disturbed by the clash of swords. Isolde gauged the progress of the fight from the combatants' labored breath, and reckoned every blow from the groans of pain. She saw Tristan's head running with blood, and recoiled. *Goddess, Mother, spare him—spare my love.*

The clearing was turning to mud as the fight went on. Minute by minute and hour after terrible hour, the two knights attacked and fell back, feinted and came again. Isolde heard and counted every stroke and knew that Tristan could not escape unscathed. Soon Tristan's breastplate was covered in blood and one arm swung numbly at his side.

But Greuze himself was in even poorer shape. The big knight was floundering like a bull at bay, swinging his heavy head to and fro. Tristan had gored him with many deep wounds, and he was swaying from loss of blood. As Isolde watched, Greuze's lifeblood ran down, puddling with the mud around his feet, and he fell to his knees.

Strike—now . . . Kill, kill!

"Have at you!" Tristan screamed.

He had one last moment, he knew, before his strength failed. He threw down his sword and staggered forward fumbling madly for his dagger, and took his enemy's head in the crook of his arm. The only sound was a soft departing breath as Tristan found the gap at the base of the helmet and drove home the blade. A spout of blood issued from Greuze's neck, and his body slumped to the ground.

"My lord—"

The leader of Greuze's knights fell to his knees. One by one the rest of the men followed him. Tristan stumbled toward Isolde, covered in blood.

"Your Majesty," he gasped, "your enemy is dead! I lay this triumph at your royal feet."

"And we accept it," Isolde proclaimed. Turning to the knights, she gestured to the figure on the ground. "Your lord is gone. I am your lady now. By the fortunes of war, I claim this castle for Sir Tristan, King of Lyonesse."

The leader of the knights nodded his close-cropped head. Slowly he stood up, a short, stocky figure with a battle-hardened air, bowing first to Isolde then kneeling to Tristan. Reversing his sword, he offered up the hilt. "You have won this combat in all chivalry. We accept defeat at your hands."

Tristan laid one hand on the weapon, swaying on his feet. He did not feel his blood running down to the ground. "So, sir, your name?" he rasped.

"They call me Yder, sir."

"From the Welshlands, lady," Brangwain muttered. Her own accent was very marked.

Yder overheard her. "From Caer Narvon itself," he proclaimed with open pride.

Brangwain treated him to a flinty smile, then turned back to Isolde. "A land of true men, lady: tight, but true," she said quietly. "If he'll serve our lord, you may trust him with your life."

Isolde saw the knight's face flicker into a smile. "You heard that, sir? Then what's your reply?"

Sir Yder fell to his knees and offered up his sword. "Receive my allegiance, lady, you and your lord. And I swear I speak for the rest of the men. We took service with Sir Greuze in the Holy Land, before he began on these evil tricks." He pointed to the body of La Pauvre, lying in the grass, and looked away.

Isolde felt angry tears rising at the back of her throat. "Alas, poor lady—we must bury her with the honor that is her due."

"Take heart, madam," Tristan said hoarsely. "She has what she must have been praying for all along, the freedom to escape her tormentor and be with her love . . ."

His voice trailed off. Isolde looked at him. His eyes were dilated and his skin very pale. "Sir Tristan . . ."

Sir Yder saw it too. "My lord—" he began in deep concern. As he spoke, Tristan crumpled to the ground.

Isolde vaulted from her horse. "Forward, all of you!" she cried. "Bring him up to your castle as fast as you can."

"This way, Majesty!"

Two spears and a shield made the kind of litter knights used to carry their dead from the field. Four of the strongest took up the burden as Yder led the way deep into the wood. Greuze's retreat was nearer than Isolde had thought, but without Sir Yder and the knights, they would never have found it at all. Hidden deep in a hollow, and built into the side of a hill overgrown by trees, Castle Pleure was a secret locked away from mortal eyes.

Indeed any traveler might have passed it unwares. There were no towers, no battlements, no flags, and the whole edifice was more of an ancient, rambling forest grange than a fortress for defense. Even the door was mantled with thick ivy, hiding the way in. Isolde nodded grimly. With his evil way of life, Sir Greuze had had good reason to bury himself here. But how would she find help for Tristan in such a remote place?

Stifling her fear, she stepped over the mossy threshold into a wide hall. After the chill of the forest, the place felt kinder than she expected, with a warm fire twinkling through the soft, greenish gloom. On either side she could see into well-furnished apartments with bright rugs on the floor, all glimmering with the same woodland light.

She turned to Sir Yder. "Where are the women? Who runs the household here?"

Sir Yder smiled. "There are none. We fend for ourselves."

"Then where's your infirmary, sir?"

Yder laughed. "Infirmary, lady? We have no such thing."

Isolde looked at Tristan and her heart dropped. "Where do you heal your sick knights?"

"In the guardroom, lady."

"No, that will never do. Show me where you keep your herbs or any healing salves you have."

"We have none." Yder shrugged. "Sir Greuze wanted no weaklings among his chosen men. If our wounds festered, he let us die."

"Your best apartment then, somewhere with light and air!" Brangwain exploded. She gestured toward Tristan. "Gods above, man, don't you see how bad he is?"

Isolde nodded, dry-mouthed. *A chamber for Tristan, yes, must get him to bed.* She lifted her head. "Show me the cleanest and most peaceful room you have."

Sir Yder fixed her with a gaze that spoke his grief. "This way, madam—this way. . . ."

She turned to Tristan. He was breathing hard and his face was very cold. His wounds were red and gaping like open mouths, but his flesh was already turning gray from lack of blood. One cut in his groin was slowly welling with blood. Isolde staunched the flow and felt for his pulse.

Brangwain pursed her lips. "I'll take care of him, lady, while you go and see what they've got. Then I'll scour the forest for herbs as soon as it's light."

Isolde nodded. "We'll have to stay here till Tristan's well again." She paused. "Although Mark's sure to be suspicious of any delay."

What will he suspect? Will he guess that I'm prolonging the journey to linger out of the way?

To be with Sir Tristan. With my secret love.

Isolde felt the dark shadows gathering like bats. She glanced at the bloodless figure on the makeshift bier. "But we can't move Tristan, and we can't leave him behind. What else can we do?"

chapter 10

Like mother, like daughter?

Was one queen who had always been in love with herself to be replaced by another who followed her own will, even when her country was hungering for her return?

No, he would not—dare not—think of Isolde that way!

Cursing himself for his lack of faith, Sir Gilhan drove his horse onward into the wood. The dank air and rotting vegetation beneath the trees lowered his spirits still more, but the gray winter of his surroundings must not cloud his judgment now. Isolde must have had good reason to delay, and her absence had not provoked any threat to the country that he could see.

For dangerous though he seemed, Breccan had not shown a dangerous hand. Indeed, to the best of Gilhan's knowledge, the truculent young knight had done nothing at all. He had been away from court out hunting with his brother and his knights, amusing himself as harmlessly as any man in the land. If things continued as peaceably as this, Ireland could safely wait a while longer for her rightful queen.

But ye Gods, he mourned, where is the darling girl? A slim, laughing child with a fall of flame-colored hair danced across his mind, and he laughed to find his old eyes rheumy with tears. Girl, you old fool? he chided himself. She's over thirty now. Will you always be thinking of the fine little imp she was?

Well, wherever she was, he mused, he had to keep the land safe. True, Breccan was carrying all before him at court, with every one of the younger knights his sworn follower now. But outside the court there was another world, an older universe of love and trust. In the heart of the forest, they kept the Old Faith. Here he would find the allies he needed now.

Still, he had to move with care. He had not sent to Cormac to announce his coming, for even in the forest, creatures had ears. He had no doubt he would find the Chief Druid here, for Cormac never left his sacred grove. And the only other soul who would attend was a man Gilhan would trust with his life. All might yet be well.

A watery sun struck downward through the trees. The short afternoon was fading. He should hurry on. Not too far ahead through the greenish gloom, the sacred grove lay basking in a pool of light. Gilhan emerged into the clearing from the damp and dripping wood, shivering with relief. Even in the dead of winter there was warmth here at the heart of the forest in the great circle of ancient oaks breathing out their wisdom to the world. The old knight drew the green fragrance down into his lungs and felt his soul expand. How fresh it was after the stale, sour air of the court!

Oh Gods, the court . . .

Unwittingly, he smelled again the raw odor of vaunting young manhood, sharp as cat's gism and rank to his old nose. He growled in distress. Even away from court, Breccan and his young lions were hard to forget. But that was why he was here. "Onward!" he muttered. "No faltering now."

A raven was croaking ominously overhead. Gilhan dismounted stiffly and tied his horse to a tree. Already his nagging doubts were turning into fears. Where was the familiar figure in his fleece-white robe? What business could have taken Cormac away?

In the heart of a thicket stood the Druid's cell, a round dwelling underneath the mossy oaks. Walled with bracken and ivy and roofed by sweet leaf-mold, it was as much a part of the forest as a fold of the living earth. Here Cormac slept and prayed and passed his days worshipping the Great Mother, his only love. Here he received his pupils and taught those who cared to learn the Druids' lore.

Approaching, Gilhan saw the door standing ajar. A handful of cold ashes blackened the hearth, and a wooden trencher with the remains of a meal lay upturned on the floor. From the dry crusts of bread and withered herbs, a week or more had passed since the Druid had sat by the fire for his frugal repast.

Gilhan picked up the bread and crushed it in his fist. What happened here? he demanded of the empty space. Moments later he was fumbling for his sword. With a terrible clarity he knew there was someone behind him *now!* Then the point of a knife dug deep into his ribs as a hand seized his wrist and twisted his arm behind his back.

"Easy now," came an angry grunt as the attacker tightened his grip past the point of pain.

The breath of the assailant was cold on the back of his neck. Gilhan closed his eyes and made the old soldier's prayer: let me die standing. Let me see my death.

"What's your business here?" demanded the hostile voice. "Come to revisit the house of the man you killed?"

Gilhan gave a sharp barking laugh of surprise. "Is Cormac dead?"

"You know he is." He felt a venomous jab of the knife in his back, and the blood began to trickle down his skin. "You know where he's buried. You put him there."

The knife moved again. Gilhan could take no more. "Gods above, man!" he burst out in a rage. "I came to seek his help! We both serve the Queen, I'm an old friend of his from court."

"Who are you, then?"

"I'm the head of the Queen's Council, and her champion long ago. Gilhan is my name. And I need Cormac alive."

"How so?"

"I want him to stand with me against her foes. And if he's dead, the trees of this forest know more of it than I!"

There was a heavy silence. When the unknown voice came again, it had changed. "You came for his help to support the Old Faith?"

"I swear it by the Great Ones themselves," Gilhan spat. "On the soul of the one I love best. And that's myself!"

There was a snarling laugh. "That's a good oath."

Gilhan felt himself spun round. Before him stood a young Druid, a burly well-set figure in an indigo robe. His broad face was flushed with passion and his eyes burned with honest truth.

Gilhan could see the Druid mark pulsing between his brows. His eyes widened. "You're one of Cormac's followers. Don't you know where he is?"

A look of confusion crossed the bold young face. "No. He's been gone a week and more."

"But I thought he was always here."

The young man frowned. "Sometimes he takes to the mountains to worship the Great One and renew his love."

Gilhan shook his head firmly. "He would not wander now."

"Why not?"

"The land's in peril since the old Queen died. He'd never put his moon-longings above our need. And he'd want to be here when Queen Isolde comes."

"Where is she, then?"

It was Gilhan's turn to frown. "She left Castle Dore in Cornwall, we know that much."

"And now . . . ?" prompted the young man.

"I wish I knew." Gilhan gave an angry sigh. "Lingering like this, she puts all our lives at risk."

The young eyes widened. "Of what?"

Gilhan eyed him levelly. "If she doesn't come forward to assert her claim to the throne, we may see a time when the Mother-right is no more."

"Never!" the young Druid scoffed. "Not as long as men love nature and understand what gives them life."

"Men like Sir Breccan, you mean?"

"Who's he?"

Gilhan laughed harshly. "Pray to the Great One that you'll never know." He gazed around the clearing, his senses as sharp as a fox. "He's been here, I know it. And if he has, he's taken Cormac away."

There was a shout from across the clearing. "Who's there?"

Emerging from the trees was a spare figure of medium height, mounted on a great roan charger, heavily armed. His battle-hardened body and close-cropped gray hair announced him as a knight of more than middle years. But his cool gaze had lost none of its force, and his scarred hand still knew how to grip a sword. He was clad for combat in leather and hammered bronze, and as he dismounted and strode forward, Gilhan's spirits soared.

"Fideal!"

To his horror, Gilhan felt tears pricking his eyes. Bluffly, he clasped his old friend to his chest. But Fideal stood back from his embrace and pushed him off.

"Why am I here?" he demanded. "Why did you send for me?"

Gilhan carefully surveyed the stony face. "I wanted to meet Cormac here with you. I need a few men who will defend the Great One and the faith we serve. And Isolde, our Queen, as she must be."

Fideal stared bleakly around, taking in the young Druid as he moved away. "Where is Cormac, then?"

"Disappeared."

"He's not the only one, from what I hear."

Gilhan started. "What d'you mean?"

Fideal smiled grimly. "Young Breccan has been hunting 'round these parts. He paid a visit to Odent of the Peak, and Odent had a fatal apoplexy as they talked. Then his brother Tolen, the Queen's last chosen one, perished in a riding accident on the way back—"

"Oh, so?" Gilhan released a dry bark of mirth. "Tolen? The best rider in the land?"

"He was drunk, they said." Fideal looked Gilhan in the eye. "But all the world knew he stood in Breccan's way. He was too loyal to the Queen and the old ways. His death is a lesson to one and all. Those who want to survive must embrace the rising sun."

"Gods and Great Ones preserve us!" Gilhan groaned. He reached for Fideal's hand. "Stand by me now. I need your help, old friend!"

Fideal shook his head. A shadow of long-ago pain crossed his face. "I have forsworn the court."

Gilhan spread his hands. "The Queen betrayed you, man, we all know that. But think of Isolde. She never did you any harm."

"I cannot." Fideal shook his grizzled head. "I broke my sword and cast it into the sea. I swore an oath that I would never return."

Gilhan played his last card. "When terror strikes like this, no man is safe. Breccan and his dogs could come for you."

Fideal laughed. "If Breccan cared about me, I'd be dead by now. He has already dismissed me from his mind." He straightened up and gazed off into the dusk. "He knows that nothing will draw me back to the Queen's side."

Gilhan paused. "Not even at her death?" he asked gently.

"Above all, not now." The clear gray eyes were fixed on something Gilhan could not see. "I hear the Otherworld calling. I'll be with her soon enough." He moved across to his horse.

Gilhan pounded his head in grief. "Gods above, man, won't you think again?"

"Farewell." Fideal swung up into the saddle and turned toward the west. He stared out into a sunset wreathed in blood. "Where's Isolde? She's the only one who can save you now."

Gilhan's heart congealed into despair. "If only we knew."

The young Druid had long disappeared. Gilhan watched until Fideal was no more than a distant figure between the trees, then turned to go. As he did so, he heard the crack of a twig underfoot and a horse's soft sigh.

Now the shadows on the edge of the clearing were taking on human form. Darkness settled on the forest, disguising the menacing figures gathering around.

"Who's there?" Gilhan cried out in fear.

"Friends of Lord Cormac the Druid," came a low chuckle. "He's waiting for you, sir. Shall we take you to him now?"

chapter 11

à *vous, madame! Pour l'amour de vous!"*

Blanche strode into the Great Hall, her skirts rustling furiously around her feet. The shouts of the tournament were still ringing in her ears. *For you, madame—all for the love of you . . .*

Goddess, Mother, how dared her father invite this King here to court without her consent? Yes, he was a brave and handsome knight who had done so well at the joust that all the crowd had cheered him to the core. But...

She bit her lip. But my knight will be coming from Lyonesse with his sword in his hand, and he won't be the handsome King Amaury of Gaul!

She checked herself for a moment to gather her breath. The Great Hall lay before her, decked out for the midwinter feast, bright with holly on every pillar and glossy green ivy rambling around the beams. A great ball of mistletoe hung from the arch of the roof, and posies of the soft pearly berries appeared over every door. The flagstones were green with fresh rushes and rosemary, and pots of burning herbs sweetened the air. Two mighty Yule logs warmed the massive hearths, and countless candles lit the dais ahead. The tables were laid for a hundred guests, and King Hoel himself stood waiting to greet them, with her brother at his side.

And here they were, knights, lords, and ladies arriving for the feast, all greeting her with curtsies and admiring bows. Complacently, Blanche stroked her fine hair and pushed back her veil. Exquisite in ice-white silk and silver lace, with a cloak of silver satin and a crystal coronet, she knew that she would be the queen of the feast. She would be the most beautiful woman there tonight, beyond compare. And she would dance, perhaps even with the King of Gaul . . .

She hailed a passing servant and glanced around the hall. "Where are the musicians?"

"Here, lady—at your service." A lean-faced, intense man stepped out of a group by the door and pulled off his cap. "What's your will?"

What did she want? Irritably, Blanche threw her eye over the troupe. Standing in the front of the men with their instruments was a pale, frog-like boy with bulging eyes. "What an ugly child!" She laughed. "Where did he come from?"

The leader reached out for his dearly loved only son and swiftly tucked the child away behind his back. Bowing low, he produced a practiced smile. "Ah, Princess, wait till you hear him sing."

"Very well..." Blanche pursed her lips and waved them toward the dais. "Take your places and begin."

"As you wish, lady." The little group bowed and moved off.

Blanche turned toward the door. Now the guests were thronging in, ladies in rainbow silks attended by knights in silver and lords in velvet and furs. All down the hall the red berries of the holly pulsed like drops of blood, and the servants were making their rounds with flagons of wine. At the far end, with his dogs around his feet and a brimming goblet in his hand, King Hoel stood warming his back against the fire and pondering the mystery of a woman's heart.

"Has she said any more about Tristan?" he growled to his son.

Kedrin shook his head. "Not since King Amaury arrived."

"And in fine style, eh?" Hoel brightened. "With a hundred knights and banners and pipes and drums, surely enough fandangle to win any girl. D'you think he can replace Tristan in her heart?"

There was a pause. Speculatively, Kedrin eyed his sister as she smiled and greeted the guests, shimmering her way around the hall in crystals and lace. "Not unless we tell her that Tristan will never marry her. That he'll always be Isolde's, body and soul."

"Do we know that?" Hoel challenged. "Do you know he's Isolde's lover? Does any man?"

Kedrin considered, pushing back his hair. "We know that he's served her devotedly these last ten years," he said crisply. "And they say that in all that time, no woman has come into his bed." He laughed and stroked his mustache. "Of course there could be another reason for that."

"A boy-bender, then?" Hoel groaned in disgust. "Worse and worse! My daughter will bring a back-scuttler into our kin."

"Sir..." Kedrin drew a breath. "We don't know that either."

"We know one thing for sure," Hoel said with grim emphasis, lowering his voice as his daughter approached. "Whatever he is, he's not for our Blanche."

Her father and brother together, head-to-head: were they talking about her? Blanche bore down on the two men with an icy glint in her eye.

"Come, sister," Kedrin rallied her, "where's your smile?" He scanned her silver-laced gown and sparkling crystals with a brotherly regard. "Tonight you'll be loved and admired by all."

"Oh, brother, do you think I care about that?" Blanche smiled sweetly at Kedrin and turned away. If Kedrin thought he could get around her, he was wrong.

"Alas, my love..."

The plaintive note of recorders filled the air. Soaring above them came the boy's pure treble, aching with love and loss. Blanche tossed her head. What nonsense it was, all this wailing about heartbreak and grief! A sensible woman made sure of the man she loved and took care not to love a man she could not win.

The music changed to a sprightly Gaulish air. At the far end of the hall King Amaury entered, surrounded by his knights. In a tunic and cloak of royal velvet with a deep circlet of gold holding back his hair, he looked modest yet kingly too, and she had to admit he was a handsome man. Tall, like her brother, he was slim and gracefully built, and his dark eyes were seeking hers the moment he came through the door. Seeing her, he moved forward with a heartfelt smile.

For you, madam, all for the love of you...

A cloud of doubt and discontent dampened Blanche's soul. Was she wrong to cling to Tristan in her heart? Here was a man in love, young, ardent, handsome, and a king. Even his voice with its husky, broken accent was pleasing to her ear. Why then did another shadow darken her mind? An older, stronger figure, more remote—yet a man in truth whom she had never seen?

"My lord..." King Hoel strode forward and ushered the King to a chair. "Let us show you how we feast our guests in France!"

He raised an arm and the music struck up again. The food followed, wave after steaming wave of roast boar, broth, and brawn, borne by armies of sweating menservants and scurrying maids. Seated beside Amaury, Blanche smiled politely as she picked at a piece of pork and nibbled on a fig. Time enough to eat when the wretch had gone.

Kedrin leaned into his father, careful not to let Blanche overhear his words. "She seems to like him, Father."

King Hoel threw down a drumstick to his favorite dog. "You know Blanche. The King of the Fair Ones himself could court her and she'd find fault." He heaved a sigh. "But let's hope."

Hope . . .

Dared he hope?

Amaury glanced at the perfect profile with mounting concern. Why did the Princess keep turning her face away? He had answered King Hoel's invitation with an open mind, but as soon as he saw Blanche he had lost his heart.

There was no one in Gaul with that pale, tender face, that long white neck, that delicate air. Perhaps it was only her silver-white dress, but her skin had the gleam of ice in the winter sun and her body was long and lovely beyond compare. He reached for his wine. Tomorrow he must return to Gaul as her betrothed or else live forever as a broken man. *Pour l'amour!* he told himself, shaking inwardly. He reached for his wine and threw it down his throat. *Speak, man! Speak, or die!*

"Princess, will you give me your hand?"

In marriage? hung between them like a sword. With maddening slowness, Blanche turned her shapely head. "D'you dance, sir?" she parried.

He looked into her eyes. "As well as any man. But I'll dance better when I dance with you."

Blanche looked at him coldly. "I don't want to be your teacher, I want a man who can tutor me. Have you ever crossed swords with Sir Tristan of Lyonesse?"

Is he my rival? Amaury's soul darkened. Gods above, then I am doomed. He steadied his voice. "I have indeed."

"They say he's the most peerless knight in all the world."

"Queen Guenevere would say that about Sir Lancelot of the Lake. But Sir Tristan serves the Queen of Ireland. He is not free to seek a bride like other men."

Blanche's eyes flared. "But women can seek too," she said hotly. "And a woman of spirit must seek the man of the dream."

Amaury gazed at her in deep wretchedness. "And what do you seek, madame—may I know?"

Blanche looked at Amaury's flushed cheeks, his anxious eyes, his uncertain air. Goddess, Mother, why was she fooling with this callow youth when a hero like Tristan lay in her stars ahead?

She drew a long, cool breath. "I seek a man, sir," she said with cruel emphasis, "not a boy. A proven hero of many tournaments. And I shall find him. He will come to me." She rose to her feet and dropped a curtsy of farewell. "I wish you and your knights a safe return to Gaul."

She gathered up her skirts and left him there. Surging down the hall, she made for King Hoel's throne. The deep curtsy she gave her father was for all the hall to see. But her look of angry purpose was for him alone. "At the next tournament, sir, let Sir Tristan be the honored guest. I shall never marry King Amaury as long as I live!"

chapter 12

F ather?"

"What is it, my son?"

The old monk raised his milky eyes from his prayers as he felt the rush of air into his cell. He knew without sight that the forceful presence and hurried, limping steps belonged to Dominian, his former pupil and dearly loved foster son. Bedridden now and a breath away from heaven, the old man still remembered the small stunted body kneeling in prayer at his side and the hard little paw, warm and trusting, in his hand. Dominian might be head of the community now and a man of growing might among Christians everywhere, but the old monk would never forget the lost child he had loved and saved.

Even today he could hear in Dominian's urgent tones haunting echoes of the half-savage he had been. Hated by his mother and cast out to die in the woods, the seven-year-old had thought that he was cursed. His sisters were his mother's only joy, and as a Goddess-worshipper in a land where women ruled, she rejected him because he was merely male. Jerome sighed to himself. No wonder Dominian now persecuted the Mother with all the fury of a poisoned heart. The blows and bruises of his early days, his empty belly, uncouth speech, and starving mind, had all been cured. But the primal wound to his soul, the old monk thought, no force on earth would ever be able to heal.

"News, Father!" He felt the short body drop onto the chair by his bed and heard the triumphant slap of a scroll against Dominian's palm. "Word from Rome."

"From the Holy Father?"

"From the Pope himself." Dominian unfurled the scroll with a flourish, his dark face alight. At times like this, even the never-ending pain of his crumpled spine seemed worth the burden he was forced to bear.

"The first word is for you," he said, his eyes aglow. No one would ever know how he loved this man, but he had made sure that they knew his worth in Rome. "'Greetings to Jerome, our beloved son in Christ,'" he read out joyfully. "See, you are mentioned by name!"

Jerome allowed himself a smile. "You feed my vanity. What is the word from Rome . . . ?"

"The word is 'Strike!' We are ordered to move against the pagans with all speed."

The wasted figure in the bed stiffened. "Move against—how?"

Dominian held up his hand, raising the hard, brown fingers one by one. "Root out the worship of the Great Whore they call the Mother, and put down her shrines. Convert her followers to Christ, by the sword if need be, and secure their so-called Hallows for our use. Leave no trace of this Goddess-evil in this place. Scour through the islands with tempest, wind, and fire, till she's not even a memory to aftertimes."

The old man raised a trembling hand to his forehead. "Now God defend us!"

Dominian turned sharply. "Why?"

"This persecution is against our faith. Our God is love."

"What would you have us do?"

Jerome struggled to sit up. "Work with the people here and learn from them. Their priestesses teach that religion is kindness and all faith should be love." The old man's unseeing eyes gleamed with tears. "Why take from any soul the comfort of that?"

"Priestesses, you say?" Dominian scoffed.

"And more, my son, much more." A light from the Otherworld crossed Jerome's face. "Once, long ago, I was on Avalon. I saw the green hill crowned with blossoms and the Sacred Island rising above the lake. The Lady that ruled there was a miracle."

"Lady?" Dominian struggled with a feeling he could not name. "We have another such Lady here, the Lady of the Sea. They preach thigh-freedom for women and deny the right of a man to call his wife his own. I call them whores." He reached blindly for the scroll from Rome. "And we are ordered to destroy them all!"

"Son, only think!" Jerome begged. "Could you in your conscience put innocent souls to the sword because they worship another Higher Power than ours?"

"We have it in Holy Scripture." Dominian's smoldering eyes sparked into fire. "Our God Himself has commanded, 'Thou shalt have none other gods before me.'"

Jerome shook his white head. "Jesus said, 'Whatsoever you would have men do unto you, do you likewise unto them.' And did not He teach us to love one another, even to the smallest child, 'for of such is the kingdom of God'?" He fixed his blind eyes on Dominian, burning with tears. "You call them pagans. You yourself were reared in the faith of the Mother and were just such a benighted soul when you came to me. You resisted every word of our Christian truth. Should I have put you to death?"

The younger man clenched his fists. Never had he been so at odds with his mentor before. "You oppose this? You do not see the need?"

Jerome laid his hand upon his heart. "Not on God's earth."

Dominian felt something tearing in his breast. "You have been too long among these pagans, Father," he said brutally, winding up his scroll. "They ask in Rome what we are doing here, why we delay the righteous work of God. They say the way to win souls is not through weakness, but through deeds." He threw a hostile glance around the small whitewashed cell bare of all but a wooden beaker of water and a cross over the door. "But perhaps you've withdrawn too far from the world."

Jerome bowed his head and spread his hands. "What deeds?" he asked in a low voice.

Dominian smiled like a wolf. "The Queen set out for Ireland, weeks ago. But she never reached the port. God willing, she's been overtaken by outlaws or ravished by some rogue knight. But wherever she is, God has given us time to work on the King."

He rose from the chair and knelt beside the bed. Taking Jerome's papery hand, he placed it on his head and noted the old man's tears beginning afresh.

"Give me your blessing, Father," he muttered in hot tones. "King Mark is the key to the kingdom now that Isolde has gone. When I have him in my hand, all this land is ours."

ALREADY THE BRIEF DAY was closing in. The salt mist was rolling mournfully off the sea and the crying of winter-starved birds echoed overhead. Daylight had left the towers of Castle Dore not long after noon, and endless hours of darkness lay ahead. Andred sighed, and set down his wine in deep content. Shallow souls might love the summer or the weak, piping spring. But was there any better time of the year than winter, when life itself ran down to its very roots? When the ghost of the sun struggled each day to be born and died weeping before dark? When lesser men huddled like dumb creatures in their dens and no one saw what sharper men chose to do?

So yes, he could bear the darkness and all that midwinter brought, the long hours of drinking in the knights' hall with their raucous braying and their lightning brawls, their stupid boasting and the smoke and the stink. He looked around the Great Hall and smiled to himself. He could even bear Mark because Mark was his, the darkness in Mark was his, and he could work with it any way he pleased.

And he had won that right by learning to please Mark. This midwinter feast and the revels he'd arranged now had all been devised to tickle the King's lightest whim. What did it matter that the older lords were not pleased, Sir Nabon openly dissatisfied, and old Sir Wisbeck and the pompous Sir Quirian frankly at a loss. They all remembered the fine feasts of the past when the whole of the Great Hall became a living bower. When holly and ivy filled the great vault of the roof and the red and white winter berries were everywhere.

But such beauty meant nothing to Mark. He loved to see a blazing yuletide hearth making the air thick with tallow, smoke, and sweat. He wanted to watch his dogs nosing among the rushes and fighting for scraps, and laughed uproariously whenever one of them lifted its leg or added its droppings to the waste on the floor. All he demanded was his favorite wine, a ruby liquor as meaty as bull's blood. And whatever the King desired, the King must have.

"Enjoy the feast!" he drunkenly harangued his knights. "We shan't revel like this when the Queen returns!" He turned to Elva with a roguish wink. "Eh?"

"Too true, my lord," Elva smiled, lowering her eyes.

Elva, too, Andred reflected with the old catch of pain, even his own lover was for Mark's love and use. Well, Elva knew what to do. He had to rely on her to carry it out.

Elva caught his swift glance and sent back a silent reply: I will, my love, never fear. Turning, she leaned in toward Mark, rejoicing in the cool kiss of the earrings brushing her neck. So Isolde lorded it at the High Table in emeralds for Ireland and pearls for the Mother's tears? Elva laughed. Tonight she had the place of honor beside the King, resplendent in jasper and agate and jade from across the sea. Her gown was the black-green of winter holly gleaming against the fiery whiteness of her skin, and she knew she was the finest in the hall. Reaching for her wine, she assessed Mark covertly over the rim of her glass. Time to get to work.

"Here's a health to the King!"

Two or three knights were raising their glasses and staggering to their feet, carrying their drunken revels into the body of the hall. Mark rubbed his distended stomach and looked around with delight. See how the men were enjoying themselves!

"On you go, lads!" he bellowed, raising a slopping goblet in the air. A blood-red splash landed in Elva's lap and lost itself in the scaly black markings of her mottled silk gown. Mark gave a drunken laugh.

The knights in the hall were wrestling each other to the ground. "A show! A show!" Mark crowed. He turned to Andred. "Is there a show for us?"

Andred leaned forward. "Tumblers, mummers, dancers, and pageant-men, whatever Your Majesty desires."

"Remember, sire, we must have all seemly here!" The dark figure of Dominian leaned forward across the table, a warning finger upraised. "This is the birth of Christ. Our Lady lay in a stable at this very hour, travailing to bring Him forth."

"Yes, yes, Father," Mark snapped, his good humor gone. Gods above, would these Christians never cease? "But men also need beef and ale in their bellies at this time of the year. How else will they keep up their strength for the hunt?"

"You are right, my lord," Elva soothed. "And you show your joy in Christ by feasting his birth."

"Yes, I do, don't I?" Mark brightened at once.

"Indeed, sire." Elva took a breath. "And let us pray that the Queen is also keeping Christ's Holy Day.

"Yes, indeed," Mark agreed. "Wherever she is."

"Surely, my lord, she has sent you word?" wondered Elva, wide-eyed.

"Not one," Mark confirmed with a baleful glare.

Elva put a puzzled finger to her cheek. "Then where can she be?" She paused. "Your Majesty equipped her so well. Surely she could find one messenger from a whole troop?"

"You're right!" Mark's small eyes narrowed. "You're saying she's insulted me, that's it?"

"Never, sire," Elva returned in solemn tones. "You know I admire the Queen, as everyone does. Why, the people adore her, they flock to her healing hands—"

"That's another thing!" Mark broke in resentfully. "She gets all their love by involving herself with them. She takes away what should rightfully be mine."

"Your generosity means nothing to her," agreed Elva sorrowfully. "It is the way of Queens."

Mark stared at her, baffled. "What?"

"Her Majesty your Queen was born to rule. It's the same with your overlord, Queen Igraine. They both claim the power of the Mother to queen it over one and all." She paused again. "Perhaps it's time for Your Majesty to show yourself a king."

Gods, it was hot. Mark tugged at the neck of his gown. "What can I do?" he railed.

Elva dropped her eyes in delicious deference. "A king can do anything."

Mark's soul soared. Here was a woman who knew how things should be. Not like Isolde, his precious roaming wife.

"Well then," he said, greatly daring, "I shall—I shall—" He shook his fuddled head. "What shall I do?"

She was ready for this. "Your Majesty may at least ask where your Queen is. And her knight, for Sir Tristan must be with her too."

Dominian leaned forward. "They may be lost, sire, have you thought of that?"

"Indeed!" Elva widened her eyes. "Perhaps they've been attacked by outlaws, or waylaid."

Mark laughed in scorn. "There's no one in that forest."

The priest shook his head. "But Your Majesty must make sure that your Queen is safe."

"Must, must?" fretted Mark. "Why should they come to any harm?" He turned to Elva, putting on a careless shrug. "And if they're in a hurry to get to Ireland, why should they send word?"

She could smell his uncertainty above the rank odor of the wine. "You are the King. They owe their faith to you."

"Send after them, sire," said Dominian forcefully. "Find out what's going on."

Thank you, priest! Purring inwardly, Elva pressed her advantage home. "Tristan at least should return at your command. He owes you an explanation of the reason for their delay."

Mark hesitated. His head swam. God Almighty, what to do?

"Well, sire?" Dominian cut in.

"Well what?" snapped Mark. "I'm sure Isolde can take care of herself. And if she's lost, what am I to do? Queen Igraine is the overlord of the forest, not I."

Dominian's eyes flared. "Why should you be subject to the old Queen? A man should rule his kingdom—and his wife."

Mark clenched his fists and turned an ugly red. "Are you saying I don't?" He called the nearest servant. "Tell the Captain of the Guard to get a galloper here." He nodded to Dominian and Elva. "I'll send to the port to see if they've taken ship. I'll show them who is King!"

"Your Majesty is wise." Elva preened herself like a snake in the sun, writhing her long hard body under Mark's gaze.

Mark eyed her sharp, high breasts, lean waist, and boyish flanks. He had done his work for the day and could take his reward. "Come, lady," he said thickly. "Let's go to bed."

chapter 13

*C*astle Pleure?

Now I know why they call this the Place of Tears.

Isolde raised her weary head from her arms and rubbed her eyes. Truly Sir Greuze's retreat was well named. How many tears had she shed in the short time here? How many nights had she watched by Tristan's bed, with only the bats and screech owls for company?

Brangwain, loyal to a fault, had to be ordered to her own bed at night, for her strength would be needed when Isolde could go no more. Tristan lay before them like a carving on a tomb, and his ragged breath rustled like dead leaves through the darkness of the night. And still Isolde was haunted by the fearful thought, *Goddess, Mother, tell me how bad he is.*

Wait and see was the bleak answer, from the moment the knights carried Tristan's unconscious body into the hall.

Isolde closed her eyes. Would she ever forget how hard it had been to get Tristan's poor tortured body into a bed? Built into the face of the hillside, its chambers burrowing back into the rock, the castle had no open, airy apartments where the sun poured in. Ivy mantled all the windows and every room was bathed in greenish light. Still, the rooms were warm and dry, and a sweet forest fragrance hung in the air. So the place was wholesome enough—but if only they had been in Dubh Lein ...

At first she wanted to put Tristan in the best room in the house.

"Where did your master sleep?" she questioned Sir Yder as they climbed the stairs.

Sir Yder threw open a handsome pair of doors. "Here, lady."

Isolde moved forward. The rooms themselves were wide and gracious enough, floored in mellow oak and looking out through green curtains of ivy into the heart of the wood. But as she entered, Greuze's blood-stained armor hung on every wall, his double-edged swords crossed with his daggers and killing spears. On the floor lay the hideous trophies of his evil ways, long hanks of women's hair in chestnut, fair, and dark with even a few pitiful, tangled tufts of gray. One side of the bed was stained with tears and blood, and the terrible smell of madness filled the air.

Tears filled her eyes. "Thank you, sir."

She turned sharply on her heel and hurried away. Tomorrow she would have the whole apartment scoured from ceiling to floor. Then these rooms could be habitable again. But put Tristan here to recover? Never! She fought down her rising stomach. "On, sir, on!"

At the top of the castle was a disused attic chamber empty of all but the old wooden frame of a bed. Rambling away under the eaves, it caught all the sun that reached the ancient grange. Its round windows gazed out through the drifting tops of the trees, and the gentle movement of the branches might help Tristan sleep.

She turned to Sir Yder. "A mattress and clean linen, and a full set of hangings, sir—and I may beg you, on Tristan's life, your very best?"

The night was long, watching over Tristan's body as his fever rose. A dark-faced Brangwain kept the vigil beside her, her lean frame coiled like a cat ready to spring.

At length the loyal maid could bear no more. "We need healing-stuffs, lady. If there's anything here, I'll find it tonight!"

She was gone for a long time. But when she returned, Isolde was reminded again why they called Brangwain "Merlin's kin."

"Here, madam!" cried the maid, erupting into the chamber with a pot of salve. "Sir Greuze forbade all such potions, but I knew one of the knights must have his own remedy for cuts and hurts." She grinned in triumph. "They all swore they had no such thing, but I found it in the end."

Isolde opened the lid. The salve was rich and glossy, brownish-black, and stiff enough to hold a knife upright. It smelled of poppy and all-heal, lavender and thyme, with a strange seductive hint of something unknown. She peered at it suspiciously. "Did they say what it was?"

"From the East, was all they knew. But they swore it had saved more lives among them than one."

Isolde hesitated. Could she risk using this? Yet what else was there if she rejected it? She cast a stricken eye over the figure slumbering like death at her side, and dug into the paste. They never knew if it helped Tristan or not. But he did not die that night.

⁂

THE NEXT DAY they buried the Lady La Pauvre and Sir Greuze. The poor lady was laid to rest in the little chapel adjoining the castle, and Isolde herself led the funeral rites. As the candles bloomed like white roses on the walls, she called on the Mother to bring the lost soul to peace. As she did so, her sight shivered and she saw two souls walking in starlight on the astral plain, wrapped in each other's arms, each comforting the other with tears of joy. Then Tristan's words came back to her with new pain: *she has what she wanted. Her spirit is with her love.*

But they could not lay Greuze in the earth, for the Mother would never take him to Herself. Nor was it right that he should rest forever beside the lady he had wronged. When the bodies were brought up from the forest, Isolde decreed that Greuze should not be admitted to Castle Pleure, but was to pass the night outside, guarded by four of his knights.

More than one of his knights, Isolde knew, slipped out in the long hours of darkness to bid their lord farewell. She guessed others would weep privately for the knight he once had been. But none challenged her decision with a word or a look. Greuze had banished himself from the company of decent souls and must be buried as the outcast he had made himself in his life.

At dawn Isolde had him carried deep into the wood, with all his knights marching in front and behind. Greuze was laid to rest in a sheltered hollow underneath the trees, wrapped in his banner, with his sword at his side. With none to praise his life or mourn his death, the ceremonies were brief. Then the knights covered him with a cairn of stones. Very soon the woodland would take the unmarked grave to itself and Greuze would sleep undisturbed in his stony bed.

They turned to go. Standing at the side of the cairn, Isolde saw an older knight leaning heavily on his sword, his head bowed in grief.

"He knighted me," he said simply. "I was a green lad, and he saw what I could do. He taught me chivalry, everything I know. But in the Holy Land, a bolt from a crossbow caught him in the head. After that—" he struggled to master himself. "We all prayed he would recover his mind one day. He was a true knight once."

Isolde felt tears burning the back of her throat. "May that be his epitaph. And may his soul make its way to the arms of the Mother in the end."

The knight stared out into the rising sun. "Let us hope, lady. Let us hope."

chapter 14

"ℎow is he now, Brangwain?"

"Much better, lady, I believe."

Coming slowly back to consciousness, Tristan recognized the voice of the maid. But Brangwain would probably say that, no matter how he was.

How bad was he, rambling through these endless regions of pain? He laughed to himself, and back the answer came: you cannot know. But Isolde would know, and so would Brangwain. That was all he had to care about now. He drifted away on a cloud of content.

Isolde my lady—Isolde my only love . . .

He wanted to tell the world, shout it aloud. But he knew he must protect her name with his life. Not a word, then, he told himself owlishly, not a word . . . Yet his mind played on.

My lady . . . oh, my love . . .

Tristan heard his own voice singing in his head, and came to himself bathed in greenish light. I have drowned was the sweet thought filling his brain. The Lady of the Sea has come to take me home. He floated in warm abandon, loose as a child. His lifelong prayer drifted gently through his mind, I pray you, lay me with my mother, she died for me.

Then he felt a hand he knew on the back of his neck, and the edge of a cup nudged briskly at his lips.

"Drink this," said the voice he would have obeyed through all three worlds, and he drank and slipped back into the arms of the sea.

But one day he heard a robin scolding as she scoured the wintry forest, then he caught the pattering of a mouse in the wainscot, followed by the furious scratching of a cat. When the night was at its lowest, he listened to the slow ticking of the deathwatch beetle at its mournful work.

Then at dawn came the blessed crowing of a cock, and he knew he was not dead but alive and on earth.

But which earth? Cornwall, Ireland, or a foreign land? Wherever he was, she was with him too. Every day he felt the hard little hands at work, feeding him sops, dressing his wounds, or cooling his forehead to drive the demons away.

Then came the moment when he opened his eyes and knew where he was. Smiling, he drew a great breath of air and tried to speak.

Isolde swallowed her rising tears of joy. "You have kept us very busy, sir," she said huskily, "Brangwain and I. You ran a fever from your injuries, and we lost you for a while."

He found his voice. "What are my wounds?"

She regarded him gravely. "Almost too many to count."

"And the worst?"

"This." Delicately, she traced a long raised scar on his thigh. "The blade pierced you to the bone."

And struck into the groin; he could tell it from her face. He flexed his leg and knew at once how long it would be before he walked again or was able to ride.

Or before he . . .

A primal fear of manhood shook him from head to foot, and he forced himself to put the thought away. Time enough for that, he schooled himself with gritted teeth. He forced a lopsided grin. "Your knight gave a poor account of himself, it seems."

She leapt to his defense. "Greuze was fully armed, and you were only equipped for the road! He had—"

"I know." He tried to sit up and was defeated by the trembling in his limbs. "How long have we been here?"

"Long enough to enjoy the peace of this castle of yours. But I've sent ahead to the port, to command a ship for when we're ready to put to sea."

He looked at her quizzically. "This castle of mine, lady?"

"Yours, sir," she said firmly. "Won by the rules of war."

He laughed with delight. "Then if it's mine, I shall call it—" He paused, while a thousand little winged joys fluttered round his head. "—Bel Content. I don't want to own a place of weeping and tears."

"Castle Bel Content." Isolde rolled the name around her mind, relishing the sound. "Your knights will say their new lord has chosen well."

"And what does my doctor say?"

"That the patient has talked enough for one day." She stooped down with a smile and stopped his mouth with a kiss.

But he would not be silenced for long, Isolde knew, and soon he insisted on trying out his strength. White and sweating, he forced himself around the chamber, leaning on Yder's shoulder all the way. That night he moaned in torment in his sleep, and Isolde sat watchful and wakeful, suffering through it all.

But each day became easier, till the great shuffling figure, huddled over like a sick old man, returned step-by-step to his former self. Before long he had made his way to the stables to visit the great gray who had carried him down the years, and both horse and rider wept on each other's necks. At last he had the strength to join Yder and the knights at the hunt, and joyfully stayed in the saddle from dawn to dusk. Isolde watched the color come back to his dear face and felt the blood returning to her heart. The old year was dying now from day to day, but like the green man of the woods, Tristan waxed and grew strong.

At length they came to the moment that Tristan had feared. But Isolde knew what he dreaded, and in her arms he found the comfort that drives away fear. Alone at the top of the castle, with the faithful Brangwain keeping the world at bay, slowly and tenderly they renewed their love. In the sweet greenish light of the trees, lulled by the wind in the branches singing them to sleep, they lay together all night, drowsing in bliss and waking in each other's arms.

Even then they knew it was a special interlude. Love's time is not like other hours and weeks, and they lived a lifetime of joy in the days they had. At Mark's court or in the castle of Dubh Lein, a thousand eyes saw everything they did, and the dread of discovery ran through their lives. Here they could be together without fear, to walk in the woodland by day and whisper by candlelight at night. Every morning brought new pleasure, and each twilight a warm glow of content. Yet always the thought hung between them like a shadow from the Otherworld: *one day soon, love, we must be on our way . . .*

And still the days wore away to the death of the year. Now the snows came down, and the earth lay bound in frost. The forest was roofed with white, casting an Otherworldly light on the ground below, and snow crystals glittered like diamonds on every tree. Indoors, too, the frost left its traces on the windowpanes. As she went from room to room, Isolde found written in the ice mantling the green glass, *Isolde my lady* or *My lady and my Queen.* Then she knew that Tristan was himself again.

One day when they were quite alone he said, "Lady, we should celebrate the midwinter feast. I want to see you revel and dance like a queen."

Then she knew why she loved him, and him alone. "The midwinter feast?"

He looked at her and saw her dancing eyes. "To mourn the death of the year," he affirmed, "and bring on the birth of the new. The midwinter revels drive the darkness away."

He reached for her hand and brought it to his lips. The touch of her melted his heart, and he heard music and laughter and the singing of her soul. He saw her radiant in jewels and velvet, fragrant as midsummer, dancing in her winter court. None of this came to him in words he could say. "A feast," he repeated stubbornly, "a feast."

"A feast?" Brangwain did not hesitate, her dark eyes dancing with glee. "You have your harp, sir, and there'll be some here, I swear, who can raise a tune." She laughed with delight. "And not only my countryman from the land of song."

Brangwain was right. Fighting man though he was, Sir Yder bore the music of his race deep in his veins. Most of the knights could also carry a tune, and a few were proficient on flute and tabor too.

But the knights were reluctant to enter into the spirit of mirth.

"The heart has gone out of them, lady," Tristan said sorrowfully. "They lost the joy of merrymaking years ago."

Isolde shook her head. "Every man hopes for delight in his soul," she said firmly. "We'll send them into the greenwood for holly and ivy, and whoever does best, we'll make him the king of the feast."

The next morning a laughing, jostling procession made its way into the wood. That night the hall was decked like a forest bower, redolent with the sharp green scent of the woodland and hung about with great globes of mistletoe glowing like the moon.

They began the music as soon as the food was done. As Tristan led, Yder followed and the little band of musicians struck up a lilting tune. One refrain led into another as they recalled songs of their boyhood, their adventures as young knights, and sweet serenades of their courtship days. Note after note filled the candlelit hall till the scene faded and Isolde saw wide sunlit meadows, bustling tournaments, and highways teeming with life. At the foot of a tower stood a knight harping of love, to a lady who leaned down from her window and threw him a rose.

The ballad came to an end. Tristan passed his harp to Yder and rose to his feet. Immediately the Welshman plucked out a lively air, and the rest of the musicians took up the beat of the dance. Tristan crossed to Isolde, bowed, and held out his hand. "Honor me, Your Majesty?" he inquired softly.

"Oh, sir . . ." Isolde smiled into his eyes. "The honor is mine."

For the rest of her life the first notes of that tune would always take her back to that candlelit hall, that time of joy. Tristan danced as he fought, deft and sure and strong. His hard hand in hers was all that she desired, his brief touch on her shoulder or waist a promise of more. Borne up by the music, they leapt and swooped and soared, rising like birds above the everyday world. Moving as one, their spirits left the world, bound for the regions high above the stars. For a moment they touched the place where souls go hand in hand and lovers never part. And that night they returned there again in each other's arms, heart-to-heart and naked soul to soul.

The next morning dawned gray and the sun hid its head. Shrouded within the great bed, Isolde closed her eyes. *The sun cannot bear to watch what we have to do.* By her side Tristan slept lightly like a hunter, his face shadowed by the early morning light. Lovingly, she eyed the smooth lines of his strong-featured face and resisted the urge to stroke his powerful jaw. The warm, familiar smell of him rose to greet her as she carefully snuggled her body closer to his. *How can I live without this?* stabbed her to the quick. She reached out to him for comfort, then pulled back, her heart darkening like the day. *I must learn to live without you. Tomorrow, love, we will wake alone.*

As they left, all the knights turned out to bid them farewell. Yder had agreed to take command of the castle, and there was no reason to delay. On the edge of the forest, Isolde thought she heard a voice calling from the depths of the old grange, *return when you will, you will find me here.* But she dared not let herself look back.

Now every hour brought them to the port. Step by step the air overhead grew sharp with the tang of salt, and the mournful cries of the gulls beckoned them on. Isolde read Tristan's bleak face and threw him a glance. *Soon, love, we'll be in Ireland, where no man can say me nay. And there we'll be happy again as we were at Bel Content.*

They came to the top of a hill. As they climbed the ridge, it began to snow. On the crest, a great flock of magpies rose squawking from the ground, a flash of blue-black and white, and glittering, staring eyes. *One for sorrow . . . seven for a secret that must never be told . . .*

Isolde shivered. Gods above, magpies were ill-omened birds. She looked around in alarm. Below them lay a sheltered inlet with two or three ships at anchor, surrounded by the armored guards of the king. A lean, sharp-faced captain stood at their head, and Mark's royal standard was flying over them all.

Isolde felt her heart choking her throat. *Goddess, Mother, is Mark here? Will he know that Tristan has just left my bed?*

The reins of her horse lay idle in her hands. She took them up in a dream of dread and forced herself down the slope. The captain began to speak as they drew near.

"King Mark greets the Queen of Ireland, his loyal wife," he proclaimed. "He wishes her a good voyage to Ireland and all speed in her state affairs. And he orders his royal nephew and liege knight, Tristan of Lyonesse, to turn back to Castle Dore. Matters of state demand his presence there, and the King will take it as the act of a traitor to refuse."

chapter 15

There was no sound but the crying of the gulls. Isolde felt the blood draining from her face and thought all the world must hear the clamor in her heart. The captain stood watching her with all his men as she sat on her horse amid the drifting snow. She gazed back at the wall of staring eyes and dared not look at Tristan at her side.

"You shall not go," she muttered, numb with shock.

A great wave dashed against the dock, and a fine freezing spray fell on their faces like tears.

"Think, lady!" he ground back, suppressing a groan. "If I defy Mark and take ship with you, won't the whole world know whose knight I am?"

She nodded furiously, *yes. It would tell Mark that we are lovers and care nothing for him.* And it would put a weapon into Andred's hands that the jealous knight would not hesitate to use.

She moistened her dry lips. "What does he want?"

"Mark?" Tristan gave soft and savage laugh. "What else but to part us, lady, and to cause you pain?"

She did not want to believe it. "Matters of state," she insisted. "He said—"

"Lies!" Tristan spat. "He only wants to demonstrate his power."

"Over me?" Her eyes flared. "I am Queen of the Western Isle in my own right. Even in Cornwall every woman has the freedom of the Mother-right. Mark cannot touch me."

And that is why he hates you, and always will. Tristan choked back an angry sigh. He nodded toward the men drawn up on the quay. "Come, lady, let us give them what they want. Let me see you aboard and then be on my way." As he spoke he felt his heart crack like a bone.

"Rest here tonight," she said, frantic to change his mind. "It's snowing, and you'll never find the way. You'll be lost in the wood if you try to ride in the dark. If I sail at dawn, that will give us a few more hours."

The dying sun was plunging into the sea. Tristan watched it dissolve in a cauldron of red and gold and steeled himself not to melt with it too. "Mark's orders were that I should return at once."

"Through a midnight forest? At the risk of your life?" she flung out furiously, then bit it back. Nothing was gained by pressing him to delay.

Overhead a pair of gulls wheeled and cried, then parted lamenting into the setting sun. The sky was bathed in blood like the death of hope, and banks of dark cloud draped the horizon in black. The sea called out with a slow departing roar and the wind plucked at her garments, *come, Isolde, come . . .*

The evening star was blooming in the west. She could hardly speak for pain. "So we must part?"

"Only in body," he said in low, fervent tones. "My soul is yours, my spirit, my sword are yours. Every evening I shall look on the love star and pray for you. Every dawn I shall call down the love of the Mother on your head."

"And I you." She bowed her head. "And with every breath I shall draw you back to my side."

"And I you."

"So, then . . . ?" She could not say it.

"You to the sea, and I to the lonely sky," Tristan muttered through pale lips. "I must go back to the forest and find my way."

He had the look of a deer in the midnight woodland, wild and strange. *Already you have left me, my sweet love.* She wanted to weep.

He turned moonstruck eyes upon her. "A thousand years ago the Great Ones set this suffering in the stars. But our coming together again will be written too. One day I shall be with you, never to part. Come, lady, let me bring you to your ship."

THE WOODLAND LAY around him, dark and deep. The stars had fled behind the louring clouds, and the glimmering moon could hardly light the way. And it was cold . . . so cold . . .

Snow lay everywhere, turning the world to white. A deep frost had made all the forest a labyrinth of ice, and he had long ago lost all sense in his hands and feet. He reached forward to pat his horse's neck. "Farther, old friend?"

The great gray swung back his head and nuzzled Tristan's boot. You're the master, sir.

I know, Tristan nodded. And I should have done better by both of us than this!

He heaved a furious sigh. Why had he chosen to travel on a night like this? And why had he left the straight track that he knew and struck off through the trees in search of a shorter route?

"Go with the Goddess," she had said, her face as stripped of emotion as a sea-bleached bone. But loving her as he did, he knew what lay beneath. And he had never felt anything as naked and raw as her grief, unless it was his own.

Yet he, too, had to hide all he felt. "Farewell, lady" was his wooden reply.

Then he bowed and left her on the windswept deck and watched from the jetty as the sea bore her away. She is gone, ripped through him like a severed nerve. When shall I see her, hold her, kiss her sweet eyes again?

Yes, yes, he told himself, shivering, that had been pain indeed, almost beyond his power to endure. Still, what a fool to leave the greenways that were old when the Romans came, and strike off into the trackless wastes of the wood. It was colder now than he could have believed, every twig cracking as the frost tightened its grip, every tree bowed down with the weight of snow and ice. As he nosed his horse forward it came to him like a cold branch in the face, I could die here. I could lose my life.

On plodded the gray, on through the frozen night. Cold as he was, he felt tiredness overtaking him with every step as his overstrained body nudged him to the edge of sleep.

Sleep . . .

He laughed, a strange, rusty sound. On the road, he often slumbered as his horse went along, knowing the faithful creature would find the way. Indeed in those far-off, glorious tournament days when he chased the sport of arms from place to place, the gray had known the great highways of France, Spain, and Gaul better than he had himself. But if he slept now, they would never see the dawn. No, sleep must wait till he lay in a fine feather bed, hung with royal emerald satin and embroidered with the white trefoil.

Till he lay in Isolde's arms . . .

A faint fragrance reached him through the drowsy air. Greeting his starved senses in that midnight wood, it seemed the sweetest thing in all the world, and he turned his horse toward it in a dream.

"Gods above!"

The gray stumbled heavily, jolting him awake. Cursing, he vaulted from the saddle and groaned. If the gray went lame, they would perish here. Time to go on foot and lead his loyal mount.

On . . .

Must get on . . .

What was that?

Ahead of him a light flickered and was gone. Was it real? Trembling, he cast around in an ecstasy of hope. Where was it? Over there?

"Where are you?" he cried out. "Show me again!"

All around him the forest lay dark and cold and still. Tears as hard as diamonds stood in his frozen eyes. It was only a will-o'-the-wisp after all, the spirit who came to torment a lost traveler's last hours. So that was his fate, then, death?

So be it. He laughed a frozen laugh. He would not be the first to lose his way in the wood, and pay for the misjudgment with his life. The pulse of life was still thundering through his veins. But the Dark Lord was approaching, he could hear his tread.

He fixed his eyes on the place where the light had died, and filled his mind with joy. One thought alone would transport him to the Plains of Delight.

Isolde, my lady . . .

My lady and my love.

chapter 16

a ray of light shone out through the gloom. Tristan held onto the reins for support, staring like the dead. With painful slowness he closed his frozen eyes then opened them again. His heart lurched wildly. The light was still there.

"Look, look!" he mumbled in crazy excitement to the gray. He pointed a trembling hand. "And another over there?" He fumbled at the reins. "Get on, while we can still see it—on!"

But the gray took the bit between his teeth and refused to move, tossing his head and digging in his hooves.

"Gods above!" Tristan groaned. Was this a time to delay? Roughly he drove forward toward the light. But his strength was waning now with every step, and he cried out in fear as the distant gleam flickered, then died away. Just as he was about to stumble to his knees, a brightness lit the midnight path ahead and he saw the lights of a castle glimmering through the trees. Weeping, he threw an arm over his horse's furry neck.

"Saved!" he rejoiced. "We're saved."

All at once the air seemed warmer and he smelled the sweet fragrance again. It came from the dark dwelling he could see ahead, its outline getting clearer as he drew near. The ground was rising toward a tree-lined crest and it stood proudly on the horizon, its black facade starkly outlined against the fleeting moon. For a moment he took it for a shape with no substance, then told himself that the high walls and delicate towers must be solid enough. How else would a castle appear in the middle of a forest at night?

Now the gray was suddenly fearful again, shying away and whinnying with distress, as if it feared to face the way ahead. Slowly, he coaxed it from the shelter of the trees. They came out into a clearing, a wide expanse of white under the pale winter moon. Tristan stared. All around the castle the snow lay undisturbed, as if nothing had passed that way for weeks. Yet in winter like this, when food would be running low, surely the knights must go hunting every day?

Tristan shook his head. Time enough to puzzle this out later on. For now—he raised his eyes from the ground and caught his breath.

The whole of the castle was bathed in a glimmering light. A pearly sheen danced off the snow-covered ground, and frost glistened on every stone tracery and parapet. The great doors of the gatehouse stood open below, and a warm glow seemed to beckon weary travelers in. Venturing through the gates, he found himself in a wide courtyard, where forty stables stood open around three sides of a fine cobbled square. Tristan looked around, at a loss again. In any other stables at this hour, overworked lads would be scrambling to deal with mud-spattered riders and horses loudly whinnying for their feed. But here there were neither men nor horses to be seen.

Tristan shrugged his stiff shoulders: no matter. On the road he always looked after his horse himself. He led the gray into the nearest stall and unsaddled and rubbed him down with unusual care. But still the horse shivered and rolled his eyes, breathing as hard as if he scented blood.

"What's wrong with you, snorting and skittering like this?" Tristan demanded fondly, fetching his old friend a whack across the rump. "Nothing that a bale of hay won't cure."

At last he left the stable and made his way up through the yard. The stars were out and a fragile moon smiled down upon a world of ice and snow. Ahead of him a glittering archway gave onto a grand courtyard with torchlit cloisters shaded by ivy and yew. As he made his way forward, the sweet fragrance came to him again. Be calm, he schooled himself. But still his pulse beat faster and he could feel the excitement gathering in his soul.

Far off now he could hear high-pitched voices and tinkling laughter, and faint strains of ethereal music overhead. Light poured into the courtyard, and a pair of great bronze doors swung open to reveal a handsome hall with slender, brightly clad shapes drifting to and fro. More candles than he could count burned around the walls, and the flames of a roaring fire danced on the hearth. The fragrance he had followed from the forest came to meet him, catching his heart, and he thought of his lost mother, frail, lovely, and fleeting, and too young to die. A vast yearning filled him, and he wanted to stay forever in this glittering space where brilliant, beautiful creatures wafted to and fro. One thought alone suffused his wandering brain: I have come to the place where the Fair Ones live.

In a dream, he stepped over the threshold and entered the hall. Now he saw that the long chamber was hung with tapestries and every scene depicted seemed alive. In one, a proud queen embraced a unicorn on a golden chain and spurned the handsome lover at her side. In another, she commanded a suitor to be gone, banishing him from the sunlit orchard where she held court. In the last, a young man lay dying on the ground, all alone in a withered forest where no flowers grew. A few faint words were issuing from his mouth, but at this distance Tristan could not make out what they were.

He closed his eyes. That scent again—what was it? The faint smell of blossom reached him, and he turned his head. At the far end of the chamber stood a great bowl of blood-red roses, flourishing their dark heads. Roses in winter? Tristan looked again. Strange, that these artificial blooms could look so real, and even smell so too. Real? He shook his head. He had not realized how tired he was.

Drifting around the hall, clustered together or moving in ones and twos, were twenty or more slender, laughing young women, each lovelier than the last. Tristan sighed with relief. Here at last were the people of the castle—but where were the men?

Now the girls had seen him, and he found himself the focus of many pairs of curious eyes, all the sweet-faced, willowy girls giggling and whispering as they looked him up and down. Their bright silks rustled as they talked and they nodded their heads together like a garland of flowers. Tristan drew in his breath and gave thanks that his love for Isolde was true, or he might have found it hard to resist the sideways glances and inviting smiles.

"Sir . . ."

The tallest of the maidens came toward him with a gliding tread. She was as slender as a hazel-twig in March and robed in pale, filmy garments the color of catkins in spring. She had long, glossy hair in a vivid chestnut brown, and the coloring to match. Her veil flowed around her shoulders like a woodland stream, and her smile lit up the night. She dropped him a low curtsy. "Welcome, sir, to the Castle Plaisir de Fay."

Plaisir de . . . pleasure of what?

Fay . . . fayerie . . . floated through his mind, but it made no sense. He put a hand to his head. His brain would labor no further today. "Madam, how may I call you?"

The nut-brown maiden smiled at him again. "Falsamilla, lord."

Falsa—what? Another name to conjure with. Manfully, Tristan pressed on. "Will you lead me to your lord and lady to make my greetings to them?"

"My lord?" A cascade of shrill laughter filled the air. "We have no lord, sir. Our lady rules here alone."

"A widow, perhaps?" Tristan asked, and earned another high-pitched laugh.

Confused, he took in the sumptuous hangings on the wall, the rich carpets underfoot, and the regal dais at the end of the hall. Beneath a deep canopy of mulberry silk stood a low but elegant chair like a royal throne. Tristan turned back to Falsamilla. "Is she a queen?"

The maiden glanced up at him with mischief in her eyes. "Our lady will tell you all you need to know."

Another of the gorgeous girls was at his elbow, holding a pitcher of silver and an ornate goblet of gold. "You'll take some wine, sir? Our lady will be here very soon."

Tristan bowed his head, mesmerized by the stream of ruby liquor pouring into the gold. "Thank you, yes."

He stared at the gaggle of young women, whose excitement seemed to be reaching a fever pitch. "Tell me about your Castle Plaisir de Fay," he demanded brusquely, to cover his unease. "Who is your lady?"

An odd, husky voice sounded in his ear. "They call me Duessa, sir."

He had not heard her come in. Gods above, he thought wildly, these women must move on wheels instead of feet. Unless it's a fetch, a spirit of the place . . . He forced himself to turn.

But the figure standing before him looked mortal enough, and womanly too, from the tip of her headdress to her fine satin shoes. Her gown was of black silk damask, rich and plain, and cut like a nun's habit in its simplicity. She wore a tall pointed casque of black velvet, and around the base gleamed a coronet of red gold. Over it all floated a silver-spangled veil, and behind it he could see no more than her eyes.

Her eyes were like dark stars. Tristan felt his mind slipping away. Was it the headdress that made her so imposing, or her lean, fierce frame? Her soft shoulders or her hard, jutting breasts, straining against the severely modest gown? He shook his muddled head. Gods above, what was she, widow or Queen? Neither, or both?

Slowly she put back her veil. "Welcome, sir."

She stood calm and unsmiling, waiting for him to speak. In silence he absorbed her shapely presence, large dark eyes and ivory skin, till her sharp white teeth flashed in a sudden smile. Yet still he thought there was something secretive about her deep-set eyes, and wondered if the long, pale face had ever seen the sun. And a sweet secret it seemed to be too—a pleasure crying out to be enjoyed. Her dark, puckered mouth was like a wild loganberry waiting to be picked. Without warning, he saw himself feasting on her overripe lips, nipping them with his teeth till the juices flowed . . .

Goddess, Mother!

Hot with shame, he turned his face to the fire. "My lady," he forced out, "I find myself benighted in this wood. May I crave the shelter of your roof tonight?"

"Oh, sir . . ."

She put out her hand. Her low, husky voice wrapped him around in warmth. "Sir Tristan, my maidens and I are honored to greet you tonight."

He gasped. "You know my name?"

"Oh, sir," she said gravely, "all the world knows you. The great hero who rides the gray horse is known far and wide." Her long arms floated out to embrace the hall. "Even here, where my maidens and I hide away."

"Hide away?" Tristan cried impetuously, "why should you do that? Your maidens are the fairest to be seen, and your ladyship would grace any court on earth." He gave a self-conscious laugh. "Lady, how should I address you? I would not wish to insult your dignity."

For a second he thought that a whole life flashed violently behind the brooding, coal-black eyes. She turned her dark gaze upon him, and a shudder passed through him as he felt its force. The next moment she was herself again. "'Lady' is the finest title of them all." She lifted her hand. "Let us eat."

Within minutes, the maidens had raised a handsome trestle on the dais and dressed it for a feast. In a few airy passes the table was set with linen and silver and bowls of flowers and fruit. Plates and goblets followed, and candles and pitchers of wine. Then, out of nowhere, it seemed, a royal seat appeared for him, and the Lady Duessa, smiling, took her throne.

Seated beneath the rich red canopy, the lady raised a ruby-studded goblet and the wine in her cup gleamed in the candlelight like blood. "To the health of our guest, Sir Tristan of Lyonesse."

"Sir Tristan, Sir Tristan!" Standing around the table, the maidens rustled together like flowers in a field. Tristan rose to his feet to accept the toast. "And to you, lady—blessings on the Castle Plaisir de Fay!"

Never in his life had Tristan seen roast pork so succulent that it fell apart under the knife, or beef so richly marbled that it melted from the bone. Dish after dish of jelly, broth, and brawn appeared and disappeared in the deft, whisking hands. Meanwhile salads and nuts and cheeses and a thousand sweet delights came to keep them company on the groaning board.

The lady ate sparingly, Tristan noticed, and drank even less. She's right not to drink, he thought owlishly, as he felt the warmth of the wine spreading through his brain. As she picked at her food she spoke of a hundred things, and her hot, husky voice flowed in and out of his head. Now and again she fell silent, smiling into his eyes. Before long a thought took shape in his mind: this lady lives alone, without the company of men. Lives alone, sleeps alone, but seems to desire some other fortune tonight...

Again he felt the unwelcome pricking in his loins. Goddess, Mother! he choked in silence. Have you lost your mind? As a knight on the road, such things had come his way, but never since he swore his faith to Isolde had he turned aside to take these casual pickings when they arose. Never once had he yielded to the pleas of a lovesick virgin or stooped to pleasure the lady of a castle when her knight was away.

And could he forget his vow to Isolde now? He groaned inwardly. Out, man! Get out! Once safely away from here, he could relate this whole adventure to her without shame. He could tell her all, because there would be nothing to tell.

His mind racing, he hastened through the remains of his meal. The lady, he noticed, had stopped eating a while ago. He waved a hand toward her and sketched out a bow. "Madam Duessa, I am keeping you from your rest. And I myself—" He pretended to yawn, then gallantly covered it with his hand. "Forgive me, lady, if I forget all courtesy. I have ridden too far today, I must retire."

"Of course." She gave a gracious smile and rose to her feet. "My maidens will escort you to your rest."

"Thank you."

He leapt up with alacrity and crossed to draw back her chair. As he did so, the tapestry on the wall caught his eye. He saw a tormented knight lying on the ground, holding up his hand to a lady dressed all in black. Now he could read the dying man's last words: "La belle dame sans merci has me in thrall." And the lady had deep-set eyes and a secret, mulberry mouth like the lady here—

Goddess, Mother, and all the Great Ones, I was not wrong!

Changing color, he recoiled with a violent start and realized his mistake at once. The lady, he saw, had gone unnaturally pale.

"Till tomorrow, then," he cried too eagerly, backing away with an awkward bow. "I hope I do not offend you, lady, by retiring now."

"No offense at all. On the contrary."

Something unfathomable passed behind her eyes. Smiling, she moved toward him and gave him her hand. He bent his head to brush it with his lips as she spoke again.

"Sir Tristan, in a house of women, I have made it my custom to take passing knights to my bed. My maids will bring you to my chamber tonight."

The next moment she was caressing his temple and stroking the side of his neck. "You are a hero, Sir Tristan, the greatest who ever wandered into my wood. Let us show you how my maidens and I welcome a man like you to Plaisir de Fay."

chapter 17

a wave of disgust broke over Tristan's head. *Gods above,* he cursed with slow-rising anger, *you have had nothing from me, lady, to encourage this!* Carefully, he withdrew himself from her touch and straightened up to look her in the eye.

"Your ladyship flatters me beyond my deserts," he said as coldly as he could. *Gods, Gods, Gods, if only he had not drunk so much wine* . . .

"Oh, sir . . ." She glimmered at him, her dark eyes like moons. Sick at heart, he saw two fathomless pools of desire, hungry black pupils dilated in the hope of what was to come.

He shook his head. He wanted to stride away, brush her off like the town cat that rubbed up against his leg. But he had taken her bread and salt, and the shelter of her roof had saved his life. He drew himself up and bowed.

"Madam, I may not abuse your hospitality that way," he said stiffly. "In all honor, I am bound to you as a knight—"

"Honor?" She was no longer smiling, but feral and dangerous. "Honor is a code among men. In a house of women, d'you think we care for that?"

"Usssss? Care for thaaaaat?"

Belatedly, he saw that all the maidens had drawn closer to Duessa in angry ones and twos, their flower-like faces as dark as their mistress's eyes. He shuddered and came to himself, aware that a sticky sheen of sweat was covering his face.

"Lady, my honor is all that I possess. It is against my oath of chivalry to pay for my bed tonight with bed-service to you. I shall always remember that you saved my life, and for that I shall be your champion till I die. Call on me ever afterward to defend you against the wrong of any man."

Duessa raised her hand and gave him a tremulous smile. "Forgive me, sir, if I offended you." She dropped her eyes. "Loneliness makes savages of us all."

"No offense, my lady," he replied hastily. "You are Queen here. It is your place to command."

She showed him her white teeth. "Then allow me to command you to your rest. You are overworn for one day."

Free, Gods be thanked! "Madam, I owe you more than words can say," he said fervently, pressing her hand.

"Till tomorrow," she said, waving him away. She raised a hand for the maiden. "Falsamilla will take you to your chamber."

Tristan had never bowed more devotedly in his life. "Thank you, lady, and goodnight."

Rejoicing, he followed the wavering candle of the maid through miles of dark corridor and up a flight of torchlit stairs. At last Falsamilla paused and threw open a door.

"Your chamber, sir," she proclaimed.

Was it safe? Tristan stepped forward cautiously, still half expecting a trick. But the apartment before him was furnished for a king. Vast tented hangings hung over the great bed, like a knight's pavilion in the Holy Land. The chairs and tables hewn out of massive black oak would accommodate any man's bulk, and an armor-stand loomed in the corner for his helmet, sword, and shield. Tristan released a slow sigh of relief. He had not been brought to Duessa's chamber after all.

A low fire was glowing on the hearth. Falsamilla gestured to a hand-bell by the door. "If you require anything, sir—"

"Nothing, thank you." He ushered her to the door. "Not even a cup of water in the morning to break my fast. Your lady will understand I must leave at dawn."

Leave at dawn . . . *yessssssss.*

Thankfully, he rested his back against the door, threw back his head, and closed his weary eyes. Bed . . . Get to bed . . .

He was almost too tired to move. Stumbling, he made his way to the window and opened the casement on the starlit sky. The face of the heavens was studded with pinpoints of gold. He fixed his eyes on the love star and began his devotions with a flowing heart. *My lady, oh my love . . .* As he prayed, his soul left his body and his spirit sped like an arrow to

Isolde's side. For a while they wandered on the Plain of Delight. Then, grieving, they parted and came back to earth again.

Oh, my lady...

Groaning, he made ready for bed. Clumsy with fatigue, he unstrapped his sword and kicked off his boots, then pulled his tunic and shirt over his head. As he fumbled to turn back the covers, a last thought made its way through his wandering brain.

The door—bolt the door.

He was halfway across the room when he caught a sound. What was it? Straining his ears, he reached for his sword and glued his eyes to the door. Inch by inch the latch began to lift.

Without warning the fire on the hearth leapt into life, throwing up writhing flames of green and blue. The air in the chamber thickened till he could hardly breathe, and the door swung back on its hinges without a sound.

Duessa stood on the threshold, no longer darkly clad like a pious widow or a simple nun. Her body was sheathed in a gorgeous chamber gown of red fox fur, with a high standing collar and sleeves touching the ground. Beneath it she wore a wisp of flame-colored satin and embroidered slippers with low, velvet heels. For the first time he saw her hair, indigo black, and as deep as a starless night. It coiled in a lofty diadem on top of her head, secured with an ivory pin like a great cat's tooth.

"Sir Tristan."

She stepped into the room. With an onrush of rage, he saw himself through her eyes, half naked and trembling, brandishing a sword. Afraid of a woman? An unarmed female in a chamber gown?

Gods, what a fool he was making of himself! He threw down his sword. "Lady—" he began thickly, trying to calm his racing heart.

"No words."

She moved up on him with all the confidence of a wife, and reached out a practiced hand. "You are mine, sir," she murmured, showing her teeth. "You knew it from the moment we met."

Tristan recoiled. "No!"

Duessa laughed. Then she shot out a hand and gave his nipple a painful tweak. "You're a hunter, Tristan, and you know the sport. It adds to the conquest to play with such noble game."

Tristan closed his eyes to master his choking rage. "I am not game for you or any woman in the world. I have given my sword and my soul to another for these last ten years."

Duessa released a rich, condescending laugh. "Poor little Isolde, you mean?" she said indulgently.

"The Queen of Ireland, yes," he said evenly, "I am her sworn knight."

"Not in my kingdom. Your vows mean nothing here." With deliberate slowness she raised her hand to her head, pulled out the ivory pin, and threw it to the floor. Coiling and uncoiling, her hair fell around her like a cloak. Blue-black and shimmering, it only half concealed her glistening flesh as she laid open the front of her gown to expose her breasts.

"Look at me, Tristan," she triumphed, "and drink your fill. Tonight you will exchange Isolde's love for mine. With me you'll be able to live free from deceit and hold up your head as a knight again."

No more lies and deception, but unashamed joy and delight?

A cloud of bright visions flooded Tristan's mind. He saw himself walking openly with his love and going freely to her bed. He would regain the honor he had lost when he broke his oath to Mark. Gods above, he betrayed his uncle every time he lay with his wife—

The next second, he caught Duessa's eye and saw the temptation she offered for what it was. Maddened, he fought not to look at the great red nipples or the mounds of gleaming white flesh. Anger came to his rescue. "Lady, you must excuse me from your bed!"

"Never, sir." Smiling her secret smile, she shook her head. "No man refuses me in Plaisir de Fay."

"Then forgive one who has no other choice."

He took her arm to thrust her from the room. But as he touched the cold-as-marble skin, she shot out a hand and gripped him by the throat.

A vicious pain shot through him. Gagging, he tried to break free, but she held him with an Otherworldly force. Madly he tore at her fingers, to no avail. "Lady!" he screamed.

She tightened her grip and the agony renewed. Even her voice had changed, hissing like a cat. "You are lucky, Sir Tristan, that my revenge stops here. You are the first to refuse me the custom of Plaisir de Fay."

With the strength of a man she threw him to his knees, and the door slammed behind her sweeping form. In an ecstasy of fear he threw himself at the oak planking and drove home the bolt to keep her out. As he did so, he heard a key turning on the other side. Duessa's voice dropped to an angry growl.

"You will learn, sir, that I mean what I say. You are mine now, and you are here till you give me your love. And only you can decide how long it will take."

chapter 18

ow long will it take? Gods above, man, who knows the secret of a woman's heart?"

Furiously, King Hoel tugged at his thinning beard and favored his old friend De Luz with a red-eyed glare. And what a friend the King of the Basques had proved, he thought remorsefully, making the long journey over the mountains at this time of the year. Hoel looked across the small private chamber at his guest and was heartened to receive a forgiving smile in return. All might yet be well.

"More wine?" he offered. "Sweetmeats? Nuts?"

He must make much of De Luz. A journey like this was always hard and no man wanted to leave his lands when winter was at last giving way to spring. But good man that he was, De Luz had heard and heeded the cry of an old friend. He sat now, grave-eyed and understanding, as Hoel opened the subject of his quarrel with Blanche.

"Marriage is a weighty thing," De Luz said in comfortable tones. "Every woman needs time to make up her mind."

"Not Blanche." Hoel groaned aloud and reached for his goblet of wine. "You know she refused King Amaury de Gaul? Sent him packing with a flea in his ear?"

De Luz nodded gravely. "The whole of France knows that."

There was a moment of heavy silence between the two. If the story had reached the Basque country, Hoel reflected savagely, then De Luz must also know that they'd been lucky to escape the threat of war. Hearing of Amaury's treatment at Blanche's hands, his enraged mother wanted to avenge the insult to her son. Aged as she was, the old battle-queen of the Gauls was still a formidable foe. Only a formal embassy with Prince Kedrin at its head, delivering fulsome flattery and gifts of gemstones and gold, had served to appease her wrath.

And it must not happen again! Hoel made up his mind. "Help me, old friend. Give me your advice."

De Luz opened his arms. "With all my heart."

"Blanche wouldn't marry Amaury because she wants another man."

"Ah," said De Luz, who was not surprised. "Has she said who?"

Hoel took a gulp of the thick red wine and sluiced it dolefully around his mouth. "She's set her heart on Tristan of Lyonesse."

"But Sir Tristan," De Luz said gently, "is—"

"Yes, yes!" Hoel broke in. "Sworn to the Queen of Ireland these ten years and more. Her knight. Her—whatever you call it . . ."

De Luz nodded. This was worse than he feared.

Hoel looked at his old friend, breathing heavily. "So you understand. She needs a flesh-and-blood suitor, not some romantic dream. And we must find her one. A man who will love her, as you loved Roxane."

"Roxane, yes . . ." De Luz thought of his long-dead wife with a sadness as fine as the mist on the mountains of home.

"Think, then, man!" Hoel pressed him. "Who do you know? Give me some names."

"I shall certainly consider it," De Luz said quietly. "But you know we can do nothing without Blanche's consent. We're not Christians, remember. Our women are not chattels to be given away."

Hoel sighed. "Just speak to her, will you, De Luz? Turn her mind toward marriage if you can. And if you can't, at least talk some sense into her!"

There was another pause.

"Let me go to her," De Luz said at last. "Where is she now?"

THE WINTRY DAY was drawing to a close. In the square, whitewashed room, the white-clad attendants were lighting the evening lamps and mending the fires. The clean healing smell of herbs hung in the air, mingled with the sweetness of beeswax on the tables and floors. Looking around, Blanche felt the familiar upsurge of pride. No matter that none of this had been her work, or even her thought. It was how an infirmary ought to be, and she wanted the best. She smiled a satisfied smile. Clad all in white, swathed in a large, important apron with a brisk headdress and a white veil holding back her hair, she fancied she looked like the Goddess Herself at work. The sick were lucky who found themselves in her care!

As this one was now. Fluttering her eyelids in exquisite sympathy, she leaned over the withered ancient in the nearest bed. A gentle sleep had softened the lines on his face and he breathed easily, his crabbed hands at peace on his chest.

By his side stood a tall, stooped man with a careworn face and troubled eyes. With him was an older woman in a spotless white apron and head-cloth, holding a vial.

Blanche nodded to him. "So, Doctor, how is he now?"

"Going gently to join the Old Ones," the doctor replied. "His race on earth is run."

Blanche raised her head sharply. "But I thought we could save him."

The doctor shook his head. Why did the Princess always refuse to accept the limits of human power? "Madam, there is no saving men from natural death. This old one has lived his life, and the Mother is calling him home."

Blanche's mouth set in an unpleasant line. "What about this?" She gestured to the tiny bottle in the woman's hand. "A draught of great power, you say."

The doctor took a breath. "Of great power, but sadly little use. Its only function is to arrest the onset of death. It cannot cure or prevent what nature has determined must occur."

"It arrests the onset of death?" Blanche widened her eyes into a strident stare. "And you say it's of little use? Ask the old man what he thinks of that."

The woman leaned forward earnestly. "Lady, I've nursed many to their deaths. When the Mother calls, old souls are glad to go."

Blanche eyed her with disfavor and pointed to the vial in her hand. "Is that why you kept the knowledge of this from me?"

The doctor frowned. "Lady, this tincture buys life at a heavy cost. Yes, the sufferer wakes and lives and speaks again, it's true. But the spirits that possess his body are not his own. When Merlin used it to keep Uther Pendragon alive, the King spoke in other voices and lost his mind."

"Uther may have lost his mind already, dying young as he was and

leaving a war-torn kingdom without an heir," Blanche returned sarcastically. "But what do I care about Uther? I want to see how this works." She
reached for the flask, pulled out the stopper, and dropped the entire contents into the old man's mouth.

Within minutes a flush of warmth had returned to the withered gray
skin. The old man's breathing deepened, and they saw the signs of movement returning to his limbs. As they watched, his eyes opened and fastened on Blanche in a glance of adoring love. "Lady—" he began.

"There you are!" Blanche made no effort to keep the triumph from her
voice. "Now we'll see how he goes on. Watch him closely, Doctor. I'm
relying on you."

With a sweep of her snowy skirts she turned away, in time to catch a
new arrival at the door. Smiling, she moved forward to greet her father's
old friend, the King of the Basques. "Your Majesty," she cried, curtsying.

"Princess Blanche," he responded warmly, kissing her hand.

She rose to her feet and raked him from head to foot. *I know why you
are here,* her bold scrutiny conveyed. *And why should you think you can
persuade me when others can't? Kedrin, too—I know my dear brother
has a hand in this.*

She forced herself to sound cold. "My father sent for you to talk to me,
I think?"

His quizzical face took on a gentle air. "My old friend only seeks your
happiness. Every father hopes to see his child fulfilled, not led astray by
false hopes and dreams."

"They aren't false!" Blanche cried, to her fury feeling the tears rising
in her throat. "My knight is true. And he will come to me."

Suddenly, she was a lost child again, crying for her dead mother,
Daddy, I want . . . He had given her anything she wanted then, and he
would now.

De Luz saw the overbright eyes and trembling lips, and yearned to
take her in his arms, comfort her sadness, stroke her pearly skin. All
at once he saw how Amaury de Gaul had lost his heart. *Beware, De Luz,
beware. This maiden will love only once in her life, and you are not
the man.*

"Let me never come between a maiden and her dream," he said
huskily, aching with tenderness for her stubborn, wounded heart. "Our
dreams are sent us by the Great Ones themselves, to teach us how to

love. But lady, when you dream of a man so far out of your reach, you may never hope to possess him in this life. You condemn your spirit to walk the Otherworld, pining for joy and fulfillment that can never be."

"You think so, sir?" Passionately she brushed him aside. "Why should I listen to you? I wouldn't allow Sir Tristan of Lyonesse himself to take charge of my life and tell me what to do."

He could see her face quivering with anger and hurt. "Let me promise you that no man will try to—"

"I shall see to that!"

De Luz felt a chill of fear. "What will you do?"

"It's done!" she triumphed. "I've sent word to King Mark of Cornwall that a tournament will be held for the hand of the Princess of France. And if his nephew sees fit to be there, the Princess is likely to smile upon his suit."

Alas, poor Tristan. And poor Hoel, my unhappy old friend. But above all, poor, willful, deluded Blanche. Gods above, where will this end?

"You've invited Sir Tristan by name?" De Luz drew a breath. "Will he come?"

"Will he come?" Blanche let out a harsh, mocking laugh. "What finer alliance for Cornwall than the throne of France?"

"The throne of France!" came a wild echo from behind. The sick man Blanche had left only minutes ago was fighting to sit up, shouting and crying out. The doctor and his assistant were struggling to hold him down, and the breath rattled in his throat as he spoke.

"Cornwall will be here!" he screeched. "Lyonesse will attend. King Mark will command it. The knight will come!"

His eyes were bulging as if they would burst from his head, and the sinews were standing out in his scrawny neck. "Here! Here! Lyonesse will be here!" With one last cry, he coughed up a pool of blood, then fell backward and lay still.

"Goddess, Mother, take this child of yours . . ."

Moving forward to the bedside of the dead man, De Luz folded his hands and gravely began the ancient prayer of farewell. Frowning, the doctor and nurse straightened the old man's limbs and closed his eyes. But Blanche sped out of the infirmary with joy in every step. Tristan is coming. My knight will be here.

chapter 19

Ireland.

Erin.

Home.

Isolde stood on the deck and filled her lungs with the sweet soft air of the beloved land, a breath of beauty like nothing else in life. For the first time in all these dank and dreary weeks she could smell the coming of spring. But whenever she came back to Ireland, it was always spring.

"When the Old Ones made the world," her mother used to say, "they chose this island for the finest people on the earth. They gave it green hills and valleys and the leap of the salmon and the kiss of the silver rain. They filled it with fighters and talkers and princes and poets and those who love the craic. Then they gave it to the Goddess, who gave it her own name, and entrusted it to a line of Queens to love and care for as only women can."

And now they were racing home with a stiff wind in the sails and every rope and mainstay dancing a joyful jig. Ahead of them Dubh Lein lay smiling a welcome through a lavender twilight tinged with green and gold. Wheeling above the cliff, a great sea-eagle dipped its white tail in salutation, and roamed away across the sky, dwarfing the little figures on the quay below.

Ireland.

Erin.

Home.

But could it be home without Mother? Or Ireland without the Queen? Isolde paced the deck, staring out through the dusk. She swallowed a sigh. When she was alive, the Queen's only answer to questions had been a toss of her head, and she would never answer now.

"The Queen!"

"Queen Isolde!"

"The Queen!"

Isolde stepped into the prow and raised her cloaked arms like wings as she scanned the waiting throng. In the front stood a troop of armed men, their lances glinting in the last light of the sun. At their head she could see a handful of the old Queen's knights, the veteran Sir Doneal gleaming in silver mail, and Sir Vaindor smoothing back his hair. And was that Sir Tolen, standing at the back? No, the tall figure shading his face was another man and Tolen was nowhere to be seen. Did he think he had to keep out of her way because he had been her mother's chosen one? Well, he'd soon learn he had nothing to fear from her. But where was Sir Gilhan, her own counselor and friend?

Blithely, the ship came to rest at the dock. As the sailors handed her down into the waiting crowd, the first knight to kiss her hand was one she hardly knew.

"Your Majesty," he cried with a dazzling smile.

The prowl of a wild cat, a predatory gaze, the feral smell of danger, hot and strong . . . Beware! Briskly, she drew her hand out of his grasp. "Sir Breccan, I think? When I saw you last, you were still a boy."

His handsome young face darkened. "Boy no longer, my lady, as you see." He gestured to his men. "You know my chief knight, Sir Ravigel, of old? And his nephew, Tiercel, another of my kin?"

Ravigel was the tall, broad-shouldered knight she had mistaken for Tolen from the ship. He bowed his head and greeted her on one knee, but Isolde could tell at a glance what he was. Scarred hands, eyes of stone, and a killer's smile—what was a man like this doing at her court?

A grim foreboding settled on her soul. She turned back to Breccan. "Where is Sir Tolen? I expected to see him here."

"My poor brother?" Breccan's well-shaped face took on a tragic air. "Alas, he's dead."

Isolde suppressed a start. "Dead? How?"

"He fell from a clifftop—such a loss . . ."

You killed him came to Isolde like a blow. She looked around. There was Vaindor, yes, still stroking his thinning curls, standing next to Sir Doneal with his weather-beaten face and blue-eyed stare older than the mountains of the moon. *But where was . . . ?*

She set her chin. "And Sir Gilhan?"

Another doleful sigh. Breccan shook his head. "No man knows."

She could not suppress her anger. "What do you mean?"

His gaze flickered to Sir Ravigel at his side. "They say he has disappeared."

She snorted with disgust. "No man disappears, sir, in this land of ours. Least of all the Queen's chief counselor and a lord of state. When was he last seen?"

He laughed openly, and she felt the first chill of fear. "Setting off into the forest to take counsel of the Queen's Druid, Cormac. Now both of them are lost, no man knows where."

Isolde's heart turned to ice. *No man but you, sir.*

Breccan stepped forward. "But you have other men to serve you, lady, men with younger minds and stronger swords. And Ireland can only be grateful for new blood 'round the throne."

"Men like you, sir?"

"Myself above all. My knights and I are yours, body and soul, sworn to serve you in the legions of death."

He bared his strong white teeth in a winning smile and the smell of wolf was all around them now. She looked at the other men standing on the dock, and one by one their glances slid away. All her mother's knights and lords were afraid of him. *So be it.* She nodded to herself. *There is not a soul here that I can trust. No man to fight for me, not one.*

She drew a long, steady breath. *Then I'll fight for myself.*

"Come, sirs," she cried gaily, "why are we lingering here? I'm longing to set foot in Dubh Lein again."

Vaindor thrust himself forward. "Yes, Majesty!" he cried. "Let us bring you home!"

"Bring the Queen home!" came the chorus on all sides. Young and old now rallied around to pledge their allegiance and offer her their swords.

But it was Breccan, she noted, who gave orders to disembark the ship—Breccan who shadowed her half a pace behind as she greeted the rest of the crowd on the windswept quay—and Breccan who com-

manded the ring of steel that encircled her every step as she made her
way up from the harbor and entered Dubh Lein.

A MISTY BLUE TWILIGHT had settled over the hills. The evening winds
had lulled themselves to sleep and the birds had long ago tucked their
heads under their wings. The two-legged world had also gone to its rest.
But Isolde prowled the vastness of Dubh Lein sleepless and alone, with
nothing but fear to keep her company.

At last she came back to the Queen's house, chilled to the bone. Glittering coldly in the moonlight, the great white building loomed up ahead
of her like a reproach. *If only I had come back sooner . . . I should have been
here. If I had been, Cormac and Gilhan would be safe.*

Sir Gilhan would never betray her, she was certain of that. If he had
gone, it would have been against his will. He had fought for the Mother-
right all his life—had he died for it now?

And Cormac? Was he dead too? Her skin prickled. If he were alive he
would certainly be here. Nothing but death would dim that mystical
light. *Well, I shall find you, sirs, and give you burial.*

And they were not the only men lost and gone. Feasting in the hall,
with all Dubh Lein gathered to toast her return, she saw gap after gap
where her mother's knights used to be. This one had left court to travel,
she was told, others were trying their skill at foreign tournaments, and
still others had joined a quest to the Holy Land. Many had left quietly to
live on their own estates. Did she remember Sir Odent, or old Sir Fideal?

Of course she did. But her mother had driven them away with her
rampant demands and voracious sexual greed. *And now I am alone and no
knight will raise a sword in my defense.*

She groaned aloud. *Goddess, Mother, send me some good men!*

One above all, Great Mother.

Send me back my love.

Gods above, where could Tristan be?

She rose to her feet and surged over to the great bay window, threw
open the casement, then set a candle to shine out through the dark. *Forgive me, love, that I did not do this at dusk. I know you'll have made your
remembrance of me tonight, you never fail.* With a pang of guilt, she pictured

Tristan out on the road, cold and hungry, sleeping on the ground. She had the warmth and attention of a court, he had nothing but his faith and love for her.

Trembling, she lit the candle and made a prayer. *Gods and Great Ones, guide my true love's path. Speed his steps and bring him safe to me.*

"Madam!"

The door burst open and Brangwain flew into the room. "Sir Breccan is here to see you with a troop of men."

"He wants an audience?" Isolde stared. "At this hour?"

Brangwain shook her dark head. "Send him packing, lady. There's nothing can't wait till tomorrow. He has no right to be here."

And spend a sleepless night not knowing what he planned? Isolde shuddered. "Admit him, Brangwain."

Brangwain crossed to the door. "This way, sir."

"Thank you."

His scent came before him into the room, hot and musky like a stag in rut. His long thick hair had been perfumed and groomed into sleek, smiling curls lying on his shoulders like living things. His own smile was respectful, and he came toward her with a modest air. But there was no mistaking the triumph in his eyes.

Calm, stay calm . . .

He was coming in a blaze of red and black, dark wool breeches tucked into black leather boots, a red leather jerkin studded with garnets and gold. His shirt, as white as his smile, was of fine cambric, embroidered with gold thread at the neck and sleeves. A gold ring hung from one ear, and the gold torque of knighthood encircled his strong neck, fashioned like a snake devouring its own tail.

"Your Majesty."

He bowed and gave her his hand. The back of it was cross-hatched with silver scars, a sharp reminder of his fearlessness in close combat and many battles fought and won. She set her teeth: know your enemy. Breccan was a fearsome adversary in peace or war.

And worse—his sinewy grip and flashing smile were disturbing her now in ways she would not admit. With a rush of anger very close to shame she found herself watching the prowling figure, compelled by his every move. Not as tall as Tristan but superbly made, he had the shoulders of a warrior and lean horseman's hips. His narrow waist was defined by a broad leather belt, and his muscular brown forearms were marked like his sword hand with scars.

"It's very late, Sir Breccan," she said distantly. "What brings you here?"

He smiled winningly. "Only the desire to serve you, my Queen."

She bowed. "Your loyalty does you credit."

He took an easy step closer. "Your Majesty will have need of every sword. These are dangerous times."

Isolde stood her ground. "Only if we allow them to be."

"Ah, but danger lurks unseen."

Subtly he had drawn himself nearer still. Isolde drew herself up and looked him in the eye. "I beg you, keep your distance, Sir Breccan. Let me say, too, I don't wish to have your advice. Beltain is coming, I must bury the Queen and take up the reins of the kingdom as Queen myself. Till then, I give you leave to withdraw."

"Withdraw?"

A peal of mocking laughter filled the room. "No, lady, I am here to stay." He stretched out his hard brown hand and gripped her wrist. "You forget I come from the clan of the Companions of the Throne. My brother was the Queen's last chosen one. I am the last of the line till my sons are born." He paused, breathing hard, his handsome face faintly bedewed with sweat. "Born to you, Majesty, as it must surely be."

"Born to *me*?" Gasping, she flung off his grip. "You forget yourself, sir. A queen makes her own choice of the man she loves and I made my choice, many years ago."

"But the old ways change. Nowadays the people demand a king to rule alongside their Queen."

"Not in my lifetime." She took a contemptuous step backward. "Go now. You have already said too much."

Breccan did not move. A light she could hardly endure had come into his eye.

"Come now," he said huskily, throwing back his hair. "One man alone cannot sustain a queen, your mother taught you that." He laughed with all the cruelty of youth. "Old men weaken and their manhood fails. You need a young man to refresh your rule." One hand idly played with his sword while the other unselfconsciously rested on his thigh. "No one else in Ireland can match me in bed or battle, come what may. Therefore I must be King, and you will be my Queen."

"Never!" she swore. *What, am I dreaming this?*

He laughed. "How long did you linger in Cornwall?" he demanded insolently. "Every day you were away I built up my power."

"Your power?" She laughed in his face. "You have no power! Only the strength of the bully to spread terror on command."

He leaned back, idly studying his fingernails. "You were asking about Sir Gilhan . . ."

Isolde froze. "Where is he?"

He gave a malevolent laugh. "In good company."

Her heart plunged. "With Cormac."

"The Druid indeed." He smiled with delight. "Your mother's cherished adviser—and yours."

She could scarcely control herself. "So you imprison an old man, and a man of the Gods?"

A soft chuckle was his only response. "Only to show you—"

"What?" she spat.

A dark glory spread across his face. "That I'm King already, in all but name." He paused and drew a deep breath. "But more than that, madam . . ."

She stood gripped by the flare in his eyes.

"You are mine," he went on in a cold passion, "mine to take and use as I wish. That's what women were created for, and Queen or not, you were made the same."

"So then," Isolde breathed, "I must be Queen as your plaything, or not at all?"

With a swift and brutal move, Breccan pulled her into his arms and held her fast. "And which do you choose?"

chapter 20

don't fight.

Don't move.

Think!

His mouth was so close she could taste the sourness of his wine. Sighing, she placed a light hand on Breccan's chest and disengaged herself as winningly as she could.

"Not yet, sir," she breathed with a tantalizing smile. "No hunter enjoys what is too easily caught."

Breccan's frown changed to a wolfish grin. Gods above, how he loved a woman who loved the game!

"True enough," he said huskily, feeling a welcome warmth spreading through his thighs. Appreciatively, he surveyed her lithe figure and full breasts, relishing the joy of her body to come. And she was right, the chase should not be rushed. *You've tumbled too many kitchen sluts and chambermaids,* he chuckled to himself. *Only a fool would try to force a queen.*

"You'll take me for your chosen one?" He gave a lazy laugh.

"And more." Isolde steadied herself, conscious of the powerful body not two feet from hers. "I'll go back to Cornwall and leave you here as my knight. Then you can rule unchallenged in the Western Isle."

"Go back to Cornwall?" he snorted derisively. "And let you raise an army to reclaim your land?"

"Not at all." Isolde summoned up a flattering smile. "I have to return to Cornwall. I am Queen of two kingdoms and I have no knight." She forced a self-pitying sigh. "I'm all alone."

So! Breccan's mind raced. He had done what they all said he would never do. Isolde was his.

His! Again the promise of pleasure warmed Breccan's loins. Then a tendril of doubt made its way into his mind. He frowned. "How do I know you're not just playing with me?"

How young he is, she thought. She widened her eyes and soothed him with a smile. "You know that a queen can't rule without a knight. All the other knights answer to you, so if you refuse, no man in Ireland will draw his sword for me."

That at least was true. "Not a single one," he agreed.

Isolde reached for her most honeyed tones. "There's no man in the whole of the island to compare with Breccan."

Breccan stroked back his hair. "True again," he purred. "I can kill any man alive. So, lady—"

Once again an iron forearm was around her waist and a hot red mouth was groping toward hers.

She closed her eyes. "Forgive me, sir," she murmured. "But this is not the time. Like all women, I am subject to the moon . . ."

Her voice trailed off. Cursing lightly, Breccan let her go. "Till the new moon, then." He grinned. "When I shall return." He turned toward the door.

Is it over? She hardly dared to hope. "Brangwain?" she called.

"My lady?"

Briskly, Brangwain ushered Breccan out, then stepped back into the room. In silence they listened as he gave orders to the guard, and shared a glance of despair. Was there nowhere in Dubh Lein his power did not reach?

Isolde turned to Brangwain. "You heard what he wants," she forced out.

"I did."

"What are we to do?"

The maid's lips compressed into a thin line. "Leave it to me, lady— leave it to me."

THEY LEFT AS THE STARS were shedding the last of their glow and the glittering sky was fading toward dawn. The owls in the bell tower had come home to roost, and every soul in the palace lay asleep. Veiled in gray to blend into the night, they slipped through the shadowy corridors like wraiths. As silent as mice, they moved down and down, through Dubh Lein's dark passageways to the place beneath.

In the heart of the ancient citadel lay the Throne Room of Queens. Isolde led the way into the great vaulted chamber and paused before the throne on its lofty dais. Made of black bog oak that had been old when the world was young, it loomed stark and forbidding in the light of the moon, pulsing with secret power. Beneath it rested the stone of destiny, the treasured *lia fáill* handed down from the earliest dwellers in the land. Slumbering until a new queen awakened it, the stone never failed to cry out when the rightful ruler took her predestined place. Isolde's sight faded, and she saw her mother seated once again upon her throne, her black eyes snapping with delight, her lovely, powerful face vibrant and alive.

Oh, Mother, Mother . . .

Tears of loss choked her throat. Then she felt Brangwain's hand on her arm. "She has come to bless our venture."

Isolde shivered. *Or to give a warning of disaster ahead?*

"This way, madam."

Firmly, Brangwain drew her down the room and around the back of the throne. A low archway in the wall behind the dais led down to a darkness deeper than night. Isolde groaned. Suddenly she was a frightened child again: *This way, Mawther? Oh, it's dark down there!*

No fears, Isolde. This is the way of Queens.

Where are we going? Why are we going down there?

No tears, no fears. Remember you will be Queen.

What's down there, Mawther? Tell me, tell me, please . . .

The Dark Pool, child. The gift of the Goddess to Dubh Lein.

Tell me, Mawther—

I've told you—

Tell me again, Mawther, please . . .

Once, long ago, when the world was young, the Shining Ones wove our island out of sunshine and rain. Then its beauty caught the eye of the Great One herself and she made it her chosen place and gave it her name. She called it Erin the Fair after herself, and filled it with wise women and poets and Druids and heroes and queens. Then other lands needed her and she left with the Shining

Ones for the Plains of Delight. But she gave us the sun and the softest rain in the world, and when these two kiss, the rainbow they make is the Mother's pledge to the world.

Pledge of what, Mawther?

Religion is kindness. Faith should be love.

A long-ago feeling of peace filled her heart. "So, Brangwain . . . ?"

She took the maid's hand and they left the moonlit chamber, making their way downward without fear. The darkness enfolded them like a mother's arms, and they knew they were not alone in the warm, echoing void. The air around them was full of gentle murmurings, and the sweet smell of sacred water rose to welcome them.

Now a faint glimmer was reaching them from below. As their eyes adjusted to the dark, they saw a great underground lake, the Dark Pool from which Dubh Lein took its name. Serene and gleaming, it lit the darkness like the face of the moon as it silently beckoned them on: This way . . . this way . . . do not be afraid . . .

At the foot of the steps lay a silver expanse of sand, and beyond it the sweet water that gave Dubh Lein its life. Isolde felt her feet sink in the soft sand with another spring of hope. On, on . . .

Slowly, they circled the still, glassy lake.

"There, lady!" came Brangwain's triumphant tones.

"Where?" Isolde strained to see.

Brangwain chuckled with satisfaction. "Where I told them to be."

A dark barge lay drawn up on the farthest shore, lost in the shadows of the endless night. A short, shaggy creature clad in damp, shiny pelts stood upright in the prow, eyeing them as shyly as a water vole in the reeds. At his feet crouched a boy who might have been any age, his eyes like moons in his head, his wild, starved face at one with his animal wraps.

Brangwain nodded. "So, sir? You are here for my lady and me?"

The boatman surveyed them with a friendly gaze. His eyes fell on Isolde, and the soft, coughing sound of the Old Tongue whispered through the air, "You are the Throne Woman, seeking the Lady of the Sea. We will take you where you want to go."

Murmuring to the boy, he held out a sinewy paw to help them into the barge. Then he drew a deep breath of the sweet air into his lungs and poled off strongly into the darkness ahead.

chapter 21

The only light came from the moon-like face of the lake. The boat slipped over its silvery surface to the back of the cave where the rocky roof met the water and there seemed to be no way through. But the boatman tossed his pole to the left, to the right, then back again, till he flicked the unwieldy barge through a crack in the rock hardly wide enough to let them through.

In the next cavern they encountered darkness absolute, primeval night. They glided on through cavern after cavern, over lake after lake, till Isolde lost all sense of time in the glimmering dark. On they went, through the purple-black void, through the kiss of the velvet silence and the warm, fragrant air. The thought of Tristan came to her like a dull ache, and she hopelessly craved to hold him in her arms. *Tristan, where are you? Where are you, my love?*

Now they could see a faint light ahead. The boatman gave a sharp laugh like an otter's bark, and his dark face lit with joy. Talking excitedly in the Old Tongue, he drove the barge onward with powerful strokes. Imperceptibly their steady rhythm gave way to a slower, deeper sound swelling up behind. Isolde tensed. It was the low persistent call of the sea.

In the distance lay the edge of the lake and a shining semicircle of golden sand. Farther back, scattered heaps of rock tumbled up to meet the walls of the cave. And nestling everywhere—

Isolde caught her breath.

My mother's emblem.

The spirits of Ireland itself.

Gathered on the sand, or half hidden in the rocks, were countless swans, some lying with their heads beneath their wings, others watching their approach with unblinking eyes. In the forefront a queenly female rose to greet them, spreading her vast wings. *This way,* she said without words, craning her long white neck, *this way, my dears.*

In silence the boatman handed them onto the shore. Brangwain nodded toward the swan. "They knew you were coming, my lady. I'll wait for you here."

Isolde pressed her hand and turned away. Mutely, she followed the direction of the swan's pointing beak and made her way forward through the rocks. As she left the shore, the scattered stones began to take on recognizable shapes, like those who might guard the approach to the Lady of the Sea. Here were a circle of maidens and there a pair of mighty sea eagles, brooding over a tangle of porpoises at play. Once again she felt the low, strong pulse of the tide. *This is sweet water still, but we are drawing near to the heart of the sea.*

Now the guardian stones seemed to lean aside and a jagged archway appeared in the cavern wall. The darkness deepened. She ducked her head and shouldered her way in. With a thrill of fear, she felt the walls of the narrow passage closing in.

Resolutely, she drove herself forward. *On—get on . . .*

Before long she caught a shaft of broken light and heard a strange whirring sound she could not place. The singing of the sea grew louder now, borne on the throb of the warm briny air. A few strides later she stepped out of the rocky passage into a warm, lighted space and caught her breath.

She stood in a low cave, its roof and walls bright with gray, green, and mauve crystals in all the shades of the sea. Fine white sand made a welcoming carpet underfoot. A sea-coal fire crackled on a nearby stone and a torch on the wall lit the rosy gloom.

"Greetings, Isolde."

Whirr, whirr . . .

At the side of the cave sat a girl at a spinning wheel, her foot plying the treadle up and down, her busy hands teasing out the thread. Startled, Isolde took in a young maiden on the tender brink of womanhood, with the clear-eyed look of a virgin and a body still unawakened to the joy the Goddess gives. Her bright hair was looped back from her temples with seed pearls and shells, and her skin had the sheen of spindrift off the sea. She wore a gown as light as the froth on an ocean wave and a misty,

floating veil. A girlish delight shone from her sea-green eyes as she nodded to Isolde and beckoned her in.

"You did well to find us," she said in kindly tones. "You are truly welcome here."

Us? Isolde looked around. There was no one else in the cave.

"I came to see the Lady," she said stiffly. "Where is she?"

The girl's eyes danced. Her laughter had the surge of an ocean wave.
"The sea is everywhere. She has left me here in her place."

Bleakly, Isolde surveyed the girl's foamy draperies and the sweet,
grave features half hidden by the veil. Who was this busy little spinner,
hardly more than a child? And how could she take the place of the Lady
of the Sea?

The young girl was regarding her with a glance of timeless age. "You
have brought your sorrows to the right place," she said gently. "We can
help you here."

We again? thought Isolde in distress. She drew a weary hand across
her eyes. "Maiden, I—"

Tears of sudden hopelessness caught at her throat. "I want to talk to
the Lady," she said stubbornly.

Whirr, whirr . . .

The wheel spun on and the capable hands flashed to and fro. "The
Lady thought I could help you. Young women have their store of wisdom too."

Isolde clenched her fists. "I beg you, maiden, tell me where the
Lady is."

"As you will." The girl bowed her head and gestured to the wheel.
"Watch."

Isolde frowned. *Watch the wheel?* The girl heard her thought and nodded her shining head. Her right foot plied more vigorously up and down
and the thread spun out faster as the pace of the wheel picked up.

Whirr, whirr . . .

The only sound was the hissing of the wheel. Isolde fixed her eyes on
the flashing spokes and watched the fine filament of wool spinning out
around the rim. Soon the hissing and spinning dissolved into one and
the cave around them began darken and fade. As she watched, it seemed
to Isolde that the maiden was weaving her thread from the sand at her
feet and forging the shining grains into a silver web.

Whirr, whirr . . .

The spinning wheel spun on, growing bigger with every turn. Now the spider-fine net was studded with silver stars, weaving its way across the roof of the cave. Star by star the roof itself melted into the void, and the little spinner was a maiden no more. Her slight figure shivered and swelled till her head touched the stars and her womanly body filled the astral space. The flimsy wraps quickened and lengthened, veiling the towering form from head to foot. From behind the gauzy draperies came a well-loved voice.

"Ah, Isolde! Do you not know me?"

Isolde felt herself spinning with the wheel. "Lady!"

"Who else?" There was a mellow chuckle.

Isolde laughed for joy. "How could I forget you are maiden and mother and wise woman in one?"

The tall form inclined her head. "Open your heart, then. Speak."

"Oh, Lady—"

Isolde felt herself drowning in a tide of woes. "Lady, I have come into my kingdom and it is not mine. My mother ended her life in disarray, and now her enemies beset me on all sides."

The great head moved sorrowfully up and down. "One above all."

"Breccan, yes!" Isolde spat. She could hardly bring herself to say his name. "He wants to make himself my knight. But I have a knight, faithful and true to me."

"Tristan?" There was a sigh like the wind off the sea. "Ah, little one, knights may fail. Men weaken, their flesh decays, and even the best go down to the darkness in the end."

"I know that!" Isolde cried, feeling the floodgates of her grief give way. "It was not Tristan's fault he had to go. But now I'm alone and no man in Dubh Lein will take up arms for me."

There was a long silence before the Lady spoke. "There are always men who love the Mother-right. In the mountains above Dubh Lein there is one who will give his heart's blood for you."

"One man?"

The shrouded head nodded. "Put your faith in him. He will not fail."

Hope and anguish leapt together in Isolde's heart. "How shall I find him?"

"He will come to you."

Isolde felt herself overwhelmed by despair. "One man alone against Breccan and his knights?"

A sad smile reached her through the layers of filmy gauze. "Every man in the world had a mother once. Awaken those who love the Mother-right, and he will not be alone."

"But Breccan—" Isolde could not hold back a flood of furious tears. "Can you stop this madness, Lady? Can you make him believe in a faith of love, not death?"

The Lady shook her head. "Breccan's fate was spun a thousand years ago. Even the Mother cannot hold back the wheel." The honeyed tones darkened. "Every man chooses the path his feet will tread. Breccan is not your concern."

"Not Breccan?" Something in the words stabbed Isolde with dread. "Then what—?"

The Lady bowed her head and did not speak.

Isolde's heart seized. *"Tristan!"* she gasped. "Is he dead?"

"Not dead, nor dying, no."

"But in danger?"

Another aching silence filled the air.

Isolde felt the blood rushing to her head. "Tell me!" she forced out. "If Tristan is doomed to die, I want to know!"

"Alas, child . . ." The Lady's voice was growing deeper with every sound. "There are more ways than one for a man to die. If a man loses his honor, then he suffers the double death of death in life."

"Loses his honor?" Isolde felt her mind giving way. Her sight shivered and she saw Tristan between two women, the first as dark as midnight, the other pale and fair-haired like a child. As she watched, a third woman appeared. Slowly, slowly, Tristan leaned his head down to the chestnut-haired newcomer and kissed her on the mouth.

Goddess, Mother. No!

Tristan unfaithful? No, it could not be.

But the echo of the Lady's words rang in her ears. *Every man chooses the path his feet will tread. And even the Mother cannot turn back the wheel.*

What would Tristan choose? She hid her face in her hands and began to sob.

"Save him, Lady! He's more to me than all the Western Isle. I'd give my whole kingdom to keep him from harm."

"Little one, little one..." The Lady's stern voice reached her through a mist. "You cannot give up your kingdom for Tristan. Every woman must live her own life to the full."

She could not bear it. "Lady—"

Again she saw the shaking of the great head. "You are here to bury your mother and to claim your throne. When she is laid to rest on the Hill of Queens, you will make the mystical marriage with the land, as all the Queens of Ireland have done before. That is your task now."

Isolde raised her swollen face. "But Tristan...?"

"Never forget you are married to the land. You are the Sovereignty and the spirit of the Western Isle. That is the burden that you may not escape."

To her horror, she saw the great form beginning to fade. The sonorous tones rolled on. "In return you are granted the three joys of the Goddess—the bliss of your body, the suckling of the child at your breast, and the knowledge of a life well lived."

The Lady's wraps were melting into the mist. "Two of the three are yours without dispute. For the third, only the Mother Herself holds that key. Hold fast to what you have and keep the faith."

Isolde poured her heart into her cry. "Don't leave me, Lady!"

There was no response. Slowly, the last wisp of gauze faded from sight. But like a great bell, the wondrous voice tolled on.

"Go, Isolde, and do the duty that lies nearest to your hand. Your work lies here. And like every man, your Tristan must fend for himself."

chapter 22

You will learn, sir, that I mean what I say. You are mine now, and you are here till you give me your love. And only you can decide how long that will take.

TRISTAN CAME TO HIMSELF in a bleak winter dawn with the voice of Duessa hissing in his ears. What, he groaned to himself, still here? All night long he had fought to keep fearful thoughts at bay, in between snatches of fitful sleep and broken dreams. Yet he was lying in a fine chamber, warm and safe in bed. What could the lady do to him, after all?

He yawned and stretched, taking stock of the thin gray fingers of dawn curling around the edges of the shutters like dead men's bones. Time to be on his way. He threw back the bedcovers and swung his long legs to the floor. Soon he'd be miles away from this cursed place, and all that happened last night would be just a bad dream.

He dressed and pulled on his boots, then made his morning toilet as best he could. Strapping on his sword, he crossed the room with rapid strides and was not surprised to find the door still locked. So! He grinned, the lady had her pride, and now, it seemed, he must beg for his release. Well and good. Let the penitence begin. He reached for the bell by the door and rang it long and hard.

Before long he heard the light tread of female feet. The door opened, and Falsamilla stood on the threshold, her face wreathed in a smile, holding a shining silver bowl breathing out a sweet mist of rosemary and rue.

"Your toilet water, sir," the lady in waiting chirped cheerily. "May I come in?"

"Lady Falsamilla," returned Tristan, charmed by her approach, "by all means."

Falsamilla moved forward and set down the bowl.

"Madam, I must leave you with all speed," he said courteously. "Will you send to the stables to have my horse prepared?"

Falsamilla laughed. "Oh, sir, you must know that there's no leaving now."

Tristan's jaw dropped. "What do you mean?"

"Last night you refused to take my lady to your bed. That means you're her prisoner till you change your mind. Surely you can't have forgotten that?"

Tristan reached for a nonchalant air. "Indeed," he said, giving a manly laugh, "your mistress joked about that with me. But great ladies often amuse themselves with such things. Today I shall beg her forgiveness and kiss both her hands, then be on my way."

Falsamilla laughed with him, shaking her head. "She won't receive you again till you give her your love."

Tristan's temper flared. "Never!"

"Then you'll have to stay."

Tristan threw back his head. "Lady, I know this is all some elaborate game—"

"No, sir." The maid fixed him with an unfathomable gaze. "Castle Plaisir de Fay is another world. My mistress is a great queen of necromancy, and those who love her pass a night beyond compare. Her skills outclass any woman in the world. By morning all her lovers are her slaves for life."

Tristan caught his breath. Unbidden, Duessa's naked body flashed before his mind, the red fox fur cradling the ivory flesh, the throbbing nipples hungering for his touch . . .

The blood thundered through his head. *Out, man! Get out!*

"Forgive me, lady!" burst from his throat. His hand on his sword, he leapt wildly for the door. Tearing it open, he surged through. *Free! Free!*

The corridor outside was lined with knights, a wall of swords, shields, and helmets as far as he could see. A drawn sword pricked his throat, and he felt real fear. Goddess, Mother, there are men here, whatever the women said. He heard Falsamilla's voice cold in his ear. "I told you, sir. Now d'you understand?"

Wildly, he surveyed the the knight who held him at bay. There was no glimmer of humanity in the eyes behind the iron grille. To the knight's left and right were thirty or forty of the same, all with swords drawn, all ready for combat, and hungry, he could smell it, for blood.

His blood.

He spread his hands. "Sir—" he began hoarsely.

The knight in front of him flexed his grip on his sword. With a thrill of horror Tristan caught sight of his opponent's hand. Small, pale, and hairless, quite unscarred, with round pink nails. *Almighty Gods, it's a woman! They're women and killers, every living one!*

Fear deep as vomit rushed into his throat. Hopeless, he knew that he could never smash his fist into a female face or strike out at soft breasts and bodies made for love. Head bowed, he felt Falsamilla seize his wrists and bind his hands.

One thought obsessed his brain.

I have betrayed my lady and my love. I came into this castle like a fool, then like a traitor, I let another woman come into my mind. And see now . . .

Isolde . . .

"Still harping on Isolde?"

The savage cry cut through the air like a knife and the ranks of the women knights parted like the sea as Duessa approached. From her tall headdress to the hem of her hissing silks, she was clad all in black, and her eyes burned with a graveyard fire. She wore a man's silver breastplate like the rest of her armed band, but the hard silvery shell only emphasized her high breasts and narrow waist. *Gods above, man,* Tristan groaned to himself in abject disgust. *What, thinking about her body even now?*

Duessa laughed exultantly, and he knew she had heard his thought. "Do you know, sir, what you despised and cast away?"

He stared at her, numb with shame. "Lady, no more—"

"Yes!" She gave a horrible laugh and threw out both her arms. "Yours, Tristan—all yours!" came her plangent cry. "But you scorned me, and threw all this away."

Without warning Tristan saw the face of a child, quivering with age-old hurts too deep for tears. What had happened to wound her soul like this? And who had done this wrong? "Not I, lady," he said wearily, "not I."

"Yes, you!" she shrilled in a passion. "You and your kind! Merlin, Arthur, Tristan, you're all the same. And you'll live to regret you were born of the race of men. Our dungeons are deep here at Plaisir de Fay. And down there you'll waste your wretched life and die!"

chapter 23

*n*o tears, no fears, Mother.
So you still hear me, little one?
I hear you. And I shall listen for the rest of my life.

THE LONG CAVALCADE straggled forward over the plain. Isolde eased her stiff body in the saddle and stared out at the line of chariots, horses, and men journeying into the eye of the rising moon. Once before, the Queen had brought her here as a child. Now she was bringing her mother to her last home.

The Hill of Queens had stood on its sacred plateau guarded by a ring of high mountains since the Great One Herself had raised it from the ground. Seen from below as they rode in from Dubh Lein, its vast contours swelled up with deceptive gentleness, like the Goddess asleep. As she watched the great green flanks rising from the turf, Isolde thought there was no sweeter place to lie.

Especially in a tender, hopeful spring, when the earth was pulsing with the promise of new life. Soft winds sighed through the air overhead, and every returning swallow sang of love. Never had the grass looked greener, blessed and renewed by the gentle rain. Mile upon mile of green lawn ran before them bright with white and gold, as the daisies and celandines put forth their starry heads.

Ahead of them lay the entrance to the Hill of Queens, a dark opening in the gathering dusk. Beside it rested a great black disk of stone, ready to seal up the door when the last rites were done. The long chamber running into the hillside was lined with white quartz and aligned to catch the rays of the morning sun. When the Mother smiled on this great work She had made, the rising dawn spangled the space with fire.

Not a soul knew how many Queens lay here, or how many chambers the vast mound contained. This secret was held by the Keeper of the Hill, a woman Druid as old as the hill itself. Like her mother and all her fore-mothers, she was born into the sacred role of the Guardian of the Queens. She was waiting to greet them now, with her women on either hand. Robed in dark blue with the Druid mark between her brows, her tall, craggy form seemed part of the mountains themselves and her great face had seen ages come and go.

The procession wound forward to greet them at the foot of the hill. At the head was the Queen's chariot bearing the Queen herself, resting on a bed of green trefoil as if she were asleep. Pale as marble, her hair newly burnished with henna to copper and red, she was as lovely as she had ever been in life. Her long body was fragrant with all the herbs and oils her Druids had used to preserve it from decay. She lay now clad in rich silks of crimson and black, with her beloved ropes of jet at her neck and waist. A gold helmet with silver wings covered her head, and her breastplate bore a pair of fighting swans carved in silver and gold. Her head was pillowed on the bronze dome of her shield, and her faithful sword and war-axe lay by her hand.

Goddess, Mother, thanks—wherever Cormac was now, at least the Queen's Druid had been spared for the last essential office of her life, anointing her body to preserve it from decay. Among the sweet herbs and oils from the East, Isolde caught the scent of patchouli, and had to turn away. Then her mother's voice dropped through the evening air: *No tears, no fears. I am with you still.* She breathed deeply and took strength from the familiar scent. The Queen's undying favorite would be her fragrance now. *Yes, I hear you, Mother. This is the way of Queens.*

Around the Queen's chariot rode a handful of old men, the remains of her onetime band of lovers and knights. The oldest of them all drove the chariot, a knight shriveled like a cricket, no more than skin and bone. Isolde watched these faithful ancients with wondering eyes. *May I be served no worse when my time comes.*

And that may be now. For Breccan's knights were around her on every side, wave upon wave of bronze and shining steel. Breccan already held the island in his hand. And before dawn tomorrow he would make himself King.

Goddess, Mother, help me!

The familiar flare of panic caught her by the throat. Yet who could say what would happen in the hours ahead? At least she would become Ireland's Queen. Darkening every inch of the turf around the Hill of Queens were those who would bring it about, tribespeople in their hundreds and thousands gathering here for days. Squat, earthbound creatures with small, sturdy women and hobgoblin children flashing sweet, broken smiles, they were the kin born of the land itself. And scattered among them she saw with wonder those who surely traced their descent from another race, men and women who could have been kin to the Fair Ones, tall, dark, and unsmiling in the secret night.

There . . . and there . . .

Catching more than one fleeting gaze of burning brown eyes, Isolde held her breath and allowed herself to hope. Could some of these lean, mysterious strangers even be the Fair Ones themselves, coming from their green hills and hollows to grace her great day? The next thought was not far behind. *Or to fight for the Mother-right? Is the knight the Lady promised me already here?*

But the valley belonged to the land kin, she could see that. Camped on the slopes of the mountain they reveled and sang, their fires making the night as bright as day. Every year at Beltain, the God Bel came back from the house of darkness to warm the earth, and the Mother received Her lover with open arms. Then all the folk of the island came from crannog, bog, and fen, to celebrate the joy the Goddess gives.

The feast of Beltain, a queen-making, and a full moon—no wonder that so many had swarmed to join in the ceremonies on the Hill of Queens. But the full moon was the sign that Breccan wanted too, the time to claim the bargain he had made with her flesh.

Breathing hard, she slipped her hand into her bodice and felt for her mother's dagger where it lay between her breasts, silently murmuring the runic words on its blade.

morrighan they call me, and my name is death.
whoever wrongs my mistress, i drink his blood.

Be ready then, friend, she sent back, comforted, smoothing down her robe. She had dressed today for the moment of acclaim when she mounted the Queen stone in the face of all the tribes. What could she wear to be seen from every mountainside in the light of the rising moon?

They found it at last in her mother's secret store, a part of the Queen's house to which only she had the key. Through a small unused door behind a worn and dusty tapestry, they came upon jewels and gowns never seen before.

"Madam, look, look! And here!" Brangwain's dark eyes were out on stalks. From ceiling to floor, the chamber was hung with cloaks made of the feathers of peacock, raven, and swan, glittering gowns encrusted with jewels or gold disks like the face of the moon, and gossamer silks tumbling in rainbow cascades. Every garment, every mantle, every thread breathed out her mother's presence, heavy with its haunting scent of musk.

Brangwain was in her element. "Well, lady, this? Or this?"

In the end they chose a kirtle of dancing silks, its glassy green surface the color of Ireland itself. With it she wore a bodice of emeralds and gold, set with a silver breastplate of a swan in majesty. Over it came a gold overgown with a high standing collar, a queenly train, and great white sleeves like wings. On her head she wore Ireland's mighty diadem of queens, a deep circle of emeralds rumored to be the crown of the Goddess Herself. Beneath it she let her rich, red-gold hair run free. What better crowning glory for a woman of the Western Isle?

"Oh, my lady—" Looking at her mistress, Brangwain was ready to weep with joy.

"Thank you—thank you, Brangwain!"

Isolde had looked in the mirror with a pang of dread: who was this gorgeous stranger in the misty glass? Behind the sad, white, face she caught an echo of a pair of dancing eyes and a merry smile. Her heart seized. *I will never be that laughing girl again.* Then the beauty of the green and gold dazzled her eyes and she felt the first shoots of spring. A new strength came into her like the voice of the winter-bound earth. *Your springs will flow, Isolde. You will flower again.*

Flower as Queen, and be with Tristan again . . . Dreaming, she rode on.

Behind her, Breccan saw the still form and scowled. Gods above, what had got into Isolde, sitting her horse like a statue, half asleep? They were nearly there. But he should do nothing. She'd made it plain enough that his place lay behind. Time enough to change all that when he was King.

Breccan chuckled softly. So you thought I'd never be King, brother? he sneered. Well, you're justly rewarded. See me now, and despair!

Rage filled his brain, coloring his thoughts with blood, and he sent Tolen packing with a final sneer. Tonight I take your place as the Queen's chosen one. I'll have Isolde, whether she wants me or not. I'll break her down, turn her inside out.

And ... if she resists ... ?

Tell me, brother, can't women die as easily as men?

chapter 24

The Queen's chariot came to rest at the foot of the hill. The woman Druid stepped forward and threw up her arms. "Welcome, lady, to the Hill of Queens."

At her sign, the veiled women around her bowed and took up the cry. "The Queen leaves us, and the Queen comes again!"

"The Queen! The Queen!"

Now the hillsides came alive in sympathy and the bowl of the valley resounded with the call of drums. A thousand dark figures on the mountains took up the beat, while the boldest began the ancient funeral games of leaping through the fires.

"New life!" a thousand voices rang over the darkling plain. "The Queen journeys through the Beyond, and the Queen comes again."

Isolde felt the Druid's hand upon her arm. "Lady, this way."

Blazing swan-lights lit the low passageway of ancient stone, and the walls of the inner chamber flamed with crystal fire. Behind them came the Queen's waiting women carrying the comforts they had brought from Dubh Lein. As Isolde watched, they moved steadily to and fro, setting out the dainty cakes and wine to sustain the Queen on her quest, her bronze bed of state, her carved wooden throne. Soon the chamber was equipped as it had been in life, bright with the Queen's jewels and face colors, her polished glass and treasured copper comb.

"We are ready," the Druid called to those waiting by the door. Trembling with the effort, a party of the Queen's old knights carried her in on her bed of shamrock and laid her down. One by one they knelt to make their farewells, kissing her hand and blessing her sleeping head. Moments later the chamber filled with sound. The Druid led the chant in a voice like the earth itself, and Isolde followed the ancient hymn in a trance.

Goddess, Mother, take your daughter to yourself.

She knew love and war, and lay with heroes and fools. She sang with the Battle Raven in full cry and lay down with the dead and keened upon their bones.

From the hard love of men, she had her true reward, the beautiful daughter that she dreamed she would have. Speed her journey, Great One! Set her soul among the stars!

And grant us the ancient right of Queens, Mother to daughter, Isolde to Isolde since time began.

Go now, pilgrim wanderer, to begin life anew. And welcome, Isolde, to this land of Queens!

The plangent song soared to one last haunting note. In the echoing silence, the swan lamps began to flicker and die.

"Come, lady, come . . ."

She felt the hand of the Druid on her arm, drawing her forward into the night outside. A fair moon was smiling a blessing down from the sky, and she stood on the threshold, fighting tears and joy. All eyes were upon her. It was time. Her body sang, pregnant with newfound power.

"Lay the Queen to rest!" she commanded in ringing tones. "And bring me to the stone!"

Groaning, the tallest among the women rolled the black disk of granite into place to seal the door, then surged with her up the hill. Now the slopes were crowded with onlookers, the tribesmen and women jostling Breccan's knights and those who had made the journey from Dubh Lein. One above all, she thought, lean and gray-haired, seemed to want to speak to her, and she paused to read the message in his eyes. But the hand of the Druid was firm upon her back. "On, lady, on!"

The hillside lay green and gleaming under the moon. On the top stood a large, flat rock higher than a man's head, with a few rough footholds cut into its side. Alone on this eminence lay *lia fáill*, Ireland's stone of destiny for her royal Queens. Now its high mystical call trembled through the night. *Approach, Isolde, draw near, this is your time.*

Isolde steadied herself and prepared to mount. *My time?*

Time to embrace your fate and take your place in the Sacred Isle's line of Queens. Only follow the dream.

She felt her spirit laughing and dancing for joy. *I shall! And I shall find it, I and my true love—*

"Allow me, lady . . ."

Without warning a harsh voice rang like a knell in her ear. Breccan stood beside her, gripping her hand. Behind him she could see Ravigel and Tiercel and forty or so of his knights. But she was not afraid. Soul and body on fire, she thrust him away "Back!" she commanded throatily, raising her voice to echo to the hills. "Let no man approach. The Queen mounts alone."

Turning, she surged up the side of the rock, finding its shallow footholds effortlessly. *This is my destiny—mine and mine alone . . .*

She thought she heard the stone itself crying out, calling her onward, *come, Isolde, come!* Above it soared the yearning cry of the crowd, every voice resounding with the same refrain.

"Our Queen is gone—give us back our Queen!"

Your Queen . . .

Isolde stepped to the edge of the stone and threw up her arms. "I am your Queen!"

"The Queen!"

The drums of the land kin throbbed and the women keened. Sighing, the wind rose to greet her, and her upraised sleeves filled like mighty wings. Suddenly she was swan and woman, she was Queen, she was Erin herself. She was the land and the sovereignty of the land, she was the sea and the spirit of the sea. Her brothers were the black mountains and the hollow dells, her sisters the rushing rivers and the silver streams. She was every marsh and meadow, and every oak, every thorn, every shamrock was born of her flesh. Neither flesh nor fowl, no, not a tiny, hapless wren would suffer in this island if the Queen could raise her hand.

One more step . . .

Turning, she approached *lia fáill* and fell to her knees. Bending her head, she brought her cold lips to the stone. *Make me worthy, Goddess, Mother, of this crown I wear. Give me strength to bear its burdens and meet its demands. Let me not fail the least of my people's desires. May I live and die in their enduring love.*

This is my vow, Great Mother. Accept my oath. With her soul in her hands, she leapt up on *lia fáill.*

She felt the stone quake and tremble beneath her feet. *Be it so!* groaned the granite from its rocky heart.

Be it so! cried the night-flying eagle overhead.

Be it so! echoed through the golden air.

"Be it so!" howled the crowd. "*Lia fáill* has cried out!"

The cry resounded from the distant hills. "The stone has spoken! The stone has cried out for the Queen!"

"The Queen, the Queen, the stone has cried out for the Queen!"

The torrent of sound rang off the mountainside. Tearing their hair, the land women beat their breasts and opened their throats in the wild ululation known only in the Western Isle. Now, the night was alive with hectic screams and cries. In the deep purple void, her mother was with her again. *I told you, Isolde, one day you would be Queen . . .*

You did, Mawther, you did.

"A king! A king! A queen deserves a king."

She had not heard him come. Wild-eyed, Breccan had mounted the stone, bellowing his acclaim, and was striding toward her with a naked sword in his hand.

"A king for the Western Isle!" he shouted through the gloom. "And I am here—your Queen's chosen one!"

Goddess, Mother—!

A fresh burst of cries and cheers answered his words. Brandishing the sword, he reached up and pulled her down from *lia fáill.* Now she stood at his side, under the moonlit shadow of his sword, but menaced far more by his wide, white, wolf-like grin.

A hollow wind blew mournfully over the hill.

Lady, where is the knight you promised me?

And Tristan too? Has he failed me, is he dead?

"So, lady . . . ?"

Breccan was pulling her to him, his wolf's breath hot on her neck. She reached for the comfort of the dagger at her breast. *Whatever I have to do, Lady, it will be done.*

chapter 25

King Breccan...

The cries of the crowd thundered in his ears. His heart pounding, Breccan tasted the darkness within him and found it good. Good? Never better! His starved soul crowed like a cock. This was the finest moment of his life.

King Breccan. Already his knights had fallen to their knees, every man with his hand on his heart. The very hillsides lay hushed with reverence, and Breccan's spirit soared. Now at last he had come into his own.

Breccan's jaw tightened and his head began to throb. All men would respect him now, even this white-faced creature at his side. Yes, even Isolde, who thought she would be Queen. His anger peaked. She'd be the first to feel his boot on her neck.

"So, madam..."

He seized Isolde's arm and pushed her from the rock, forcing her none too gently down the steps. He was King from this moment on. If her fool of a husband dared to come to her aid, he'd be dealt with too. But a Cornish vassal king could never threaten him. There could be no denying his right to rule.

King Breccan...

His head swam as he watched her descend. Then flying like a bird, he leapt down from the rock. He was kin to the eagle, he was King!

King Breccan?

Isolde felt her way carefully down the rock. Coldly she swore an oath: Breccan would never touch her flesh again. And no man could seek to destroy the Mother-right and live. Still, calmly, now... She must not lose control. But as soon as the moment came—*kill! Kill!*

Blinded by her thoughts, she did not see the man waiting collectedly at the foot of the rock.

"King Breccan?" came a quiet voice in her ear. "Lady, is this your will?"

A sob of exultation burst from Isolde's lungs. *Goddess, Mother, praise and thanks—he has come!*

Standing before her was the man she had noticed as she climbed the hill, a lean knight in his middle years, grizzled but erect, and armed from head to foot. His piercing gaze had an Otherworldly air, and for a moment she caught the look of the Fair Ones again. *This is my knight. He has come to me.*

"My king?" she cried in a passion. "Never! No!"

Breccan stared at the stranger. "Who's this?"

The knight returned his stare. "When I served the Queen who has gone, she called me her Faithful One. My name is Fideal."

Fideal?

Breccan froze like a stag in the forest at the hunter's tread. The dead Queen's onetime champion? The old fool that Ravigel had urged him to put down?

Now Gods, be with me!

With a sharp lurch, Breccan saw that the old fool he had supposed was not so old after all. Fideal had the spare fighting frame of a much younger man, and a muscular body taller than his own. And a two-handed fighter as well, armed with sword and stabbing spear, the hardest to beat. But worst of all, Breccan saw with deep disquiet, was the look in the newcomer's eye. His pale gaze had the finality of one who had bid farewell, to life, to love, and all that he called his. Here was a man ready and willing to die.

"Go, fool, whatever they call you!" he said roughly, to cover his sudden fear. He seized Isolde's arm. "Leave the Queen. She has not sent for you."

Isolde tore herself contemptuously from his grip. "The Queen gives her own orders. And you, Breccan, will leave my kingdom, never to return."

Breccan's mouth fell open. "What?"

She leveled her eyes on his. "You are banished, Sir Breccan," she said thickly. "On pain of death. Leave my land at once."

"Never!" Breccan swore, reaching for his sword.

Fideal gave a thin smile. "The Queen has spoken."

"And a sword speaks loudest of all."

Without warning, Breccan lunged violently at Fideal. Gods above, he'd kill this old wretch, then by all the powers of darkness he'd kill this vicious queen!

The onlookers scattered in fear. Neatly evading Breccan's slashing sword, Fideal grinned mirthlessly to himself: *so!*

Everything he knew about Breccan had prepared him for a treacherous onslaught like this. His own sword was already in his hand. "Have at you, then!"

Breccan's only answer was another slash and thrust, followed by a furious hail of blows. Grimly, Fideal blocked the young knight's approach, parrying the glinting blade-strokes one by one. He was lighter on his feet than Breccan, Isolde saw with relief. But Breccan had youth on his side, and brute strength enough to beat any man down. Grunting, he drove at Fideal like a bull, his sword swinging and thrusting in a glinting arc.

Time and again Fideal deftly evaded attack as Breccan charged, overshot, turned and charged again. On the next run, Breccan whirled around, then came at Fideal sideways, like a crab. Fideal crouched to meet the sinister scuttling approach. At the last moment Breccan straightened up and sliced at the older knight's shoulder with a sickening blow. Fideal's sword fell from his hand and his arm dangled uselessly at his side. Roaring with triumph, Breccan bounded forward to plant his foot on Fideal's blade.

"Yield, sir!" he exulted. "You're a dead man else."

Fideal raised his dagger and beckoned mockingly. "Come and bury me, then," he cried. "Or do you need your brother to do it for you?"

"My brother...?"

Gasping, Breccan hefted his sword and swung it around his head. Gods, he would have Fideal's head for this! But first he would hack him living, limb from limb. Grinning, he surged in for the kill—*kill him now!*

After that, kill Isolde!

Then every voice would cheer for King Breccan...

King Breccan!

His ears ringing with imaginary cries, Breccan lunged at Fideal.

Blinded with blood-lust, dazzled by his own bright dreams, he hardly saw Fideal duck under his sword or felt the dagger slip into his armpit under his outstretched arm. His mouth was still spitting curses and boasts as the sharp blade pierced his heart.

"What—?" he began to protest, but speech and understanding had already fled.

From the side of the ring, Isolde watched as Breccan's body fell lifeless to the ground. *Farewell, Breccan. May your Gods go with you as the Lord of Darkness takes you for his own.*

Dead—Breccan's dead...

A low rising wind mourned around the mountaintop. Now the funeral cry was spreading across the hills as keening tribeswomen added their lamentations to the night.

Isolde looked up. "Who called this man master?"

"I did." Ravigel came forward, his eyes as empty as the dead man's.

Isolde gestured toward the pitiful hulk on the ground. "Take charge of your lord. Give him the burial he might have deserved."

Ravigel beckoned Tiercel and a handful of Breccan's knights. "It shall be done."

In silence she watched the knights bear Breccan away. Then she turned to Fideal with a tremulous smile. White and drawn, her defender stood holding his injured arm, watching her with an air of Otherwordly patience and something close to love.

"Sir Fideal, there are no words to repay your service tonight. But tomorrow I shall feast you as you deserve. You shall see what it is to win the gratitude of a queen."

"Ah, lady, that I know." He gave a painful smile. "Your mother honored me beyond my deserts."

And dishonored you too, as she did every man... "Oh, sir—"

He stared at her, unmoving. "I loved her and she betrayed me, a thousand times. So I left her and took to the mountains to nurse my hate. Gilhan sought me out to fight against Breccan, and my hatred was still strong and I refused."

Her eyes widened. "But what brought you here tonight...?"

"Ah, lady..." His face lit with a sweetness beyond compare. "She called me here. She has chosen me to tread the Beyond at her side."

"Sir, you may still serve her by helping me," Isolde cried in alarm. "The kingdom is threatened. I shall need your sword."

He shook his head. "My sword was hers, as my faith and my life were hers. And my life is nothing to me now that she has gone."

He raised his hand and tilted his head to one side. "You hear her?" he said fondly. "I must not delay. Give me leave to go."

Isolde nodded numbly. "And may the Mother of all the Great Ones go with you."

"And with you." Bowing low, he moved away down the hill. At the entrance to the Queen's burial chamber, the Druid's women rolled back the heavy stone. She watched as he paused to thank them, then stepped over the threshold and vanished into the gloom. Slowly the women returned the stone to its place.

At dawn, Isolde had the tomb unsealed again, just as the first rays of the sun bathed all the chamber with fire. In the farthest recesses of the chamber, still and cold, Fideal lay on a bed of trefoil with the Queen in his arms. Holding her beloved body, he had made the journey to the Otherworld. And in his strong embrace, her head pillowed on his chest, she had traveled with him to the Plains of Delight.

Isolde paused to make her last farewell. Her mother's face was soft with smiles and tears, and her fingers curled tenderly against Fideal's neck. The rich smell of incense enveloped them both. The breath of the Mother filled the sacred place.

"Seal the door," she commanded. "This is a house of rest."

The woman Druid nodded. "And what then, Majesty?"

"A time of peace," she said sadly. "A time to repair and renew."

And to find my knight—the only true love in the world. Where are you, Tristan? Where are you, my love?

chapter 26

Primroses carpeting the cliff tops like morning sun, wild violets in every valley, the hillsides alive with little stotting lambs: spring came more sweetly to Cornwall than to any place on earth. But Andred was blind to the beauty that whispered around him every day. The unfolding year meant only one thing to him: another week gone, and Tristan still not here.

"Dead!" pronounced Elva with relish, rolling the thought greedily around her mind. "Or as good as dead, or else he'd be here now."

Yes, he knew she must be right. Tristan would never disobey Mark so flagrantly. And how fine it would be if his dear cousin was rotting somewhere, so badly injured that he could not move. But Andred knew better than to allow himself to dream. People only disappeared like that in moldy old stories or children's tales. For now, it was enough that Tristan was absent, and in deep disgrace. King Mark would not forgive him for this lengthy delay.

"Is he here yet?" the King moaned every day. It was a question all his servants had learned to dread. Staggering up from his wine-slobbered couch or returning from the hunt, he could think of nothing else, and his temper grew worse with every passing hour.

"Where is Tristan, sire?" Andred composed his face in an expression of distress. "Who can say? But wherever he is, I am sure he would not betray you—"

"Betray me?" Mark goggled. "Why should he do that?"

"Oh, sire!" Elva chimed in, rolling her eyes. "Other knights may disobey your command, but not Sir Tristan."

"Not Tristan, no," echoed Andred dutifully, with just the right hint of doubt in his voice.

"You think he's gone over to Ireland with the Queen?"

"If he has, he must have had a reason..." Andred trailed off unconvincingly. Oh, how he loved playing with Mark like this! And every day brought new chances to hand.

"FROM THE PRINCESS of France?" Mark bleated, taking the scroll. "She's calling a tournament, you say?"

"And inviting Sir Tristan, as the premier knight," said Andred insinuatingly. "No one else."

Mark tugged at a stringy lock of his sandy-gray hair. "Why him?"

"You must ask that of the Princess herself."

"Isolde, is that what she's called? The same as the Queen? Why did they call her that?"

"Her father loved the Queen of Ireland, but she would not marry him. So, he named his own daughter after her and brought her up to be a healer like our Queen."

"Another healer, eh?" said Mark with interest. "Is she as good as Isolde?"

"They say she has healing hands."

"And she's invited him to a tournament? Well, he shan't go," Mark proclaimed with satisfaction. "We don't need the French to show us what to do. If there's to be a tournament, we'll have one ourselves."

"But if Tristan doesn't return—"

"He will!" declared Mark explosively. "When he hears that there's jousting in hand. He wouldn't miss that. Send out messengers to every lord and king, and get the heralds on the road."

Andred bowed, his brain furiously at work. His elf-shotten lip began to throb and he stroked it down: courage now, I will turn this to advantage, never fear.

What would Elva say? He found himself hungering for her expressive words, her long hard body, her sharp breasts. Get to her then, get to Elva right away...

Mark's voice floated after him as he hurried away. "Oh, and Andred, order our own knights down to the tiltyard at once. They've done nothing all winter, they'd better get ready at once. Wherever he is, Tristan can beat them all!"

NOW THE EARTH was awakening from its winter sleep and the fields and woods were stirring with the spring. At midday the cattle slumbered in the warmth of the sun, and the nights were alive with lovers' whispers and cries. But underground there was no night or day. Nothing but darkness and the endless throb of regret.

Tristan lay in a cell in the castle's foundations, a low chamber cut out of the primeval rock. Only rats and toads could survive in such places, he knew, and the fetid air had not stirred for a hundred years. As the day went on, a slit in the rock let in a little sun. But when daylight faded, darkness came down like a shroud, and he lost count of the hours before morning came again.

Yet a lover's heart can always tell the time. Each evening when the love star rose again, he prayed, Bless Isolde, my lady and my love. And destroy Breccan if he breaks his faith. I could have saved her from him, his soul cried. But I left her undefended. I failed her trust.

Yet how did I fail? he cried, raging, weeping, cursing, and pacing his cell. Ambushed by women as he tried to escape, he was beaten before he began. He had sworn to defend every woman, to cherish her honor as his own and to keep her from harm. To go against that would make him an oath-breaker, a rogue knight, a thing beyond shame.

Yet how could Duessa and her women claim his chivalry? They had imprisoned him here against his will, starving and growing weaker day by day. He knew he could hardly sit a horse by now, and it would be a long time before he could trust himself to handle a sword. Could he escape without doing them any harm, turn the tables on Falsamilla when she brought his food? By now he could count every step of her daily visit to his prison, and could track her descent by the rustling of her skirts. But if he tried to break free, the armed guards would not be far away.

As they must be now. Already he could hear her footfall on the stair. "Sir?"

The door opened and Falsamilla came in, set down the provisions beside him, and began to speak.

"My lady catches knights the way children catch flies. I am only sorry that I helped her catch one such as you." To his surprise, her eyes seemed bright with tears.

He shook his head. "Lady, I don't blame you for my woes," he replied brusquely. "Every man chooses the path that he will tread."

She forced a smile. "And you chose well when you refused her love. Most men leap into her arms and embrace their doom." She looked around the malodorous cell. "The rest think again when they find themselves suffering here. In time, even the strongest begs his way into her bed."

Tristan recoiled in disgust. "What pleasure can she take in that?"

Falsamilla gave a twisted smile. "Remember, my lady is an enchanter beyond compare. She transports her lovers to worlds they never knew, and they never want it to end."

"All things end," said Tristan quietly.

"Oh, they do." Falsamilla gave a smile he did not like. "The lover slips into the sweetest sleep of his life. Then he awakes to find himself alone on the cold hillside, left with a soul-sickness that nothing can cure. For the rest of his life he is fated to pine and mourn around this wood, searching for her and the castle he never can find."

Tristan closed his eyes. Out of the darkness came troop upon troop of knights, pale, hollow-eyed, sick and wasted creatures of skin and bone, haunting the hillsides, weeping on the ground.

One held up a skeletal hand in Tristan's face. "She has sucked out my soul," he cried. "Beware of yours!"

"Oh, sir—"

He heard Falsamilla weeping, and came to himself. The maid wrung her hands. "My lady would kill me if she knew I had told you this—"

"She will never know," he said hoarsely. "But what possesses her to do such evil things?"

Falsamilla gave him a brooding stare. "Let me tell you, sir," she rasped. "When she was a child, a man of lust killed my lady's father, then raped her mother and took the children away. The elder sister he married off to another king like him, but he gave my lady to the Christians when she was still a child."

"He put her in a nunnery?" Tristan knew how Christian women were ruled in those houses of theirs. "To be starved, and whipped—"

Angry tears filled Falsamilla's eyes. "And forced to worship their God when she was destined for the life of the Goddess—even to serve Her in the highest place."

Tristan found his voice. "Avalon? Alas the Gods! Who would do such a cruel thing?"

She gave him a piercing look. "Not you, sir, if I read you right. And you would not betray me."

He raised his head, baffled. "Betray you . . . ? I would never betray a lady in my life."

"I believe you." She gave a decisive nod. "Sir Tristan, if you give me your oath that you'll never reveal my help, I will set you free."

"Free?" He could hardly believe her. "Lady, why in the name of the Gods . . . ?"

Her mouth twisted in a painful smile. "The life of a good man is worth one good turn. I have years ahead to enjoy all the rest."

"But surely you'll be in danger?" He shuddered at the thought of Duessa's rage.

She shook her head, laughing openly. "D'you think my lady ever comes down here?"

He would not press her further. "When will you come?"

"Tonight, at owl-light. Listen for their call." She hurried to the door. "But swear," she cried on the threshold, "swear your faith to me?"

"I have sworn a knighthood oath!" he cried in a fury. "Do you doubt my faith?"

The only answer was the slamming of the door. Trembling, he heard the key grind in the lock. A frenzy of doubt and hope seized him. Was she playing with him, would she return?

He never knew how many hours went by, only that he paced the floor till he could go no more. When his legs failed, he crouched down by the door, straining for every sound. He heard the owls cry and she did not come. Still he kept hope alive, till he passed the hour when the last hope dies and hordes of new fears are born. In the end he fell into an exhausted doze against the wall. When a sound came from the stairs, he was instantly awake. But still he did not believe it when the door swung open and there she was.

She stood, white-faced, with her finger on her lips: be silent, or die! He made himself like a wraith as he followed her up, stumbling through the passageways as best he could. Now his long imprisonment was telling on his wasted frame. Gods above, how would he handle a horse, with his muscles already failing at every step?

And still Falsamilla led onward through the gloom, passing down into the castle's unknown depths. They slipped through low side alleys and forgotten cells, lit only by the lantern in the maid's hand. One cobweb-hung tunnel had hardly been traversed in years, till at last they came to a door. One thrust of her shoulder and she had it open, ushering him through.

Hardly daring to breathe, Tristan stepped out into the night. His poisoned lungs gulped up the air like balm, sweeter than honey after so long underground. The night was hung with a thousand glittering stars, and the Mother Herself smiled down from the sky overhead.

Goddess, Mother, thanks!

He stood outside a forgotten postern gate with a watchman's shelter and alarm bell by the wall. The little gate had once been guarded, that was plain. But the forest had long ago crept up to the castle walls, and no hand had rung the alarm bell for years.

A few yards away stood his gray stallion, saddled for the road, with his harp and his sword in its scabbard by the horse's side. He stepped forward and embraced the great beast, weeping on its neck. The horse leaned down its head and nuzzled his hand. So there you are, master. Which way now, my dear?

Far away! All the way. As far as we can go.

An answering whinny snickered through the night. Tristan turned. Across the clearing stood another horse, with Falsamilla taking up the reins, preparing to mount.

Tristan's gut heaved. "What now, lady? You ride along with me?"

She flashed him a smile of triumph. "All the way, my dear."

"But I ride alone."

"No longer, Tristan. Your way is my way now."

He struggled for control. "Madam, I shall gladly escort you to the highway. Or bring you to the safety of the nearest town."

"Oh sir, in the first town, we shall stop at the first inn and take the first bed." She paused, her eyes raking him up and down. "We can't go far tonight, you'll have to rest. After that, we'll travel at night and lie up by day."

Was he dreaming, or was there a lascivious light in her eye? A cold sweat broke out on his forehead, and he floundered for words. "Lady, I may not do as you command. I serve Queen Isolde, I am sworn to her.

And my kinsman King Mark has summoned me to his side. I must ride to Cornwall with all speed."

She waved a contemptuous hand. "You pledged me your faith in exchange for your freedom. You are my knight now."

"Hear me, madam—" He swallowed his mounting rage. "I will transport you safely from this place, and find you a refuge where you may decently live. From this moment on, if any man wrongs you, he will answer to me." His hand tore through his hair. "Whoever he is, even kin of my own, I will make him repay. All this I swear I will do for you. But I cannot do what you demand of me now."

Her face had gone very white. "Not even for your freedom?"

He tried to keep the disgust out of his voice. "There's no freedom for a man who breaks his word, and mine was given to Isolde years ago. Look elsewhere, lady, for a knight who lies and cheats—a man who'd take your body to bargain for his own."

She shook her head wildly. Tears burst from her eyes and she made a frantic leap for the postern bell. "Promise you'll go with me to the ends of the earth," she wept. "Swear to marry me and make me your lady or I'll ring this alarm till I wake the dead. The whole castle will come down on you like a hive of bees, and you'll never get away from here alive!"

Marry me . . . ?

Never hurt a woman flashed across his mind and he threw the thought away. Madly, he tore the great sword from its sheath and covered the clearing in a couple of strides. The silver blade went singing ahead of him to find the tender hollow of Falsamilla's throat, pinning the goggle-eyed maiden to the wall. Tristan's soul sang with it, every joyful move. One simple refrain was turning his brain to blood.

Kill, kill!

chapter 27

a mournful wind had risen with the dawn, driving the clouds before it like a herd of sheep. Wisps of thin white mist limply drifted through the air, wrapping the travelers in damp and cold. Standing in the courtyard, King Jean de Luz folded King Hoel to his breast, and knew it was time to leave. But he would carry with him all the way back to his lands the sight of Hoel's troubled face, tight mouth, and shoulders slack in defeat. If only he could have done better by his old friend!

But what man on earth could get the better of Blanche? No maiden modesty, no fear of rejection, would hold her back. And a girl shameless enough to woo a knight for herself would have no scruples about shaming her country too. A girl like that could hold any man to ransom, father or king.

De Luz flung wide his arms and folded the King to his breast. "Till our next meeting, then. May your Gods keep you well."

Hoel straightened his back and reached for a cheerful smile. "Let me hear from you."

De Luz gave him a keen glance. "And I from you, old friend. May your Gods be with you, whatever comes about."

It had begun to rain. Hoel fixed his eyes on the horizon and watched the slow drizzle drowning the sky in gray. He took a deep breath of the sullen air and sighed. "Whatever comes about."

WELL, THE KING of the Basques had gone. Frowning, Kedrin made his way through the palace in a deepening gloom. The visit had come to nothing, as he'd said from the start. At last King Hoel had admitted that someone should consult Blanche herself.

"If we had, we could have stopped her sending for Tristan," Hoel moaned in distress. "The Gods alone know where that piece of folly will lead! We only just escaped war with the Gauls. We don't want King Mark up in arms as well." He reached out to his son. "Put a stop to this nonsense, will you, Kedrin?"

Kedrin was not sure that any force on earth would stop Blanche. But his sister had to be consulted, so here he was. With a fixed smile and a jaunty air, he knocked on her door.

"Blanche!"

As always, his heart lifted at the sight of his sister in her dainty gown, seated before her mirror as pale and perfect as a pearl in its shell. Here in this quiet room washed with creamy loam, Blanche's narrow bed was the one she had slept in as a child, and she still used her old girlhood dressing-table and chair. The low-ceilinged chamber even smelled like a young girl's room, fragrant with lavender and rosewater. Today she wore a simple chamber gown of silver-white silk, and her hair, unbound, shone like snow in the sun. She rose to greet him with a loving kiss. "Good day, brother."

"And you, sister," he returned affectionately, settling down on a plump sheepskin settee. "So Jean de Luz has gone."

"Oh, pouf!" She waved a dismissive hand. "Father never listens to a word I say. I could have told him beforehand De Luz would be wasting his time."

Kedrin nodded calmly. "I told him that. And now you've written to Sir Tristan to invite him here? But he's sworn to obey his lord. What if King Mark won't agree?"

She caught one of the pale locks of hair around her finger and began winding it up. "It doesn't matter. Tristan's on his way."

"What?" Kedrin started. "How d'you know?"

The little hand waved again. "Oh, I know."

Gods above! Kedrin fought back a gasp of shock. "But if he doesn't . . . ?" he resumed uncertainly. "What then?"

"Oh, he will."

Kedrin wanted to weep. "Hear me, sister," he said heartily. "No princess of France should have one suitor alone. A lady like you should have legions of lovers clamoring for your hand, and knights from all over the world swooning at your feet."

The baby-blue eyes took on a soft, drifting look. "Yesss," Blanche murmured. "Yesss."

Kedrin leaned forward with an understanding air. "Now, of course, you'll have eyes for Sir Tristan alone. But believe me, sister, it keeps a man on edge to know that there are others in the running beside himself. Let other knights court you too. I'll summon them myself, the very best."

Blanche paused to consider, twirling her wayward curl.

Other men? The very best?

Other men to make Tristan jealous, to ensure that when he saw his rivals, he would not delay . . . ?

Oh yessss!

"If you say so, brother, let them come," Blanche breathed, dropping her eyes. "And if others come and Tristan beats them all, at least I'll know I've chosen the right man. And then our father will surely be satisfied," she added virtuously. "He will know I have made a careful, prudent choice."

Oh, my dear sister . . .

Blanche did not know, Kedrin would swear, that her innocent pupils had narrowed as she spoke and her innocent air of roses and lavender had been overlaid with the taint of deceit. She claimed to love Tristan, yet even before they met him, she was ready do anything to arouse his jealousy. Treachery was the element in which Blanche lived. Indeed it was not treachery to her but common sense, to make sure that she got what she wanted, whatever the cost.

Kedrin sighed. Some women are born to scheme, and you are a queen among them, sister mine. But you don't always know what you want, he thought tenderly. You're like a child crying for the red apple even though it carries poison in its heart. Well, I'll protect you, I'll look out for you.

And he would not deceive her. However she twisted and turned, he would teach her trust. "The very best men," he repeated. "But one above all."

"Yes?" She turned her face to her mirror and practiced a shy, dimpled smile.

"You'll have seen him already at some of our tournaments last year—the King of . . ."

"Ouesterland?" Blanche's head went back. "The knight they call Saint Roc?"

So she had noticed him. Kedrin suppressed a grin. "The very same. The Chevalier Jacques Saint Rocquefort, to give him his full name."

"And he's one of the knights you suggest?" Turning, Blanche saw herself in the glass, fetchingly caught between a shrug and a pout. She liked it so much that she did it again. "Well, bring him here if you like."

"Sister, it shall be."

Dropping a kiss on his sister's head, Kedrin hastened through the palace to his father's side. He found him in his chamber, staring at the wall. "She's agreed!"

Hoel turned his head. "She remembered Saint Roc?"

"At once," Kedrin laughed.

"Well, he was always the hardest fighter of the day. Not the best, but the most determined of them all."

"It's true, Tristan beat him that time Blanche saw him first," Kedrin conceded. "But he fought to the end like a wolf, he never gave up."

"Well, he's got the right spirit, if that's what we want. But is it? He can't offer much in the way of land."

Kedrin shook his head. "Blanche will have plenty of her own."

"Will he make her happy?" Hoel said doubtfully. "He's a hard man, they say."

"He comes from a hard place."

"Roc by name, rock by nature, eh?"

"It's what Blanche needs, whether she knows it or not." Kedrin drew a breath. "Trust me, sir, he's a man of weight. And he's the man for us, if he'll take it on."

Hoel bowed his head. "Send for him, then," he said in deep weariness. "This madness with Tristan is going to ruin us all. Offer him anything to change Blanche's mind!"

chapter 28

Westward, *ever onward into the west.*

On . . . on . . .

The road stretched ahead of them, white in the morning sun. The hillsides now were in full springtime green, a stinging viridian almost too bright for their eyes. Every tree was in leaf, every bush home to nesting birds, and the earth beneath throbbing with new life. Sitting back in the saddle, Isolde gave her horse its head. Any other day she would have enjoyed this ride to Breccan's estate.

Breccan . . .

She could not think of the dead knight without pain. *The Mother loved you, Breccan. You were handsome, gifted, and brave, truly favored among Her sons. One of Her blue-eyed daughters could have loved you, and given you sons and daughters of your own. You could have chosen life, Breccan, new life, not death. And instead you have gone down to the House of Death and the earth lies over your eyes.*

And now she was riding west, crossing the island with a handful of knights. Since Breccan's unexpected death, there had been no trace of Cormac and Gilhan. Today she was bringing the search to Breccan's own lands.

Breccan's? She smarted at another painful memory. Lough Larne was never Breccan's estate at all. The fine castle and rich lands around had all been given to Tolen by the doting Queen. Still, Lough Larne had become a place of delight for them both. On rare occasions at least, Isolde knew that her mother's quicksilver soul had found peace here and love.

And as they crested the sheltering mountain ridge, she could feel it too. Ahead of them the green hillside ran down to a valley with the lough at its heart. Mirrored in the still, silver waters stood the white castle, commanding the head of the valley with its airy crenellations and tall towers. Not far away was the sea, bringing the sparkling tang of salt on the morning air. For a moment Isolde saw her mother again, leaning out from her tower in welcome, her veil lifting in the breeze. *Come, Isolde! Hurry, little one.*

Her eyes blurred. *No tears, no fears.*

Onward . . .

Always on . . .

And here if anywhere, they must find Gilhan and Cormac. After so long, there was nowhere else to look. She had had the island scoured for miles around Dubh Lein, widening the fruitless search with every sweep. And every day her sense of hopelessness grew. *Cormac's a man of the spirit, how will he bear such a long imprisonment? And Gilhan's too old to be locked up, he was old when I was young . . .*

Goddess, Mother, help me.

Without her mother's chief counselor and Druid, how would she deal with a land in disarray? Wise heads and sturdy souls were needed now to bring the country back from long neglect, and avert the threat of famine when winter came. Already she had sent many of the knights and lords back to their lands, to hearten the people and prepare for the harvest to come. There was more to be done before she could leave Dubh Lein, but with Gilhan and Cormac, the country would be safe.

Leave Dubh Lein and set out to find my love . . .

She thought of him all the time. In ten years, they had rarely been apart. Being without him was like losing the use of her hands. *Tristan* was her last thought as she lay down at night and her first as she opened her eyes on another gray dawn. When the wind had sighed and sobbed round Dubh Lein, when the clouds overhead were heavy with unshed tears, she felt all the world was grieving for her loss.

There was no comfort to be had in this long delay. Nothing but death or disaster could have kept him from her side. Had he been ambushed by some rogue in the wood, as they were waylaid by the pitiless Sir Greuze? Had he reached Castle Dore and fallen foul of Andred or Mark? All these pangs kept her awake at night. But one fear above all kept her trembling in her bed. *Have you left me, sweetheart? Have you found another love?*

But Tristan unfaithful? Her one true love, so devoted for so long? It seemed to her that she betrayed him every time the thought came into her mind. As soon as she found him, she would solve the riddle of his absence, fold him in her arms, feed and fill the hollow at her heart.

Tristan . . . oh, my love . . .

But to do that she had to find Cormac and Gilhan first. What had Breccan done with them? And what a fool she had been to let Ravigel go! On the terrible night when Breccan and Fideal died, she never once thought to detain and question him. Ravigel had broken his sword and laid it with his master, then kissed Breccan's sword and taken it for his own. Blind with loss, he had mounted and ridden away, surrounded by the rest of Breccan's band. And with them had gone any knowledge of where the prisoners might be.

For they were nowhere to be found. No castle, no cave, no fortress or abandoned hermitage held the men, and Isolde was forced to acknowledge that the searchers had drawn a blank. Yet she would not give up. Time to try Lough Larne. *And if you don't find them there?* She put the thought away.

Now the castle lay before them with its tall white towers, its stables, barns, and byres. The leader of the knights gave a cheerful grin. "Leave it to us, lady. We'll find them, if they're here."

Gods above, they must be! There's nowhere else.

"The steward, my lady."

The knights were ushering forward a man of middle height with a keen-eyed, military bearing and an honest air. Isolde knew him as the castle's longtime custodian and the steward of the former Queen. Isolde bowed. "Sir, you know why we're here. Can you think of anything that might help?"

The steward shook his head. "Sir Breccan didn't come here, my lady. Sir Tolen was always our lord."

"So he never knew the place at all?"

"Oh, that he did." The steward brightened. "They were born hereabouts, Sir Breccan and all his kin. That's why the Queen gave Sir Tolen this estate. She wanted him to have his own place on the family's ancestral land."

Isolde's pulse quickened. "Then he grew up 'round here?"

"Very near," the steward confirmed. His broad face creased in a reminiscent smile. "The brothers used to ride these hills like the hobgoblins of hell, tormenting the life out of the ancients who lived 'round about."

"The ancients," said Isolde slowly. "Is there anyone here who might have known them in those days?"

The steward paused for thought. "It was so long ago that most of them are dead."

"There must be some." She tried to compose herself. "I beg you, sir, think!"

The man considered. "There's old Friya."

"Who?"

"She used to be their nurse. She served in the household and took care of every one of the boys as they came along. She worshipped them all, but Breccan was her favorite, she'd do anything for him. She's so old now that she doesn't know who she is, mad as a March hare, they say. Her married daughter in the village wants to take her in, but old Friya won't leave that place of hers on the cliff. Says she's always worshipped the Mother above Lough Larne and isn't going to end her days some-where else."

He laughed unhappily. "She's the oldest living creature for miles around, lady, but she's not much use to you. She's mad now and she sees things, those who know her say."

A disregarded soul, who lived alone? Old, mad, and loyal to Breccan all her life?

Isolde raised her head. "Where does she live? Can you take me there?"

chapter 29

On the ridge above Lough Larne a dense, untamed woodland covered the hillside as far as the edge of the cliff. The narrow pathway would only admit one traveler at a time, and no horses had passed this way for many years. Heedless of briar and bracken, Isolde gathered up her skirts and plunged in, almost treading on the heels of the knight leading the way.

"Here, madam."

Without warning, the man gestured and stepped aside. Directly ahead, rising not more than four or five feet from the ground, stood a rough hovel built of forest loam and roofed with dead leaves.

The knight eyed the strange dwelling askance. "I'll go in first, my lady, and make sure it's safe."

His sword was drawn in his hand. Isolde shook her head. "No, sir. I shall be safe enough from this lady, I think."

Stooping, she entered the low dwelling and found herself in the gloom. The hovel's one small window was covered with a tattered piece of sacking, shutting out the light. Cautiously, she took a pace or two across the floor of trodden earth, and paused to look around. There was nothing but a stool, a wooden bowl, and a pile of moldy rags heaped up against the wall. That would serve as the place both to sit and to sleep and perhaps as the old woman's clothing and bed covering too. It was a place of desperate poverty, hardly fit for human life.

But someone lived here, she could tell, and sooner or later the inhabitant would appear. Isolde turned toward the door to tell her knights to wait. As she did, a thrill of horror rooted her to the floor. The pile of rags had a pair of yellow eyes.

Mad eyes, as wild as March winds, peered out at her from beneath the heap of cloth. Meeting their frightened gaze, Isolde quelled her own fear. *Don't be afraid. I shan't do you any harm.*

She bowed her head politely. "Dame Friya?"

There was no response. Breathing hard, she tried again. "I am Isolde, come to call on you."

The pile of rags did not move. Isolde paused. All she could hear was the sound of the sea, beating on the shore below the cliff. Then without warning, a young cat with eyes as mad as its mistress slid into the room. Seeing Isolde, it arched its thin back and hissed, fixing her with a yellow, spangled stare. An odd sensation ran through her, and she began to feel dizzy and sick. Suddenly she knew that she had to get out.

She groped for the door. Then a cracked laugh disturbed the musty gloom. "Behave, Malkin, none of your mischief now. Don't scare the lady away, we don't often have visitors here."

The cat dropped her eyes and slunk off. Isolde watched uncertainly as the nondescript bundle of rags parted and an aged woman crawled out onto the floor. Slowly she heaved her skinny form to her feet. Her filthy garments were no more than rags, and her gray hair hung in elf-locks down her back. A battered black hat clung to the side of her head, lending a poignant air of lost dignity and better days. Two odd, light eyes rolled behind her matted fringe, and a strange little smile flickered and was gone. She nodded to Isolde.

A rank smell filled the room. Isolde swallowed hard. "Madam Friya, they say you've lived all your life 'round Lough Larne."

The old woman waved a filthy hand. "They say, they say," she said grandly. "What do they know?"

Her voice was crusty but supremely confident. Isolde pressed on. "Did you know Sir Breccan?"

"Know him?" An unexpected cackle startled Isolde with its intensity. "No, I didn't know him," she said scornfully, "not the finest of my nurslings, no, no, no!"

"When did you see him last?"

Friya stared. "See him here, or there?"

Goddess, Mother, she's mad . . . Isolde felt close to tears. "Where?"

"In the Otherworld. He's gone with the Dark Lord, everyone knows that. The Mother sent him to the House of the Dead. And he'll give 'em a rousting, if I know my boy!"

"But here on earth, here at Lough Larne . . . ?"

The oddly assorted eyes flashed from side to side. The old woman played suspiciously with the hairs on her chin.

"He was never here," she pronounced at last. "Never here," she repeated in a loud singsong voice.

Never here? Isolde's stomach clenched.

"My lord . . . my dead boy . . " Friya crooned, hugging herself in her skinny arms and rocking to and fro.

Hopelessness broke over Isolde like a wave. If Breccan was never here, then neither were Cormac and Gilhan. Why was she troubling this poor old soul?

"Never here," she echoed emptily.

So be it.

Time to go.

She took a step toward Friya to bid farewell, and was startled to receive a flashing smile. The old woman was nodding and winking like one possessed, her ancient elbows twitching with nudges she could not hold back. Twice she opened her mouth and twice closed it, unable to speak.

"You have something to say?" Isolde asked, bewildered.

"No, it's forbidden!" Friya shrilled. Then her face dissolved again into a brilliant smile. "But I can tell you. You're one of them. Tall and shining, I knew you at once."

"One of whom?"

"You know," cried the old woman irritably. "The Shining Ones. You're one of them."

"Tell me, then." Isolde felt herself trembling. "You can tell me."

The old woman lowered her voice. "The Fair Ones are here. Right here. But you know that."

"Here? Yes, of course."

Friya gave a mysterious smile and waved her hands. "They came here to live with me."

"The Fair Ones have come here to live with you . . ." Isolde shook her head. *Madness, all of it. There was no sense in a word Friya said.*

Alas, poor soul, we must take care of her. She has a daughter, didn't the steward say that? She should be left with her. Or else in some kindly hospice where the aged like her may find peace at last.

Dimly, she heard the old woman's voice running on, mingling with the distant roar of the sea.

"...yes, Fair Ones, tall and unsmiling in the night, but the one with the mark, he was a Shining One, I knew him as I knew you..."

Isolde did not move. "The one with the mark...?"

Friya treated her to a glance of utter scorn. "Between his brows, shining, you've seen it, you know—"

"Yes, yes, I know." She could hardly breathe. "How many of them were there, these Fair Ones, when they came?"

"Two!" Friya hooted vigorously. "Two of them, and many more mounted men."

Isolde made her voice as calm as she could. "And where are they now, the Fair Ones? Where are they living, these dark, shining men?"

THE OLD HERMITAGE lay halfway down the cliff, a large cave with a natural stone ledge before it jutting out over the sea.

The only way down the sheer face of the rock was by the long, rickety ladder, lying now on the cliff top at their feet. The hermit would have used it to descend to the platform of stone, then drawn it down after him to protect his retreat. But without it, for any unfortunates marooned on the rocky ledge, there was no way up. Or down: the cliff fell away sharply beneath the ledge, and the sea prowled hungrily on the rocks below.

Beside the ladder lay a capacious wooden bucket with a long rope attached to its handle—for lowering food and water to men in the cave below...?

Isolde surged to the edge of the cliff, fire in every limb. Gathering up her skirts, she threw herself to the ground and leaned over the edge. "Lord Cormac and Sir Gilhan," she called, "are you there?"

"*Areyouthereareyouthereareyouthere...*"

A mocking echo tore her voice away. There was no answer from the cave below. Trembling, she tried again, stretching farther over the cliff edge.

"Lady," cried her leading knight, "beware!"

She took no notice and called again. Far below came a rustling inside the cave, like creatures in hibernation stirring from a long sleep. Then came the words she would treasure all her life.

"Your Majesty?"

It was Gilhan's voice, rusty and cracked, but firm. "Is there a ladder up there, by any chance?"

A WEEK LATER Isolde stood with Sir Gilhan on the deck of the Queen's ship. "Sir, we are safely embarked. We have a fair wind for Cornwall, and a full tide. I shall return as swiftly as I can."

"And in the meantime, you may safely leave Ireland to me and to Lord Cormac, lady," he responded quietly. "We shall repay your care. When you rescued us, we had almost given up hope. The Gods only know how much longer we would have received our daily bucket from the ancient dame."

Isolde nodded. "And what a miracle that poor mad Friya never forgot her instructions or failed her trust. She was the only one who knew where you were."

Gilhan drew a sharp breath. "Yes, Majesty."

She looked at him and feared she had said too much: no man wanted to be reminded of a violent, unjust arrest, weeks of imprisonment in fear of his life, and eking out a miserable existence in a cave, with nothing but the rocks and the sea below. Yet both her old friends had come through their ordeal intact.

"Well, sir," she resumed, "the Gods and Great Ones brought you and Lord Cormac back to me. I know the Western Isle will be safe in your hands."

"I will tell Cormac so." Gilhan smiled. "Now may the sun and the wind speed you on your way and bring you what you seek."

What I seek . . . ?

A sudden wind whipped over the purple sea. The air shivered, and Isolde heard the Lady's voice. *Ah, Isolde, beware of what you seek. If a man loses his honor . . .*

Her sight faded and three female faces floated up from the sea, one fair, one dark, and the third with chestnut hair. All opened their soundless mouths at the same time, and their eyes filled with fire. *Love me,*

Tristan, their hungry lips intoned. Their red lips were ripe for kissing, and she thought she saw Tristan's head leaning down to kiss one of them.

She closed her eyes, shaking from head to foot. Who were these women to invade her mind and try to steal her love?

Why do you haunt me like this?

Go away!

"My lady? Are you well?"

It was Brangwain, her eyes alight with concern. Isolde stood very still. *No, I am not well. I am sick for Tristan, and this sickness is my love.*

With an effort of will, she forced herself to smile. "Away with us then, Sir Gilhan," she cried gaily.

Sir Gilhan nodded. "Godspeed then, madam," he said slowly. "And away with you."

The sun was sinking in a pool of fire as the little ship ran out of the bay with the tide. Gilhan stood on the quay, hand upraised in farewell for as long as he could see Isolde and Brangwain standing on the deck. A dark misgiving gripped him, body and soul, and his prayer soared with the seabirds following the ship.

"May all your Gods go with you, lady. May you find what you seek— and nothing more, nothing worse!"

chapter 30

Kill! *Kill!*

A red mist drowned Tristan's sight. All he could see were two eyes like lakes of darkness and an open, quivering mouth. The silver point of his sword drove forward without his command and drew blood, dancing in the white hollow of a woman's throat.

A shuddering moan reached him from far away. "Don't kill me! Don't—"

It was the maid Falsamilla, on her knees before him, weeping at his feet. He could see half a dozen tiny sword-cuts in her neck. Had he done that? Gods above, to treat a woman so . . .

"Let me be your lady," she implored through swollen lips. "Let me only follow you . . ."

Drops of blood were pulsing from her throat. He could not look at her. *I have hurt her like this, and still she begs me to love her, and grovels like a dog?* "No."

"On my knees, sir—"

He could not bear it. "Lady, it cannot be."

She looked at him, speechless, desolate. Averting his gaze, he plowed on. "The Great Ones decide who will go hand in hand through all the worlds. For us, it was not written in the stars. You gave me my freedom, and I shall honor you all my life. But from this moment, our paths lie apart."

Falsamilla bowed her head. "Go, then," she muttered. "But at least give me something to remember you by."

He started and backed away. "What can I give you?"

Her eyes were like desert moons. "A kiss."

"A kiss from me?" he gasped. "Why?"

Now it was her turn to look away. "No man ever kissed me in my life," she said stonily. "I want to know what a kiss is before I die."

Alas, poor lady . . .

Pity flooded him. She saved my life and all she asks is this? Aching with sorrow, he looked at her lovely face, her soft body ripe for awakening. and felt an angry shame on behalf of his sex. Where is the man who will warm this woman through? Where is the knight that she can call her own?

She was trembling like a child after a beating, staring at the floor. Without thinking, he took her in his arms, cradling her in his cloak. With a shock, he felt her heart thudding against his breast. Lowering his head, he gave her a gentle kiss. But he was not surprised when her lips parted and her red mouth fastened desperately on his. She clung to him so greedily that for a moment panic touched him with one fearful thought, *she will suck out my soul!* But the next second, he tasted the salt of her tears and knew that this was no enchantment, just a woman's breaking heart.

They kissed, and kissed again. At last he broke away.

Oh, Isolde, I have betrayed our love . . .

"I must go," he said, lost in despair. She nodded, staring at him with huge and empty eyes, and he felt her misery in his own soul. "What will you do?" he asked awkwardly.

She gave a crooked smile. "Ah, sir, the world is wide. I shall find my way."

"Alone?"

Her smile grew bitter as she looked at him. "Unless you'll change your mind."

"But the highways are full of rogues and lawless men."

"Have no fear. Duessa taught us all to take care of ourselves."

He watched unhappily as she took her horse and climbed into the saddle, all her brightness gone. She pointed to where two tracks diverged in the wood. "You that way," she said bleakly, "and I this." Then she turned away without another word.

"Farewell, lady," he called out desperately to the retreating back. "May the Mother Herself watch over you as you go." But there was no reply.

Only the mocking whisper of the wind, echoing the shame and disgust he felt.

You swore to protect all women, and to be true to one. You have betrayed Falsamilla and deceived Isolde tonight.

You have broken your oath. You are no true knight.

Failed again, Tristan, failed. Gods above, where will it all end?

MANY EYES SAW the knight on the gray riding in. First came the watcher in the tree, who was soon on horseback to gabble out the news. "Lord Andred, he's here—the knight you ordered me to watch for all these weeks..."

After him came the women at the ford below Castle Dore. Five or ten of them, bare-legged in the water, were washing their linen in the crisp running stream when one caught sight of the newcomer and cried out, "He's here!"

"The lost Prince?"

"Not any more, girl. See for yourself!"

As they ran to see, more than one noticed that the knight was as white as the sheets they'd left floating in the ford, his handsome face bleached with weariness and pain. But still he had a courteous word for all of them, and a tired smile. Then the men in the fields rushed to kiss his hand, and the castle-dwellers came pouring out of kitchens, cellars, and attics to welcome him home. Smiling through it all, Tristan swung down from his horse in the courtyard, his legs trembling with fatigue. Gods and Great Ones, he vowed with a humble heart, thanks and blessings for bringing me safe home.

But one look at Mark's face told him there was no safety here.

"Tristan?"

Surrounded by his entourage, the King was bearing down on him with an unpleasant smile. "We have missed you, nephew," he said in spiteful tones. "You were due back here weeks ago. Where have you been all this while?"

Tristan took a deep breath. "Sire..." he began, and launched into his tale.

But Mark was not minded to believe a word he heard. "Oh, indeed," he sneered. "Delayed by a lady, you say, held against your will? When I had sent for you urgently, commanded you to be here?"

Andred leaned forward. "At least Sir Tristan's back in time for the tournament."

Tristan shook his head. "What tournament?"

"Ah, you don't know, you see," Mark cried triumphantly. "That's what you get for staying away so long. You were invited by name—you alone, nephew—to a tournament in France. Well, I couldn't have that. So we're holding our own tournament here . . ."

"Sire . . ." Tristan felt a muscle jumping beside his eye. "What is all this to me?"

Mark rolled his eyes. "You were summoned to France by their princess, no less."

Tristan was baffled. "The Princess of France?"

Andred nodded. "They call her Blanche. She's the King's only daughter, and a great healer, they say."

"Is it so?" Tristan closed his eyes. There is only one great healer in the world, his soul lamented, and it is not this maid.

Mark gave a jealous leer. "And she's a great admirer of yours, nephew, it seems. Wanted you to joust for her alone. But we don't need the French to show us what to do. We've had heralds proclaiming our tournament far and wide. Now don't pretend you didn't know." He winked at Tristan then gave a broader wink to Andred. "We knew you'd return as soon as you heard the call."

Tristan paled. "Sire, I may not compete. I have lain in a dungeon now for many weeks. And more than that, I must go to Ireland at once to be with the Queen. She's new to her throne and she'll have need of me—"

"Nonsense, nephew!" cried Mark balefully. "Isolde will do very well without your help. And every knight is out of condition in the spring. What makes you think you're any different from the rest?"

"Sire, I haven't ridden in weeks, I haven't handled a lance—"

Mark waved an uncaring hand. "You're still the champion here and the best knight we have. You'll beat them all with one hand tied behind your back."

Tristan gathered the last of his strength. "Alas, sire, no," he said forcefully. "I'm unfit to compete. And what strength I have, I owe to the Queen . . ."

Mark's eyes bulged. "To Isolde? I forbid you to mention her name! You were my knight first. Your allegiance is to me!"

"And I have honored it!" Tristan cried in desperation. "I obeyed your command and came as soon as I could."

"Oh yes, the lady who held you against your will?" Mark sneered. "I'm sure you came as soon as you could get out of her bed." He gave an unconvincing imitation of a doggish leer. "Ugly, was she, and old? Covered in warts, with hairs sprouting from her chin? Fat and greasy-haired? Boss-eyed, one-eared, and lame?"

"My lord . . ." It was Andred, smiling unctuously at Mark. "Sire, in all honor, Sir Tristan may not speak of his paramour to us."

Tristan wanted to kill him. "She was not my paramour!" he burst out. "I never came into the lady's bed."

Andred's knowing smile grew broader. "Of course you have to defend a lady's good name—"

"Tell the truth, nephew," Mark sniggered. "She was a beauty, wasn't she, and a witch between the sheets? Well worth risking my displeasure to dally with and delay?"

Tristan grasped at his horse's pommel for support. "Forgive me, sire. I have to go to the Queen."

Mark's good humor vanished. "Go to Ireland?" he snarled. "Not if you value your life! I've trumpeted this tournament far and wide, and all the world knows you're Cornwall's champion. The heralds have returned, the contestants are on their way, and you think you can ride off to Ireland and shame us all?"

"Cousin, take this chance to redeem yourself," urged Andred soulfully. "You can prove your loyalty to the King and show your worth."

"Hear me—" Tristan gasped in despair.

But Mark was already turning away. "Be ready, nephew, for tomorrow week," he caroled. "I'm counting on you. Beware you don't let me down!"

chapter 31

never had a week passed so slowly yet vanished so fast. Day by day in the tiltyard Tristan struggled, sweated, and swore as his arms failed him and his legs fluttered like a girl's. Even the sweet, sharp smell of the newly mown turf in the tiltyard failed to raise his spirits as it always had. Mastering his sword and shield seemed impossible, and his lance felt like a tree trunk in his weakened grip. Yet still the days slipped through his fingers like sand, and he counted them off every night, alarmed at how swiftly they went.

When the day of the tournament dawned, he could sit a horse with assurance once again, and his ravaged frame had thrown off much of the lassitude of the prison cell. But as he armed himself to face the day's affray, the sickness gripping his stomach told him the truth. If your Gods are with you, you'll survive this joust. If not, get ready for broken limbs, or worse.

"Sir Tristan! Tristan of Lyonesse!"

The cheers hit him like brickbats as he rode out of the castle gate.

"It's the champion. He'll slaughter them all, you'll see!"

"Tristan! Tristan! *Tristan!*"

"Sir Tristan!"

Dimly, he heard the chamberlain's cheerful call. Staff in hand and robed in his finest furs, the head of the King's household was waiting to greet the contestants as they entered the field. "Welcome to the joust, Sir Tristan. It looks as if we're assured of a fine feast of arms," the old courtier chirped.

Running down from the castle mount, the fields were as bright as water meadows in May. Dotted over the grass, the knight's pavilions flourished in yellow and white, silver-red and speedwell-blue. The same shades of spring appeared in the combatants' flags and shields as they rode up and down, each fighting to hold down his snorting steed. Others had turned out in the colors of blood and death, with armor and banners in mulberry, charcoal, and jet. Looking on, Tristan felt the ghost of a smile. He knew them all. They held no fears for him.

He drew a breath. As long as his strength held out. Still, none of them knew that. They had only heard Mark boasting of Tristan's strength, that his lusty nephew had neglected the King's command to sport in bed for weeks in a lady's arms. Pray the Gods Isolde never got to hear of it!

But he had never lied or deceived her, she knew him too well. Sooner or later she had to know that he had betrayed her with a kiss. Without warning, Falsamilla rose like a torture from the well of memory, and there she was, chestnut hair, red lips, and black eyes. Red lips? Tristan's head reeled. Gods above, that sucking mouth—would that one wanton kiss ruin his whole life . . . ?

The call of the trumpets split his reverie.

"Sir Tristan to the field!" howled the Lord Marshal as the heralds let fly. "All take the field after the King's champion, Sir Tristan of Lyonesse . . ."

The King's champion, the champion, the champion, rang in a desolate chime through Tristan's heart as he led the procession of kings and knights around the field. You have failed and failed again in recent days, he berated himself. Now is your chance to redeem your misdemeanors with an open heart.

The greensward lay before him like a dream. No fence divided the jousters, Tristan noted with foreboding: Mark wanted the combat to be close and bloody today. As he slammed down his visor, he heard the harsh clatter of rooks rising from the trees: beware, Tristan, beware!

Seated in the viewing gallery high above the fray with Sir Andred and the Lady Elva, Mark smirked with delight upon the crowd below.

"On, nephew, get on," he shrilled, lolling on a massive throne-like chair as his hand nursed a goblet in his lap. "Remember you fight for your King and Cornwall today, and don't let me down!"

"He won't, my lord," Andred put in jovially. "Sir Tristan will go for you to the last drop of blood."

Oh, he will, will he? Tristan gritted his teeth. What was Andred's game? He bowed and flourished his lance. Whatever his dark-faced cousin was brewing up as he stood sleekly smiling and stroking his mustache, there was no time to worry about it now. In the distance a horseman curvetted to and fro, fighting to hold back a frothing roan. Who was the knight he'd be fighting very soon?

He narrowed his eyes. Silver banner flying from a golden stave, and the sign of a lion rampant engraved on his shield.

"Sir Gervase of Saint Katz," shrilled the heralds, "to the fray!"

Leaning forward, Tristan lightly touched the powerful neck of the gray and the great beast leapt snorting into the lists. Three passes later, winded in every one, Gervase threw up his visor and tossed his lance to his squire, humorously signaling his retirement from the fray.

"On then! Get on!" Mark shouted from the viewing gallery, draining down more wine. Poised and attentive behind the King's chair, Lady Elva silently directed a servant to replenish the King's glass. Andred covered a smile with his hand. What a woman she was! Half of his own soul.

"Next man in!" intoned the marshal.

The heralds swarmed back into action. "Sir Losiwith!" they cried.

And "Sir Kennot!" and "Sir Chandler" and "Sir Eamonn of the Ridge!" And "Next man in!" and "Next!" and "Next!"

"Next!" . . .

One by one they came at him, and one by one Tristan lightly put them down. In sparing them, he knew he was sparing himself, and his conscience pricked him for fighting like an old man, dealing out nicks and taps rather than the full-blooded combat the knights had come here to enjoy. Yet he knew he could not risk a full-scale onslaught and survive.

Next man down . . .

And another . . .

Down and down . . .

How many more?

The heralds paced forward and the trumpets brayed. "King Systin of the Chapel!"

Last man in . . .

A dark figure took shape before Tristan's flickering eyes. Clad in coal-colored armor and riding a blood-red roan, the knight came hurtling toward him in a blur of black and red.

"Have at you!" Tristan cried, spurring on. With a grunt he took the satisfying impact as his lance caught his opponent on the breast and tossed him out of his saddle like a rag doll. Cantering on, he turned at the head of the lists. The last challenger lay supine on the ground.

The crowd erupted in one continuous roar. "Sir Tristan for champion! Sir Tristan wins the day!"

Staring, Tristan could hardly believe that his ordeal was at an end. Every muscle he had was twitching with pain and fatigue. Goddess, Mother, is it over? For the love of the Gods, can I lie down and sleep?

"Sir Tristan! Sir Tristan the champion!" caroled the ecstatic crowd.

But others were booing and hissing the fallen knight. "Ride him down!" bellowed darker voices in the throng.

Tristan's heart clenched like a fist. The figure on the ground was stumbling to his feet, and raising his gauntlet in the air to carry on. No other knight had challenged him to fight on foot. This was the trial of strength he had feared to endure.

Ride him down...

Now, do it now, his inner demons urged. Unhorsed and staggering, his enemy was fair game, and one blow would send him reeling to the ground. Then the contest would be over and he would have victory.

Tristan, Tristan, his soul groaned. You never took advantage of an opponent in your life. Will you start now?

"What's the matter, man? Ride him down!" Mark's petulant cry reached him from far away.

Never.

With a show of careless valor, Tristan vaulted from his horse, drew his sword, and moved forward onto the field. But King Systin had taken full advantage of Tristan's delay and was already on the attack as Tristan drew near.

"To the death," Systin shouted, the hoarse bravado rattling in his throat as he raised his sword and swung it around his head.

Come, friend, Tristan called on Glaeve from his soul.

Here, master, Glaeve replied with a soundless hiss.

Beyond thought, beyond pain, Tristan swung and slashed, cutting and thrusting to wear his enemy down. You are mine, sir, he chanted to keep his spirits up, I shall overcome. But another voice whispered, Beware, Tristan, you are losing too. His overstrained muscles were twitching with his fading strength, and his will to win burned lower with every stroke.

Just as he thought that he could go no more, he saw his enemy drop to one knee and offer up his sword.

"I yield, Sir Tristan," Systin cried out so that all the crowd could hear, "but I beg you, grant me my life! I challenged you to the death—have mercy on me now!"

He's yielding? Tristan fought down a hysterical laugh. If only you knew, Systin, how near you were to defeating me!

"Rise, sir, take your life," he said huskily. "And you fought honorably. You may keep your sword."

Once more the crowd renewed its ecstatic cheers. "Sir Tristan for champion! Sir Tristan beats them all!"

Mark leaned down from the viewing gallery with a dangerous smile, a goblet swinging from his hand. "Well, Tristan, you proved that you're the finest knight we have."

He raised his hand to the heralds and gave a drunken wave. "Proclaim Sir Tristan the champion!"

"Sir Tristan! Sir Tristan is champion!" The Lord Marshal strained his lungs like bellows as the heralds spat into their trumpets and flourished the end of the day.

Ye Gods, is it over? Can it be?

Trembling with relief, Tristan turned his horse's head toward Castle Dore. The contest was finished and nothing could keep him here now. Sleep first—Gods, let me sleep!—then away to Ireland, to Isolde, on the first tide . . .

Isolde, my lady . . .

My lady and my love.

Thoughts soft as thistledown wrapped him in their embrace. Closing his eyes, he saw a cloud of red-gold hair glowing like the dawn and the light of a smile that could live among the stars. His sight faded and his spirit slipped away, roaming the vastness of the astral plane. Isolde came to him through space, through time, her loveliness warming the cold glittering void. She was robed in the beauty of a cloudy night, and a crown of stars formed a circle around her head. He reached out to take her in his arms. Then, without warning, a cry arrested his ears.

"Stand, Sir Tristan. I challenge you to the lists."

Stand?

Challenge?

He could not take it in. Slowly, he swung around and struggled to believe what he saw. The newcomer was armored in burnished bronze from head to foot, and equipped with the finest horse and weapons a knight could desire. A silver-gilt banner fluttered over his head, and his horse's trappings were heavy with gold and silver plate. But perched on the lordly stallion was a slight and misshapen figure, grinning with a strange light in his eye. His short body and dwarfish limbs seemed to rule him out for combat, yet he rode into the ring like a champion and displayed an air of savage self-satisfaction as he surveyed the field.

"Announce me!" he called out to the heralds in a high, arrogant tone. "Sir Plethyn of the Pike."

Plethyn of the Pike? Tristan paused. The mists of memory parted and brought back fragments of gossip from years ago. The old Earl Plethyn was too proud to mix his seed with common clay, so he had sent for a Princess of Iceland to bear his sons. But the thin, chilly maiden who arrived could bring forth nothing from her icicle thighs. Enraged, the old earl gave her to a wise woman famed for her power with herbs. Dosed and drugged by day and plowed and furrowed every night, the pale creature at last delivered the longed-for son and gave up the ghost.

But the earl shed no tears, for a son was worth a wife. His delight lasted till the child could walk and talk. Then those around him began to mutter and would not meet the earl's eyes. Many nurses, tutors, and doctors later, the earl was forced to accept that the old witch's potions or the anger of the Gods had brought forth a changeling, both in body and mind. The child's stunted frame would never grow to a man's height, and his mind would be an unknown country forevermore. Yet he could not escape the fate to which he was born. He was sole heir to an earldom and had to be brought up as such, trained for the knighthood he could never adorn.

Alas, poor soul. Well, he would receive nothing but chivalry here. Tristan bowed courteously. "Forgive me, sir, but the heralds have blown the last fanfare of the day. The lists are closed."

"Closed?" A familiar drunken braying filled the air. "Not if I order the heralds to blow up again."

Goddess, Mother, no!

Tristan rode up to the viewing gallery and came to a halt. "I am over-battled, sire. I can go no more."

Mark leaned down with a disbelieving glare. "You're the King's champion. You go at my command."

"Sire, I must decline this battle. I shall only give a poor account of myself."

"Decline?" Mark's eyes narrowed to red and angry slits. "Do you want to shame me in front of all the world?"

"No, sire, I—"

"Then get on!" An impulse of open cruelty twisted Mark's face. "He's a tadpole, less than half your size. I want to see you hang him out to dry. Now hold your tongue and get on!"

Tristan's head reeled. Sickness gripped his throat. How could he honor Mark and keep his own honor intact at the same time? Glaeve shivered in his grasp. *Only one more* came the high, silent call. *Then you and I can rest for today.*

So be it, friend. Tristan bowed his head. He would make one ceremonial pass for courtesy's sake, saving both Plethyn and himself from a full assault. That would obey the King's order and still cheat Mark out of his desire to enjoy Sir Plethyn's pain. Circling his horse, he rode back to the head of the lists.

"Come on," Sir Plethyn flashed out in his odd, inhuman voice. "I'm ready for you, sir!"

"One pass," Tristan cried to the heralds, "for honor's sake."

Sir Plethyn's strange eyes bulged. "Three, three, I demand it!" he shouted furiously.

The Lord Marshal stepped forward. "The champion has the call. One pass it is."

The peal of the trumpets silenced Plethyn's angry cries.

Tristan leaned forward and stroked the neck of his horse, stark and stiff now with sweat. *Another run, old friend? Will you go for me one last time?*

Go again? Fondly, the gray nodded his ponderous head and broke into a steady, loping stride. Moving down the field, Tristan saw Plethyn hurtling toward him with the reckless fury of the damned and evaded the wavering lance with consummate ease. Drawing level with the odd little knight, Tristan raised his lance in salute and cantered on. *Merciful Gods,* he sighed from the depths of his soul, *duty done, honor paid to* knight and King alike, now for Ireland and Isolde, my lady and my love . . .

He did not see the madness striking his opponent's face like a thunderbolt. He did not hear Plethyn's uncontrolled protests and the venom welling from his malformed soul. The distant threats seemed no more than the cries of homecoming birds drifting away on the evening breeze.

The first he knew was the volley of warning shouts from the horrified crowd.

"Behind you!"

"Sir Tristan, beware!"

Dazed by the sudden uproar, Tristan turned too late to avoid Plethyn's attack. The vengeful knight's lance struck the back of his head and pierced his skull. A starburst of light exploded inside his brain, and he toppled to the ground. With the screams of the crowd still ringing in his ears, he lay and watched the lights in his head fading away to blood, then gave one last shuddering groan and was gone.

chapter 32

"Captain, what news?"

"No news, Majesty—and I beg you, get below!" Dashing the spray from his face with one red, raw hand, the harassed seaman pointed to the cabin door. "Down below—that's the safest place for you and your maid. When the wind changes, you'll be the first to know."

Isolde shivered, straining to hear his voice over the thunderous roar and clash of the breaking waves. "Till then we ride it out?"

"Unless you can rule the sea as well as the land!" The captain turned away with a sardonic laugh. The rising wind whipped the words from his throat. "Bosun!"

"Sir?" came a distant call from above.

"Take in the topsail. Lower, man, have a care!" He swung back to Isolde, his face knotted with concern. "Madam, forgive me, I have to—"

"Of course." Isolde bowed her head and let him go.

She stared out over the sea, its wild gray waves a perfect mirror for her heaving soul. *Where are you, Tristan? Have you left me, my love?* More and more these days she thought he must be dead or dying, for nothing else would have kept him from her side. Yet if his dear spirit had slipped that rare body of his, the body she had worshipped for so long, surely she'd have known?

And if he'd died, that would be only what Druids called "the little death." The great death was betrayal, when the beloved gave himself to another love. That brought madness and loss and the death of the heart. Had Tristan done that? *Goddess, Mother, spare me . . .* She gasped for breath. *Have you left me, Tristan? Is there another woman in your heart where I used to be?*

Her last sight of him came back to her in a bright flash of pain, and the howling gale cried out like a dying man. Huddling herself into her soaked and salt-stained wrap, she paced angrily to and fro. Gods above, why were they still at sea? She should have been in Cornwall long ago!

Had the Goddess turned against her, to keep them apart like this? Three times they had sailed out bravely from Dubh Lein, only to be driven back.

"But I thought we'd escaped all the winter storms" she complained to the captain on the third attempt. She gestured to Dubh Lein's green hills. "See, spring has come to every bud and bower." *And I need a calm sea to bring me to my love.*

The captain threw a sour glance at the sky, where a skein of black swans flew into the setting sun. "Winter's not gone yet, lady, if the wild birds fly that way."

She could have struck him. "When shall we reach Cornwall, sir?" she demanded. "Tell me when."

He scanned the tormented ocean for signs of peace, then raised his eyes to the moon sailing high above. "When it pleases the Lady," he growled. "The Lady of the Sea."

PLETHYN'S ATTACKED HIM, and he's down . . . Now Gods, if you love me, may he never rise again.

Andred crossed the courtyard of Castle Dore, reliving the joy of the moment when Tristan fell! Even now, a week later, the passage of time had not taken the edge off Andred's delight. To see Tristan down, blood pouring from his mouth and nose—oh, it was good, so good . . .

And as the days passed, it got better still. Soon they learned that Plethyn's lance had pierced Tristan's skull. Would he live? The grave-faced doctors would not say. But doctors and laymen alike knew what happened to knights who took such wounds to the head. And the news from the sickroom today was every bit as bad as Andred could desire. The wound in Tristan's skull had festered, oozing out a stream of pus and gore. His body was burning with fever and every day brought more damage to his injured brain. Now he hovered in the vale of the undead, and the slender thread of his life must soon give way.

"May God forgive me!" Mark threw himself down on a sofa and struck his head. "I should never have ordered him back into the ring."

"Oh, sire . . ." Elva hastened forward and knelt at Mark's side. "How could you have known things would turn out like this?"

Mark scowled at Andred. "That wretch has been dealt with, you say?"

"As you ordered, sire," Andred went on smoothly. "Stripped of his knighthood and banished to his lands, banned from all tournaments and jousts from this day on."

"He dishonored me." Mark's voice quivered with uncontrolled venom. "God blast his eyes, and rot his dwarfish bones. I thought we'd show the French, and he's made us a laughingstock to all the world. And their princess, what's her name?"

"Blanche, sir," replied Andred. "In fact, Isolde—"

But Mark had lost interest. "Whatever she's called, God knows what she'll make of this. Plethyn has ruined our reputation with this disgrace."

"He'll pay for it, sire, never fear," Elva cried. "And his father the earl has offered blood gelt to you—"

"But all the earl's gold won't help Tristan now." Mark surged furiously to his feet, and the ready tears started again in his eyes. "And if I lose him . . . Gods above, Andred, what a blessing you were here!"

Andred composed his face in a devoted smile. "Why, Uncle—you know my only desire is to be useful to you."

"Take me to him," Mark wept.

Before he dies hung unspoken in the air.

Outside, the noonday sun was turning the world to gold and filling the courtyard with the soft fragrance of spring. But inside the infirmary the air was cold and sour. As they came in, stricken faces greeted them, and the echoing space was heavy with the presence of death. Tristan lay alone in a low, arched cell, with a bevy of white-clad attendants clustered around his bed. Next to him was a squat, dark figure with a black-lettered book. The sonorous music of Latin hung in the air, and the heavy odor of incense crept out to the walls.

"*Salve, Domine*—save this soul, O Lord . . ."

Savoring every word like finest meat, Dominian gave Tristan the last rites of the Church. Take his life, Lord, he prayed fervently, speed this pagan on his way. Hearing the last rites, men often died from terror and despair. Until then, they had not known how ill they were.

"Oh, Tristan!"

Mark surged noisily toward the sick man's bed. Following him,

Andred saw that Tristan's eyes were on fire, and the skin of his face burned with a hectic sheen. When he spoke, his voice was a dry husk. "Send me to Isolde . . ." they heard, "before I die."

To Isolde . . . ?

A dark vision bloomed inside Andred's head. Send him to Isolde, yes, of course. It was perfect, it was flawless, it could not fail . . .

". . . before I die," Tristan gasped with the last of his breath.

"Die?" yelped Mark, throwing up his arms. "You're not going to die. Talk to him, Andred. Tell him he'll pull through."

"Ah, but will he, sire?" Andred said mournfully. "The doctors admit they're defeated. It may be time for a fresh look at the case."

"What?" Mark mumbled.

"At least we should honor a dying man's last wish."

Mark tugged unhappily at his beard. "Send him to Isolde, you mean?"

Andred nodded. "He says it's what he wants."

"Well, she's a great healer," Mark muttered, his eyes red with tears.

"And as you said, sire, we need a fresh pair of hands on the case."

"Did I say that?" Mark demanded, surprised at his own wisdom. "Then that's the best thing, of course. If we send him to Isolde, we know he'll be in the right place."

"Oh yes, indeed, sire," Andred said with deep feeling. He hugged himself with glee. Yes, Tristan, the best place on earth for you, my friend.

Mark's dull eye caught fire. "Let's get him to the quay and on board a ship. He could catch the evening tide." He moved back to Tristan, feeling a fresh fit of tears coming on. "We'll get you to Isolde, never fear."

Andred stepped forward. "Sire, leave it to me. You have suffered enough."

Mark looked up hopefully. "I have, haven't I?"

Andred nodded soulfully. "And you have to think of yourself. You should be in the Great Hall, giving comfort to your guests." Liquid comfort, he did not need to say. "The honor of Cornwall requires that you feast them tonight. You may trust me, sire, to see Tristan embarked."

"Yes, yes, of course." Mark was starting to feel better. What a good soul Andred was! He nodded grandly. "See to it, then, Andred. Just let me know when he's safely at sea."

"Oh, I will, sir, I will."

And indeed the word was soon borne back to the King as he sat at the

High Table with the first of many glasses in his hand: "Sir Tristan is afloat and a fair tide is carrying him over the sea." This was the signal for many brimming bumpers of wine, and the health of the King's nephew was toasted to the skies. The day jolted on through feasting and revelry till all decent men had long ago gone to their beds and the stragglers had passed out and vomited where they lay.

But no one, least of all Andred, told the owl-eyed King that Tristan was bound not for Ireland, but for France. In the distress of the moment, it seemed, Andred's orders had been quite misunderstood by the captain of the ship. Honest but confused, the good seaman was sailing not west, but due south, bearing the patient not to La Belle Isolde, but into the arms of Isolde des Blanche Mains.

Only the seagulls haunting the sky overhead saw the ship with the dark sails of Cornwall slipping out to sea. But many eyes on the quay saw Isolde's ship sailing in, passing Tristan's ship unawares in the gathering night. High and low in Castle Dore heard the return of the Queen as the people ran down to the harbor to greet her with rousing cheers. But not even the sailors on the ship sailing for France heard Tristan as he lay alone below, calling Isolde's name to the uncaring air, his glazed and sightless eyes turned upward in his head.

chapter 33

*t*ristan, Tristan, Tristan . . .

Are you here, my love?

Isolde paced the deck in a dream of misery, careless of the blinding, wind-borne spray. The salt spray in her eyes turned the world to tears. Isolde gripped the rail blindly, hearing cries of "Land ahead!" How could they tell the mist-covered mountains from the gray-green, heaving sea? Soaked from head to foot, a lean, weather-beaten figure in the prow wrestled with the wheel. She laid a frozen hand on his arm. "Are we there, sailor?"

The mariner shook the spray from his face with a beaming grin, and nodded into the wind. "There and beyond, my lady—home."

Isolde nodded dully. *There is no home for me if Tristan is away.* "Cornwall, then?"

"Castle Dore."

She turned away. On the edge of her vision another ship was running out of the harbor with the evening tide. Rigged with the dark sails of Cornwall, it was reefed to catch the last of the night wind sighing over the sea.

What is it? Fear clutched at Isolde's heart. Her sight shivered and she saw crows and ravens nestled in the dark ship's shrouds, both carrion birds, both harbingers of death. *Tristan, Tristan* flashed into her mind. Then the ship was gone with the wind, taking its secret with it like an evil dream. Why did it make her think of Tristan with such fear? Soon she would see him and find out what had kept them apart. Soon she would hold him in her arms again, and make up for this long separation, this loneliness and loss.

Gods above, to see his face again . . .

"Hurry, Brangwain!" she called madly, pressing forward to get off the ship. "I must get to the castle, Tristan will be there . . ."

"Madam, have a care," Brangwain cried in alarm as Isolde leapt over the gangplank before it was lashed to the quay.

But Isolde did not hear. *Hurry, hurry—are you there, my love?*

Castle Dore loomed before them in the evening mist, its great bulk dark against the dying light. Scarcely pausing to acknowledge the startled greetings of the guards, she flew through the courtyard and entered the Great Hall.

Ye Gods, the stink! The court was in the throes of a feast such as only Mark could give. Below the fine tables and the food fit for a king, puddles of red wine lay in the hollows of the floor. Scratching between the guests' legs, the court dogs were gorging on splashes of vomit, then crouching with quivering flanks to drop on the rushes below.

At the head of the hall, Mark sat in kingly state with Andred on his right hand and Elva on his left.

And Tristan was not there.

"Isolde!" Mark bellowed down the hall.

"Your Majesty . . ."

It was Elva. What was she doing in the seat of Queens?

Isolde fought for breath. All sly eyes and insolent smile, Elva sat beside Mark, robed in shining green satin with a golden train. Great clusters of jade and jasper gleamed on her head and swung on gold chains from her waist. Her long earrings clattering loudly against her neck as she snaked her eyes over Isolde, then covered her mouth with her hand.

She's laughing at me! She saw herself through Elva's eyes, poorly clad in a thick, sea-stained mantle and bedraggled gown. *I am Queen of this country, and the fishwives of Castle Dore look better than I do.* Why had she rushed in so blindly? *Fool, Isolde, fool!*

And why had she thought she might greet Mark as a friend, share a meal with him, take a glass of wine? Had she forgotten the hours of drunken revelry, the coarse banter, and as the night went on, the foul stupor they all fell into, one by one? *Fool again. Fool!*

"The Queen!" yodeled one high-flown reveler, raising his glass. "A toast to the Queen."

Mark leaned forward. "So, Isolde," he said sarcastically, "we thought you were too full of affairs in Ireland to think of us here. What makes you grace us with your royal presence now?"

Ask him about himself, feed his vanity, she told herself. But she could not do it. Gasping for breath, she took her soul in her hands. *"Where is Tristan?"*

Mark shuffled his feet. "You've missed him, Isolde. He sailed on the evening tide."

The dark ship going out. Yes, I knew it. "He sailed away? Why?"

Mark gave an uneasy glance. "We had a tournament and he took a wound to the head. Oh, don't look like that! It was nothing much, but he wasn't getting better here. Our doctors were not having much success with him."

She forced herself to stay calm. "So you sent him to me in Ireland?" *Never fear, sweetheart, I'll follow you on the first tide.*

"Ireland?" Andred leaned forward with an air of deep concern. "Oh, sire, you ordered he should be sent to France."

Mark started. "I did? Why did I do that?"

Andred furrowed his brow. "Surely you remember, my lord? We were talking about the Princess Isolde of France—the lady they call Blanche Mains—and you said she's the best healer, send him over there."

Isolde's soul seized. She could not speak, her tongue lay dead in her mouth.

Tristan sick and taken away from me.

Sent over the sea to another woman's care.

Is this my rival? The dark witch or the fair, the black swan or the white, or the woman with chestnut hair? Goddess, Mother, give me back my love!

"Yes, that's right," Mark cried, a smirk of reassurance spreading across his face. "He asked to be sent to her, I remember it now. That was where he wanted to go."

Isolde put a hand to her throbbing head. "To the French princess? How did he hear of her?"

Mark laughed. "Oh, he's a dark horse, Tristan. You know he found a lady on the way home? And he stayed with her for weeks, so God only knows what they got up to all that time." He turned his eyes on Elva, who returned his gaze, rippling her bosom at him suggestively. Locked onto each other like snakes, the two of them shared a slow smile.

Isolde watched them and a dull shock ran through her brain. *This woman has taken my place.*

And Tristan not here to defend me in my hour of need.

She felt a howl like a banshee rising in her throat.

He's betrayed me! He's deceived me, he's left me for someone else.

Shaking, she saw again the sight that had haunted her dreams, Tristan caught between two woman till a third came between them, and Tristan kissed her on the mouth.

Gods above . . .

She closed her eyes. *Save him, Lady, save him from all of them. Take my kingdom, if it will keep Tristan safe!*

But the Lady's words rang again and again in her ear. *Every man chooses the path his feet will tread. And even the Mother cannot turn back the wheel.*

chapter 34

Was there any country in the world as fine as France? Or any castle to compare with the court of King Hoel and its honey-colored sprawl of turrets and towers?

Smiling, the Chevalier Saint Roc strolled out of the castle gatehouse and into the warmth of the sun. Before him lay wide, well-tended garden walks, winding their way between neat tangles of knot-grass and flowering shrubs with succulent beds of fragrant herbs beyond. All along the sunlit castle walls, stands of ancient roses were fumbling their way to life. Spring came early to this sweet southwestern kingdom, he noted approvingly, and on every side he saw the tender green shoots lit with shafts of gold. He sighed with contentment. Was not a king's garden a fine place to be on a warm April day, when the sun himself was making love to the blushing earth?

Making love? Saint Roc permitted himself an ironic grin. These tentative overtures and soft sighing winds were not what a Frenchman would call the sport of kings. Let the English have their horses, cats, and dogs. We in France prefer women, and our women want to be loved.

Yet perhaps this shy, sideways approach of spring, so gently warming up to the full-blooded heat of summer, had a message for him on his mission here. That was how a virgin should be approached by a man of the world, a man who loved women, as he had come here to do.

He chuckled softly and fondled the hilt of his sword. Oh, Madame Blanche was a virgin, he had no doubt of that. Of course she had greeted him as a woman well versed in courtship, and he laughed again to recall her disdainful manner and the toss of her small fair head.

"The King of Ouesterland?" she had said as they met, making his kingdom sound like the very end of the world.

"Jacques Saint Rocquefort at your service, madame," he had said, highly amused. "But they call me Saint Roc."

Then he had made a brief bow and walked away, letting the knight behind him take his place. Gods above, it was the oldest trick in the book. When it piqued her interest, as he thought it would, he knew how green she was.

Green, yes, but gamesome too. That night she held the whole court to ransom with dancing and games, involving every soul there in forfeits and fooling and all kinds of fun. And what simple pleasure she had shown and shared, setting aside her royalty like a cloak. Ah, what a woman! His spirit stirred to recall how freely she moved between princess and child.

"Where is the King of Ousterland? Here, sir," she had called imperiously as she took the floor, beckoning him to the place at her side.

"Alas, madame," he had replied, fingering his thigh. "An old war wound troubles me. I cannot dance."

She flushed sharply and turned away. But as she did, he caught the hurt glance of a child. What's the matter, don't you like me? Why won't you play with me?

And it had touched his heart.

Your heart, Saint Roc? came a sardonic inner voice as he reached for a rose on the wall and picked the first bud. Could that gnarled, half-forgotten organ he once called his heart, battered and misshapen by too many women and wars, be brought back to life by the look in the eyes of this child?

Child? scoffed his inner voice with growing delight. Look again, Saint Roc. Tripping out of the gatehouse with a girlish air was a tall womanly figure, her straight back and the purposeful set of her head betraying her determination in every step. From her baby-blue gown and lace headdress to the tips of her dainty kid shoes, Blanche was a portrait of sweet simplicity. But Saint Roc had known whores like this, pure-faced girls who would take a man in their arms, only to stab him all the better in the back. On guard then, Saint Roc, he grinned, feeling his blood rise.

Blanche came straight toward him like a bee to a flower. "Greetings, sir," she caroled sweetly. "What a pleasant surprise to meet you in the garden today."

Surprise? He had no doubt that she was looking for him. He played idly with the rose he held in his hand. "As well as can be expected, Princess," he sighed.

Blanche swept him from head to foot, noting with growing approval the lambskin tunic slashed with ochre and black, the well-fitting breeches and hand-worked cambric shirt, and knew that all this was for her, and her alone. Yes, he would have been finer without the scars on his sword hand and that questioning, ironic glint in his eye. And when Tristan came, he would be bigger too, as a hero should be, not like Saint Roc, of average height and build.

But the body before her was hard and well-honed and trim, and one that many women would welcome in their bed. Only fair men could be truly handsome, as Tristan was. But still there was something about a thick head of glossy dark hair, cropped like a soldier's and neat as a tutor's black cap. Yet what could it be, if she only liked fair men?

Unsettled, she went on the offensive again. "You sound like an old man. How old are you?"

"Old enough," he said grimly, thinking of his checkered past.

"But young enough to dance," she returned, staring at him hard. "When your leg gets better, I mean."

She dropped her eyes demurely, and he had to laugh. What a girl, what a woman she was!

She returned to the attack. "So you're king of a great kingdom?"

"Whoever told you that?" He laughed quietly to himself, enjoying the joke. "My kingdom is one of the smallest and meanest in France. One half lies in the shadow of the mountains, while the other lies open to the wind and the sun. Our crops are meager and our cattle half starved. If you're counting my assets, lady, count again. But our people have the stoutest hearts on earth."

He gave a reminiscent grin. "And Gods! How they love to fight. A wilderness like ours produces wild men. I have made it my task to settle their disputes, and stop them killing each other for the sake of a few sheep or goats."

"A fair aim." Blanche looked at Saint Roc's steady gaze and was impressed. "Why have you never married?" she shot back.

His answer surprised both of them, and himself most of all. "I was waiting for you."

In silence he presented her with the rose. Gasping, she took it from his hand. Then her eyes flared in alarm. "Is that true?"

He held up both hands in surrender: lady, don't ask.

There was a lingering silence. Blanche bit her lip. "Then I must tell you to set aside your hopes," she resumed shakily. "You and I will never marry."

He glimmered at her with an air of mystery. "Never is too long a word to say."

She drew back sharply. "Sir, I have given my heart to another man." Slowly, she let the rosebud fall to the ground.

To her fury, she saw signs of amusement crinkling the corners of his bright black eyes. "And has he given you his in fair exchange?"

How dare he? She struggled to find the right words. "All that concerns you, sir, is that your suit is dead."

He was laughing openly now. "Oh, I don't think so."

Why was she bandying words with this arrogant fool? "Then think again!"

Saint Roc fixed his eyes on the rose rambling around the wall. "Your brother tells me that you summoned Sir Tristan here."

Blanche stared at him. "Indeed I did."

"And did he reply?"

"What is that to you?"

Saint Roc saw the ice forming in the pale blue eyes and was undeterred. "You can never enjoy Tristan. You will never have his love. He loves the Queen of Ireland, and her alone."

"Is that all?" Blanche burst into mocking laughter to cover her relief. "Every knight loves his lady. That's part of their courtly oath."

"Not as he does."

Blanche's heart gave a violent leap. "How?"

There was an endless pause. "Forbiddenly."

"Forbiddenly?" She was fighting for breath. "Tell me what you mean!"

Oh, my poor girl. Saint Roc took in the startled eyes and trembling mouth, and felt a spring of pity he did not know he had.

"It is not known for sure," he began carefully, "and Sir Tristan himself would never speak a word. But those who hear the whispers in the night say that he's the Queen's chosen one. Her companion of the couch. Her bed-slave, if you will."

A flash of revulsion distorted the angel face. "I don't believe it!"

"Oh, you will, madame, you will."

Reaching for his dagger, he cut a fresh rose from the wall. For a moment he studied its fragrant, half-open heart, then brought it to his lips.

"You are the rose of France, my Princess," he said, half mockingly, half in a tone that neither of them understood. "And whether you like it or not, I will marry you."

"Pouf!" She blew him away, her long white hands flapping madly, her face dark with distress.

"As you wish, madame."

Still smiling, he pressed the rose into her hand. As he did, they heard a servant calling from the castle gate.

"Lady, they're searching for you all over the castle, you must come at once. There's a ship of Cornwall lying at the dock bearing the King's nephew, Sir Tristan of Lyonesse. He's sore wounded, the sailors say, and he's come here to you for your care."

Goddess, Mother, thanks!

Blanche threw back her head in triumph and turned on Saint Roc. "You'll marry me, you say, when I'm destined for Sir Tristan himself? Who but the Great Ones could have brought him here?"

He bowed his head. "Madame, enough."

But she could not hold back. "Did you think you'd appeal to me by attacking Tristan? And did you think for a minute that I'd believe those lies? You're jealous of him, of course, I understand that. But you're wasting your time, you have no future with me. I wish you good speed on your journey back to your lands. Go with your Gods, sir, farewell."

"Go?" He was laughing, his sallow face alight. "Why should I go?"

To her fury, she saw that his expression was more sardonic than before. "Sir, don't you understand a word I said—?"

He held up a peaceable hand. "Madame, I shall leave you now. But you must allow me to stay here at court to pursue my suit. I can wait on the will and pleasure of a woman like you. And I can't wait to see this wooing between you and your new love."

She was blazing with rage. "We shall see about that!"

His laughter reached her as she strode away. "We shall indeed, madame—oh, we shall."

chapter 35

"Send me to Isolde," he had said. Why then had he awoken in this strange place where they were all speaking in French? And how had he come by this hideous pain in his head, a cluster of lights and sharp stabbings every time he moved?

The last thing he remembered was leaving the field on his horse. After that, only fragments of sensation filled the void. Aching shoulders, yes, and his body worked beyond endurance, the reins lying loose in his hands as he gave his horse its head: he could feel it now. But what reins? What horse? What field? What country even, what joust? At this fearful thought, his riven mind collapsed and slid away into the cold beyond.

And there he met himself, or rather his other self, weeping and holding out her hands, and he took her in his arms and called her by her name.

Isolde.

Yes, that was her name, and without her, he could never be well again.

Because he was sick, he realized that too. He lay in bed like a dead man, unable to move. Only his senses were alive and they told him he was in an herb-scented sickroom, brought here for his wound to be healed. At this, the panic and dread began again. What sickroom? What country? What healer and what wound?

He drifted in terror, not knowing who he was. Yet whatever he was, where was Isolde now? And who was the being who attended him, all in white? The first day he managed to open his seething eyes, he saw her white hands fluttering over him like doves. Lightly they landed on his burning head and cooled the fever that was burning him alive. Then he saw a gown of filmy white and a white face above it, wimpled like a nun. Escaping from the white headdress were wisps of fine hair like the feathers of a swan, and he wondered if this creature was a swan-maiden, still bearing the curse of her enchanted kin.

But nun or nurse, angel or swan, she cooled the flames in his head by day, and chafed the warmth into his feet and hands at night. Her very skin had the sheen of mother-of-pearl, and her young body had the innocence of the unpossessed. It came to him that in the days of his youth, passing from tournament to tournament, he had learned how to tell a virgin from a woman of the camps. Floating now, he giggled to himself. *So you have been a knight errant, then, in your time? You knew the tournaments, you knew the game?*

Then he knew why he was here in this spotless white space smelling of herbs and salves. He had been injured in a fearful joust and brought to the castle's sick bay to be healed. But where? He had to ask. The next time he saw the white creature swanning by, he marshaled the tongue lying dead in his mouth and jumbled out a few misspoken words.

A sweet face was instantly at his side. Startled, he thought he saw lovelight in her eyes, and his mind misgave.

Isolde? he tried to say, but nothing came. His skin crawled. Had Isolde changed her shape into this maid? Why else would she love him and hang over him like this?

"Where are you?" he heard a soft, attentive sigh. "You're in France, sire, at the court of King Hoel."

"Sire?" He started violently. "You may not call me that! I am not a king. My father lives, the King of Lyonesse."

A look of deep pity filled the forget-me-not eyes. "Your father died years ago, my lord. You have long been King of Lyonesse in your own right."

Am I so? wandered through his brain. Well, then, so be it. He drifted away on a fathomless sea as snatches of speech hung about him in the air.

"...quite common, lady, after a blow to the head. Men can forget their names and even who they are."

"Will he get his memory back?"

"Very likely, given time. You must help him to rebuild his shattered mind."

What did it mean? He sank beneath the pain. But when the billows that rocked him brought him again to shore, he tried again, his lazy tongue flubbing every sound. "How did I get here?"

"You asked to be sent here," the white maiden purred. "You asked for me by name."

How could that be, Tristan wondered, since he did not know her name? But this was only one of the mysteries that beset him now.

And this creature in white was his only way out of the mist. She was his lifeline, his all. If he ever hoped to get back to Isolde, it would be through her. She fed him, she talked to him, she had saved his life.

He was not to know that the hands that washed him and fed him and turned him were not hers. He did not see the nurses who labored while he lay unconscious, under strict instructions to call Blanche and disappear the moment he stirred. He did not hear the words of the doctor in the infirmary, battling to protect the sick man from Blanche's consuming love.

"The cordial, Doctor—when shall we try that?"

When we want to kill him, Princess. Remember the old man? the doctor did not say. Sighing inwardly, he forced himself to flatter her, or the knight's life was at stake. "Lucky is the man to have such a gifted nurse. Your royal touch is all that Sir Tristan needs."

"Thank you, sir."

Blanche basked in the doctor's approval, warming to the keen-faced man and his thoughtful air. And he was right, she preened herself, about her healing touch. Day by day the patient grew stronger, till he could work his slow tongue around the next great question, "Lady, who are you?"

Oh, she had waited for this! Blanche's heart bounded, and her vanity raced away.

She held out her hands and waved them before his face. "You may call me Blanche, sir, but that's only my nickname, because of my white hands. My real name is Isolde, Isolde des Blanche Mains..."

The comatose figure in the bed came violently to life. "Isolde?" he cried thickly, lurching up. "Is she here?"

She could not believe it. "Isolde here...?"

"She's not here? Then where is she, do you know?"

She could see the agony of loss on his face and hear the hope catching desperately at his throat. An ugly impulse of vindictiveness invaded her soul. "She's not here," she said trenchantly. "Nowhere near. Queen Isolde is far away in the Western Isle."

He was sweating and trembling like a stallion in a trap. "I must go to her. I must send her word."

Go to her? Blanche felt her jealous soul boil with rage. She set her lovely features in a foxy smile. "All in good time, my lord."

He fixed her with a wandering, feverish glare. "I must write to her."

She gave a brittle laugh. "But you can't write! You can't hold a spoon, let alone a pen."

A vivid flush of shame crept up his neck. "It's true that I cannot do much for myself," he said with difficulty. "But I could write something. And my lady would be glad to have it, I know."

"And so she shall," Blanche said heartily. She could see the beads of sweat standing on his brow. "As soon as you're stronger."

"Tomorrow, then?" he pressed, feeling his strength fading with every word.

"Tomorrow, perhaps," she agreed in warm tones, "if you go on as you are."

But tomorrow came and more tomorrows after that, with no sign of the pen and paper he asked for every day.

"YOUR LETTER TO Queen Isolde, sir? Yes, to be sure. As soon as you're stronger . . . as soon as this is done . . ."

Tristan nodded, trying not to awake the great pain in his head. So many steps toward his recovery, and every one seemed so long—

"You can't remember, sire, why you asked for me?" Blanche would demand, her baby-pale eyes aglow. "Surely you'd heard of me, and my skill with my hands? I've been known for their beauty all my life."

She cocked her head on one side like a hopeful child, and he could not say no. Yet she wasn't a child, she had to be twenty at least, only ten years younger than he was, perhaps even less. Why then did she seem young enough to be his daughter? And why did he care?

"Princess—" he began awkwardly.

But Blanche was blind to his hesitation. "And now you've simply forgotten who I am," she pressed on grandly. "I'm famous as a healer throughout France. You must have known that, or else why are you here?"

He shook his head. He had no idea.

Blanche leaned forward, plaiting her long sinuous fingers into a knot. "You must revisit your past, sir, and tell me all you see."

He had to recover his memory, she told him every day. So all the time he was working to regain his strength, the trickle of subtle probing never stopped. Day after day he would struggle to oblige. I owe her my life, he made a solemn vow. And whatever comes after, I must not forget.

Yet try as she might, hour after torturous hour, she could not get from him more than any knight would say. And his courtly reserve only increased her desire to know more about her rival for his love. Tell me about Isolde! she wanted to scream.

But he would not do it. "War came early that year," he would say, "so I had to leave. Nothing happened after that." Or, "Queen Isolde was with her mother in Ireland, dealing with a threatened invasion from the Picts. There is no more to tell."

And Blanche had to leave it at that.

At times like this it was very hard to bear the knowing smiles of Saint Roc and his laughing eyes. Her sardonic suitor was everywhere, it seemed. When she hurried to the sickroom at the start of the day, she would meet him on his way to the stables for his morning ride. When she left Tristan, there he was again, as if blown into her path by the evening breeze. At night in the Great Hall, he was always the first to raise his glass in a humorous toast to her health. When the minstrels played and the court danced, she could count on his quizzical glance as he stepped forward to offer her his hand: "My old wound sleeps tonight, lady, will you dance?"

Was he mocking her? To her fury, she could never tell. At times she would see an open grin of amusement on his sharp face. Yet there was no sign of malice in the nosegay of white blossoms, the posy of tiny sweetmeats, or other delicate favors he dropped in her way.

Yet still she felt that he scorned her, and smoldered in secret under his supercilious smile and knowing air. Soon she discovered that Tristan felt it too. The first time he left his bed, Saint Roc happened to be strolling airily past. With a tunic of fighting-cock red and a jaunty feathered cap, the knight Roc cut a dashing figure, as he clearly meant to do.

Tristan stiffened. "Who is that?" he demanded with narrowed eyes.

And Blanche's small soul leapt to hear the raw note of male rivalry in Tristan's voice.

Tristan heard it too, and sweated at the sound. Saint Roc's hard-eyed, cynical stare pricked at his soul, and he loathed his own slow, limping progress and gasping breath. Does it please you to see my weakness? he snarled silently. D'you want to taste my strength? Yet he knew that he could not challenge a kitten, he was still so weak.

One night Blanche had him taken down in a carrying chair to feast with her father and brother in the Great Hall.

"My lord!" King Hoel rose to greet him, tears in his eyes. At his side, Prince Kedrin bowed deeply to Tristan, clasping both his hands. "We are honored, sire."

Clumsily, Tristan heaved himself out of the chair. "The honor is mine." Cursing, he felt his foolish legs give way, and surprised himself by sitting down again. But he had found his feet. He would walk again, and even ride and handle a sword in time.

Gods and Great Ones, thanks . . .

And now if it please you, bring me to my love . . .

Farther down the table, a lady in waiting was flirting with Saint Roc. Panting lightly to make her breasts flutter under his gaze, she stared boldly into his eyes and licked her lips.

"Look at her! Look!" Blanche was hissing like an angry swan. "That silly slut will find herself packing before the night is out. Any lady in waiting who flirts with her own lady's suitor is no use to me."

Tristan studied Saint Roc with new interest. "Is he your suitor?"

Blanche dropped her eyes and twisted her hands in her lap. "May I trust you, sir?" she breathed.

Why did she ask? Tristan felt his brain creaking like an overladen boat. "Lady, on my oath as a knight—"

"I hate him." She raised great, sad eyes to his face and shed a tear. "But my father is forcing me to marry him."

Tristan stared at Blanche. What, King Hoel, his gracious host, the kindly faced man across the table, talking easily to one of his lords? But fathers often wanted to dictate to daughters, he knew. And when thrones and dynasties were involved . . .

"That must not be," he said roughly. "Not while any man can raise a sword in your defense."

Blanche smiled then and seemed comforted, and soon after he heard her purring as a swan does when her egg is laid. After that he noticed Saint Roc looking at Blanche, and wondered what had provoked that sarcastic smile.

And if Blanche hated her unwanted suitor so much, his limping mind wandered on, why did she care if her lady in waiting courted him? But his head was throbbing. It was all too much for now. Tomorrow he would try to fathom it out.

And tomorrow, please the Gods, he would write to Isolde.

chapter 36

The next day Blanche came dancing through the door.

"Do the people in your kingdom go Maying at this time of the year?" she demanded, her pale blue eyes alight.

At this time of the year? he pondered. Yes, in truth it was April, going into May. The feast of Beltain, with its fires and flowers, when the doors of the Otherworld stood open for love.

"Indeed they do, lady," he replied, beguiled by her roguish smile and mysterious air. "Our maidens go to the woods and bring back armfuls of May blossom to deck their houses and hearths. It gives them the blessing of the Goddess for the year ahead, and Her help in knowing which of their young men to choose."

She held his eyes in a glimmering, secretive gaze. "Then tomorrow we'll go too."

The next day at dawn they set out for the wood. At Blanche's orders, two men at arms were standing by, but he walked by himself to the litter at the door. The great carrying bed in the courtyard was covered with a tasseled canopy and curtained with hangings in rich, creamy brocade. Four soft-eyed, heavy horses bore its weight, and its huge pillows were sweetened with lavender and rose. Trembling and sweating at the effort he had made, Tristan sank gratefully into their downy embrace.

Early as it was, the castle was alive with pink-faced maidens, stout matrons, and the village menfolk too. The motley procession moved off with the children larking in the front, followed by the maidens, everyone dressed in green. Behind them came the minstrels playing ancient woodland airs, then the people of the castle, young and old. Blanche rode beside Tristan's litter on a milk-white mare, and an army of servants and laden mules marched in the rear.

The woodland lay before them, clothed in white. At its heart were mighty stands of rugged oak, hornbeam, and ash. But its verges were garlanded with hawthorn in full flower, and the raw tangy scent reached out to welcome them.

"Here, sir!"

A small grubby face appeared at the side of the litter, and a grinning urchin tossed a spray of hawthorn into his lap. Yelping with glee, others followed. Tristan picked up the thorny blossom and the years dissolved. Without warning he was a child again like these, running in unselfconscious rapture to the woods. He smiled across the years at his younger self. My first Maying, yes, when I was no older than this.

And oh, the joy of being in the woodland again! In wonderment he felt the sun on his skin and drew the warm scent of the loam into his lungs, feeling at one with the creatures of the earth. Silently, he communed with the wayside hare and the hawk on the wing: greetings, little mother, and you, brother, the blessings of the Great One on you all.

Above the trees a herd of woolly clouds gamboled like sheep across a field of blue. A golden midsummer sun sang in the sky, and the birds caroled too, till the arch of the heaven resounded with their song. Farther in, the woodland ways narrowed and the air became warm and still. Shafts of sunlight poured through the forest roof like burning gold, and every mote in the air sparkled with fire.

They came to a clearing at the forest's heart, a green circle where sunlight puddled like honey on the green grass. There, the revelers dispersed to gather blossom, and Tristan's litter was set down while the servants laid out a feast as grand as any in the Great Hall.

Blanche came to his side and pressed a goblet into his hand. "Red wine," she commanded. "It will renew your blood." Somewhere out of sight, skillful fingers plucked at a harp and the sound of a love song trembled through the air.

Without warning, he felt Isolde at his side, galloping through the woods as they always did, her hair flying and her strong face flushed with joy. The only wine they needed then ran in every stream, and the thunder of horses' hooves was the music they craved. They had no care for food when they had each other, and the days were never too long.

Trembling, he brought the goblet to his lips and took a deep draught. Oh, Isolde, Isolde, my lady and my love.

As the warmth of the blood-red wine spread to his heart, he drank again and did not notice when the servants filled his glass. Blanche helped him from the litter and made him comfortable on sheepskin cushions in the shade of a tree. All around lay heaped platters of cheese, meat, and fruit, and the ever-attentive servants hovered with more wine.

More wine, yes. Tristan nodded, holding up his glass. "Good for the blood."

"Yes indeed ..." Blanche's voice trailed sadly away.

Tristan squinted at her. "Lady ... ?" he began.

"Oh, sir ..."

A flood of words cascaded round his ears. He struggled to make sense of what she said. "You're being forced to marry against your will?"

There was a heartrending sob. "Very soon."

The wine sang in his veins. "I shall defend you, lady!"

There was a sudden quickening in her eye. "What will you do?"

What would he do? He had no idea. "I shall be your knight," he said thickly. "My lady will understand."

"Your lady Isolde?"

"There is no other." As he spoke, a dark cloud of failure enveloped him. "I should be with her," he said lamely. "I should write to her."

"If she is your lady," Blanche said with a quiet venom, "why doesn't she write to you?"

He stared at her in distress. "I don't know."

"Perhaps she has another knight, now that you're not there," said Blanche, her head cocked unpleasantly to one side. "Or else her husband King Mark is claiming her time and attention these days."

Tristan felt a chasm open before his feet. Another knight? Her husband? Either or both of them taking his place?

His head was splitting. "Pen and ink and paper, by your leave, Princess," he said harshly, "in my chamber—tonight."

She could not refuse. Putting a good face on it, she got through the rest of the day, and the Maying procession wound slowly back to town. But the paper she sent him to write to Isolde that night was back in her own hands again within the hour.

"Leave this with me," she ordered the servant. "You may go."

Before the door closed, she was tearing open the parchment and breaking the seal. The wandering script danced before her eyes. Tristan must have struggled over every stroke, and she could only guess at what the effort had cost. Then she fell on the contents and devoured them like a banquet of spiders when there was no other food.

With a sharper pain than she had ever known, she read:

> *To La Belle Isolde, Queen of the Western Isle,*
> *Forgive me, lady, that I have not returned to your side. I took a hurt in Cornwall, and heal myself now in France. I shall leave as soon as may be. Look for me then.*
> *You are still my lady.*
> *I am still your knight.*
>
> *Tristan of Lyonesse*

They were lovers, then.

Blanche stared at the letter, the misshapen characters burning her eyes. Sparse though his words were, and written for any eyes, Tristan's heart spoke through his ill-written hand and betrayed his love.

And where was she herself, Blanche, in all this?

Nowhere to be seen. He did not even mention her name. Like a deer hurt in a forest, Blanche held herself tight, afraid to breathe or move.

And leave, he said?

No, he must not leave. Panting, she felt her heart shrivel in her breast and tighten into a hard, pitiless knot.

You won't leave me, Tristan.

I am your lady now.

You are my knight.

chapter 37

Yes, God was good. There was an inescapable purpose in all His works. For there she was again, haunting the headland above Castle Dore.

Stepping out through the monastery gates in a rain-washed dawn, Dominian looked out across the hillside toward the quay. For weeks he had seen Isolde waiting there, watching the ships as they came sailing in. Hopeful at first, the white-clad figure now drifted like a wraith from the Otherworld, showing a heartsick sadness in every move. Good, good! The little monk rubbed his hands and allowed himself a smile. God in His wisdom had parted Isolde from her knight, and who cared if the Queen suffered? It was His will.

And who cared why Isolde missed her knight so much? Dominian sniffed. It was nothing to him that the Queen's pale face and troubled air had given rise to rumors that Sir Tristan meant more to her than he should. Let the gossips and idlers whisper what they liked, he had no intention of demeaning himself with such stuff. The King, he reminded himself, is where the power lies. His black eyes took fire. Get command of the King, and the rest will follow as night follows day.

Smoldering, Dominian looked into the future and renewed his vows. Lord our God, Maker of Heaven and Earth, I swear to You that in times to come You shall see a Christian priest in every parish and a Christian church in every town. He snorted. Yes, of course, the blindworms who favored the Old Faith would cling to the Mother-right and insist that King Mark must be subject to Queen Igraine. But the old Queen in Tintagel might as well be dead for all they saw of her. Mark was King here, Mark commanded the army and controlled a powerful band of knights.

What if he had lost his champion, Tristan, to France? Others were already jostling to take his place.

And here they were, all the fine fighting boys, the priest observed with sour disdain. At the entrance to the lower courtyard, a group of younger knights were lounging against the wall, swapping low banter and idle talk in the morning sun. Behind them a troop of scurrying stable boys labored to make their horses ready for the hunt. Both knights and horses could be in for a long wait, Dominian reflected with disgust, if the King was slow to rise from his mistress's bed. But rain or shine, Mark would be riding out, and one of these young men would be at his side.

Now, which one? Dominian appraised the group coldly as he hurried along. Sir Fer de Gambon came of a good line, but his bowlegs and receding chin showed that the heroic strain had run its course. His cruel mouth, slippery glance, and sneering grin suggested, too, that the knight was no stranger to dishonor when it served his turn. The young giant beside him, Sir Taboral, was impressive enough in body, but his dull eyes and slack, foolish face said little for the brains within. Dominian scanned the rest of them and shook his head. They were all much the same. Well, what did he expect? Who but a weakling, a coward, or a poltroon would serve a king who was all those things himself?

Still, Mark was king of Cornwall and ruler of the land. Dominian entered the King's House and pressed on to the Privy Chamber with a resolute tread. If the work of God was to advance in this land, Mark had to be brought to his duties as husband and king. And with Tristan away and Isolde left alone, there could hardly be a better time to strike.

"Step aside, fellow! Out of my way."

Brushing aside royal guards and servants, Dominian found Mark in his inner chamber, pulling on his breeches and tucking in his shirt. To judge by the unmade bed, the half-sheepish, half-angry look on Mark's long face, and the unmistakable smell of sex lingering in the air, it seemed that the lady Elva had not long left.

"Sire?" Dominian began ominously, looking around.

Mark turned to greet him, his nondescript chin thrust out. "Yes, Father? What brings you here?"

"Concern for your kingdom, your kinfolk, and your good name," Dominian returned trenchantly. "What news of Sir Tristan?"

"Not a word." Guiltily Mark remembered that all the time Elva had been working her wondrous way with him, Tristan had been nowhere in his mind. Tears rose to his eyes. "I don't know if he's alive or dead."

Dominian saw his moment and moved onto the attack. "Whether Sir Tristan lives or dies, the kingdom needs an heir."

"What?" Braced for a sermon on his unseemly lust, Mark had not expected this. He gaped at Dominian. "But you know that Isolde and I— I mean, the Queen—"

"Yes indeed, sire, you will need to call upon your wife," the priest proclaimed with an intimidating frown. "Queen Isolde has a duty in this too. Marriage is ordained for the procreation of children and the relief of sin. Concupiscence is abhorrent to the Lord."

"Concupiscence?" Mark struggled to take it in. Was this a lecture about Elva after all? He cleared his throat. "Father, I—"

"This is your duty, sire. Think of the needs of your kingdom and the state of your soul. Isolde is your Queen. Only the creation of children can make this marriage good in the eyes of the Lord."

Children? Mark's eyes bulged. God Almighty, what was the matter with these priests? Did Dominian think Isolde would lie down for him and bear children on command? "And if the woman is not willing, Father, what then?"

"Willing or not, it's of no account. In Christian wedlock, women are not granted free will. They give their bodies to their husbands in the marriage act. They are bound ever after to obey their husband's will."

"What?" Mark could not believe it. "You mean that once they are married, they can never refuse a husband his natural rights?"

"Never," said Dominian firmly. "Queen Isolde must honor your command in this regard."

"Well..."

There was a hushed silence while Mark worked his mind around the idea and wondered how the Christians had ever persuaded free women to agree.

Dominian drew a breath. "If the Queen cannot furnish you with an heir, the laws of God permit you to put her away. Then God will send you a good Christian virgin to bear Christian offspring pleasing unto Him."

Mark scratched himself hopelessly. God in Heaven, the morning was wasting and he'd never get out to the hunt. He reached for a confident smile. "Hear me, Father. I don't care about heirs of my body. God has given me two fine nephews to deal with the kingdom after I am gone."

Dominian nodded heavily. And the kingdom would choose Tristan, the shameless pagan who never darkened a church. Under him, the True Faith would be dead. Tristan, no, in God's name, it cannot be. Yet Andred would not be much better. He might pretend to help and support their holy work, but Andred served only himself.

And as long as Mark thought he had Andred and Tristan as his heirs, he would never trouble himself with Dominian's careful plan. What to do, then? Work against both of them. First Tristan, and then Andred. Dominian nodded to himself. In the back of his mind he had always known it would come to this.

But how to do it? The priest engaged his labyrinthine mind. If Andred could be enlisted against Tristan, then he might move against Andred himself—

He was aware of Mark's interested gaze. "What, Father?"

"Sir Tristan and Sir Andred," Dominian said brusquely. "You are blest in them both."

Mark preened himself openly. "I am, aren't I? Well, they come from fine kin."

Not yours then, Dominian thought grimly. He folded his hands in his sleeves. Mark had gone as far as his brain would take him for one day. "God has smiled on you, sire. Like as the giant whose quiver is full of arrows, so is the man whose gate is full of sons."

"True," Mark agreed, uncomprehending. He reached for his hunting spear.

Dominian raised his eyes to heaven and launched into a prayer. *Confitebimur tibi* . . . We give thanks to Thee, O Lord . . .

Has he finished? Mark sighed with relief. Already he could hear the hounds in full cry, smell the stag running through the summer wood, and feel the silken thrumming of the stallion between his thighs.

"God be with you, Father!" he cried, scurrying away.

Dominian raised his hand and sketched a savage blessing in the air. "And with you, my son."

Brooding, the priest brought his hands together in prayer as he watched Mark making his exit with unkingly haste. What was to be done? He paced out into the corridor deep in thought, and did not hear the soft footfall approaching behind his back. "All well, Father?"

Turning, Dominian was aware of an ironic scrutiny. Smoothly he covered his sense of unpleasant surprise. "Sir Andred—I did not see you there."

Andred bowed. "I am attending to the King's affairs while he is at the hunt."

Now it was Dominian's turn to bow. "I know you place the King's interests above your own."

Then you know more than I do, little man. Smiling to himself, Andred nodded soulfully and laid his hand on his heart. "My uncle the King is more than kin to me," he murmured. "But the Queen—?"

Dominian pricked up his ears. Did Andred know something new? He folded his hands. "I fear she is not well."

Andred paused. "I know she haunts the quayside, watching for ships, or sends her maid down there at all hours."

"Waiting for a letter that never comes," observed Dominian with the passionless relish of inborn cruelty. "In all courtesy, her knight should have sent her word. But Sir Tristan has forgotten her, it seems."

Andred raised his eyes to the ceiling. "The French King's daughter is a beauty, they say."

"Is she so?"

"And a famous healer, like our own Queen." He smiled. "But a lot younger, and unmarried too."

"Not married?" Dominian moved his lips in the ghost of a smile. "Then she has that in common with Sir Tristan himself."

There was a pause. The same thought made its way through both men's minds. Dominian was the first to speak. "If Sir Tristan were to marry the French princess and remain in France with her, how very fine and fitting that would be . . ."

In the distance, a lone bell began the call to prayer. Dominian raised his head. "How excellent are Thy ways, O Lord our God," he remarked cheerfully. "Let us pray. Farewell, sir. I commend you to your concerns."

"And you to yours, sir." Bowing fulsomely, Andred waved Dominian on his way. Your concerns, priest? What do you and your fellow eunuchs fret about? What business could you have that compares with mine?

Tristan, now, he concerns me—

What was that? Andred froze. A disturbing noise, a sudden threatening shape: Gods above, it was Isolde! He laughed to himself. Andred, Andred, are you ready for this?

She came surging toward him down the corridor, her heels clacking on the flagstones with a sound like doom. Her tall queenly figure had lost none of its power, and she bore down on him as fiercely as her warrior foremothers must have driven the Romans from the land. But she had aged ten years and more, he saw with delight, her brightness dimmed, her shadowed eyes showing sleepless nights. Good, good! May her grief for Tristan waste her body and rot her mind.

She laid her gaze on him with the force of a curse. "You sent Tristan away," she said ominously. "You sent him to France."

Andred held up his hands, palm outward, and shook his head. "It was a mistake, my lady, nothing more."

"Oh, sir—" She waved a hand and laughed openly in his face. "If the King believes that, he's more credulous than I thought. Tristan would ask for me with his dying breath. You tricked them both."

"I, madam? Now why would I do that?"

There was no mistaking the tightening of his jaw. Isolde felt her temper rising to meet his. "Why? Because you hate Tristan and would gladly see him dead. Because you never tire of causing pain."

Andred forced a smile. "Madam, you are not well—"

But there was no stopping the torrent of reproof. "Above all, because you're rotten to the core. Evil is the element in which you live."

"Lady—"

"Don't speak to me." She held up her hand and turned contemptuously away. "From now on you are my sworn enemy."

She turned on her heel and paced unhurriedly away. Her gait put Andred in mind of a she-wolf on the kill, and she did not look back.

My enemy, eh? Well, well.

Andred watched her go, his mind racing in time with his thudding heart. Words, words, he tried to tell himself, furious at the sight of his trembling hands. She's talking nonsense. All this will pass.

But an inner voice whispered that things had changed, and Isolde most of all. She's grown older and harder since she's been away, he thought, shivering. Whatever happened in Ireland has given her a new edge. And he'd thought that she'd lose her power along with her looks, that grieving for Tristan would undermine her strength? Wrong, wrong! She has learned how to hate. She has embraced me for her enemy and she will not hold back.

But the Great Ones still rewarded those who strike first. Like an adder preparing to attack, Andred moved into the King's apartments with a new purpose darkening his mind. Pen and ink, he resolved, and a letter to France. By the fastest messenger. He knew the man.

To my faithful knight, he began composing in his mind. Or *my wandering knight*, perhaps? No, he needed something more cutting than that. *Sir* . . .

He knew the Queen's hand. Now how did she make her *T*s?

chapter 38

The June twilight bathed all the sky in gold. The high halls of heaven sighed with the dying light, and all the creatures of earth breathed in the sweet incense. The last strands of fading, silvery light drifted like cobwebs through the violet haze. And in the tower room that Blanche had made his home, Tristan pressed his fingers to the side of his head and sat down to write to Isolde once again.

> *Oh my dear lady—*
> *My lady and my love*
>   *I think I shall never see you again in this world. But my love for you will last through all three worlds and beyond.*
>   *Wait for me, sweetheart, where all roads lead to one, where all rivers run together into the sea. I languish here a prisoner in silken bonds, enfeebled by a weakness in the head. But every day I strive to recover my strength and my only thought is to come to you.*
>   *Yours and no other,*
>
>   *Tristan of Lyonesse*

How many times had he written this letter to her? Or had he only written it in his mind? In truth, he did not know. But he knew he wrote to her all the time in such tones of love and loss.

Other times, anger seized him and shook him like a rat. The letters he wrote then were accusing, hot, and harsh, the ink boiling like brimstone and the paper saturated with the smell of rage.

> *Lady, why don't you write a single word to me? Why no letter to your faithful knight?*

Do you think I have failed you? Forgotten you, my Queen?
Abandoned my oath of knighthood, left you on a whim?
    I may be weak and foolish, all men are. But I have never
betrayed my only love.
    Nor will never.
    Never, never, never, never, never . . .

After twenty misshapen nevers, deeply underlined, and other odd scribbles besides, he came to himself and knew he was not well.

Yet he had to keep writing to Isolde.

Isolde.

Yes.

Tristan kneaded his temples and rested his head in his hands.

"Sir Tristan?" The door opened, and a lean, gray form appeared.

Tristan raised his head. The doctor, of course, he knew who the visitor was. The healer he had met in the infirmary after Blanche had made him well.

The doctor moved quietly forward to Tristan's side. "How are you, sir?" Much thinner, looking ravaged, not good, ran swiftly through the doctor's mind.

Tristan forced a smile. "Oh, better every day."

"May I?"

The doctor's cool, clever fingers moved to the back of Tristan's neck and gently circled the site of his great wound.

"It's healed very well," he remarked in grave tones. "But you're still getting pains, you say, and flashes of light?"

Tristan shifted imperceptibly in his chair. "Not as much as before."

No better, then, the doctor noted silently. He knew the ways of knights too well to believe what they said. He tried another tack. "And how is it when you walk or try to ride?"

Tristan shook his head and abandoned all pretense. "Why am I still so weak?" he demanded hoarsely.

The doctor nodded, unsurprised. "Are you sleeping?"

There was a pause. "No."

"Eating well?"

Tristan turned his face away without a word.

The doctor drew a breath. "Sir, I can see that something is preying on your mind. Any care or concern will stop you from getting well. It's essential to keep as quiet as possible and avoid all strain."

Which was not an opinion he could share with Princess Blanche, he resolved with a sigh. His royal mistress was agog to take the care of the patient into her fabled white hands. If he told her what he saw, she would want to apply some willful remedy for Tristan's suffering that he could not approve.

"Sire, my care is not only for your body, but for your mind," he resumed heavily. "I could call myself a great healer indeed if I could lift the weight that holds your mind in chains."

"Thank you, sir." Tristan looked at the shrewd eyes and kindly face. What was he saying? And who was he again?

The doctor came to a decision. This man should be back in the infirmary, that was plain. The Princess had rushed him back into the world too soon. He needed peace, and a respite from her. Then, with the aid of herbs that promoted sleep, he could be brought back to himself again.

The doctor stepped forward. "Sir, by your leave—"

"A letter for the King of Lyonesse . . ."

The door opened and another gray figure appeared. Tristan lunged forward, his heart in his eyes. "A letter?"

"From the Queen of Cornwall," the messenger confirmed.

Hungrily Tristan snatched the missive from his hand. "May all the Gods rain blessings on you, good man." He brought the letter to his lips, and a glow of wonder lit his ravaged face.

The doctor watched his color improve and rejoiced. Gods and Great Ones, is this the good news he craved?

"Farewell, my lord." The messenger bowed and withdrew.

Eyes closed, Tristan stood clasping the letter to his heart as tears of joy ringed his tightly closed lids. Moved to the point of pain, the doctor bowed. "I'll leave you to your letter then, sir."

Closing the door behind him, the doctor strode away. Gods, if only all his patients could have medicine like that! Love and joy were the finest healers in the world.

HE WAS ALMOST BETTER, she knew it. Oh, not quite himself, anyone could see that, but it was only a matter of time. Blanche stared into her mirror, drew a strand of hair fetchingly over one eye, and arranged her mouth into a seductive smile. Tristan would make a full recovery as soon as he forgot Isolde and settled down with her.

And that would be soon. Everything was moving in the right direction, just as she would wish. Tristan had promised to save her from Saint Roc. She only had to make this unwanted marriage come true, and Tristan was hers.

And now this message had come from Isolde . . .

She glanced sharply round her chamber, weary of its innocent tints of lavender and rose. As Queen of Lyonesse, she would have palaces in royal blue and gold and private apartments throbbing in purple and red, colors that a queen like Isolde must surely favor for herself.

And whatever Isolde could do . . .

Blanche set her chin and folded her flower-like mouth. All this she would have when she was Tristan's queen.

Now, how to persuade Tristan? Every word of it was ready in her head. Her father had been with her, she would say, raging and threatening and insisting she married Saint Roc. She could not withstand him, beg and plead as she might. The wedding would take place within the week. She tousled her hair, pinched her cheeks, and studied the result. Sad enough? Oh, yes, the red blotches were very touching and forlorn. And when she added a few tears . . .

She left the room and hurried down the corridor, getting ready to weep. Years ago she had lost her little dog in the wood and thinking of that always helped her to conjure up tears.

Ready then? She burst through Tristan's door.

"Sir Tristan! Oh, sir—?"

He stood in the window, staring into space. A closely written parchment dangled from his hand. He turned to her with eyes of madness and despair, but when he opened his mouth, he was unable to speak.

With a compulsive twitch, he threw the letter at her feet. Blanche snatched it up and read it, her eyes out on stalks.

To my lost knight, Sir Tristan of Lyonesse:
I looked for you in Ireland, but you did not come. In Cornwall I
learned that you dallied with a lady along the way. They tell me

now that you took a great hurt to the head. Yet still I have no word of truth from you.

Meanwhile King Mark welcomes me to his arms. I have wearied of your delay and made myself his wife. My time to bear children grows shorter every year. Now I look to bear fruit before the year is out.

Farewell, my faithless friend. Go where you will, this world of ours is wide. But from this day forward, never see me again. Never come where I come, or go where I may go. On your honor as a knight, never dare to call again on the love of your onetime lady,
Isolde, Queen of the Western Isle

"Alas, sir!"

Assuming an air of tragic sympathy, Blanche read and reread the letter with secret delight. She found she was enjoying Isolde's words all over again, even more than when she had read them the first time. Indeed, she liked them better now than before, when the letter had been delivered, and she had had to survey the contents before she could allow it to be given to Tristan.

So he had had it and taken it badly, she could see.

Good, wonderful, the best!

"Oh, my lord . . ." She sprouted a few fresh tears. "You and I both share a great sorrow, it seems."

Tristan stirred. "Lady?" he said.

His eyes were glittering, and he held the side of his head. Blanche saw it, and pressed on. "Oh, sir!" She let out a shrill wail and was rewarded by a dark shaft of anguish in Tristan's shadowed gaze. "This marriage I told you about, to the knight Saint Roc," she wept piteously, "it's being forced on me now."

"Now?" He looked stunned.

"Before the end of the week."

"What can I do for you, lady?" he muttered like a man in a dream.

"The only way to rescue me from this marriage," she began, her heart in her mouth, "is—"

"Rescue you?"

"You swore!"

"I—?"

"Yes, to rescue me from Saint Roc—"

"Yes—"

"And the only way to set me free from this marriage—"

"—is to marry you myself!"

The sound of his laughter chilled her to the bone. He clutched his head.

"I'll do it!" he said madly. "Tell your father, choose the church, set the day. Call up the minstrels, let the whole court revel and dance!"

His skull was cracking, but he did not care. "And we'll have a feast," he raged on, "to end all feasts, till the end of the world."

Blanche found herself shaking. "Do you mean this, sir? Will you marry me?"

"Within the week." Tristan tore his sword from its sheath and kissed the hilt. "On my honor as a knight." He seized her hands. "I will save you from this man."

His hands were as cold as death. "And I will make you love me. I will replace Isolde in your mind," Blanche cried rashly, treading down a sudden violent fear.

He stared at her like a ghost. "There is no replacing Isolde in my mind." He gestured wildly at the letter. "But she has forbidden me her company in this world. I must wait for her then, till the next world and the next. And in the meantime, lady, I will marry you."

chapter 39

dispatches from Ireland? Tell me, Sir Gilhan is well?"

The fresh-faced young knight shouldering in through the door gave a cheerful smile. "Never better, Majesty, and Cormac, your Druid, too."

Isolde gave an answering smile of relief. "Sir Kerrigan! What a pleasure to see you here."

She watched as the newcomer's eyes traveled approvingly over the spacious, well-furnished apartment fragrant with midsummer flowers, then came to rest on the writing table with a half-written letter lying plainly in view. Beside it rested other sheets covered in rough jottings, crossings out, and marks that were plainly tears. He hesitated on the threshold. "Am I intruding? Should I come back later on?"

"Not at all." She stepped back and welcomed him into the room.

"Then here you are, madam." With a thankful sigh, Sir Kerrigan deposited a heavy satchel at her feet. "Documents from your Council. There are many questions that you alone can decide. But no grave issues lie in wait for you."

"Come then, sir." Isolde turned back toward the table, pushed aside her papers, and gestured to the knight to draw up another chair. "Don't stand on ceremony, sit down and tell me all you know. What has been happening in the Western Isle?"

He smelled of green fields and silver rain, of the wind at sea, of the wild woodland and fresh horses at dawn. He smelled as Tristan did when they rode out. *What news from Erin for a hungry heart?*

"Nothing but good, my lady," returned Sir Kerrigan stoutly, arranging his long legs with care as he took a seat. "Of course, your lords have had a good deal to do."

"Cleansing the land of Sir Breccan and all his deeds?" Isolde asked quietly.

Sir Kerrigan nodded. "Still they come forward with their pitiful tales, women widowed by his men, children orphaned and driven from their homes. Your Council of lords has sat late into the night, striving to right this endless flow of wrongs."

Oh, my poor country. Isolde nodded, tight-lipped. "Is there any way to make recompense?"

"Yes indeed, madam." Sir Kerrigan's chuckle filled the room. "Sir Breccan left money enough and more. His brother's estate had come down to him, and your mother the Queen had made Sir Tolen a wealthy man. Sir Breccan had been adding to his own wealth too. Sir Gilhan came across an heiress he had taken from her parents by force, planning to marry her as soon as she came of age." He grinned with honest delight. "You may imagine how overjoyed her parents were to get her back unharmed."

"Indeed, I can." *When a loved one is lost, who knows the suffering?* She suppressed a sigh. "And the old woman, Breccan's nurse, who took care of Sir Gilhan and Cormac? What's become of her?"

"Dame Friya? Safe in the arms of her daughter, warm, clean, and well fed. No more living alone in the wood, but tucked up in a cottage in the village, where she keeps them enthralled with her tales of lords and knights."

Isolde gave a watery smile. "And the Fair Ones, don't forget. They came to her too." She pointed to the leather satchel packed with documents. "What must I deal with first?"

Sir Kerrigan fixed his earnest young eyes on hers. "The Council has some concern about the Picts. Their king is ailing, and there's a fear that their young Prince Darath may be tempted to try his strength. Of course, they could never take our towns or approach Dubh Lein, but the outlying crannogs are vulnerable to attack. Should they be fortified for their own defense? Sir Gilhan has written about the whole question to you. The Council awaits your decision and your command."

"And they shall have it," Isolde promised. She rose stiffly to her feet. "Thank you, sir, for your service on Ireland's behalf. Now if you'll excuse me, the court will soon gather for dinner in the Great Hall. If you will attend me there, I shall present you to the King."

Sir Kerrigan jumped to his feet. "Till the dinner hour then, madam. I shall be honored to kiss the hand of the King."

Isolde stood as he bowed himself out. "Farewell, sir."

Outside the window, the sun was dissolving into the bowl of night, its silver-pink beams yielding to purple and gray. Dreaming, Isolde leaned out of the casement and fixed her gaze on the sky. The roses in the Queen's garden below were in their midsummer glory, and now, as evening approached, sighing their hearts out in the soft evening air. Lapped in their tender fragrance, she waited and watched.

At last she saw it, tiny and low in the sky. On the far horizon, the evening star bloomed like a golden rose through the gathering dusk. Turning to the table at her side, Isolde lit a candle with a silent prayer. *Tristan, do you see the love star rising too? Or have you forgotten my love, wherever you are?*

She could see his face now as it was on the night they met, a face of astonishing beauty and power and grace. That look, that sweetness, that sense of the heart coming home, she had always thought would be hers till she died. But now . . .

She felt her soul shrivel with grief and dread. Was this the pitiful end of every great love, nothing but distance, estrangement, and the slow, sad forgetting of every sweet memory that had bound their two souls closer than skin?

No more tears. Soon, very soon, she would know. The end of this long dreary waiting was in sight.

Turning, she made her way into the inner chamber, where Brangwain was making ready for the evening in the Great Hall. The maid had two or three gowns set out on wooden stands and was busy matching jewels, girdles, and headdresses to each.

Isolde hurried forward and closed the door. "Did you speak to the captain? Is the boat ready to sail?"

Brangwain paused in her sorting and nodded. "The last of the provisions are being loaded tonight. Tomorrow I can sail with the first tide, and away." Her sharp face softened with concern. "Then at least we shall know what is going on."

"Do it, then. You have all you need?"

Brangwain gave a grim smile. "Lady, you've given me enough gold to ransom a king. When I get there, I'll be able to hire the best horses in the land. And the ship is the fastest in the Cornish fleet. I shall fly like a bird to France and back again."

Then at least I shall know . . .

Enough! She forced herself to turn to the full, heavy gowns, each standing stiffly to attention like a life-sized doll. Silk, satin, and velvet, shading from the blue of a cloudless sky to a midnight sea. Isolde remembered Sir Kerrigan and her sad heart yearned. "Where's my green silk, Brangwain? I'll wear that tonight."

"Green is for Ireland, and blue is for Cornwall here," said the maid firmly. A waterfall of jewels tumbled from her hand. Sapphires, aquamarines, and beryls spilled out before her, each beguiling her, wear me, wear me. Brangwain's brisk voice reached her from behind. "You want to be as fine as the Lady Elva tonight."

"Finer." Isolde's face hardened. "Tonight and every night, Brangwain. There is only one Queen in Cornwall, and she has forgotten that. Now, show me what we have."

Soon a stranger's face looked out from Isolde's glass, her eyes and complexion enhanced by Brangwain's skill, her mouth ripened to rich shades of peony and plum. Her gown fell in folds of thick velvet to the floor, her full skirts whispering to the long train behind. A deep collar of tourmalines circled her white throat, and the gold of her crown gleamed in the candlelight.

Brangwain stared at her, entranced. "Lady, the Queen of the Sea never looked so fine."

The sea, the sea.

My love lies over the sea.

My love lies with his fair eyes . . .

Did my love lie to me?

Again she struggled to pull her spirits around, *Smile, Isolde. A queen must always smile.*

"Ready, Brangwain?"

Breathing deeply, Isolde swept out and down to the Great Hall with Brangwain following behind. *Ready, Isolde? Prepared to encounter Elva and stare her down?*

But Elva was not the first to accost her in the crowded hall. With a palpable buzz of interest, all eyes were keenly turned to greet her as she came in.

What's happened? There is something here I don't know.

"Your Majesty."

It was Sir Nabon, stepping forward with a bow. Isolde's heart eased. The grizzled warlord might be Mark's chief adviser and the head of the King's Council, but he had always been a good friend to her too. Anxious for the King to be married, Nabon had counted Isolde as a pearl above price. And unlike others, he had shown a deep understanding when Mark had proved himself to be a husband she could not accept.

Sir Nabon was talking with two lords of the Council, Sir Quirian and the aged Sir Wisbeck, who had served Mark's father and who was rumored to be older than Castle Dore. Nabon drew aside from his companions with a low bow. "My lady, a word in your ear."

He gestured across the shadowy, candlelit hall to a small group of courtiers clustered around the King. Foremost among them was a short, squat, black-clad shape, standing four-square and impassive at Mark's side.

"The King's confessor Dominian?" Isolde surveyed the monk, then turned back to Nabon.

Nabon fingered his chin uneasily. "It seems that the Church is taking an interest in your affairs."

Isolde tensed. "How so?"

"A whisper has reached me that the King's priest is urging him to make good his marriage vows."

"Is it so?" *Is that why the whole court is aflame with excitement tonight?*

No, that could not be it. This would not be the talk of the court, not yet at least. Again she felt the force of a hundred eyes, some pitying, some amused, some with an openly malicious air. *There's something else. What is it?* Her stomach tightened as she looked around.

Not far from Mark, Andred stood with the Lady Elva at the center of a busy, chattering throng. *Andred will know.* She bowed to Sir Nabon. "Thank you, my lord, for your kind advisement of this. Let us talk further when I've considered it." She glanced behind her. "Come, Brangwain."

"Forewarned is forearmed, my lady," Sir Nabon said grimly. He took a breath. "There's another matter I should mention too . . ."

But Isolde was already striding away. Nabon watched her go with pity in his eyes. "She won't like it," he growled to Wisbeck under his breath.

Wisbeck's ancient face showed his sadness too. "How can she?" he said gruffly.

The crowd around the King parted as she approached and Andred stood grinning in the center of her view. Beside him Elva was wreathed in a snake-like smile.

"Good news, Isolde," Mark cried boisterously.

What's good for Mark can only be bad for me. "What news, my lord?"

"It's Tristan," Mark brayed in triumph. "You know we thought he was on the brink of death? Well, the rogue has a surprise for us yet." He laughed and released a belch. "You'll never guess."

Oh, I think I can. What else could give you all such enjoyment at my expense?

Mark waved a brimming goblet, and bright drops of red wine fell through the air like blood. For the rest of her life, whenever liquor was spilled, Isolde would see her heart breaking and her life's liquor running out.

Behind her Brangwain breathed, "Courage, lady." She took her heart in her hands.

"Tell me, my lord," she cried gaily. "Whatever it is, it will be welcome. We all wish Sir Tristan well."

Mark goggled at her with a foolish grin. "He's going to be married, Isolde, to the Princess of France. Now what do you think of that?"

Then he swung his goblet high in the air again. Isolde watched her heart's blood fly away. "A toast!" he proclaimed, "a toast."

Standing behind Isolde, Brangwain watched the immobile form as her mistress absorbed the extremity of pain. But Isolde did not need to move or turn her head for the maid to hear and obey her mistress's thought.

Fly to the dock, Brangwain, take ship tonight. Order the captain to sail on the evening tide and get over to France to find out if this is true!

chapter 40

It was the finest day of that long, hot summer, a day of golden glory, made for joy. The sun shone, the birds sang, the flowers bloomed, the people rejoiced, and Tristan walked out like a dead man to marry the Princess of France.

To the cheering crowds, he looked as fine as the day itself, shining like the sun. Blanche had commanded a wedding tunic for him in silver and white, made of pearly leather patterned with silver studs. Over it swung a cloak of white lined with silver, and chains of silver from King Hoel's treasury. From the same source had come the heavy gold crown he wore, in token of his kingship of Lyonesse. With a savage amusement, it came to him that out of every stitch covering his nakedness, only his boots and his breeches were his own. Those, and the torque of knighthood around his neck, the fatal sign and symbol of what had brought him here today.

On my oath as a knight, he had said, *I will marry you.* He had kissed her white hand and told her to name the day. But no sooner had she left the room than a voice like Isolde's had started inside his head.

Traitor . . .

Coward . . .

Faithless wretch . . .

You have failed your knighthood oath, and now you have failed me.

A shaft of white light ran like a skewer through his brain. He struck at his head for relief, and the pain increased.

"Failed? Failed again?" he cried, beside himself. "I shall make amends!"

Bursting from his chamber, he ran through the palace to the royal apartments and hammered on Blanche's door, kneeling at her feet. "Lady, forgive me," he gasped, "I cannot marry you. But I shall challenge Saint Roc to single combat and set you free."

Blanche froze. "You will not marry me?"

"Making false vows endangers your honor and mine. You want me to prevent your marriage to Saint Roc. And I can beat him on horseback at the joust, on the ground, anywhere!"

"Oh, sir—"

There was no measuring the depth of Blanche's contempt. "You'll fight for me, when you can't sit a horse? When you can't raise a lance, or even hold a sword?"

Tears started to his eyes. In a frenzy, he leapt to his feet. "Madam, I—"

"And now you mean to shame me before all the world?"

"Shame you?" His head was splitting. "How?"

Blanche reached for the lie with a lifetime's ease. "I've told my father that you've proposed to me. He's gone to announce our marriage to all the court."

Devils and darkness . . . Tristan held his head. "Is it so?"

Remorselessly Blanche pressed her advantage home. "It will be proclaimed far and wide."

A monstrous abyss was gaping at Tristan's feet. "But lady—I can't marry you without love."

"Many couples marry without love." She gave a seductive smile. "Love comes afterward."

Tristan's stomach heaved. "I can never love you, maiden, you must know that. I have taken a vow to the Queen of the Western Isle."

Blanche paused. Isolde again? Well, sooner or later he'd forget her, it would only take time. And they would have time, as soon as the knot was tied. As long as she could make Tristan stick to his vow.

She thought of her little lost dog, and the tears flowed. "Sir, if you'll only keep your oath, I'll be safe from Saint Roc. After that I swear I'll make no further demands on you. I'll get the marriage annulled as soon as I can. Till then we'll be like brother and sister, friends in chastity. A white marriage, we call it in France."

Could he trust her? He did not know. "On your oath, lady?"

She widened her eyes and brought both her hands to her heart. "On my mother's soul."

Still he was wavering. She leaned toward him, wringing her perfect hands. "You gave me your word. On your honor as a knight." Gently she eased her tears into helpless sobs. "Will you break your oath? Will you fail me now?"

Tristan gazed into the tearful blue eyes, and his senses drowned.

On my honor as a knight, I fail and I fail . . .

Fail Blanche, fail Isolde, fail, fail, fail . . .

His gorge rose, and sickness swept him from head to foot. And now he was walking to the church, still dreaming mad thoughts of escape and flight. Fool! You can't draw back now, hammered through his brain. There's no way out. He gave a hurtful laugh. What, leave her at the altar, all dressed up in silver and white?

As you are too. He looked at his ludicrous outfit and laughed again.

What was this?

What was Tristan laughing at?

Walking at Tristan's side, Kedrin eyed him with deep concern. A bridegroom was expected to be happy, not emitting odd, mad little chuckles like this. But the wedding was ill-starred, Tristan must know that.

Did Tristan also know, Kedrin wondered, that he had challenged Blanche as soon as the wedding was announced?

"He does not love you, sister," he had said.

She had laughed then, a long, low disturbing sound. "Oh, he will. He is mine now. And he will marry me. You and my father were wrong."

There was no resisting Blanche's triumph and her joy. King Hoel's protests had been likewise brushed aside and the wedding went forward at a furious pace. Kedrin had been elected as Tristan's groomsman, since the knight had no other friend in the whole of France. Within a week they were walking to the small chapel below the castle where Blanche would arrive with her father at her side.

Kedrin groaned inwardly. He'd agreed to stand up beside Tristan in church, but he'd rather be throwing his friend to the wolves. Why was he so sure that this marriage was destined to fail?

Fail, fail, you failed.

Failed then, failing now.

Trying to do right, doing so much wrong.

Traitor . . .

Coward . . .

Faithless wretch . . .

You have failed your knighthood oath and now you have failed me.

Where was he? Lights flared behind Tristan's eyes. Walking out of the castle, yes, and into the sun, down the hill and into the tree-sheltered grove. Little church beside water, and therefore once a holy lake, sacred to the Goddess before the Christians came. A Christian church, then? Another wild chuckle rose to Tristan's lips. Another betrayal of Isolde, another disgrace.

He stumbled over the threshold, straining to see. Who were all these people, all these foolish, festive faces, grinning away? Strange that a man would not know a single soul among those who had gathered on his wedding day. He could feel the mad laughter rising again in his chest and willed himself to hold it back. At least the wretched Saint Roc was not here. The villain who had been the cause of all this grief had at least had the grace to make himself scarce today.

Was that the altar ahead? Tristan pondered. So then, what now?

What now indeed, bride-man?

Saint Roc stood unseen at the back of the church and laughed silently at the folly of the world. So Blanche was trying to make him jealous by taking Tristan? Foolish girl. The task of deflowering a virgin was little but a chore, and he was happy to leave it to the King of Lyonesse. The only man who desired a virgin bride was one who feared comparison with other men. A man of the world looked for women who understood pleasure, and Blanche would know more about that when Tristan was through. Saint Roc gave a sigh of content. Blanche would be his, he knew it. This so-called marriage would not, could not last. All he had to do was wait.

Cantate Domino: O, sing unto the Lord a new song . . .

The church was cool and dim after the sunshine outside. A choir of boys sang like angels in the shadows, and the soft gloom helped the pain in Tristan's head. But the sickly smell of incense choked his throat, and for a moment he could not breathe.

A white shape came toward him veiled from head to foot, and he felt another flare of fear. *This ghostly creature is your bride, Tristan. Did you think she would fade away, like a bad dream?*

And this was the priest, gowned and mumbling, smelling like his church of the incense from the East. What was he saying? Take this woman? No escaping now. Only one answer. Yes.

Her hand was cold. Perhaps his was too. But the wedding ring sat like a hoop of fire on his hand. Why was it thick and solid like a glittering shackle, not looking like an object of love and joy? Why was it so different from the ring on his other hand, the love token Isolde had given him years ago?

Isolde, sang the cracked voices in his head.

Traitor.

Wretched failure.

Recreant knight.

What had he done, he wondered, mad with despair, that the Gods had resolved to torture him like this? The thought obsessed him, weaving in and out of the sounds only he could hear. Sometimes he heard a low, sad echo, sometimes a cacophony of sobbing, whistling, and catcalls. It came to him; you are losing your mind.

And perhaps he had lost it already, for he hardly knew where he was. The world had shrunk to two black pinpoints of pain through which he peered about as blind as a mole. Blink, and he was in the Great Hall, at a great feast. Blink, and an hour had passed, then many more. Hands guided him about, sat him down, pushed a brimming goblet into his hand, carved and set before him the choicest cuts of peacock, beef, and swan. One pair of white hands seemed to be everywhere, and he had no difficulty in knowing whose they were.

"Bring the bride to bed!"

He knew what that meant too. Fool, Tristan, worse than fool! Every wedding ended in this coarse revelry, when the ladies prepared the bride for her husband's embrace, and the groom was led to her chamber with a thousand ribald jests. Why had he never thought that this would come and made sure to avoid it somehow, anyhow?

Blanche vanished from the table and from the hall, surrounded by giggling ladies with armfuls of flowers. The young men of the court swarmed around Tristan like flies, each armed with some crude comment or suggestive joke. Jab, jab, jab they came, stinging like rapier points. More wine somehow found its way down his throat. The knights' belches and belly laughter filled the air with stale, stinking breath.

Goddess, Mother, save me . . .

A dull monotonous throbbing ran through his veins.

"This way, sir!"

Rough hands fastened on him like crabs and hoisted him aloft. One face seemed to leap out from the throng. Gods above! Saint Roc? Reeling, he felt himself hoisted onto drunken, unsteady shoulders and fell backward, dropping like a tree.

"He's drunk!" yodeled a thick voice in his ear. "Let's hope he can still do his duty by the bride!"

Caught and carried forward like a sack, he was bundled through a door and set upright on his feet. As his swimming senses returned, he saw a large, square chamber bright with candles, and a row of long windows giving out on the warm night.

The knights pounced on the ladies and chased them squealing from the room. Alone in the candlelit silence, he could hear nothing but the roaring in his skull. Then he lifted his head and knew what he had to fear.

At the end of the chamber, marooned in a bed of state, Blanche sat arrayed in a nightgown as white as her soft flesh. Her long pale hair spilled down over her shoulders, and her eyes were very bright. The flimsy gown scarcely covered her breasts, and she was panting lightly, her pink mouth ajar. One hand played with the flowers covering the bed. The other was raised in command, beckoning him.

"Come, sir."

He could not look at her. He saw again the ring Isolde gave him when they pledged their love, and the monstrous wedding hoop of greenish gold. You've betrayed her, Tristan. Failed and failed again . . .

"Tristan? Can't you hear me?"

The white figure slipped determinedly from the bed. Terror and pain nailed Tristan to the floor.

"What's the matter?" She was at his side.

He rallied his forces and bowed. "Madam, let me bid you goodnight."

"Goodnight?" She laughed in his face. "You're my husband now. You know what that means."

He could feel a film of sweat gathering on the back of his neck. "Lady, we had an understanding. You agreed—"

She moved into him with a seductive shrug, rippling the flimsy gauze covering her breasts. "It's every woman's right to change her mind."

Terror gripped his vitals. "A white marriage!" he said hoarsely. "You made a vow—"

Blanche gave a lascivious laugh. "The more fool you for trusting to a woman's vow."

"I have an old wound," he cried desperately, striking the top of his leg, "here in the groin."

"Then I shall make it better," she returned implacably. She reached out a hand.

Outside the window, the moon floated in the sky. A shimmering silvery light poured through the great mullioned casements standing open to the night. Tristan scented the cool air rising from the forest below, and a desperate resolve formed in his ruined brain. Get away. Must get away.

"Madam—" he began with the last of his strength.

But she was not listening. "Come here, sir."

The grin she wore seemed to stretch from wall to wall, and he trembled at the hot glint in her eye. Her breasts, all too visible, struck him like evil things, and her nipples seemed to stare at him like eyes, great animal lights from another, crueler world. Hissing like a swan, she spread her long white arms, and he felt her enfold him in her scaly wings. The next moment her mouth fastened wetly upon his, sucking, pulling, dragging out his soul. He thought of Isolde and lost his last shred of hope.

Traitorcowardfaithlesswretchfailed failed failed . . .

His mind split open, and a great darkness loomed. Blindly his body followed his spirit into the void. Bounding like a stag across the floor, he jumped up onto the window ledge. Then as Blanche gaped in horror and ran crying for the guard, he leapt into the night.

chapter 41

darkness favored lovers, everyone knew that. So the wedding celebrations at court only swelled in volume as the sun went down. In the town, too, the revelry had been rising by the hour. Huddled in the shadow of the castle wall, the town alehouse was crammed with roisterers toasting the newlyweds' health.

"A toast to the Princess!"

"She's Queen now—Queen of Lyonesse!"

"Well, here's to the Queen and her King—"

"—and a toast to the young prince or princess that they're making right now!"

Nothing like a wedding to bring the drinkers out, the alewife thought happily, slipping more coins under the counter into the well-filled leather bag now bulging like her hips.

"More ale over there," she ordered the little drudge who labored as her maid.

She moved forward to clear the nearest table of its load, a jumble of tankards and goblets all drained to the dregs. As she did so, a disheveled creature appeared in the open door.

The alewife eyed the stranger's travel-worn garments and dusty cloak. "Come far?" she said.

"Far enough," came the low rejoinder. "Can I rest here?"

The alewife nodded, sizing up the signs of desperate strain and fatigue on the haggard face. Too far for one day, that was clear. Slowly she assessed the newcomer's well-cut but somber gown and fine woolen wrap, the aura of quiet authority and respect, the heavy purse at her waist, the ringless left hand. A lady in waiting or high-born gentlewoman, on some errand of sad importance for her lady or her lord. A death or a dying, she pronounced to herself. Or a bastard child. As long as life went on, there would always be both.

"A drink, is it? Or a bed for the night?"

The newcomer hesitated. "I suppose it's too late to get to court tonight?"

"Tonight?" the alewife guffawed. "Yes, indeed."

"Then a bed for the night, if you have room."

"To the King!"

Behind them another round of drunken cheering rang out, shivering the cobwebs in the smoke-blackened roof.

"The King of Lyonesse! May he bring new blood into our royal house!"

"And his Queen—our Princess—blessings on her too!"

The newcomer gasped. "So it's true," she cried out in a sharp, lilting voice. "The King of Lyonesse has married your Princess?"

"Married her today," the alewife confirmed with a gap-toothed smile. "Wedded and bedded her, too, by now, I don't doubt."

The stranger brought her clasped hands to her lips. "Goddess, Mother, no!"

The alewife sniffed. What was wrong with the woman? Why couldn't she be happy for the Princess like everyone else? She felt a wave of dislike for the sallow, sour-faced thing. "So you didn't come to see our Princess married, then?"

The newcomer looked as if she had swallowed a toad. "No, I did not."

"Then you missed the most beautiful sight you ever saw. She was all in white, our Princess, she's called Blanche, you know. She had him got up all in white and silver too; you never saw such a pair. Outside the chapel, when the knot was tied, King Hoel had ordered a flock of white doves released. So they were all fluttering 'round as the King and Queen came out, like a blessing on them from the Great One Herself."

"King and Queen, are they?" muttered the lady furiously, tossing her head to and fro. Her face had flushed, the alewife saw, and her eyes were glittering.

Gods above, what if the wanderer had brought a fever into the house? Worse still, the plague? Better lay her up in the lean-to hovel outside where gypsies, lepers, and other creatures of the road took shelter when her dogs didn't get there first to drive them away.

She moved forward and took the stranger by the arm. "A bed for the night, lady?" she said brusquely. "This way."

⚓

"DON'T TELL ME THAT! You're just not searching hard enough." Twisting her hands, Blanche furiously paced the floor.

The captain eased his bulk back on his heels and kept his eyes fixed stolidly ahead. His dear wife would never believe him when he told her all this. She loved Princess Blanche, everyone did, and she'd hate to know that the poor girl's wedding night had turned out this way. "Like I said, lady." He waved at the open window with a beefy hand. "When he went out of there, the Gods only know what became of him."

Blanche turned on him, white with rage. "But he must have left some sign. Surely you've found something, after all this time?"

"You can see where he fell, all right," the captain conceded. "There were a few broken branches, and plenty of blood on the ground. But after that, nothing. It's as if the Fair Ones popped up and flew him away."

Blanche felt a surge of fear from her very depths. Fair Ones? What nonsense, all of it! But where could Tristan be? Did he hate her so much that he had to run away? And now surely he'd be injured again too? She strangled the urge to weep. "But you have trackers—dogs—"

"We've had 'em all out since dawn. Even the best of the dogs couldn't pick up a scent."

"Well, search again," Blanche ordered trenchantly, pacing to and fro. "He can't have gotten far." Gods above, how could he do this to me? she moaned inside. And on our wedding night too? Why was he so offended by her approach? Wouldn't any bride have expected to be loved?

"Well, no, he can't," the captain agreed cautiously. "Not if he was drunk, like you said, when he fell out."

Blanche stopped her pacing by the great fireplace and kicked out at one of the dogs dozing on the hearth. "I told you he was. That's how he lost his balance." She rounded on the captain again, her eyes ablaze. "How else would a man fall out of a window, tell me that?"

The captain bowed. "Let me order another search, lady. And we'll keep it secret, as you ordered before."

"Yes!" Blanche's pale face flared with desperate intent. She bore down on him like an angry swan. "I'll hang any man that breathes a word of this."

"Yes, lady."

"Tell them to widen the search. I want all the inns and high roads watched, anywhere my lord might take shelter to recover himself. There's a thousand crowns for the man who brings him to me!"

"Lady, it shall be done."

The captain backed to the door and made a speedy escape. He'd have plenty to tell his dear wife when he got home, and none of it made any sense. Lord Tristan so drunk that he couldn't stand up? And then fell out of a window and flew away without a trace?

"Tell that story to the Fair Ones, my lady," he muttered under his breath. "And get them to find him, for I fear we never shall."

chapter 42

The rising sun streamed in through a little window of greeny glass. A summer dove was cooing in the tree outside, and the smell of new bread rose from the kitchen below. Brangwain woke in the finest room in the alehouse and for a second felt warm, free, and safe. Then the memory of last night descended like a dead weight on her soul.

They were married, then. There was no denying it. Sir Tristan had gone to church of his own free will and wedded the Princess of France. The whole court and kingdom of King Hoel could bear witness it was true, not just one of Andred's mischief-making lies.

But how? Brangwain moaned and tossed in the wide bed. Lord Tristan loved Isolde with his life. The Princess must have put a spell on him to change his mind, or else the Fair Ones had stolen his soul away.

Well, today she would find out. At least she had had a fairly good night's sleep, once she'd sharply refused the wretched outhouse where the poor and lazarous creatures lay. A little gold had secured the best room in the house, and a decent bed it was too. Groaning, Brangwain stretched her weary limbs. Flying across the sea, taking horse after horse as she raced here from the coast, she had not rested in her efforts to reach the court of King Hoel before the wedding took place. And at my age, too, she grumbled.

And she had failed. So what now? She frowned and tried to think. Get up to the castle and try to see Tristan? How would she get to speak to him alone? Write a letter, then, and give it to one of the servants? But how would she know he got it? And Gods above! He was only married last night. He was still in the first flush of his honeymoon. Yet how could he betray my lady and marry like this? Brangwain buried her face in her hands. Goddess, Mother, help me . . .

There was a heavy thumping on the stairs. Brangwain dried her tears and managed a thin smile. So the fat alewife was bringing the breakfast herself. Well and good. Let the day begin.

Another series of thumps, and the chamber door flew back under the rough impact of the alewife's foot. "G'morning, lady," she observed with a toothless grin.

"Good morning." Sitting up, Brangwain watched as the bulky figure entered with a tray bearing a bowl of figs, a tankard of creamy milk, and a sizable chunk of passable-looking bread. She gave the goodwife a smile. "How are you today?"

The alewife set the tray down on the bed. "Better than them downstairs lying on my floor! Thick heads and yellow eyes, groaning and puking, it's a sight to be seen. And the stink! Still, they enjoyed the wedding, they'd have to say that."

Brangwain tried to keep the bitterness out of her voice. "All the world loves your Princess."

"Well, why not?" The alewife peered at her, spreading her hands upon her ample hips. "She's been a favorite here since she was a child. And then the Mother sent her our new King."

Your new King. Oh, very fine. Brangwain looked at the food on the tray and her stomach turned. *How can I tell my lady that this is true? How can I say that my lord has proved so false?*

She favored the alewife with a cheerful nod. "Let me break my fast, then we'll speak again."

"As you wish, lady." The alewife lumbered off, throwing a gummy smile over her shoulder as she went. "I'll send the maid up for the tray in a while."

"Very well."

Brangwain drank a little milk and picked at the figs. She should eat the bread, she knew, for strength later on, but she rarely felt hungry, and didn't feel hungry now. Time to act. She swung out of bed and hastened to get dressed. Just as she was securing her headdress and veil, she heard a mouse-like scratching at the door.

"Come in."

It was one of the alewife's young maids. She had the face and body of an orphan child, and the stink of poverty and despair seeped from every limb. Her threadbare gown was too small for her, and her head was covered in a greasy cloth. A worn dishrag served her as an apron, and she stood in the doorway twisting it nervously in her work-worn hands.

Brangwain beckoned her in. "Tell me, girl, what's your name?"

The maid buried her chin in her chest and refused to look up. "I'm nobody, lady. Just sent to fetch your tray."

A lifetime of taking care of such creatures flooded Brangwain's veins. Unhurriedly, she watched the girl cross over to the tray and read her starving eyes.

"Before you go, girl," she said briskly, "did you breakfast today?"

The drudge could not stop looking at the food. "Not us, ma'am," she said with a sharp laugh. "The mistress says we get sleepy when we eat. So we gets our rations at the end of the day. By that time we're sleepy anyway, so we don't need much."

"Come here, then, and eat this for me," Brangwain ordered. She dipped the bread in the milk and held it out. "I don't like to waste good food."

One snatch and the bread was gone from Brangwain's grasp and vanished down the girl's gaping throat. Brangwain pointed to the figs. "Finish it all up."

Moments later the tray was bare and a dull glow was warming the girl's thin face. Brangwain looked away.

"Is it far from here to the castle?" she asked casually.

The maid shook her head. "No more than a mile."

"And does King Hoel keep an open court? If I wanted to catch a glimpse of your new King, where should I go?"

"The new King? Oh, ma'am—! The King's run away."

Brangwain stared. "Run away?"

The little creatures shivered and dropped her voice. "My sister's married to the captain of the palace guard, and she's says he's gone."

"Gone? How?"

The girl ran the tip of her tongue over her cracked lips. "Lost his balance and fell out of the window and ran away."

Fell out of the window? Brangwain put a hand to the side of her head. "Go on, girl. What else did your sister say?"

"Well, he was drunk and he slipped, the Queen said, and here's the funny part. Any mortal man would have crashed straight to the ground. But they've searched all night and found no trace of him."

"Gods above, girl, what else could he have done?"

The girl gave a sideways smile. "He flew out of the window, that's what. They say he was one of the Fair Ones, too fine and handsome to be mortal like us. I saw him when the Princess took him Maying in the wood. And the smile he gave us, oh lady, if you'd seen that smile..."

The pinched face took on an ethereal look. Brangwain watched the girl's eyes drift into a memory she would cherish all her life.

"I can imagine," she said with difficulty. "Well, girl, may the Mother go with you. Run along."

So, what now?

Dazed, Brangwain found her way to a chair. Gods above, whatever did this mean? No happy husband leapt out of a window on his wedding night. No bridegroom in love ran away from his bride. If Tristan had fled from Blanche, had he lost his mind?

Goddess, Mother, I have to find him.

Where?

She sighed with relief. Where else would he be? Soon afterward she stood in the stable yard, waiting for a horse. A golden summer day was blooming all around. Whistling through his teeth, the groom saw another traveler mounted, then approached with a friendly grin.

Brangwain looked out through the alehouse gate. "Fine country," she observed casually. "You must have some rare forests and greenways around here."

"Miles of 'em," grinned the groom, "take your pick."

"If I wanted to explore your woodlands, where would I go?"

The groom gave a reflective tug on one grubby ear. "Some'd say one thing, some another. But I'd say the Lady Wood. It's so ancient that folk 'round here say the heart of it has turned to stone." He laughed again. "Of course, none of them's ever gone in to take a look. They say the Great One keeps it for Her own."

Brangwain pursed her lips. A petrified forest, and sacred to the Lady too? A place so deep that no one would venture in?

He was there, she knew it. Where else would Sir Tristan seek refuge than the deep greenwood where he first saw life?

She set her small pointed chin and took up the reins. I'm coming, sir. Hold on.

"A horse, then, lady?" came the voice of the groom.

Brangwain nodded. "A good goer, if you please, a stout cob or such-like, deep in the chest and strong enough to bear two."

"To bear two?" the groom chuckled, thumping the saddle down on the horse's back. "You hoping to find the King of the Fair Ones and bring him home?"

Brangwain fixed him with her Otherwordly eye. "You never know, my lad," she said grandly. "You never know."

chapter 43

Sometimes it was like a sickness, then a sharp, scalding pain. That was like childhood when she stumbled too near the fire or knocked a boiling pot over her hand. But most of the time it felt like nothing at all, because she refused to believe it was happening.

And to her—Blanche, Queen of Lyonesse? No, it was ludicrous. Tristan hadn't meant to fall, wasn't every red-blooded groom as drunk as a lord on his wedding night? And there was no reason to think he had hurt himself overmuch. He'd soon be back with his tail between his legs, and then she'd make him pay for doing this.

Arranging her face in a serene smile, Blanche called for her maids, left her chamber, and proceeded in stately fashion to the Great Hall. The whole day had passed in a fruitless search for Tristan while she lay in her chamber and waited for him to return. Since he hadn't, she would face the world alone. And what better time than now, while the glow of the wedding still lay over all the court? Whatever happened, a bride and bridegroom were forgiven everything in the first flush of wedded bliss.

Now the Great Hall lay ahead, tender with the magic light of the hour when day reluctantly hands over to night. The last of the sun lay like gold on the polished floor, while banks of candles beamed down from the walls. Massed heaps of summer blooms flamed on the wide hearths, roses and peonies, foxgloves and guelder flowers, all filling the air. Dotted throughout the high-vaulted chamber, the court bloomed too, ladies fragrant in flower-like silks, knights and lords richly clad in silver and satin, velvet and ancient furs. She might have stumbled upon a fairy cave.

"Yesssss . . ."

Blanche gave a hiss of satisfaction. With or without my husband, this is my place.

"The Queen of Lyonesse!" bellowed the chamberlain as she stepped in.

All eyes were upon her now, and she knew she had never looked better in her life. Her white satin gown shimmered with crystal and pearls, and the gossamer veil gleamed with silver filigree. Fine ropes of seed pearls adorned her long white neck and glistened on her wrists and encircled her waist. But best of all was the tall, queenly crown she wore as a sign of her new royalty. Another treasure from King Hoel's ancient store, it sat like a tower on her small round head, its high gold walls blazing with stones like fire.

"Your Majesty—"

"Your Majesty—"

"Oh, madame—"

Nodding and smiling, Blanche progressed through the court, accepting the congratulations on all sides. Ahead of her, King Hoel and her brother Kedrin stood waiting on the dais, sharing looks of unease. Where was Tristan? was written on their knotted brows.

"Madame, let me touch your robe . . ."

An ancient dame reached out a trembling hand. "Bless you, Princess. Once a woman's married, all the secrets of the Mother are hers."

Once a woman's married . . . ?

And there it was again, the stinging distress. Were they all thinking that? Suddenly she thought all the courtiers were giving her sly glances and greasy stares, the men at the back grinning behind their hands, the women sharing coy blushes and the bold-eyed, curious stares of those who longed to know a man and now took her for one who had. But it was false. She was married and not married, she was a virgin yet she'd been naked in a bed, alone with a man.

And the man she loved had willfully put her in this predicament?

Had he ever loved her at all?

Her head swam. Had she ever loved him?

Gods above, how the roses stank! The oversweet savor was more than she could bear. Faces pressed in upon her, surrounding her on all sides. She had to get out.

"Ah, Majesty—what a sight you are."

Saint Roc, it was Saint Roc. Blanche turned to him with a wild impulse of relief. But she mustn't encourage him. She felt her hand seized and raised to the wretched man's lips as she groped for a cutting response.

"You are magnificent tonight," he purred. "But where is your husband? Where are you hiding him?" He raised his eyebrows and sardonically scanned the hall. "I was hoping to pay my respects to the King of Lyonesse."

Respects? She stifled a hysterical laugh. "The King is indisposed," she said distantly. "The excitement of the wedding was too much for him. He's suffered a slight recurrence of his injury."

"Alas, alas," said Saint Roc without a trace of regret. "So we commiserate with him, no? And in the meantime, we enjoy your company?"

He was still holding her hand. Was she dreaming, or were his fingers playing with her palm? He was certainly staring too deeply into her eyes. To her horror, she felt her blood stirring under his questioning gaze. Could he possibly know what had happened last night?

Last night ...

Why had Tristan fled from her embrace?

Why?

A dull, unhappy flush spread over her neck. "So, sir," she forced out with a hollow gaiety, "did you dance at my wedding? Did your bad leg hold out?" Resolutely, she twitched her hand out of his grasp.

Saint Roc arched his eyebrows and prepared to enjoy himself. She had married Tristan to make him jealous: he was entitled to a little sport at her expense. "Dance, madame?" he sighed. "I could not dance. The pain I suffer lies not in my leg."

"Where, then?"

"In my heart. You have broken my heart."

"How so?"

Another soulful sigh. "You were too good for me. I offered you my all, but it was not enough. A lady like you, a beauty, and a healer too ..."

"Alas, it's true ..." In spite of herself, Blanche was enjoying this.

"So I lost you," he pressed on. "To my eternal grief."

Somehow, Blanche noticed, he had recaptured her hand. Well, he was suffering, to be sure. She felt moved to comfort him. "Oh, sir—"

"Why should I dance last night," he broke in, staring into her eyes, "when I knew that you lay all night in another man's arms?" He paused with teasing emphasis, his voice throbbing on every note. "When the jewel I craved was given to him, not to me."

My jewel, yes!

Blanche's blood ran roaring through her veins. *Any other man would be proud to make me his bride. But Tristan looked at me like a monster. I wanted to love him and he was ready to kill himself to get away from me . . .*

Her face flamed. Hard bright tears burst in the corner of her eyes. She opened her mouth to speak, and gasped for breath.

Saint Roc froze. How had he hit that nerve? What had he said? That she'd lain in his rival's arms, given him the treasure of her maidenhead . . .

Gods and Great Ones, she's still a virgin! Taking in Blanche's quivering lips and wounded eyes, Saint Roc wanted to laugh. This was not a girl who had been tenderly led into the arms of love, or a woman rejoicing in newly discovered bliss. Then pity swept him: *alas, poor child. What had happened in her chamber last night?*

He locked eyes with her again. What she needed now was some comfort and the strength to face the court. "And your marriage, madame," he picked up with new intensity, "has only increased your beauty in my eyes. All men must love you tonight. Every knight, every lord, would count himself in heaven to kneel at your feet."

Blanche's trembling stilled. Heartened, she noticed for the first time his crisp, curling hair as black as ash buds in March, his vivid brown eyes, his strong, even ruthless hands. His well-cut leather tunic was studded as if for war, and not one but two bright daggers gleamed at his waist. *This was a man.*

Not a weakling like Tristan, to take fright and flee like a girl. Well, wherever he was, he was reaping his just deserts. He could be lost in the woodland now, after falling like that. If he was, serve him right. In fact, it might be the best outcome if he never came back at all . . .

Blanche straightened her back and thrust her head in the air. *I am Princess of France and Queen of Lyonesse. A beauty and a healer, Saint Roc said . . .*

His seductive voice sounded again in her ear. "So, Majesty, will you dance?"

"Dance with you, sir?" She turned and looked him boldly in the eye. "All night, if you will."

chapter 44

With an eye on the sun, Brangwain rode out of the stable yard and made for the high road. Already she was warming to the solid, slow beast who would be her companion today. The broad-backed cob was everything she wanted, steady and strong. She leaned forward to pull the warm, furry ears and drew comfort from his wholesome grassy smell. "To the woods, then, my friend," she murmured. "Now, which way?"

The horse turned his head and good-naturedly nudged Brangwain's boot. *You have the reins, lady. You decide.*

The high road stretched before her, white with dust. Dark green on the far horizon spread the Lady Wood, covering the mountainside with oak and pine. Above it the ghost of a moon still hung in the sky, gilded by the rays of the morning sun. Brangwain smiled again, more hopefully this time. The moon, a clear sign of the Goddess, and a deep woodland running away out of sight? He was there, she knew it. *Hold on, sir. Hold on.*

She gave the horse his head. Soothed by the regular sound of his plodding hooves, Brangwain watched the forest drawing nearer step by step. With every clopping footfall, her confidence grew. *I'll find you, my lord, if you're there.*

If you're there. Shivering, she thrust the thought away.

And still the dark forest clung to the mountaintop, silent and aloof. In the valley below lay a wide shining lake, its glassy surface sheltered by an arch of trees. Weeping willow and slender silver birch leaned over the still water like praying hands.

And praises to the Great One, she was nearing it at last. Ahead of them the lake lay shimmering in the heat. A soft mist rose to welcome them as they came up. Brangwain bowed her head. Greetings to you, lady of this lake. Bless my search, I beg you, for my lady's sake.

Damsel flies danced and hovered overhead, flirting with the lordly dragon flies. Horse and rider skirted the soft margin of the mere, scattering shining clouds of little winged blue-green things, as Brangwain drew the damp fragrance deep into her lungs and studied the gaps in the looming forest wall. Tell me, lady, which way? As she pondered, the horse set off without urging toward the farthest track. Brangwain stroked the muscular, comforting neck. Yes, you know the way, my friend.

The air was cool and fragrant under the trees, a welcome relief from the blazing heat of the sun. As they went farther in, the vast woodland was alive with the drowsy hum of summer insects on the wing. Tall trees soared like pillars on every side, supporting a dense leafy canopy overhead. Brangwain fell again into prayerful thoughts. She was in a living temple from an older world.

Now the sun was at its fiercest, and all the earth reveled in its hot embrace. Above her head the forest was roofed with fire, the leaves filtering the sun's white-hot rays. Nestling among the boughs were pink-breasted wood pigeons and white-winged doves, roosting out of the heat of the sun. The air was heavy with the scent of pine, and the loam underfoot seemed to sigh with bliss.

She traveled onward, mile by laborious mile. The day was passing, she knew, but she could not tell the time because the trees were too dense to give her a sight of the sun.

Ride a little . . .

Cast around . . . Dismount . . .

Slowly, the air grew cooler under the trees. The dazzling sun had gone from the forest roof, and soon it grew harder to see in the light.

Now she could not silence the inner whispering. You can't search the whole forest, you know. He could be anywhere, miles away from here. And if you do find him, will he still be alive? With all he's suffered, he could be dead by now.

Her heart grew cold. I know.

At a fork in the path stood an ancient oak, its trunk densely covered with ivy and honeysuckle. Ten years slipped away, and Brangwain heard again the pledge Tristan had delivered to Isolde with shining eyes. *As the ivy and the honeysuckle so are we. In the heart of the darkest forest, they flourish as one. And so it will be with us, two hearts, one soul, our lives so entwined that each line and curve of one follows the outline of the other in deepest love.*

Brangwain felt herself dissolving into tears.

Oh, my poor lady. Oh, my lord, my lord . . .

She hung down her head and wept. When she opened her eyes, the light was almost gone and the first dews of evening were rising from the ground. She could not seek for Tristan in the dark. Soon she would be benighted in the wood.

Goddess, Mother, help me . . .

There was a light scuffling in the wood behind. Turning, she saw a great deer among her offspring, regarding her steadily from a nearby glade. As tall as a six-point stag, she stood poised and erect, her russet flanks dappled with pale love-spots like all her kind. Sensing a stranger, her brood kicked up their heels and were gone, but the doe held her ground, her large dark eyes fixed on Brangwain.

Silence filled the forest.

"Greetings, Mother," Brangwain heard herself saying in a reverent voice.

The graceful creature nodded. Greetings to you. She swung her head: this way.

Brangwain slipped from the saddle and tied the horse to a tree. A few strides and she reached the doe's secret glade. But already the deer had moved on. Brangwain gasped in fear. Don't leave me, don't go! Roughly, she set about pulling herself around. There's a reason for this. I know my lord is here.

She began to work her way around the clearing, lifting the bracken, probing the briars with a stick. After a while she took to feeling her way forward, sweeping the earth with her hands. Night had fallen on the forest, and the creatures of day had taken themselves to their beds. The evening dew had settled on the ground, and each plant, each leaf, felt cold and clammy now, like a dead man's hand.

When she found it then, she hardly knew what it was. Something cold and sinewy and tightly curled. A man's hand wearing a ring. It's the ring my lady gave him when they fell in love. It's Tristan.

Oh, my lord . . .

The thought came to her like a blow: he buried himself in this leaf-mold because he had no hope. He came here to die.

Brangwain threw back her head. Gods above, how can I tell my lady that you're dead? In a fury she grabbed at the wrist and felt for a pulse.

The night mist was falling, its cold fingers caressing her face and chilling her to the bone. The scent of decay rose from the loamy earth, and a faraway raven cried out to the rising moon. Her trembling fingers could feel no sign of life.

"Gods and Great Ones, help me!"

Cursing, weeping, careless of torn flesh and broken nails, Brangwain sank her hands in the earth and began to dig.

chapter 45

*a*lready the memory of his face was beginning to fade. Strangely, the tips of her fingers remembered its planes and hollows, the tender stubble of his jaw, better than she herself could recall how he looked. His voice was fainter too. Every day, Isolde thought of a thousand things he said. But the way he spoke, the rhythm of his tones, slipped like water through the fingers of her mind.

Tristan, Tristan . . .

But the pining, the pain, these did not fade at all. At night she dreamed he was with her, and woke in a cold empty bed, crying to dream again. Yet the dream itself was a dream, since they had so rarely been together in that way, or known what it was to sleep in each other's arms.

Some nights she had dreams of terrifying violence in which she watched him being waylaid and killed, and saw him lying dead in the heart of a dark wood. Yet even that was hardly as bad as waking each morning in the mists of ignorance that were drowning her now.

Where was he?

Was he injured, was he dead?

Had he married the French princess, or was that just Andred's desire to hurt, with no truth at all?

Andred . . .

She laughed bitterly to herself. While the man she loved was nowhere to be seen, her hated enemy was everywhere. Dawn and dusk he stalked the court, all smiles, dancing attendance on the King, feeding Mark's vanity, fulfilling his every whim. Yet Andred was also watching her, and she laughed at that too.

What can you do to me, Andred, more than you've done? You took my love when you sent Tristan away. Now he's gone, spy on me all you like, there is nothing to see. I am innocence itself these days.

And I am Queen of Ireland and Cornwall too.

So every morning she held up her head and looked the world in the eye, and every night she dressed herself regally and came down to the Great Hall to dine. In truth, she found eating as hard as sleeping, when one thought filled her mind. *When will Brangwain return?* But as long as she came to the High Table, Elva had no reason to queen it in her place.

And every night she was rewarded with a warm greeting from Sir Nabon and the rest of Mark's lords and knights. They at least were pleased she had returned to bring some order and decency to Mark's court. All the ladies too would happily cluster around, admiring her gowns of royal-blue and green, her veils of Irish lace as fine as the foam of the sea, her moonstones and gold. She found a special word for each of them in turn, and even the shyest would repay her with a shining smile.

Mark, however, took no pleasure in Isolde's return.

"What's the matter with her?" he grumbled to Andred at his side, watching Isolde's pale face as she toyed with her food. Soups and salads, whitebait in damson jelly, peacock broth and trenchers of roasted quail failed to interest his wife. Even great mouth-watering slabs of a whole roast boar dripping with fat, garlanded with apples, and piping hot from the spit, could not tempt Isolde's appetite. Mark was mystified.

"The Queen, sire?" Andred leaned forward attentively. "I fear she has not been herself since she returned."

Mark paused with his mouth half full. "What d'you mean?"

"They say she misses her knight."

"Tristan? Why should she miss him?" Mark waved his goblet at the knights' table farther down the hall. "There are a hundred here at her command."

Andred drew a careful breath. "But none, it seems, who can do for the Queen ... all that Sir Tristan did."

What did Tristan do? Mark stared at Andred, perplexed. "Well, there's none as big-built as Tristan, I grant you that."

"And Sir Tristan was so ... attentive."

"I suppose he was," Mark pondered. "Yes, he was always at her side."

Andred's black eyes gleamed. "Night and day, sire," he murmured. "Night and day."

"Yes, well . . ." Mark shuffled uneasily in his chair. What did Andred mean? He put the thought away.

"Some say Sir Tristan was everything to her," Andred insinuated.

"What?" Mark glowered. "Not as long as I'm her husband and she's my wife."

"As you say, sire." Andred made a well-judged retreat. "But she's not happy here in Cornwall, that's plain."

Happy? What did that matter? Mark tossed his head. Women should be pleasing to men, that was what they were for. His small eyes roamed the tables for a sight of his mistress, seated down the hall. Whenever he looked at Elva, he was rewarded with a smile. And more, much more. Elva understood that a man should always be pleased.

He grimaced to himself. In truth, Elva was not always submissive and sweet. When she was angry, she was like a wolf in her rage, and he had learned long ago to beware of her claws. But at least he could have the pleasure of taming her then, which only heightened the pleasure she gave him in return. Meanwhile, Isolde gave him nothing at all, only distant looks and coldness every day of the week.

A foolish smirk twisted his mouth. Well, he was King here, and she should know that. He raised his arm for a servant. "Fill the Queen's goblet!" he cried.

Isolde looked at him like a woman awakening from a dream. "Thank you, sire, no more."

Mark leaned over and patted her hand. "Drink up, my dear," he said in mock-jovial tones. "Let's get some color back into those pale cheeks of yours. I can see I've left you far too much to yourself."

Isolde searched his face, taking in his muddy complexion, mean eyes, and quarrelsome air.

Oh, Tristan, Tristan . . .

The air all around her grew dim, and she saw his face as she first knew it, golden in the springtime of their love. *You're the sea, I'm the land,* he had said then. *Land and sea together make the whole earth.* Nothing could match the sweetness of his smile. Nothing could compare with the touch of his hard huntsman's hand.

"Isolde?" came Mark's harsh, cawing voice in her ear.

She came to herself with a shudder, hardly knowing where she was. "As you wish, sire," she said tonelessly.

Mark's weak mouth hardened. *She thinks because she's a queen in her own right and I'm only a vassal king, she can brush me aside. Well, she must learn that she can't, and the sooner the better, it seems.* "Oh, I do," he insisted with an unpleasant smile. "I mean to make the most of your company while you're here."

Isolde felt a wisp of fear brush her heart.

"You're my wife, after all," Mark went on recklessly. A mad impulse seized him, and he ran with it like a hare. *So Isolde insisted on clinging to the Mother-right? Nothing like a sharp reminder that the most basic power of all lay with men. And men had used the weapon between their legs to tame unruly women since time began.*

"My wife," he resumed with growing force. "Father Dominian was talking to me about that."

Isolde stirred. What was Mark trying to say in such dark tones?

"A husband has rights, Isolde, that he can enforce. A willful woman is an abomination to God. Women were born for motherhood, and so were you. It's not too late to fulfill your marriage vows."

Fulfill what?

Isolde did not move. A stunned awareness made its way through her brain. *Mark is threatening me. If I don't behave, he's saying I can be raped. Oh, he'd never admit to it. But that's what he means.*

Would he do it? No, he's too much of a coward, he knows I'd fight. But a coward can be cruel when he drinks. Or if he's driven on by other men.

Fear clamped itself like a fist around her heart. She moistened her dry lips. "Sire," she began.

But Mark was in full cry. The flicker of terror in Isolde's eyes acted on him like the moment of kill at the hunt, gone in a second, but he had tasted blood. He laughed foolishly to himself. *Of course he'd never take Isolde by force, he felt nothing toward her that way. Dominian was dreaming if he thought there'd be a prince of Mark's loins from Isolde's thighs. But no harm in keeping her wide-eyed and white-faced.* It was good to see her so unnerved.

Smirking, Mark moved back again onto the kill. "And Andred tells me that you're pining for your knight. Well, we can't have that. I'll take you out hunting in the morning myself. And see there . . ."

He pointed to the knights carousing in the hall. "Tomorrow at dawn I'll have 'em all in the tiltyard, jousting for your favor, every man. Forget Tristan. You shall have a new champion, my Queen. And after that, I'll see he never leaves your side."

Isolde could hardly breathe.

Drink up.

I mean to make the most of your company . . .

You're my wife, Isolde. And a husband can enforce his rights.

You'll have a new champion, and he'll never leave your side . . .

Whichever way she turned, there was danger here. Dominian had been preying on Mark's fears, feeding his sense of entitlement, awakening his inadequacy. And her enemy, Andred, always had the King's ear. Had he persuaded Mark to keep a closer eye on her and give her a champion to watch her day and night, making her a prisoner in Castle Dore?

Yes. That's what he means to do.

Don't argue, don't protest.

Agree and delay.

She forced a sunny smile, and gave Mark a courteous bow. "Thank you, sire, for your kind care of me. Yes indeed, let us spend a day in the tiltyard with the flower of Cornwall's knights. I shall be honored to choose a knight from such a fine array."

And all the time, her desolate soul was crying to the moon, *Help me, Mother. Help me to get away!*

"**h**old on, sir. Hold on."

Brangwain dug steadily into the earth, throwing aside handfuls of the leaf-mold covering the motionless form. Tristan was lying on his side, curled up like a child, one arm thrown over his face. His clothes were soaked with dew and stiff with earth. His face, when she touched it, felt as cold as death. Again she felt for a pulse in his neck. Nothing. In the dusk of the nighttime forest, his skin had the pallor of the newly dead.

Brangwain could see now that he had dug out his resting place beneath the oak to make himself something like a shallow grave. Anger and desperation sharpened her tongue.

"You wanted to bury yourself, did you, sir? And what in the name of the Gods would my lady do then?"

If he was not dead, she wanted to kill him herself. She fell on him in a fury, shaking him with a strength she did not know she had. Then she rubbed his wrists to create some warmth and massaged his temples as fiercely as she dared.

"Wake up, sir!" she panted madly. "Wake up and live!"

She leaned on his chest with both hands, then did it again. The breath went out of his body with a dying sigh.

"Don't die!" she cried. She pounded her fists in a frenzy on the broad chest. "Don't you dare die!"

The waiting forest seemed to hold its breath. Nothing moved in the gloaming all around.

Through the silence came a sound like a falling leaf. Frantically, Brangwain strained to hear what it was.

"Br..."

And there it was again. A faint rustle, like the sighing of the forest as the winter storms draw near. Leaning over Tristan, she caught the ghost of a groan and the sound of her own name.

"Brangwain..."

"Goddess, Mother, thanks!" Tears poured from her eyes. "Praise the Gods, sir, that you're still alive."

Again came the sound like dead leaves. "Leave me."

"What?"

"Go back."

Brangwain's eyes bulged. "And leave you here? What would my lady say?"

Another groan that turned into a bitter laugh. "Nothing."

Brangwain shook her head. "What d'you mean?"

"The Queen has put an end to our love."

"She's—? Never!" Brangwain was outraged. "Oh, sir, you're not well. When you fell from that tower, I fear you damaged your mind."

Tristan came to life with a shudder. "I did not fall," he rasped. "I leapt out of the window and into the nearest tree."

Brangwain nodded. So that was how he flew out of the window like the Fair Ones and never touched the ground. Not that it mattered now. She seized Tristan by the shoulders. "See if you can stand, sir," she panted, "then we'll get you on my horse. I'll take you to the place where I stayed last night. We'll rest there till you're stronger, then take ship back to Cornwall as soon as we can."

Tristan groaned in despair. "Brangwain, the Queen won't see me. She wrote me a letter. You don't understand—"

"Oh, I think I do, sir." Brangwain smiled grimly to herself. Enough to smell a very big rat indeed, and I can guess his name. But plenty of time for that.

Tristan heaved himself up, shaking uncontrollably

"She told me, Brangwain—" he mumbled.

"Not now, sir."

The horse was still grazing peacefully in a patch of moonlight silvering the grass. "Be good, old friend," Brangwain implored.

Good as gold, lady, the mild beast nodded. I can see the knight is hurt.

Thankfully, Brangwain drew his hairy bulk alongside Tristan. "Mount up, sir."

Whatever effort it cost him, he did it without a sound. Swinging up in front, she flourished the reins and touched her spurs to the horse. "Hold on, sir. And get on, boy, get on."

The horse set off down the track at a stately pace. Brangwain sighed with relief. Soon have him back at the alehouse and in a warm bed. "D'you hear me, sir?" she began. "You said you had a letter, sir, here at the court in France?"

"From the Queen," he said in a voice rough with distress. "Ending our love."

"And did you believe it?" Brangwain clucked her tongue disapprovingly.

"It was in her hand."

"But why should she do such a thing?"

She could feel him start to tremble behind her back. "Because I failed her, Brangwain. I thought she could not forgive."

"I swear to you, she never wrote such a thing."

Tristan gasped in horror. "She didn't write it . . . ?"

Sorrowfully, Brangwain shook her head. "Quite the opposite, sir. She sent me to find you and bring you safely back. She's never wavered in her love for you."

Cold as he was, she could tell he was sweating too. His scent, sharp and feral, filled the air, and a low moan of torment reached her ear.

"Recreant again! I have betrayed my lady and my love."

Brangwain frowned. "My lady will forgive you, sir, never fear, when I get you back."

The trees were thinning now at the forest's edge. The high road rolled out to the horizon ahead, scarring the midnight landscape like a slash of chalk. Brangwain peered through the shadowy foliage with thoughts full of hope, the alehouse, food and drink, helping hands, rest and sanctuary . . .

"Halt there, lady."

Half a dozen men stepped out of the shadow of the trees and the leader seized the reins. An iron band of fear clamped around Brangwain's throat.

"On your way, man," she ordered hoarsely. "You have no business waylaying innocent travelers through your land."

The moonlight shone down on the leader's drawn sword. And now Brangwain saw his tunic with its royal badge.

"Oh lady," he laughed. "You're our business now."

She made one last effort, driven by despair. "I have a sick man here I'm taking to the coast. For pity's sake, don't detain us now."

"That's Sir Tristan, isn't it?" The leader pointed to the silent shape behind her back. "We're under orders to bring him back to court."

Tristan twitched and came to life.

"To King Hoel?" he said hoarsely.

The captain sniggered. "To the new Queen, sir. To your wife, the Princess Blanche."

chapter 47

*a*gain! Play again!"

The tinkling command rang out above the noise of the court. On the dais above the buzzing crowd, the little band of musicians shared a silent glance. The leader took up his instrument and nodded to his son. "Warble, boy. The Queen wants to dance."

The pale, frog-faced child tilted his chin inquiringly. "She was only a princess last week."

"Well, she's Queen of Lyonesse now, and she wants us to play." He gave his long-suffering fellows a wry smile. "Come on, lads. She'll pay well for this, and you'll get to your beds in the end."

Briskly, the musicians moved into a lilting air. The floor of the Great Hall stirred like an eddying sea as couples picked up the tune and began to dance. Banks of bright candles danced along with them, their flames whispering and sighing all through the room.

"Again!" Blanche panted, laughing up at Saint Roc. Lifting her skirts, she twitched them flirtatiously to and fro. "Again!"

Saint Roc pulled a face. "You want to dance?" he teased. He fingered his well-shaped thigh provokingly. "Alas, my leg . . ."

"Your old wound?" Blanche giggled. She pounced on him, seizing both his hands. "I have a cure for that. You move your bad leg in time to the music, and I swear it gets better at once."

"You swear?" he murmured. He looked down into the lovely flushed face and laughing eyes, and breathed in her soft pink scent with deep content. Beware Saint Roc, he chided himself sadly, you're starting to care for this woman far more than you should.

And far more than she deserves, he reminded himself, suppressing an ironic smile. *Her husband is lying injured, and she's dancing with you? Is this the behavior of a loving wife?*

Looking around, he could see that others thought so too. Seated on the dais with the musicians, King Hoel reclined on his throne talking to Prince Kedrin, apparently at ease. But Saint Roc could detect the concern behind Hoel's casual glance as it swept the hall. It had been bad enough, Saint Roc knew, that the groom had not appeared for the festivities tonight. He had seen the King's frown of distress when Blanche airily announced that Tristan had stayed in bed. And if the King's eye fell on his newly wedded daughter laughing and frolicking in the arms of another man . . .

No, it must not be. No more dancing tonight.

"Alas, my Queen," he began, gently freeing his hands from Blanche's tenacious grip. But she was not listening. She was staring down the room, her eyes on the door.

Underneath the great stone arch at the end of the hall, a man at arms was in earnest conversation with the servant at the door.

Blanche turned to Saint Roc, tight-lipped. "I must go."

"Go?" He covered his surprise with a careless shrug. "Let me escort you, madame."

"No!" she cried. All the elation had drained from her face and two round red spots burned on her cheeks like shame. She forced a laugh. "Stay and enjoy the dancing. It will help your bad leg."

Saint Roc bowed. "Till tomorrow, then."

Intrigued, he watched her pounce on the man at arms and whisk him away. What had the man come to say? Saint Roc smiled. He would know soon enough. His fate was entwined with Blanche now, and in good time all her secrets would be his. And he had learned enough for one night to sweeten his dreams. One thing above all was now crystal clear. Blanche was not married to Tristan as he understood the word. And sooner or later, all the world would find out.

***

"WHERE IS HE? You brought him in here, you say?"

Raging, Blanche swept out of the courtyard with the man at arms and burst into the quiet infirmary. The light of the swan lamps illuminated the doctor, a couple of his nurses, and a lean, soberly dressed woman she did not know. Between them, Tristan lay on a table with his eyes closed, pale and still. The cloth beneath his body was stained with blood.

A rush of emotion seized her, though she hardly knew what she felt. An hour ago, she would have sworn that she didn't care if he never came back. But to see him lying like this—

"Tristan! Oh, my husband, my love." She rushed forward and seized his hand, kissing his lips. But his flesh was as cold as clay, and his mouth had the color and taste of newly turned earth. Blanche recoiled. "God in Heaven, where has he been?"

The doctor stepped forward. "On his deathbed, madame," he said heavily. "He was brought from the Lady Wood less than half alive."

Blanche considered. It was true that Tristan smelled loamy, like a newly made grave. But now he was here, he was safe in her healing hands. She put on a bright smile. "Well, we'll soon deal with that." She turned to the darkly clad woman. "And who are you?"

To her surprise, the woman did not curtsy and drop her eyes as those around her normally did. "I found Lord Tristan in the wood and brought him here," she said trenchantly. "They call me Brangwain, lady, and I serve Queen Isolde, the Queen of the Western Isle."

Blanche did not move. *So Isolde has not cast him off after all. She must still love him. Does she want him back?* She found another smile. "Queen Isolde sent you to look for him?"

Brangwain bowed stiffly. "My lady sent me to bring good wishes on your wedding to my lord." She pointed toward the table. "I am sorry to find him in such a bad way as this."

Blanche waved her white hand dismissively. "We'll have him right again in no time at all."

The doctor shook his head. "Lord Tristan is bleeding again from the wound in his head. And he seems to be sinking under some inner grief."

Blanche released her tinkling laugh. "No man dies of that!"

"Call it what you like," he insisted. "It is my judgment that he's lost the will to live."

"Nonsense! All he needs is a touch of my special elixir."

The doctor gasped. "The last time you employed that, the old man died."

Both of Blanche's hands were waving in the air. "I gave him too much. A drop of it will do wonders for Tristan, just a touch."

"Not one drop, madame," said the doctor tensely. A throbbing pulse beat at the side of his head. "We must clean his wounds and get him food and drink, and allow him to recover in his own time. Your remedy brings death, not life. I will not permit it."

"You will not?" Blanche's eyes flared. She gestured threateningly toward the man at arms at the door. "And who is Queen here, sir, me or you?"

The doctor stepped back, breathing heavily. "On your own head be it, madame!"

Brangwain moved to his side. "What is this?" she demanded in a low voice.

The doctor nodded bitterly toward Blanche. "See for yourself."

A curtsying nurse was placing a vial in Blanche's hand. Blanche waved to the other nurse. "Hold him up."

She opened the tiny bottle and poured a drop of the contents into Tristan's mouth. His body jerked violently and he jolted upright, arms and legs flailing as he sent the vial smashing to the floor. His eyes opened, empty and stark, and fastened on Blanche. Jerking uncontrollably, he tried to speak. A fit of coughing almost strangled his words. "This is my death."

"No!" Blanche wailed, trying to take his hand.

His eyes roamed wildly round the room. Brangwain stepped forward, mastering her distress. "Sir?"

"Goddess, Mother," the hoarse voice rasped. "Let me see Isolde before I die."

"You will not die," Blanche wept.

The doctor moved forward to stand at Tristan's side. "Lady, you and your potion have brought him to the edge of death. Send for Queen Isolde, I beg. It's all you can do for him now."

"No," Blanche cried, panic in her eyes. "What can she be to him? He's married to me."

"Hear me—" Tristan pointed a shaking hand at Blanche. "I set you free from the marriage to Saint Roc. Now I claim back my freedom from you. Our marriage is dissolved, now and evermore." He turned his head. "Brangwain?"

The maid stepped forward. "Here, sir," she said steadily. Tristan seized her hand. "The ships of Cornwall are known for their dark sails. If she comes, let her fit out her ship with white. Then I'll know that she can find it in her heart to forgive."

It was more than Brangwain could bear. "Sir, she'd come to you at the very ends of the earth. I swear to you, she'll understand and forgive."

Blanche, Falsamilla, Duessa scorched across Tristan's mind and he cried out in pain. "There's too much. If she can't forgive, let the sails be black."

Brangwain bowed her head. "I will, sir."

Tristan held out a hand to Blanche. "I pray you, help this lady all you can."

"I won't, I won't," Blanche shrilled, flapping her arms. To her fury, she felt tears coursing down her cheeks. "She can go if she likes, but Queen Isolde can't come here. You're my husband. It's not fair!"

"Then let me die."

Tristan closed his eyes and turned his face to the wall. There was a pitying silence. No one moved.

The doctor came forward. "Madame, do you want the world to say that you denied a dying man's last wish?"

"Oh, very well." She glared at the doctor and her pale face took on an ugly hue. "Have it your way, I'll leave him to your tender care."

The doctor hid his relief. "The Gods will reward you." He turned to deal with Tristan.

Blanche looked at the women in attendance and her spirit rebelled. Who were these creatures with their disapproving stares? Did they expect her to weep over Tristan or tend to him herself?

Why should she? She could not look at him. Not after he had humiliated her like this. What, to disavow their marriage, as if it meant nothing and she was nothing to him? Well, he'd shown his true colors and proved how worthless he was. He was a weakling, beneath her, a recreant knight. Why had she ever wanted him as her love?

And these wretched women with their goggling eyes!

Blanche turned on Brangwain like a striking snake. "And as for you, lady, be off, back to your Queen. But tell her that there's only one Queen at this court, and that is the wife of the King of Lyonesse!"

chapter 48

The little ship ran before the wind, its white sails flapping in the driving breeze. Hour by hour it held its course for France. And still the full-bellied clouds loomed up on the horizon as great as women with child, and labored out over the sea to shed their burden of rain. The wind-lashed sky wept with the troubled surf, and every wave seemed pregnant with untold grief. As flocks of seagulls quarreled and cried overhead, Isolde stared out from her cabin at the sorrowing sea. *All the world is in mourning for my love.*

For Tristan was lost to her now. He had married the French princess, Brangwain had told her as soon as she returned. For the rest of her life Isolde would remember the sick, shaking horror of that moment and the bleakness that gripped them both.

"What?" *I don't believe you.*

"He's married, lady. To the French princess."

"Married?" *He wouldn't do that—betray me like that.*

"He thought you'd betrayed him. He had a letter . . ."

Isolde nodded bitterly as Brangwain spoke. "Andred's work, of course. I understand. But still, to marry her—?"

Brangwain gave a desolate nod. "In church, in his finest array, before the King and all the court."

She had released her fury then in a lung-splitting cry. *"Why, Brangwain? Did you find out why?"*

"It doesn't matter why. I heard him tell her that the marriage was null and void. He still loves you, lady. It's you he wants to see."

But it did matter, it mattered terribly. Tristan could not end this marriage on his word alone. A marriage belonged to two people, and why

260

should Tristan's new wife be willing to let him go? He was Blanche's husband, and nothing could alter that.

And now he was dying and wanted to see her, Brangwain said. Could she get there in time? The call had found her ready, for when the maid arrived, she discovered Isolde preparing to leave Castle Dore.

Brangwain understood at once why she wanted to go. "The King threatening you, and Sir Andred watching your every move? Gods above, madam, you were wise to get away."

Was she? Or had she read too much into what Mark said? For all his threats, he had never tried to molest her before, and she doubted that he'd start now. *You know Mark. Always big and boastful in his drink, a prey to sudden impulses and flashes of cruelty But he's weak rather than wicked and all he wants is the easy way out.*

And Mark would not give a fig that she'd sailed away. While she was gone, he was free to hunt and indulge in all his bachelor pursuits. Her place at dinner, she knew, would be taken by Elva tonight, and Mark would not spare his departed wife a thought.

But Tristan, Tristan, are you still alive? Or has your spirit slipped its shell and begun its journey to the Fortunate Isles?

Trembling, she recalled Brangwain's account of Blanche's willful, even fatal attempt to heal.

"She said she had an elixir that would bring him back to life. But the doctor said it would poison him, and it did."

Isolde gasped with rage. "She gave it to him, despite what the doctor said?"

Brangwain nodded unhappily. "He was bad enough before, he was so ill. And afterward he was much worse."

Isolde closed her eyes. *So he could be dead by now, and I would not know.*

Yet above deck, the little ship was proudly flying a full set of billowing white sails. *White for life and the hope of love renewed. White as you asked, as a sign that I would come. Will you still be alive to see them, my love, or has the earth already gone over your dear eyes?*

These days, there was no escaping that. Seeing after seeing plagued her now, visions, fragments, pieces of unreality, fears and bad dreams. She saw Tristan lying dead in a hundred different ways, and Blanche burying him where his body could never be found. Then other times she saw him well again, strong and happy as he always was, restored to his full health.

Oh, my love, my love, I've lost you, our love is gone . . .

For whatever happened, he could never be hers again. If he died, she would never see him again in this world. If he lived, he was lost to her, too, now he'd tied himself to Blanche.

"He loves you, lady!" Brangwain had sworn fiercely as she told her tale.

"He still married her!"

Brangwain was in tears. "But he's only thinking of you. He says he'll beg your forgiveness if he sees you again."

My forgiveness? Can I truly forgive?

Yes, perhaps.

Marrying another woman, even sleeping with her?

Perhaps even that.

So, what now? What would she find in France?

A brief farewell, if he lived. And if he did not, what then? *Life is nothing to me, love, as soon as you are gone.* Would she make the dark journey too? Follow in his footsteps down to the Otherworld?

"Ho there!"

There was a confused shouting on the upper deck. The cabin door burst open and Brangwain flew in. "Land ahoy, lady," she cried. "Sir Tristan will see our white sails and he'll know you've forgiven him and still love him in spite of everything!"

Isolde stared out through the porthole at the approaching land. *Do I? Is that true?*

The white sails cracked and groaned overhead. *Yes, I do. Till all the seas run together and the waters bury the land. I'm the sea, you're the land. Sea and land together make a world. Hold fast, love, I am coming. I am here.*

The cries of the sailors sounded clearly now. "Yarely, mister—broadside on, bring her in!"

Isolde brought her hands together in a solemn prayer. *Goddess, Mother, bring me to my love.*

EVENING SETTLED ON the roofs of Castle Hoel. Unmoving, like a spider in her web, Blanche sat alone in her tower and waited for the word. It was swift in coming, as she knew it would be. She had taken care to put the lookout in fear of death.

And here he was, scuttling fearfully in. "A ship from Cornwall?" She leaped to her feet. "And the sails?"

One glance at his face prepared her for his reply. "White, lady. Like the wings of a swan."

White sails?

So be it.

Blanche's wooden heels knocked on the floors as she ran. Hurry, hurry, get to Tristan before the ship reaches the dock, no one else must give him the news.

Tears of anger and jealousy surged up to choke her throat. Tristan, who had scorned her and shamed her and refused her love. The knight she had made her own chosen one, who had chosen another woman over her . . .

Panting, she burst through the infirmary door. Standing over Tristan, the doctor held up a hand in alarm. "One moment, madame. No excitement, please—"

But she could not contain herself. "Tristan, your answer has come!"

Tristan reared up, his eyes dark hollows in his skull. "A ship from Cornwall?" he husked. "What sails?"

"Black!" she gasped out with inhuman glee. "Black as death itself from stem to stern."

"Black?" The gaunt figure on the bed stared like a madman.

"You are mine now," Blanche exulted. "No more Isolde, only Blanche, your wife."

"Isolde!" Tristan threw back his head in a long, animal cry. Then the light left his eyes and he crumpled sideways on the bed.

"Gods above, see what you've done!" the doctor cried. Urgently, he set to work chafing the cold hands and rhythmically working each of the inert limbs. "I told you a shock could be too much for him. I fear this is fatal, lady, weak as he was. Prepare yourself for the worst."

Blanche stood transfixed. No, it couldn't be. Nobody died from hearing bad news. She'd only meant to punish Tristan for the way he'd treated her. How could she have known that he'd take it like this? She squared her shoulders and mutinously set her chin. What had she done wrong?

264 / ROSALIND MILES

There was a disturbance at the door and one of the attendants appeared. "The ship from Cornwall is standing at the quay. The captain requests permission for his Queen to come ashore."

"His Queen?"

It was the doctor, his face white with outrage. "You mean Queen Isolde? She's here?"

The attendant bowed. "She is, sir, and anxious to land."

"Yes, of course she can land," Blanche blustered, desperately avoiding the doctor's eyes. "Send to the quay and escort the Queen here at once."

She threw a defiant look at the doctor: there! It's all turned out right in the end. She'll soon be here. He can see her now.

But the doctor had turned back to the still form on the bed and was shining a candle into Tristan's eyes. Moments later he confronted Blanche with an expression she had never seen before. "Madame, your healing hands have done their work. Your husband is dead."

chapter 49

The little ship nestled comfortably at the quay. Isolde stood on the deck with Brangwain, containing her soul with a desperate calm. Never had a landing seemed so wearisome, so long. Each grappling hook, every rope, every bantering exchange between the sailors and the men on the dock ate into her soul. *Help me, Mother, help me. Bring me to my love.*

The ship's captain came toward her, cap in hand. "Will you disembark, my lady? An escort of men at arms is here for you."

She had dressed for this in her simplest array.

"No need to outqueen Blanche," she told Brangwain lightly, silencing the jealous murmurings of her soul. "I haven't come here as Queen. I am here to see Tristan."

If he still lives hung unspoken in the air. *And if not, the Western Isle in all its glory is nothing to me.*

So she left the ship in a gown of plain green silk, green for the heart of the woodland, green for the sea. But Brangwain had had her way with the royal jewels of the Western Isle, and Isolde stepped out with the crown of the Queens of Ireland upon her head and ropes of crystal and emerald at her neck and waist. With the little troop of guards marching ahead and Brangwain behind, she climbed up from the harbor and followed the men through the town.

Castle Hoel lay beyond on a low hill, its back to the forest, its handsome face to the sea. The slow descent of evening silvered its roofs and towers and drifted down on its courtyards in wreaths of lilac and gray. Isolde felt the weight of her fear growing with every step. *Where are you, Tristan? Are you there, my love?*

"This way, my lady." The leader of the men at arms pointed to a low white building ahead. Isolde nodded. *The infirmary, of course.* In spite of herself, her heart leapt in her breast. *Not the graveyard nor the crypt, so there is still hope. Goddess, Mother, save him! Save my love.*

The lights of the infirmary beckoned through the growing dark. As they gained the threshold, a low, mournful sound rang out.

"What's that?" Brangwain cried.

Isolde could not speak. *It's the bell the Christians ring when someone dies. Have I come so far and missed you now, my love? Is this your death knell?*

Confronting her in the doorway was a young woman dressed in white, clasping her long white hands with a trembling air. Isolde drew a breath. Was this her rival? This pale-eyed, pouting girl, her white face disfigured with tears? *Why, she's only a girl. She'd have seemed like a child to him. He could never have loved her as he loved me.*

The young woman threw back her head and came forward with a regal air. "Queen Isolde, welcome!" she declaimed. "I am Queen Blanche of Castle Hoel and Lyonesse."

Castle Hoel and Lyonesse. It sounded like a hiss. For some reason, an angry swan came into Isolde's mind. She inclined her head.

"Greetings to you, madame," she said distantly. "I am here to see Sir Tristan."

Blanche gave an ugly grimace. "Oh, so?"

Isolde leaned forward to add weight to her words. "By his invitation, lady. Please take me to him at once."

"You came to see my husband?" Blanche let out a high, cracked laugh. "You're too late."

Somewhere in the castle the death knell tolled again. *So the bell was for you, Tristan. Oh my love, my love . . .*

The hateful voice chimed on. "He died a few minutes ago." Blanche's pale eyes flashed. "You missed him by a hair."

And that pleases you, of course. Isolde nodded. "May I see him?"

"See him?" Blanche shook her head. "Oh, no!" What, let this tall, queenly woman with the fathomless green eyes know that she herself had no access to Tristan? That as the nurses came forward to lay him out, the doctor had banished her from her husband's side?

"Give him peace in the grave, at least," he had said. Blanche winced to recall the withering contempt and knew the rebuke would be with her all her life. Well, the doctor would soon be on his way, dispatched with a flea in his ear to take his skills elsewhere. But for now . . .

She squinted at Isolde disdainfully. "You want to see my husband's body? No, that's not possible. My husband has already been taken away."

Your husband, your husband ... is he yours now forevermore?

Isolde straightened her back. "Then I'd like to visit his grave."

"He will have no grave. In this country we give our dead back to the sea." And a good thing too! she was longing to say. The sooner he's gone, the better it will be. Did I ever love him? Did I really kiss that disgusting, cold, clay-like face?

Given to the sea. Isolde nodded dumbly. *Our first mother, from which all life springs. The last circle of the Goddess for men whose graves lie there.*

Sharp unshed tears were stinging the back of her eyes. She turned her gaze on Blanche, dilated and wild. *So he's gone. And you hastened his death.*

Blanche gave a strident laugh. "I know you must hate me."

"Hate you ... ?"

How young she was. Isolde shook her head. No, Blanche would never be important enough for that. "This is no time for hate. May your Gods bring you to a better life."

"Me?" Blanche's pale face assumed a furious frown. "What d'you mean?"

What did I mean?

A tremor racked Isolde from head to foot. Her sight faded, and she saw an angry sea. Raging waves dashed themselves on rocks at her feet and spent their force against the cliff behind. She was standing in the waves, she was the waves, she was the sea. With spray in her eyes and spindrift foaming her hair, she heard a voice. *Speak for me now. You are the Lady of the Sea.*

In a voice like the tide, she began to speak. "Your nature is formed like the ocean to beat on the shore. But the ocean rages alone, though it floods the whole earth. If you seek a true partner for life, look for still waters and calmer inlets where love may rush in." Dimly she caught Blanche's sharp intake of breath. "Oh, yes! Love is coming for you, though Tristan was not the man."

She paused. "Love is waiting for you," she repeated. "He is here."

She saw a light of apprehension dawn in Blanche's eyes. "I ... I—"

"You fear to lose yourself in the love of a man. But remember, men and women together make up the world. The love of another transcends our own selfish will. Love alone will bring you to the land of your heart's desire."

She bowed and turned away. "And so, farewell. Come, Brangwain, let's be gone."

"At once, my lady."

Brangwain gave Blanche the deepest, fullest curtsy of her life. Rising to her feet, she leaned forward with a scornful smile. "My lady may forgive you," she hissed, "but the Great Ones won't!"

Triumphantly, she hurried after Isolde. "Well, lady? What now?"

The bell began to sound again overhead. Isolde paused, her head tilted to one side as she counted the melancholy strokes. "Why, nothing," she said in a voice as flat as a child's. "Unless to die."

"Die, lady?" Brangwain gasped. "What nonsense is this? You aren't going to die."

The death knell rang between them with the sound of doom.

Not die? Isolde shook her head. *When my love is dead?* She drifted out through the courtyard and down into the town. A weeping woman pulled at Isolde's sleeve. "Is it Sir Tristan?" Her frame was racked with sobs.

Isolde nodded. *So they loved you here as much as they did at home. Of course they would. All the world loved Tristan.*

Ahead of them the little ship rode at anchor in the quay. Isolde could still taste the salt of the voyage in her eyes and mouth. *So will it be for my love when they give him to the sea.*

The sea was ebbing with a dying sigh. The solitary bell tolled on overhead. Isolde made her way down through the town with Brangwain, scarcely feeling the cobbled streets beneath her feet. *On such a tide I shall leave the world. This time tomorrow, I shall be gone.*

She moved forward with new purpose, and the green mists of night took her in their embrace. *Wait for me, sweetheart, where the sea meets the sky.*

"What now, lady?"

Isolde turned. There was a new, transcendent light in her eye.

Brangwain bit back a sudden alarm. "Come, lady," she said roughly, "let's get to the ship. We should sail for Ireland tonight." Fear clutched at her stomach. *Or anywhere,* please the Gods . . .

Isolde gave an Otherwordly smile. "Let's get to the ship. It is time to die."

chapter 50

Yes, summer was on the wane. Never mind, the hunting was even
better in winter when the game was scarcer and the dogs were
more fierce. Savoring the first chill of autumn, Mark strode out of his private apartments and crossed to the Audience Chamber with a spring in
his step. What would it be today? Mark glanced idly about the chamber
as he took his throne. One or two odd souls clutching petitions,
shouldn't be hard to get rid of them. And the others? Nothing to speak
of. A few brisk exchanges, and then away to try out that new hunter, the
big bay. An awkward great thing and ugly from muzzle to hocks, but a
heart as big as a haystack, he'd go all day . . .

"Sire—"

It was Andred.

Reluctantly, Mark wrenched his mind back from the stables as his
nephew spoke. Glittering in black and silver, he cut a distracting figure
with Elva beside him shimmering in serpentine green, and Mark struggled to grasp what Andred was trying to say. "Gone?" He frowned suspiciously. "What d'you mean, gone?"

"The Queen has fled, my lord. Sailed away."

"Isolde's taken ship?" Mark's eyes bulged. He chewed on his lower lip.
"Without a word?"

Andred shrugged. "She sent a message from the dock, it seems, but
nothing to explain this sudden haste."

Standing beside Andred, Elva fluttered her silks and nodded. "Of
course, Your Majesty may guess where she has gone."

"Back to Ireland?"

Andred spread his hands. "I fear not, sire. They said on the dock the ship was bound for France."

Mark paused. "She's gone to Tristan?" A slow anger began to beat inside his skull. Already he could hear the gossip in the town.

The Queen's gone! Hopped off and left the King, gone to France, they say, following her knight.

What's the King going to do?

And then the sneering whisper, the contemptuous laugh. The King? Nothing. He can't control his wife.

He can't control his wife...

Without warning, his father burst across his mind, sword and horse-whip in hand, shouting and bullying as he'd done all his life. "Gods above, boy, can't you do anything? Where's your authority? You'll never make a king."

And now Isolde had gone to Tristan. What did it mean? Gnawing on the side of his thumb, he tried to think. Dominian would say she was not a dutiful wife. Well, that was true. He gave a bitter laugh.

But Dominian was nothing. In truth, Andred's nods and hints concerned him more. What had Andred been saying in recent weeks? That Tristan would do more for Isolde than any other knight? That he never left her side? Meaning what? Mark twitched and tossed his long legs about. Meaning something he did not want to think.

And Tristan, what was his game? He must have recovered long ago from his wound. Was he staying in France to draw Isolde there, ready to welcome her as soon as she arrived? Was his marriage to the French princess a sham? But then why marry her?

"Sire?"

Mark's brain was buzzing like a beehive in spring. "What?"

It was Andred again. "There's a letter, sire—in the Queen's own hand."

Mark's meager soul shrank. "A letter? Who to?"

"To the Princess of France. I looked into her quarters to make sure she'd gone, and it was among the papers she left behind."

Mark squinted through the window at the brilliant sky. Soon the day would be gone, and with it any chance to try out the great bay. And now this letter—furiously, he snatched it from Andred and opened it up.

To Your Highness of France
You have with you my knight, Sir Tristan of Lyonesse. To me he
is the one . . .

The rest of the sentence was heavily scratched out.

I have written him many letters without a reply. Is he too sick to
hold a pen? Too sick to read what I write, or know that I am writ-
ing to him?
    If he is, this will be a grievous loss to m . . .

More heavy blotting obscured the next words.

Now word has reached me that you and he are to wed. You should
know he was sworn to me with unbreakable oaths. If he takes
you, he breaks his vow to me. If you take him, you take him
knowing that.
    For ten years and more I have enjoyed his love . . .

HERE THE PEN trailed away and the letter broke off. The last line had
been crossed through but could still be read. The meaning was plain. *For
ten years and more I have enjoyed his love.*

Almighty God, were they lovers, then? Had Tristan been cuckolding
him for ten years and more? And during all that time, had his wife who
was no wife played him for a fool and given his marital rights away?

Malice poured like poison through Mark's veins and his brain shriveled to a seething ball. If they'd shamed him, he would have his revenge.
It shouldn't take much to show the world what they were.

"Those knights of yours," he said thickly to the waiting Andred. "Fer
de Gambon and Taboral—are those their damned names?"

"Yes, sire."

"And they're good lads, would you say?"

Andred paused, his mind racing. "It depends on what Your Majesty
wants them to do. But they'll obey your bidding, sire, no questions
asked."

"No questions asked," Mark repeated with relish. His pebbly eyes were unnaturally bright. "Good. Get them here, then. Order a supper for the four of us alone, and tell them to be in attendance for as long as I need."

"Sire." Andred nodded. What scheme was Mark hatching in his slender brain? "I go."

"And Andred..." Mark's venomous tones reached him at the door. "Command horses for us all tomorrow at dawn. Then send a galloper to—no, I'll send him myself." He gave a peculiar laugh.

"My lord..." Andred checked himself on the threshold. "May I ask what—?"

Mark threw him a filthy look. "Oh, I know you think I can't do anything without you. But you'll be surprised. We're going on a journey and I'm going to—" He laughed again, an unnerving sound. "Well, I shan't tell you what I'm going to do. But I'll do it all the same."

"Indeed, my lord." Andred struggled for control. "And then?"

Mark flared his eyes. "You'll see. And so will all the world!"

chapter 51

The sun rose in a haze of purple and gray. Troubled clouds lurked on the horizon, drawing down the day before it had begun. Isolde left her cabin and mounted to the deck, feeling the twilight seeping through her soul. *This is the evening of my life, and the darkness is near.*

The rich salty smell of the ocean came toward her, wild and free. Beyond the harbor she could see the swell of the waves, as welcoming as a woman's bosom, soft and round. She nodded to herself. *Tonight the Mother will take me in her arms. I shall sail out to sea and I shall find my love.*

A brisk rustle of skirts behind her announced Brangwain's approach. "A fine day, lady," the maid said heartily.

Isolde did not turn.

"Well, a new day," Brangwain went on hollowly. And a new life for you, lady, she wanted to say, but did not. "To Ireland, is it, on the morning tide?"

Isolde shook her head. "Into the sunset, Brangwain. To the Islands of the Blessed, when the tide runs free." *And into the arms of the Mother to meet my love.*

Brangwain moved around to face her. "I shall come with you," she said decisively.

Isolde smiled at the maid's attempts to thwart her plans. Brangwain knew that she would never take any life but her own. "I forbid it," she said clearly. "I shall go alone. You must stay behind to take word to Cornwall and the Western Isle, and tell our true story when Tristan and I are gone."

Brangwain twisted her hands and paced to and fro. "What about Ireland, madam? You're our Queen! Would you leave our land ungoverned and prey to wicked men?"

"Queens of the Western Isle have come and gone. Erin herself will endure for a thousand years. She will not lack a worthy guardian after me."

"Lady, you have had a great sorrow, but sorrows pass." And Sir Tristan was not the only man in the world, she tried to convey. *You will love and be loved again. Life goes on.*

There was a pensive silence. "Sorrows?" Isolde questioned, almost to herself. *Sorrows may pass indeed, but I am sorrow itself.*

Brangwain held out both hands. "Lady, I beg you, do not do this thing—"

"No more words." Again the Otherworldly smile. "You've helped me all my life. Stay with me now. I need an old boat, at the end of its life. Then flowers, whatever can be found now that summer's gone."

A boat? And flowers? Numbly, Brangwain trailed behind her mistress the length of the quay and out onto the sea wall as Isolde spoke earnestly to the fisherfolk and sailors busy working there. At last she settled on a small, open boat, an ancient but shapely craft in a sea-washed green. It was short work, then, to arrange for it to be moored where the evening tide would carry it out to sea.

And never had Isolde looked more beautiful, Brangwain noted with an aching heart. In her simple green gown, with her red hair unbound, she blazed like a flower of the forest that lives for a only day. Dazzled by Isolde herself as much as by her gold, the old seaman who sold her the boat was ready to fulfill her every whim.

"Holes in the sides, lady?" he queried, scratching his head.

Isolde traced a line along both sides of the hull. "Here, and here."

Brangwain nodded grimly to herself. Low enough to admit enough water to scuttle the boat. High enough to take Isolde far out to sea, where the waves were deep and she could not swim back to shore.

Isolde moved away, her eyes on the distant fields beyond the town.

"I'm going for the flowers," she said.

"Let me help you."

Isolde smiled. "I want to go alone."

Beyond the little harbor and the town, the countryside lay open to the noonday sun. Green fields and rambling meadows ran along the bay to the cliffs above. Isolde struck off up the hillside, quite alone. *Except for you, my love.*

For he was still on this earth, she could tell. His spirit was with her now, he was at her side. *You're so close, I can touch you if I put out my hand.* She gave him a dreamy smile. *You're waiting for me, I know.*

Above her a lark sang in the cloudless sky. Without warning a mighty sea eagle flew out of the sun, then glided serenely away on its rippling wings. She watched it with speechless delight. *Is that you, my love? Your spirit soared like that, proud and free. You are free again now, wherever your spirit roams.*

As I shall be, when I sail on the evening tide.

Alas, no, Isolde. You will not sleep with your love tonight.

It was the voice of her mother dropping through the veils of cloud like the song of the lark. *Your life is not yours to squander. You threw it away once when you married King Mark without love. You may not do so again.*

But to live without Tristan, Mother—without love—

Ah, little one, all lovers must live without love in the end.

You never did. You always chose love.

And do you choose to be like me?

Isolde came to herself with a shudder. *Mother, no! Your choices brought Tolen and Breccan into our land and led to the deaths of good men like Fideal.* A fearful thought descended on her like a blow. *I must choose life, not death.*

But Tristan—Tristan . . .

The wind stirred, and a cloud rose over the sea. She watched the soft mass roiling and changing shape and heard the strong, sonorous tones of the Lady rolling toward the shore.

Never forget you are married to the land. You are the Sovereignty and the spirit of the isle.

Isolde's soul rebelled. *Tristan is more to me than all the Western Isle!*

Little one, little one—the Lady's stern voice sounded deep inside her mind. *You cannot give up your kingdom for any man. You have made the mystical marriage of the Queens with the land. That is the union you may not escape.*

The land . . .

Isolde wanted to weep. She thought of Cormac and Sir Gilhan: Surely Ireland would always be safe with them?

But Gilhan is old. He may die, and Cormac too. And how long before another Breccan appears? If I am the spirit and Sovereignty of the isle, can I abandon it and leave it to its fate? Oh, my poor country, unmothered like an orphan child.

The Western Isle came before her with its black mountains and emerald loughs, its silver breezes and its sighing rain. She saw the people with their laughing eyes, the broad, short-legged cattle in the fields, the bright salmon flashing like life itself from pool to pool.

A pain sharper than any before almost took her breath. *What is all this to me, now that Tristan has gone? May I not join him? I want to be with my love.*

The Lady's voice was fading into the wind. *You will. But not now. Say farewell to your grief.*

"Lady, is that all?"

She caught a last sigh. *Hold fast to what you have and keep the faith.*

Keep the faith . . .

With Tristan, or with the land?

All afternoon she wandered the meadows and clifftops, searching for flowers. But then came a wind from the sea and the unmistakable smell of evening in the air. *Hurry, Isolde, hurry—remember the tide . . .*

As she came down the hill, she could see that her boat lay moored at the end of the harbor wall, ready for the sea. She drew a deep breath of satisfaction into her lungs. *This is for you, sweetheart. I will keep the faith.*

But hurry, hurry—the night tide will not wait . . .

She hastened down to the quay. The sailors who passed her averted their eyes, and she knew they had seen the boat and guessed what she meant to do. To them, she was an ill-omened thing, already marked out for the legions of the dead. To speak to her now would be to invite bad luck, and her spirit might take one of them on its last journey, all against their will.

But I choose life, not death.

"The blessings of the Mother be upon you," she murmured to dispel their fear.

At the mooring, she gasped with pleasure when she saw the boat. Armfuls of red-gold bracken lay in feathery heaps, side by side with fat cushions of green-black ivy, their leaves splashed with gold. Sprays of acorns, oak apple, and rose hips were all laid out like offerings to the Lady of the Sea. Isolde had not shed a tear since she heard of Tristan's death, but now she could not hold back. *Oh, Brangwain—my last true friend* . . .

There was no sign of the maid. Well, she would not be far. Isolde filled the boat with crisp, dry bracken and thick branches of glossy yew. On top of it she laid armfuls of rose bay willow herb with its silky, scented tufts, then sweetened it with clover and wild thyme. Posies of sturdy pink thrift clustered in the prow, and garlands of bittersweet took up the stern. Chanting softly, she wove a wreath of black bryony and dogwood as red as blood. *Red for our love with its heart of hidden flame, red for the truth and glory of your life.*

It was getting dark. She sang and prayed contentedly as she worked, oblivious to the shadows gathering around. As she finished, Brangwain appeared, striding along the dock through the evening mist. Isolde left the boat and joined her on the quay.

"Oh, Brangwain . . ." She gestured behind her at the floral array. "How can I ever thank you?" she said quietly.

"It's nothing, lady." Red-eyed, Brangwain thrust something thin and heavy into her hand. "For your journey."

It was a fragment of slate, marked up with ancient runes. Tracing the marks with her fingers, Isolde made it out.

> bel ami,
> si ecʒt de nouʒ
> ne vouʒ sanʒ mei,
> ne mei sanʒ vouʒ.

" 'My handsome love, this is our fate, neither you without me, nor me without you.' " Isolde hugged it to her breast. "Where did you get it?" she asked huskily.

"From a wise woman at the end of the town. I knew she'd have some-thing to—" Brangwain turned away, struggling to master her voice. "Of course, it's in the language of these parts," she said darkly, regaining her fragile control, "but you'll understand that."

Isolde smiled. "We all speak the same language in the end," she said tenderly. "And the Great Ones understand every word."

Slowly, she drew in the deep, sweet breath of the sea. The mist swirled and lifted like a curtain, and the evening star laid its beam all the length of the harbor, a silver path reaching out to worlds unknown. The waves lapped on the shingle where the quay pushed out from the shore, and a great stillness filled the bay.

Isolde nodded to herself and met Brangwain's eye. "I shall not leave you tonight. When the Mother calls me will be time enough to go. We'll send the boat out in tribute to my love. May it ease his passage to the world beyond the worlds."

"Lady, lady . . ." Brangwain's voice cracked and she dissolved in tears. "Praise the Gods! And you'll be with Sir Tristan in a better place. Then he'll never leave you. He'll serve you there forever and a day."

Isolde nodded. "In that world, there is no parting and no pain."

Did Isolde know, Brangwain wondered, glimmering through her tears, that she was radiant with beauty, alive with her own light? Elf-shining, they called that look in the ancient days, when only the Old Ones and the Great Ones had such a power. Well, one day you'll be among them, my nursling, my charge. And may the Goddess bring you to the land of your heart's desire.

Isolde looked at the boat. "Candles, Brangwain, if you please?"

"Gladly, lady." With wings on her heels, Brangwain flew to fulfill the request. Together the two women lit a dozen swan lamps and set them among the flowers. The little craft glowed with life, the flames pulsing like a living heart. Just so were you, my love, in your life. And so I will remember you to the end of mine.

"Ready?" Isolde called in a low, fervent tone.

Brangwain moved to the rope secured to its cleat on the quay. "Ready, madam."

"We must wait for the turn in the tide."

Together they listened to the song of the sea, waiting for the hungry, withdrawing cry. With a sobbing sigh, the sea began to ebb, slowly at first, but with an increasing roar.

The moon soared over the horizon, flooding the world with light. Isolde looked up at the great kindly face and her heart overflowed. I am ready.

Bless my offering, Mother.

Bring it to my love.

chapter 52

already the current was beginning to tug at the boat. Blinded by unshed tears, Isolde stood on the quay. *Farewell, my love, till we meet again.* She held out her hands in blessing. "Cast off, Brangwain," she called.

The boat slipped away from its mooring, running fast and true. Together they watched it vanish into the dusk. Then from the darkness behind them, Brangwain felt a tug on her sleeve.

"Are you Queen Isolde?" said a childish voice.

Turning, Brangwain saw a boy of no more than eight, emerging like a wraith from the mist. His bare feet and ragged clothes proclaimed him to be one of the town urchins, children of the streets who lived by their wits. An unwashed, dog-like smell seeped from him when he moved.

Isolde came forward. "I am the Queen," she said gravely. "Speak to me, little sir."

The child nodded. "If you'm the Queen, you mun follow me."

"Why so?"

"I'm sent by one to do you a good turn." His grubby face brightened. "He gid me good money for it. He can help you, he says, by the white sails and the black."

Isolde stood still. *By the white sails and the black* . . . A message about Tristan, it must be. Perhaps even one he left her before he died? She patted the boy on the shoulder. "Lead on, sir."

Already the child was darting off into the night. Isolde hurried after him, anxious to keep him in sight. Brangwain swung into step beside her, drawing up her cloak to cover her head.

"Where are we going, lady?" she asked grimly. "Do you know?"

Isolde shook her head. But the boy was leading them up from the harbor and toward the town. Behind it lay the black bulk of the castle mound. *Back to the palace, to hear of Tristan's last words?*

Closely following the child, they slipped unseen through insignificant alleys and darkened streets. Twisting and turning, they soon lost their way. But the surefooted child pressed on without looking back.

Wisps of watery cloud hung over the face of the moon. They flitted like shadows through the nighttime town, keeping careful sight of the round, bobbing head. Stumbling over cobbles, skirting foul-smelling puddles and open drains, the going was hard. With every step, Isolde's misgivings grew. *Are we still in the town, or coming to the palace now?*

They came to a nondescript door in a high stone wall.

"Are we here, boy?" Brangwain hissed. But the child signaled her to silence, then gave a low knock.

There was no answer. Isolde shivered. *Why has he brought us here?*

The boy knocked again. The door opened and a tall man appeared with a candle in his hand. "Your Majesty," he said. "I beg you, come in."

They stepped over the threshold. *All-heal and savory, rosemary and rue, and above it all, the unmistakable smell of blood.*

The infirmary.

Where Tristan breathed his last.

They were in a room at the back of the building, low and white, but golden now with swan lamps gleaming on every side. Pots and jars and posies of fragrant herbs lined the walls on overflowing shelves. A large table was covered in ingredients, books, and scrolls, with surgical knives and saws scattered in their midst. Two or three doors led off to adjacent rooms, but there were no sounds of life. A solitary chair stood by the window, waiting for the occupant of the room. Isolde looked steadily at their guide. He was a man of middle age, his eyes shrewd and caring, his face lined with pain. His sleeves were rolled up and his tunic splashed with blood.

Isolde nodded. *The doctor, of course. He looks like a decent soul, honest and kind. And with no one else to trust at the very end, Tristan might well have turned to him.*

She bowed her head in greeting. "You sent for me, sir? 'By the black sails and the white.' What did you mean?" *Words of love from my loved one? A love token? A last wish?*

The doctor leaned forward earnestly. "I heard you were getting ready to end your life. But there are still those who can try to repair your hurt. I have one such, here in our infirmary—"

So there's no word from Tristan, no secret to learn. It's nothing but a trick.

"Sir—" She held up her hand and firmly shook her head. "Let me go. The Mother calls me back to my own land. I must not delay."

The doctor shook his head. "Our man is a noted healer," he said stubbornly. "He has seen much—learned much—"

"Alas, sir." She drew a ragged breath. "There are some hurts that the Gods themselves can't heal."

He paused, and she watched him choosing his words with care. "Sir Tristan thought well of this man before he died. Talk to him, I beg."

"Tristan?"

She fixed her eyes on the ceiling. She wanted to weep. "Tristan thought well of me, sir, and doubtless of you, but still he died. Thinking is nothing now, and talking is even less."

A great weariness seized her. *Wait for me, love, on the Silver Plain. The road may be short or long, but I shall be there.*

The doctor cleared his throat. "Only see him for a moment." He gestured toward the nearest door. "He's right here."

She nodded to the doctor. "Do what you will."

"You won't regret it, madame. If you'll follow me . . ."

Yes, yes . . .

She willed herself to go forward, beyond feeling, beyond hope. *Oh, Tristan . . .* The loss of him came over her with a pain like death.

"This way, madame." The doctor opened the door and ushered her through.

Oh, my love, my love. What can this healer say to cure me of you? The only cure for a love like ours is death.

Silently, she began a prayer to ease her distress. *Star of the East, give us kindly birth. Star of the South, give us love. Star of the West, give us gentle age. And Star of the North, give us peace.*

One candle alone lit the inner room. As she entered, she felt her soul tremble and break free, soaring and wheeling in the shining gloom. *Goddess, Mother, give us love and peace. No more pain and confusion, but freedom and flight to the astral plain.*

And now Tristan was coming toward her through the darkness, robed all in moonglow, his head crowned with stars. She stared at him and laughed with pure delight. *Have I died, then, my love? Are we together now?*

Then the tall, starlit figure took her hand and she knew his touch. She saw his eyes, Tristan's eyes, and heard his familiar voice. "You came to me with white sails. Can you forgive me, my Queen?"

chapter 53

Oh, my love, my love . . .

The shock was almost too much. "Are you alive?" she gasped.

In answer he lifted her hand and pressed it to his lips. "Never more so."

His voice was warm and husky, his grip strong. He was clad in a smooth leather tunic and freshly laundered shirt with the old torque of knighthood gleaming at his neck. Yet now she could see the deep shadows under his eyes, and the signs of recent suffering on his face. With a fresh shock she saw that the gleam on his skin she had taken for the glow of the moon was the pallor of strain.

"How are you? What's happened?" Babbling, weeping, she plucked at his shirt front. "Blanche told me you were dead!"

His face tightened. "She gloated to me that the sails you were flying were black. I passed out and the doctor said I'd died to stop her from trying to revive me with one of her remedies."

He was swaying on his feet.

"Let's sit down," she said anxiously. *Oh, my love, my love.* Joy and doubt raged to and fro in her mind. *Are you truly alive? Or is this all a dream?*

He drew her to a sofa against the wall. As her eyes adjusted to the dark, she made out a small, low chamber, little more than a hermit's cell, with a bed, a beaker, a table, and a chair. But in truth she could not see much through her tears. Weeping, shaking, she could not let go of his hands. *You're alive.* She gave an uncertain laugh. *I'm going mad. I must stop talking to you inside my head.*

"Tell me everything that's happened," she said in a tremulous voice. "When I got back to Cornwall, you'd just sailed away. I know you asked them to send you to me, but Andred sent you here instead. He told me he thought you meant Isolde of France." She could not hold back a bitter laugh. "He was lying, of course."

Tristan nodded tensely. "I know. As soon as I came 'round, I realized I'd been tricked. I wrote to you every day—"

"You wrote to me?" she interrupted incredulously. "I wrote to you, and you never once replied."

"Oh, lady—" Tears stood in his eyes. "I never had a single line from you. Then you wrote to tell me that our love was at an end—"

"Brangwain told me that." *Oh, sweetheart. Our love ended?* She could not catch her breath.

"—and that you were reconciled with Mark, and a child was on the way—"

"*A child?*" Now she was gasping with rage. "I didn't know the details. The letter said I was reconciled with Mark? And you believed it?"

He stared at her earnestly. "After so long without a word from you, yes, I did."

Isolde stared back at him, baffled. *How could you believe it?* Then came an unhappy thought. *I was more faithful than you. I never gave up hope.* But she could not say that now.

"It was Andred, I'm sure," she said furiously.

"Who else?" She watched Tristan intently as he pieced it out. "And Blanche must have intercepted the letters we wrote. All the messengers reported to her as they went to and fro."

"Blanche." Isolde clenched her fists. *There she is again. There's no avoiding it.* She took a painful breath. "Your wife."

"Yes." His eyes roamed away from her now, angry and wild. But his grip on her hands grew fiercer as he spoke. "I betrayed you, lady. Gods above, how I've failed! No man on earth could have been a greater fool."

"Betrayed me?" *So it's true.* She felt sick. "You went to bed with her."

He recoiled as if he had been stung. "Never!" he cried in a fury. "I never touched her. I only married her because she begged me to. She said it would save her from a marriage she could not bear. She swore she'd get it annulled as soon as she was free."

"But she broke her side of the bargain?"

An ugly flush of shame disfigured Tristan's face. "Yes, she did," he said with difficulty. "On the wedding night, she wanted me in her bed."

Ye Gods, why don't men ever know the way women's minds work? Why don't they understand the power of female desire?

"And that's when you jumped out of the window and got hurt again?" *Gods above, this man!*

"I deserved it," he said savagely.

Isolde struggled to stay calm. "You shouldn't have married Blanche, we both know that. But if nothing took place between you—"

"That's not all." He leapt to his feet and roamed around the room. "There's something else . . . something you don't know."

"Maybe I do."

Painfully she recalled Mark, Andred, and Elva, all enjoying a lecherous chuckle at Tristan's expense. *He's a dark horse, Tristan . . . the filthy wretch found a lover and holed up to pleasure a lady for weeks on end.*

"Mark told me you were delayed in a castle," she forced out. "With a lady. And her maids."

"Castle Plaisir de Fay. The lady's name was Duessa. The lady Falsamilla was the chief of her maids."

Duessa, Isolde pondered feverishly. *Falsamilla.*

"It was the lady's habit to take passing knights to her bed. She threw me into her dungeon when I refused. Then Falsamilla offered to help me to escape. But in return she wanted—"

I know what she wanted. "She wanted the same from you as her mistress had."

Slowly, she turned her face away from him. She could see it all. "So you did betray me," she said hollowly. An anguish worse than the fear of his death caught her unawares.

"Yes, I did!" he cried. "But not as you think. She wanted a kiss, that's all, for letting me go."

"You kissed her? Falsamilla?"

"Yes."

Isolde nodded. *The brown-haired woman. I knew.*

Tristan crossed the floor and slumped heavily in the chair. "I betrayed you."

A heavy silence fell. Isolde's heart was burning. *Ah, love, after we were true to each other for all these years?*

Tristan heaved a groan from the depths of his soul. "I failed you, lady. And my knighthood oath." He buried his head in his hands.

"No!" Isolde found herself surging to her feet. *Should he suffer for one kiss? When the woman he kissed saved his precious life?*

"You're my love," she burst out, giddy with sudden joy, "and you're alive! You were right to get out of that cell. Don't you think I'd rather have you here, now, in my arms?"

Tristan looked up, a gleam of hope on his ravaged face. "Can you forgive me?"

"When I have you back with me again?" Gently, she reached for his hand and brought it to her lips. "Oh, my love, it's not much to forgive."

He took her in his arms. Neither could say which one of them wept first, but they both felt their tears falling like healing rain. After a while they kissed, heart-hungry but tremulous too, like lovers who have suffered more than they know.

They sat for a long time in the candle's glow. Beyond happiness now, Isolde gazed steadfastly into the flickering flame, sheltering her soul within the strength of his.

At last she raised her head. "I have a ship at the dock, ready to sail. We can leave for Cornwall at once."

Tristan frowned. "I have to see Blanche first."

Her eyes flared in alarm. "Can we trust her, after all she's done?"

He laughed harshly. "Not in the least. But sooner or later, she has to be told I'm alive. And I have to end this marriage. She must set me free."

"But the doctor . . . ? Blanche will know he deceived her. Won't she punish him? Make him pay for it?"

Tristan gave a crooked smile. "I asked him about that. He says he's the King's doctor and the Prince's too, and he's sure they won't let him suffer because of Blanche."

"So we deal with Blanche." Isolde forced a smile. "And afterward?"

Tristan gripped her hands and kissed her again. "We put to sea, my Queen! The open sea!"

chapter 54

She made a beautiful widow, it had to be said. Smiling behind his hand, Saint Roc watched as Blanche wandered around her apartment, a picture of grief. Some might find her fragile skin too pale, her eyes too large, her mouth too sorrowful, he could see that. But her child-like air of loss, her swollen eyelids, and tearstained face still tugged at his heart. And he had to admire the vigor with which she was mourning a man she hardly knew. Yes, Blanche was certainly making the most of Tristan's death.

Indeed, it was plainly the best part she'd ever had. Already he could see her exquisitely clad in black, accepting condolences, with her brother or himself hovering attentively at her side. This was a role she could play for the rest of her life. But he was not born to dance attendance: the Chevaliers of Saint Rocquefort were adventurers and kings. Still, what was he doing now but awaiting her pleasure, dangling about in her chamber like a tassel on her gown?

And why had she summoned him to tell him about Tristan before informing anyone else, even her father the King? It meant he was Tristan's chosen successor, to be sure. But as what? Would she ever allow him to grow into a partner, lover, and husband?

"Oh, Tristan . . ."

A fresh burst of anguished crying filled the air. Blanche buried her face in the sofa, dazed with fear. Tristan was dead. Dead! She still could not believe it. How had it all gone wrong?

Trembling, Blanche peered between her fingers at the pensive Saint Roc. Why wasn't he paying attention? Tears filled her eyes again. Didn't he know that she'd only called him here to comfort her distress?

"Sir?" she called out in a shaky voice.

"Madame?" he responded with a formal bow.

"I shall never forget him! He was the most wonderful husband a woman could ever have. Oh, Tristan—" Blanche rose unsteadily to her feet. "And now I must tell my father and all the court—"

"And notify his kinsman King Mark in Cornwall." He paused. "There will be others too."

She put a hand to her head. "It's all too much. You'll help me, won't you?"

"Only if you promise to be guided by me," he said gravely, his eyes fixed on hers. "I am not here to serve you, you have many good souls for that. I am here, as I was from the first, to win your hand."

Blanche's face filled with color and she caught her breath. She could not decide if she was flattered or outraged. Gasping, she made a play for the upper hand. "Will you make love to a widow while her husband's still warm?"

"Yes," he replied simply. "When I know that the widow was hardly a wife at all."

"Hardly a wife?" she flared up. "What do you mean?"

He pressed on undeterred. "I know, too, that Sir Tristan was no real husband to you. He never knew you as I do, and therefore could never partner you as you deserve."

"As you can, I suppose?" she cried out in rage.

He gave a sardonic smile. "Only if you hear me and heed my words."

"Heed your words?" Blanche widened her eyes and madly puffed out her cheeks. "When you speak so rudely as this to a woman who has lost her husband, a poor widow—"

Widow, widow, widow—there's your answer, Saint Roc. He held up a hand. "I shall leave you, madame, to your widowhood."

"Leave me?" Blanche's mouth fell open. This was not what she planned. Her world of certainty slipped on its axis again, and she felt the abyss at her feet. Misery gripped her. What's happening to me?

"—see the Princess now."

Muffled voices sounded in the corridor outside and there was a sudden sharp confusion at the door. A frightened attendant appeared, wringing her hands.

"Don't be angry, madame. I know you gave orders you weren't to be disturbed, but I couldn't refuse the King—"

Blanche leapt forward. "My father?" she cried in alarm.

"Your husband, madame."

Since this was the only time he'd use the word, Tristan had resolved to give it full value now. His reward was to see Blanche gagging with horror and Saint Roc rooted to the ground as he came in leaning on Isolde, with the doctor and Brangwain at his side.

He fixed his hollow eyes on Blanche, breathing heavily. "You wronged me, madame, with a grievous lie, and it almost cost me my life." He gestured to the doctor. "But for this good man, I would have died at your hands. He recovered me, and he must not suffer for that."

Blanche could not speak. Tristan read her bloodless face and pressed on. "But I wronged you too. I should never have promised to marry you without love." He glanced at Saint Roc. "I could have set you free from this man in some other way. But it seems freedom from him is not what you seek now."

"I—I—" Blanche gabbled. She could not look at Tristan, at Isolde, at Saint Roc. Even the doctor's calm gaze stung her like a whip.

Tristan took a deep breath and steadied himself on Isolde's arm. "From my heart, madame, I'll make amends for what has passed. Call on me if you suffer any wrong, and I'll do all that I can in honor to set it right."

There was a breathless pause. "And on your side," he resumed, "you must swear to get this mock-marriage annulled. You know that I never came into your bed. Nothing passed between us to make us man and wife."

Saint Roc stirred. I knew it. What sadness, what madness, they must have endured that night.

Blanche found her voice. "Annulled?"

Tristan nodded gravely. "You must go to your priest and get the marriage set aside. All the world must know that our marriage is null and void."

All the world? More gossip, more shame . . . Blanche cried aloud in pain.

And suddenly Saint Roc was at her side. "Courage," he said in a low voice, taking her hand. "I'll help you. I won't leave you now."

"You won't leave me?" Blindly, she turned her naked face up to his.

"I promise. But you must promise too."

Blanche turned to Tristan and Isolde. "I promise," she faltered. "I'll do what you say."

Isolde stared at her earnestly. "You've broken your word before. Can we trust you now?"

Saint Roc laid his hand on the hilt of his sword. "You have my word." he said clearly. "And the doctor will not suffer for what he has done; I'll take care of that too."

Tristan bowed. "Thank you, sir." He turned to Isolde. "Come, my Queen."

And as suddenly as they had entered, they were gone. Saint Roc moved back to Blanche and lifted her hand to his lips.

"Another great shock, my Princess," he said as lightly as he dared. "But all for the good."

Blanche nodded dumbly. She did not trust herself to speak. But she knew Saint Roc understood.

"Now there's much to do," he resumed. "We must go together to your father and tell him all this." He gave her his sardonic grin. "Or as much as you decide. I don't think he'll want to know more. Then we'll put through the annulment, and you will be free. After that—"

He broke off. She lifted her eyes to his face. "What?"

There was not a hint of humor about him now. "After that, you must tell me when I may court you, woo you, and win you, and take you away to my kingdom as my Queen."

"Now. Let's start now."

Even her voice was different, Saint Roc noticed with a lift of his heart. He eyed her cautiously. "Life in my kingdom is harsh. You'll have to change your ways, my Princess."

"And so will you," she retorted with a flash of her old fire. "I know what old bachelors are."

He took her in his arms. She smelled of salt tears and sweet wispy hair and lavender and rose. The road ahead would not be easy, he knew. But she was the woman he wanted, come what may.

"Changing together," he murmured. "That's what marriage is. Kiss me, Princess."

He kissed her very gently. Blanche threw back her head. Bride, wife, and widow, and she'd never encountered this? She reached up to touch his lips with her white hand.

"Kiss me again."

chapter 55

*O*h, *my love, Tristan, my love* . . .

At first she could hardly let him out of her sight. She was only content when he was close to her and she could touch his face, kiss his eyes, and hold his hand. She marveled at the lift and turn of his head, his fearless gaze, and the smile that lit up his face, as if she were seeing them all for the very first time. Most of all she treasured the scent of him. It was something she never knew she'd missed till he returned.

But as always, they had to beware of the gaze of the world. "Never forget, my lady," Tristan reminded her sadly, "that a thousand eyes always follow a queen."

And on board as they were now, sailors and attendants were never more than a few feet away. So Isolde remembered to nod coolly and dismiss Tristan, and he would bow and withdraw, despite his desire to take her in his arms. It was a harsh restraint on both of them. After the long cruel winter of the months apart, the return of spring brought too little time in the sun.

Yet Tristan was alive when she'd given him up for dead! Every morning now as Isolde came to consciousness, the uprush of happiness almost took her breath.

And every day he was recovering his strength, another cause for joy she kept hidden in her heart. He had suffered far more than he knew, and even to her he would not admit how badly hurt he was. But the healing began as soon as the ship put to sea. The gentle rocking of the waves, the fresh salt air, and the calm, unchanging rhythm of the days all brought him back to himself.

Watching him, tending his beloved body, was her greatest joy. When the spray dashed its salt in their faces, when the moon shone on a sea of silver as still as glass, her blood thrilled in her veins and she found herself wanting him. How long was it since she had taken him to her bed? Alone at dawn or preparing for sleep at night, she hungered for his body, for the touch and the feel of him. But a strange fragility hung about him still, and nothing must compromise his recovery. And every night when they parted for the sake of propriety, he to his cabin and she to hers, she fell asleep blessing her good fortune and calling down prayers on his name.

And so the days passed. Dusk and bright morning, morning and shining dusk, slipped past like beads on a string. Floating between Castle Hoel and Cornwall, they crossed an ocean of unfathomable bliss. This enchanted interlude would be all too brief, she knew. But for the rest of her life she would never forget those sweet, irreplaceable, windswept days at sea.

Yet they could not sail on forever, they both knew that. They had not bid farewell to their cares on shore.

And shadows on Isolde's side lay between them too. In the dead of night, when all the ship slept except for the lookout on the topmost mast, she sat in her cabin holding Tristan's hand and told him of Mark's hostility before she left. A solitary candle held them in its glow, and the shadows cast up by the sea seemed to listen as she spoke.

Tristan heard her out in silence, reviewing her story in his mind. Mark's insistence on exerting his marriage rights, his angry bullying, and the threat of a new knight who would guard her night and day, all sounded as if his suspicions had been dangerously aroused.

"We must be on our guard," he began grimly. "If Mark thinks he's been injured, he'll strike back. He'll put revenge above pride, above reason, even his self-respect. And—"

He broke off and fell silent, gripping her hand. It was left to Isolde to put his fear into words. "And he's probably planning it now."

"Encouraged by Andred, of course." Tristan gave an angry nod. "So we can't arrive back together. Sailing into Castle Dore on the same ship would only fan the flames."

"You're right." Already she could hear the gossip Andred would put about. *Sir Tristan was married in France, but the Queen flew over there like a mad thing and dragged him back!*

Tristan frowned. "We should land where we can, then I should go straight to Castle Dore to pay my respects. Then when you come back to court, I should go away, at least for a while."

"You're right." She returned his grip with a sigh. "And as long as you're with Mark, I should stay away, until you convince him that he has nothing to fear."

"Where will you go?"

Isolde paused. Where could she go? Who could she turn to without demeaning Mark?

Someone above the fray . . . away from Castle Dore . . . living in a place of peace and repose . . .

Mists swirled around her mind. Then a face of great beauty glimmered through the dark.

"Igraine," she said with quiet certainty. "Queen Igraine."

Tristan's eyes widened. "Arthur's mother in Tintagel?"

"Yes." Isolde nodded. "And Mark's overlord."

She could see that he understood. "Queen of Cornwall in her own right," he said slowly. "So Mark cannot object to your visiting her, queen to queen. And she's wise beyond wisdom, they say."

"Yes, and more. Some say she is the Lady of the Sea. The Lady is seen in many places, but Tintagel is her home."

Tristan favored her with the smile she loved so much. "Queen Igraine will take care of you. Perhaps she'll be a friend to you, too, when I'm gone."

When you're gone.

Isolde came to herself in pain and fixed her gaze on him. Now the snug cabin with its wooden walls, its sheepskin couches and canopied royal bed, seemed to mock the brief happiness they had encountered here. *Must I lose you again, my love? When we've only just found one another, after all this time?* "We're like Guenevere and Lancelot," she said in desolation. "He takes to the road to protect her good name."

Tristan's tone was as bleak as hers. "As I must, too, for the sake of my Queen." He raised his hand and touched the side of her face. "The most beautiful queen in the world."

Tristan . . .

She looked at the candlelight gilding the hairs on his hand with a joy like grief. Then she turned to him and took his face in her hands. Half desperate, half transported, she fastened her lips on his.

*Oh—oh—*She tore herself away, and kissed him again.

The scent of his manhood reached her, and she heard him groan. "My lady—oh, my love."

His tunic was smooth beneath her fingertips. *Kiss me, my love.* She traced his forehead, his eyes, the outline of his lips, and knew them again, as she had the very first time. She had forgotten the wonder of his mouth. *Kiss me, kiss me again.*

They came together like two waves at the place of magic where the ancients say the Otherworld meets the Great Sea. *Careful, careful—it's too soon* came into her mind, and she drew back. But Tristan held her fast and would not let her go. His voice was thick with emotion in his throat. "Love me," he said.

Oh, my beloved . . .

She took him in her arms. All about them the winds sang in the sails, the candles and sea-shadows danced, and the night closed upon them as they rode the rolling sea.

chapter 56

The angry sea hurtled toward the shore. The little ship edged boldly through the waves toward the great wild, black mass of Tintagel ahead. All around them the mast, the sails, the rigging, creaked and groaned in the wind, and the sailors' cries echoed above it all.

"Easy there, mister."

"Yare, sir, yare!"

Isolde shivered. Coming to Tintagel by land was an awesome sight, she knew. As a new arrival crested the bluff and looked down from the top of the cliff, the great rock lay surrounded by water many feet below. Crowned with its ancient castle and cut off from the land, it loured like one of the Old Ones, defying time.

Ring after ring of fortifications protected the approach by land. Watchtowers and high walls guarded the inner courtyards, and a strong garrison kept the world at bay. After that came the most fearsome thing of all, a narrow flight of steps across the void. A ribbon of stone, hardly worth calling a bridge, it was the only link between Queen Igraine's castle and the land. One man with one weapon and one arm could have held it against all comers for as long as he wished. It was the best-defended place on earth.

Yet by sea Tintagel looked even more impregnable. Rising sheer from the water, the black mass with its ragged, jutting crags seemed to offer no place to land. Only the skilled eye of a Cornish captain could have discerned the narrow causeway concealed in a fold of the rock and brought the ship alongside. From the little quay, a path ran up to the castle with many twists and turns. It was guarded by stout iron gates, and, like the stone stairs arching from the land, had been built to be defended by one man alone.

"Come, my Queen."

With formal courtesy, Tristan helped Isolde to alight. She nodded with equal politeness as she stepped off the boat. From this moment on they must be lady and knight, no more.

Yet they must not come to Tintagel like guilty souls.

"You are a queen, and a great one too," Tristan had insisted, his eyes flashing, as Tintagel drew near. "And I am a knight of Cornwall and Lyonesse. We shall show Queen Igraine the respect due to her. But we must never allow Mark or Andred to make traitors of us."

Gods above, how she loved him! Isolde could not hold back a beaming smile. *You are fresh from my arms, we are only just starting the day, and already I want to take you back to my bed.*

Oh, Tristan . . .

Later he had spoken earnestly to Brangwain, urging the maid to turn her mistress out like a queen.

Brangwain gave him a frosty stare. "I always do, sir."

And Isolde herself had had to hide a smile. Yet when she stepped off the boat, she had to admit that Brangwain had wrought an extra miracle. The maid had come up with a gown of Irish green silk handwoven with tissue of gold and matched it with a cloak of gold shot through with shamrock green. Her hair had been tamed and braided into two thick ropes, glinting like copper in the morning sun. Ireland's ancient Crown of Queens secured her veil, and a fall of lacy white trefoils foamed out behind. Her wrists and fingers flashed with emerald and gold, and emeralds the size of pigeon's eggs adorned her neck.

Head high, she stepped onto the causeway and looked around. The great bluff of Tintagel soared above them. Overhead they could still hear the moaning of the wind, but here in the shelter of the rock the air felt warm. The sea sucked and sighed at their feet, surging furiously through the channel between the great rock and the land.

At the foot of the cliff opposite, the waves thundered in and out of a vast cavern, its ragged arch like the entrance to some mighty cathedral of the deep.

Tristan gestured toward it. "Merlin's cave?"

Isolde nodded. "Or the Lady's. Or a haunt of the Old Ones before Tintagel was born."

A mailed figure appeared behind the iron gate. "Your Majesty? Welcome to Tintagel. We were glad to hear of your safe arrival from France."

Isolde received the greeting without surprise. Queen Igraine had chosen to hold aloof from the world, but its doings seemed to reach her just the same. Knowledge came to her, they said, on the wind, and in every silent ripple of the sea.

The gate swung open and a young knight stepped through. He gave a courteous bow. "Will it please you to ascend?"

Together they climbed up the path. Emerging into a courtyard at the top, they saw a wide cobbled space surrounded by high walls. Ahead stood the castle, its graceful arched entrance approached by a steep flight of steps.

"This way, Majesty . . . this way . . ."

They passed under the lofty archway into an echoing Great Hall, where there was no one to be seen. Did invisible hands tend these halls and corridors, Isolde wondered, these elegant cloisters with their fine columns and marble walls? Did the same unseen helpers who brought news on the wind and waves take care of Igraine and answer her every need?

Up they went, and up. Each airy hall gave onto another, and another, each leading to an elegant flight of stairs. They passed high passageways, galleries, and side chambers without number as their guide led them on. "This way, my lady . . . this way."

And all the time, everywhere, came the sound of the sea. The roar of the surge was stronger with every step, its song more intense. Below it beat the deep pulse of the ocean, its steady, rhythmic pounding like the heart of the world. Isolde smiled and felt her spirits return. Queen Igraine would never feel alone in this sea-girt house.

One by one the passageways were narrowing down. The last one they entered came to an end at a fine arched doorway, set low in the white-washed wall.

The knight bowed and opened the door. "Queen Igraine awaits you."

Tristan returned his bow. "Thank you, sir." Taking Isolde's hand, he escorted her through.

After the dim corridor, the room was filled with light. Ahead of them stretched a great sunlit chamber, its wide windows giving out onto the sea. Igraine's eyrie was right at the top of the castle, a place high in the heavens and floating beyond the stars. Slowly, Isolde adjusted to where they were. *I remember this.*

A deep, vibrant voice filled the room. "Greetings to you both."

Before them they saw a tall, stately woman, still strikingly lovely in spite of her great age. The gown she wore ebbed and flowed like the sea, its blue, green, and gray shadows whispering about her feet, and her gold cloak and veil were sunlight on the waves. A circle of pearls and moonstones crowned her white hair, and a strangely wrought wand of gold hummed in her hand.

And her eyes . . .

Once seen, never forgotten: even Tristan's eyes could not hold so much depth and meaning or such undaunted love. The old Queen was clearly no stranger to suffering, and a thousand sorrows had left their mark on her deeply chiseled face. But nothing had destroyed the spirit that had formed the strong features and undefeated chin. The brightness of her soul shone through her frail flesh, illuminating her with an inner joy that seemed to echo from Avalon and beyond.

Isolde gazed at her, lost in wonder. *Goddess, Mother, grant that I may look as Igraine does when I am old.* Curtsying, she struggled to recover her manners and her voice. "Queen Igraine!"

The air inside the chamber was blowing in from the open sea. White horses reared and danced on the distant waves.

"Queen Isolde." Igraine inclined her lovely head toward Tristan. "And my lord of Lyonesse, I am glad to see you both. You are welcome here."

Simple words, Isolde pondered. How did Igraine infuse them with such warmth?

"Thank you, Your Majesty," she said earnestly. "I have come to you for shelter and advice."

A shadow passed over Igraine's face. "Alas, Isolde, the time for counsel has passed."

Goddess, Mother, what now? "Your Majesty?"

The mellow voice rang out like a bell. "It seems you have made an enemy of King Mark."

Mark! For the thousandth time, she blushed for his lack of shame. Or was it the malice of Andred pursuing them now? He would do anything to make her suffer and Tristan too. What was it now?

Isolde reached for all her strength. "My lady, I know nothing of what Mark may have said. But I'm sure that I have given him no offense. As soon as I get back to Castle Dore, I'll repair the breach."

Queen Igraine fixed her with her luminous stare. "It must be sooner, I fear. King Mark's complaint can't be dealt with at Castle Dore. Your husband is here."

Beside her she heard Tristan gasp with shock. "Mark here?" he cried.

Igraine spread her hands. "Attended by his nephew and his knights. He is loud and insistent in his complaints."

Tristan stepped forward, his hand on the hilt of his sword. "Surely my lady may give her version of events?"

Igraine paused. The golden staff sang softly in her hand. "Oh, sir, she may. But this concerns you too. King Mark has laid charges against you both, and you must answer to them in open court."

chapter 57

m ark leaned back in his chair with his hands behind his head
and had to admit he'd been treated like a king.

Queen Igraine received him graciously, and promised to hear his
complaint as soon as she could. In the meantime, she'd installed him in
this fine chamber with its handsome bed, wall hangings, and thick rugs
and offered him every comfort he could desire. Yes, he had done the right
thing in coming here.

He turned his gaze to the two men waiting in front of the fire. Well,
they were good lads, just as Andred had said, ready to do his bidding,
whatever it was. Pity they didn't have a more upstanding air. But even a
king could not make Fer de Gambon look less than shifty, or lend the
huge Taboral the semblance of a brain.

Still, they looked good, Andred had seen to that. Short and bow-
legged as he was, De Gambon gained valuable inches in height from his
handsome dark purple tunic with its long velvet coat. Head and shoulders above De Gambon, the deep-chested and long-limbed Taboral cut a
striking figure, as he always did. And the jaunty cap with the feathers
curling low on the brow was pretty successful in distracting attention
from his dull eyes and vacant, smiling face.

He squinted at the two knights. "Are you ready, then?" he cried impa-
tiently. "You know what you have to do?"

They both made obsequious bows. "Yes, sire."

"You'll go first, De Gambon," Mark ordered. Short and shifty he might
be, but he should be first into the lists. Then the man mountain, Taboral,
would only have to back him up.

Mark twitched his ungainly frame and got to his feet. "And Taboral, just remember what we discussed with Sir Andred, and stick to it," he said with an unkind laugh. "You can do that, can't you?"

The two knights exchanged a glance. For what they'd been promised, they could do that and a good deal more. Fer de Gambon stroked his rich plum-colored velvet with a loving hand. Gold and fine feathers had already come their way, and other rewards dangled like bright baubles ahead. All they had to do was make a good showing in front of the old Queen.

"Oh, we'll do it, sire, never fear," Taboral said, his beefy face splitting into a wide grin.

Mark frowned in dismay. "Well, try to look serious, man! This is treachery and betrayal we're revealing, life and death."

"Yes, sire."

Taboral obediently rearranged his face into an unconvincing scowl. Mark felt a fleeting misgiving. Could he trust these men?

"Sire!"

It was Andred, hastening in through the door. Like the two knights, he was finely arrayed in black velvet and white silk, with a black silken cap the same smooth midnight sheen as his hair. But his handsome face was as pale as his cambric shirt. Mark listened, rigid with shock. "Isolde *here*? With Tristan?"

"They are, my lord." Andred's tone was dark. "They came this morning from France. But the hearing will go forward at once, the old Queen says. We can lodge our charges and have them answered today."

Mark's mouth fell open as he struggled to reply.

"What are they doing here?" he cried out in rage. "I thought Tristan was married? Has he left his wife? Why, it's brazen! It's proof positive of everything I'm going to say."

Andred nodded. "We should be able to make something of it, to be sure."

"And coming here to get the old Queen on their side?" Mark went on, growing angrier with every breath. "Asking an ancient gracious lady, my overlord, to condone their treachery?" Mark strode around the chamber, punching the palm of his hand. "They'll pay for this. I'll have Tristan expelled from the Round Table and get him banished from the land. He'll be a recreant knight, trailing his shame and disgrace through all the world."

Andred cleared his throat uneasily. "Sire—"

"Isolde too." Mark treated him to a venomous glare. "I'll make her a laughingstock. I'd have her whipped through the kingdom if I could." He flexed and unflexed his hands. "Darkness and devils, I could lay on the lash myself!"

So Mark ranted and blustered till his spirits were restored. But storm as he might, he could not silence a rising lament. *What am I doing here, when I could be at Castle Dore? Why did I come?*

Then loudest of all. *When can I go home?*

"COURAGE, MY QUEEN."

Courage, yes, for the trial ahead.

Isolde lifted her head and returned Tristan's smile. Side by side they approached Tintagel's great hall.

"Queen Isolde and Sir Tristan of Lyonesse," cried the attendant at the door. They crossed the threshold and the vast space welcomed them in.

Light poured through massive windows on all sides. The midday sun, glinting off the sea, played glittering games with the graceful vault of the roof and its columns of white stone. Curving beams of the same gleaming stone arched overhead like the ribs of a whale, and the floor had been dressed in white sand. They might have been in a palace under the sea.

Seated on a high dais in the distance, Queen Igraine commanded the hall from a strangely wrought antique throne. Frail and ancient as she was, she looked every inch a queen. The high standing collar of her cloak, the richly lined sleeves reaching to the floor, the tall headdress and jewel-encrusted crown, all gave her an air of ineffable majesty. Her gown of gold and blue silk shimmered like the sun on the sea, and her gold wand of office gleamed in her right hand.

At the foot of the dais stood Mark with Andred at his side, and two of his knights in attendance behind. Isolde's heart tightened in her breast. Mark had dressed himself as if for battle royal, in a gold-studded tunic with a ceremonial sword and dagger at his thickening waist. The gold crown of Cornwall encircled his sandy-gray head, and his hand played importantly on the hilt of his sword. Take account of me! his attire seemed to say. I am knight and warrior, I am King.

"Welcome to this hearing, Queen Isolde." Igraine's resonant voice echoed down the hall. "King Mark has laid a serious charge at your door. Lord Tristan, you are named in the accusation too. Our purpose now is to hear these charges out."

"Thank you, Your Majesty." Isolde made her deepest curtsy to the throne, then switched the full force of her gaze to Mark. "Sire, I am surprised to see you here. Enlighten me, I beg you. What is this?"

"Adultery and treachery, lady, that's all," Mark cried. He turned to Igraine. "Your Majesty, I know they're scheming against me and plotting to do me down. They want to get rid of me and rule Cornwall themselves."

What . . . ? Isolde fought to remain composed.

Andred bowed to the old Queen with a sorrowful air. "This plot is treason against you too, Your Majesty," he said earnestly. "You are High Queen of Cornwall and Mark's overlord, and no one but you may replace a vassal king. They may be plotting against you now, for all we know." He took a breath. "Even against the High King Arthur himself, your dear son."

"King Mark . . ." Queen Igraine leaned forward. "Both Queen Isolde and Sir Tristan have their own kingdoms. Why should they covet yours?"

"Because they are lovers!" Mark proclaimed. "Oh, all the world thinks that Sir Tristan is the Queen's knight. But he loves the Queen beyond the bounds of chivalry."

Igraine leaned forward intently. "King Mark, you have raised these fears before and found them false. Some years ago you challenged the faith of your Queen and she undertook the ordeal by water to clear her name."

"This time I accuse Tristan too. He's a faithless wretch and a false traitor to me and deserves no less than to be cast out of the kingdom alive, stripped of his titles, honor, and dignity."

"Your Majesty—" Tristan's angry challenge cut through the open court. "Neither the Queen nor I ever plotted against the King. He is my liege lord and kinsman, and I am bound to him by double bonds of faith. Whoever says this, let him repeat his lie, and I will make the truth good against any man alive. My sword stands ready to defend the Queen to the last drop of my blood."

Isolde could not look at him. *Oh, my love, my love, my love . . .*

The old Queen held up a hand. "As you may yet, Sir Tristan. No one may deprive a knight of the right to clear his name. But the King has come here for a hearing, and I may not deny him that."

A seething silence set in. Isolde could see that Tristan did not trust himself to speak. She steadied herself against her mounting rage and appealed to Mark. "Answer me this, sire. What grounds do you have for making these wild claims?"

"Aha!" Mark fumbled triumphantly in his tunic and dragged out a paper disfigured with black scratches and crossings out. He bowed to the old Queen. "It's a letter, written in my faithless Queen's own hand to the Princess of France. With your permission, madam?"

He began to read in a loud, hysterical voice. "'To Your Highness of France. You have with you my knight, Sir Tristan of Lyonesse. To me he is the one—'"

He broke off. "'The one,'" he cried. "What does that mean, Your Majesty may ask?"

He resumed reading. "'Now word has reached me that you and he are to wed. You should know he was sworn to me with unbreakable oaths.'"

Tristan took a step toward Mark, his eyes on fire. "Sworn to the Queen, yes," he exploded, "as I was sworn to you, sire, at the same time. If I switched my allegiance to another king, you, too, might think I had betrayed your trust."

Mark's face twisted in a venomous grin. "That's not all." He turned back to the letter again. "'For ten years and more I have enjoyed his love.'" Glaring, he flung the letter at Isolde's feet. "Condemned by your own hand, lady. What d'you say to that?"

Goddess, Mother, help me . . .

Isolde threw back her head. "I say no more than all the world well knows. Sir Tristan has served me for ten years with steadfast love. A knight must have a lady, and a queen must have her knights. All who know and honor the rules of chivalry understand that."

Tristan fixed his eyes on Mark. "And chivalry also demands that a knight give faithful service to his king. I swore my allegiance to you and have never broken that oath. You are my liege lord and my King."

"Hear me, sire." Isolde strengthened her voice. "Sir Tristan has served you as faithfully as he has served me. Would you not call the service he has given you 'love'?"

The old Queen nodded. "A knight must love his lady. And in truth, a queen must have her knights."

Mark's eyes swiveled madly in his face. "What, madam, to love her forbiddenly? To serve her as a stallion serves a dam?"

Isolde felt her blood roaring through her veins. "Prove it," she said intensely. "Bring one witness to support these vile claims—"

"Or name your champion, sire!" White with passion, Tristan appealed to the throne. "Majesty, you must permit a challenge now. No man, even a king, may say such a thing."

The old Queen raised her head. "Can any man prove this?"

"Indeed we can!" Mark threw up his arm to summon the two knights in the rear. "These men will say that they have overheard Tristan and Isolde plotting against me."

Andred nodded at De Gambon and Taboral. "They will prove that the Queen and Sir Tristan planned to overthrow the King so they could rule together when he was gone. Further, they have evidence that Sir Tristan is without doubt the Queen's paramour." He bowed to Igraine. "May I question them, Majesty?"

The old Queen rose to her feet. "Allow me, sir. It will be better if I question them myself."

Andred tensed, then breathed again. Nothing to worry about. De Gambon was quick-witted and well rehearsed, and Taboral only had to echo what his fellow said.

"Very well, madam." He signaled to De Gambon. "Step forward, man."

The knight looked almost impressive, Andred reflected, with his long velvet coat concealing his short legs. And De Gambon knew the game. Isolde and Tristan were going to find it hard to wriggle out of what this young man would say.

But the old Queen was waving away De Gambon and his fine velvet coat. Her golden wand pointed to the young giant at his side. "You, sir, you come to bear witness too?"

"Me, lady?" Bursting with pride, Taboral made a clumsy bow. "Sir Taboral, at your service, Your Majesty, and indeed I do."

Stepping forward, he thrust past Fer de Gambon in his eagerness to be heard. So they thought that this little bandy-legged runt was cleverer than he was, and should give his evidence first? Now he'd have a chance to show what he could do.

"So, sir."

Queen Igraine fixed her large, intelligent eyes on the knight. There was a thoughtful pause. Her staff of office hummed and quivered in her hand and she cocked her head as if listening to what it said. At last she spoke. "Tell me, sir, have you heard Queen Isolde plotting with Sir Tristan?"

That was easy. Taboral's big body relaxed. "Many times," he said boldly.

"Most recently, when?"

When? Taboral thought hard. Tristan had been away for a long time. Better make it a good way back. "May Day," he returned.

"May Day?"

"May Day at night," he replied cunningly. "I saw them by the light of the full moon. They were strolling in the garden, arm in arm. They stopped to kiss and embrace, many times."

"Early summer, then," the old Queen repeated slowly. "At the beginning of May. You are sure of this?"

"Oh indeed, madam," Taboral said carelessly. He was beginning to enjoy himself. Who would have believed he had such a talent for this game? He looked across at his fellow conspirator and grinned. "Sir Fer de Gambon will back me up."

Behind him, Taboral heard an angry, hissing release of breath. Sir Andred, was it, or the King? He paused in unease. Why was De Gambon staring at him like that? Why the almost imperceptible shake of the head? Taboral did not know what he had said. But whatever it was, he knew he had said something wrong.

The old Queen paused. Now the wand was moving on. "Queen Isolde? Do you wish to speak?"

"Indeed I do." Isolde could not hold back. "On May Day, when this knight claims that Sir Tristan held me in his arms, he was in France. He had been at the court of King Hoel, mortally sick, for a month before that, and remained there for weeks afterward. This whole story is a pack of lies!"

The old Queen moved back to her throne. Her wand sang like a battle-axe as it swung toward Taboral. "What do you say now, *good sir?*"

"Your Majesty—" Taboral was sweating in panic. "I must have made a mistake..."

"Do you wish to reconsider?"

Taboral pressed a beefy hand to the side of his head. Reconsider? He floundered, shaking his head.

Igraine pressed on, her mellow voice chiming like a knell. "Did you see them on another occasion, perhaps?"

Could he say that? Taboral entertained a sudden, ridiculous hope. But hearing Andred's muttered curse behind brought him back to earth. No, he'd only bring more trouble down on all their heads.

He was aware that Igraine was regarding him with pity and contempt. "Is there any truth at all in your story, sir?"

Taboral gulped. "Well, I—"

"Or in that of Sir Fer de Gambon, your fellow here?"

Taboral's glance of panic toward De Gambon gave them both away.

Igraine looked at De Gambon. "Sir, do you want to speak out in your own defense?"

"No, madam." De Gambon fixed his sickly glance on the floor.

Igraine's remorseless summary embraced them both. "You are liars, then, both of you, out of your own mouths."

"I knew nothing of this, believe me, Queen Igraine!" Mark started to babble in a high-pitched voice.

"My lord," Andred interjected in a low voice. Urgently, he tried to convey his thought to Mark: leave this to me, I can still save the day...

"Hold your tongue!" Mark shrilled hysterically. "I'll never listen again to a word you say." He pointed at Andred. "He started this, lady. These men are his knights. I didn't know anything till he came to me with this tale!"

"And you came to me, King Mark," Igraine said implacably. "We are adjudicating your complaint. You asked for truth and justice. You shall receive no less."

"Truth and justice, yes." Mark was gibbering with dread. "But I did nothing to deserve—"

"What was it you demanded for Sir Tristan?" the old Queen inquired. "'He deserves no less than to be cast out alive, stripped of his titles, honor, and dignity,' you said. Is that still your verdict on faithless men?"

"Madam, I—" Mark was sweating freely, and his eyes were rolling wildly in search of help.

Isolde drew a breath. "Your Majesty, may I beg you, hold your hand . . ."

She was rewarded at once by a smile from Igraine. "Say on."

She held out both hands in appeal. "The King has always held Sir Tristan in high regard. Tristan has no other kin but the King. May I beg you to make peace between them now? I know that Sir Tristan would be reconciled if he could."

Igraine's hooded eyes seemed to survey both future and past in one sweeping glance. "Ah, little one," she said in a voice like the sound of the sea. "For thousands of years women have dreamed of peace while men have made war. But the time will come when all the world will be one, all its people living in harmony, not dying in hate." A sudden shaft of sunlight lit up her face. "And you are right, Isolde. I shall make peace today, never fear."

Goddess, Mother, praise and thanks to you . . .

The old Queen smiled. All the wisdom of her years stood in her eyes. "Let us praise the great Gods that the truth has emerged. We owe you a debt of gratitude, King Mark."

Me?

Gratitude?

Mark wanted to howl out loud and beat the ground with relief. Gods above, the old Queen could have stripped him of his kingship and banished him from the land. Then he, not Tristan, would have had to trail a lance along hot and dusty roads, drifting through foreign lands. His name, not Isolde's, would have been dragged through the mud for all men to jeer at and urchins to throw stones. He would have been . . . He would have had to . . .

Ye Gods, why hadn't he thought of this before? Panic filmed Mark's brow and filled his hands with sweat. He'd come within a hair's breadth of disgracing himself, and it was all Andred's fault. He should have warned him, advised him, saved him from all this.

Yet in fact, he'd saved himself. A glimmer of light stole back into Mark's craven eye. Now that he knew what fools Taboral and De Gambon were, he could send them packing before any more damage was done. In truth, he'd been a fool to believe Andred against Tristan, when the lad had so often proved his loyalty and was honest to a fault.

Tristan...

How he'd missed him! And how good to have him back again, fit and well.

"King Mark?"

He looked up to see the old Queen's eyes assessing him. A wry smile lit the shrewd, ageless face.

"Go, sir," Queen Igraine said gravely. "Leave Tintagel in the knowledge that your name is clear, just as the names of Isolde and Tristan are too. Neither man nor woman can impugn your honor now, or that of your nephew or Queen. And be assured that your throne is safe too. Neither your Queen nor your nephew has designs on it. You are my chosen vassal as Cornwall's King, and you will remain so as long as my faith and trust in you endures."

"Peace and joy be upon you, gracious Queen!" Mark trumpeted in a frenzy of relief. God and His blessed Mother, was he going to get off as lightly as this? Get out, man, out, as fast as you can. He contorted his long limbs into a frantic bow. "Farewell, Majesty. Your vassal kisses your hand."

In a noisy flurry, Mark and his men hastened out. Queen Igraine rose to her feet and descended from the throne. Leaning on her staff, she took Isolde's hand. The sun behind her back tipped her white hair with fire and bathed every mote of the air in liquid gold.

"Go forward, my dears, into the world of light," she said tenderly. "No danger or treachery can follow you now. You have answered your accusers and vindicated your names. King Mark must accept that you had no malice against him and these plots are false. Mark will forget all this on his first day in the saddle, as soon as he is back home at Castle Dore."

Home.

Ireland, Erin, home.

The word struck Isolde with a peculiar pain. "I must go back to my country. I cannot leave Ireland ungoverned any longer now."

The Queen pressed her hand. "Go, Isolde. The Western Isle will always be your fate. You are its Queen and the spirit of the land. It is the mystic marriage that none may break." She turned to Tristan and touched his hand. "And you, Sir Tristan, you know where you must go."

A shadow like night passed over Tristan's face. "Alas, lady, I do."

chapter 58

The little ship strained at her moorings to be free. Above her, the massive primeval rock reared up out of the sea, clinging to the land by its thread of stone. On the rock stood the castle that was old before time was born. Brooding to itself as it had done for the last thousand years, the dark mound of Tintagel hunkered down in the twilight waters against the night ahead. A mewling, weeping tide raced toward the far horizon and its dying gleam. Not a star shone in the cloud-laden sky.

Isolde heard the wandering cry of the sea birds, wailing like lost souls. *Wait for us, we are wanderers too.* Salt encrusted her lips and blinded her eyes. She hardly recognized the sound of her own voice. "Farewell."

The wind howled and wept around her mind. *Farewell? Oh, my love, my love . . .*

Tristan's voice was raw. "When you reach Ireland, will you write to me?"

Every hour, every day. "I shall. And as you ride with Mark, think of me?"

Tristan gave a bleak nod. "Every thought of my soul will be yours."

The sea raged around the rock. *Must we part?* hung between them like mist on a newly turned grave. But they both heard the soundless answer. *Yes.*

"Farewell, lady." Tristan's eyes were bright with tears. "Let me bring you on board."

In silence they mounted the gangplank and he led her to the rear, away from the bustle of the seamen as they made ready to sail. A small rosy lamp shone out steadily on the stern. "If you stand here, by the light," he said, "I can watch you from the land as long as my eyes can see."

She nodded and looked around. They were quite alone. The faithful

Brangwain was making ready below, and the captain and his men were busy elsewhere.

It will be a long, hard winter. But all winters in the end give way to spring. "When the seaways open again, I shall return to Castle Dore."

He shook his head. "I shall come to you in the Western Isle as soon as I judge that it's safe to leave."

Till then, we shall keep the faith. Holding fast to his hands, she repeated the anthem that had bound them in faith and truth through all these long years. "This love will never leave us now, neither for weal nor for woe."

"Never," he echoed, his voice breaking. "Farewell till springtime, my lady and my love. When the primroses peer and the swallows come back to the land, look for me then, among the migrant souls. I shall not fail."

She brought his dear hand to her lips.

"Look for me when the love star shows her face. Every night when she shines in the sky, I shall set a candle in my window to shine for you."

There was a sudden flurry in the prow. "Man the shrouds," came the captain's voice, "then prepare to cast off."

"Aye, sir." One of the ship's lads flew past, fleet and barefoot. A volley of further commands followed him. The evening wind lifted.

"I must go," he said.

No, stay! Stay on board with me. We'll sail to Ireland and leave the world behind.

"Yes," she said.

Step by step she watched his leaden tread as he left the deck and returned along the rocky quay. He stood on the causeway, facing her in the stern. Already he was smaller and farther away.

"Ready, mister?" the captain's cry rang out.

The answering call echoed around the bay. "Ready when you are, sir!"

"Let her run, then, out to the open sea."

The boat slipped her moorings like a hare from a trap and ran with the tide. The great rock of Tintagel, Tristan, and all the world dissolved as Isolde's eyes filled with tears.

She fixed her eyes on the lamp before her in the stern of the ship. Behind it she could still make out the tall, well-shaped body she had worshipped in a thousand acts of love. Already she was aching for the comfort of his nearness, the warmth of his hand. How long till she saw his beloved eyes again, touched his face, kissed his lips, felt him in her bed? *Too long!* Already she could feel his loss, taste her own tears.

Watch the lamp, watch the lamp. As long as you can see it, he won't be gone. She knew he would be making the same bargain, *as long as I can see the light on the stern, she'll still be with me, she won't really be gone.*

Now there was nothing but the small, rosy light of the lamp and a silence like the ending of the world. As she stood, held in time as fast as amber and afraid to move, hope came dropping through the twilight like an evening prayer, and she saw all their past and future in the tiny flame. *Even so is our love, burning as it can, yet refusing to go out. As all flames do, it will flicker in a hostile wind and shrink from the rain, but it will never die.*

She moved to the rail of the ship and leaned out into the darkness, raising a hand toward the unseen shore. *Come to me when you can, my sweetheart, my love. Whenever you come, you will find me there.*

the characters

Amaury de Rien Place, King of Gaul   Suitor to Blanche
and hopelessly in love with her

Andred, Sir   Cousin of Tristan and nephew of King Mark of
Cornwall, son of Mark's brother and mortal enemy of
Isolde and Tristan

Arthur   Pendragon, High King of Britain, son of Uther
Pendragon and Queen Igraine of Cornwall, husband to
Guenevere, father of Amir, and leader of the Round Table
fellowship of knights

Blanche, Princess of France   Daughter of King Hoel of
Little Britain in France, sister of Kedrin, courted by King
Amaury and the Chevalier Saint Roc, but determined to
have Tristan as her love

Brangwain   Lady in waiting and personal maid to Isolde,
formerly maid to Isolde's mother and nursemaid to Isolde
when she was a child, born in the Welshlands and thought
to be "Merlin's kin"

Breccan, Sir   Knight of Ireland, brother of Sir Tolen,
youngest son of the clan of Companions of the Throne,
greedy for power and determined to make himself Isolde's
king

Cormac   Chief Druid of Ireland, formerly of the Summer
Country, deeply loyal to Isolde

Darath   Prince of the Picts, only son of the King, young
warrior feared in Ireland as threatening to attack

De Luz, Jean, King of the Basques   Old friend of King Hoel and husband of the late Queen Roxane

Doctor   Chief healer at the infirmary run by Blanche in France where Tristan is taken to recover from his head wound, friend to Tristan against the impulses of Blanche

Dominian, Father   Christian priest, head of the Christian community in Cornwall and Father confessor to King Mark, abandoned as a child and cared for by Brother Jerome

Doneal, Sir   Veteran knight of Ireland, member of the Queen's Council

Duessa   Lady of the Castle Plaisir de Fay who seeks to entrap Tristan and win him to her bed

Eamonn of the Ridge, Sir   Knight of Cornwall who competes against Tristan in the tournament held by Mark

Elizabeth, Queen of Lyonesse   Late mother of Tristan, wife of King Meliodas and sister of King Mark of Cornwall, lost in the forest when her husband was imprisoned, and died there giving birth to Tristan

Elva, Lady   Mistress of King Mark, lover of Sir Andred, wife of a courtier, and enemy of Isolde

Eustan, Father   Leader of Christian community in Ireland approached by Breccan to overthrow the Mother-right, but loyal to Isolde as Queen

Falsamilla   Chief lady in waiting to Duessa, hostile to men but in love with Tristan and determined to make him her knight

Fer de Gambon   Knight of Sir Andred employed by Mark to bear false witness against Tristan at the court of Igraine, and exposed by her

Fideal, Sir   Knight of Ireland, formerly the late Queen's champion and chosen one, who comes out of retirement to defend Isolde against Breccan

Friya Nurse to Breccan and his brothers long ago, fiercely loyal to him and living a hermit's life, mad and alone

Gervase of Saint Katz Knight of Cornwall who competes against Tristan in the tournament held by King Mark

Gilhan, Sir Leader of the Queen of Ireland's Council, knight of Ireland and loyal to Isolde

Glaeve Sword of power given to Tristan by the Lady of the Sea, inscribed with runic script

Greuze Sans Pitie, Sir Rogue knight injured in the Holy Land, lord of Castle Pleure, who waylays Isolde and Tristan and is killed by Tristan

Guenevere Queen of the Summer Country, daughter of Queen Maire Macha and King Leogrance, wife of Arthur, lover of Sir Lancelot, mother of Amir and friend to Isolde from their girlhood days studying with the Lady of the Lake on Avalon

Hoel, King of Little Britain in France Father of Blanche and Kedrin, friend of King Jean de Luz

Igraine, Queen Queen of Cornwall, wife of Duke Gorlois, beloved of King Uther Pendragon, mother of Arthur, Morgause, and Morgan le Fay, and supporter of Isolde

Ireland, Queen of See Queen of Ireland

Isolde, "La Belle Isolde" Princess of Ireland, daughter of the Queen and the Irish hero Sir Cullain, lover of Tristan, wife of King Mark and Queen of Cornwall and later of Ireland in her own right

Jerome, Brother Christian hermit and holy man, foster father and spiritual counselor of the abandoned Dominian

Kedrin, Prince Brother of Blanche and devoted to her, good son of King Hoel of Little Britain

Lady of the Lake Ruler of the Sacred Island of Avalon in the Summer Country, daughter of the Lady of the Sea, and priestess of the Great Mother

Lady of the Sea Ruler of the sea, mother of the Lady of the Lake, and chief priestess of the Great Mother

Lancelot of the Lake, Sir Knight of the Round Table, lover of Queen Guenevere, son of King Ban and Queen Elaine of Benoic

Losiwith, Sir Knight of Cornwall who competes against Tristan in the tournament held by Mark

Lyonesse, Queen of See Elizabeth

Mark, King King of Cornwall, brother of Elizabeth, Queen of Lyonesse, uncle of Tristan and Andred, lover of Lady Elva, and husband of Isolde

Meliodas, King King of Lyonesse, husband of Elizabeth and father of Tristan, rescued by Merlin from imprisonment when his wife was lost in the forest and gave birth to Tristan

Merlin Welsh Druid and bard, illegitimate offspring of the house of Pendragon, adviser to Uther and Arthur Pendragon, former lover of the Queen of Ireland, and protector of Tristan

Nabon, Sir Leader of the Council of King Mark of Cornwall, supporter of Isolde

Odent, Sir Knight of Ireland, former champion and chosen one of the late Queen, murdered by Breccan for opposing him

Penn Annwyn Lord of the Underworld in Celtic mythology, the Dark Lord who comes to take his children home

Picts, the Fiercely war-like tribe of the north of modern Scotland, ancient enemies of Ireland, called Picti, the "Painted Ones," by the Romans for their custom of vigorously tattooing their faces and bodies in a variety of colors

Plethyn of the Pike, Sir Knight of Cornwall, treacherous opponent of Tristan at the tournament in Cornwall

Queen of Ireland, the late Mother of Isolde, ruler of the Western Isle in her own right, descendant of a line of warrior queens, wife of the dead hero Cullain, and lover of many Companions of the Throne

Queen of Lyonesse See Elizabeth

Quirian, Sir Knight of Cornwall, member of the Council of King Mark, much obsessed by genealogy

Ravigel, Sir Knight of Ireland, leader of the band of Breccan's knights, kinsman of Tiercel

Roxane, Queen Late wife of King Jean de Luz of the Basques

Saint Rocquefort, Jacques, King of Ouesterland Suitor to Blanche who eventually carries the day, King of a poor region in eastern France

Systin of the Chapel, King Knight of Cornwall who competes against Tristan at the tournament held by King Mark

Tiercel, Sir Knight of Ireland, follower of Breccan and kinsman of Sir Ravigel

Tolen, Sir Knight of Ireland, formerly champion and chosen one of the late Queen, descendant of the clan of Companions of the Throne and older brother of Breccan

Tristan, Sir Knight of Lyonesse, son of King Meliodas and Queen Elizabeth, nephew of King Mark of Cornwall, favored by the Lady of the Sea, and lover of Isolde

Ubert, King   Onetime lover of the late Queen of Ireland in her youth, now deceased, former dear friend and companion of King Hoel

Uther   Pendragon, King of the Middle Kingdom, High King of Britain, lover of Queen Igraine of Cornwall, kinsman of Merlin and father of Arthur

Vaindor, Sir   Knight of Ireland, former champion and chosen one of the Queen, member of her Council and hopeful of attracting Isolde

Wisbeck, Sir   Veteran knight of the Council of King Mark of Cornwall

Yder, Sir   Knight of the Welshlands serving Sir Greuze Sans Pitie who takes Tristan as his lord after Greuze's death

List of places

Avalon   Sacred isle in the Summer Country, center of Goddess worship, home of the Lady of the Lake, modern Glastonbury in Somerset

Bel Content, Castle   Name chosen by Tristan to replace the name of Castle Pleure when he becomes lord of the fortress of Sir Greuze Sans Pitie in Cornwall

Caer Narvon   Welsh town and citadel, home of Sir Yder, modern Carnarvon in North Wales

Camelot   Capital of the Summer Country, home of the Round Table, modern Cadbury in Somerset

Castle Bel Content   See Bel Content

Castle Dore   Stronghold of King Mark, on the east coast of Cornwall above modern Fouey

Castle Pleure   Ancient fortress and grange deep in the heart of the wood, retreat of the cruel Sir Greuze Sans Pitie until his defeat and death at Tristan's hands, renamed Castle Bel Content by Tristan when he becomes its lord

Cornwall   Kingdom of Arthur's mother, Queen Igraine, and of her vassal King Mark, neighboring country to Lyonesse

Dubh Lein   Stronghold of the Queens of Ireland, modern Dublin, the "Black Pool"

Erin   Ancient name of Ireland after its Goddess Eriu

Gaul   Large country of the continental Celts, incorporating much of modern France and Germany

Hill of Queens   Primeval burial ground of the Queens of Ireland since time began

Little Britain   Territory in France, location of the kingdoms of King Hoel and Sir Lancelot, modern Brittany

Lough Larne   Castle and estate in Ireland given to Sir Tolen by the late Queen, taken over by Breccan after his brother's death

Lyonesse   Kingdom below Cornwall, home of Tristan, inherited by him from his father, King Meliodas

Middle Kingdom   Arthur's ancestral kingdom lying between the Summer Country and Wales, modern Gwent, Glamorgan, and Herefordshire

Ouesterland   Kingdom of Saint Roc in eastern France

Summer Country   Guenevere's kingdom, ancient center of Goddess worship, modern Somerset

Tintagel   Castle of Queen Igraine on the north coast of Cornwall

Welshlands   Home to Merlin and Brangwain, modern Wales

Western Isle   Modern Ireland, the sacred island of the Druids and home to Goddess worship and a uniquely Celtic form of Christianity

the celtic wheel of the year

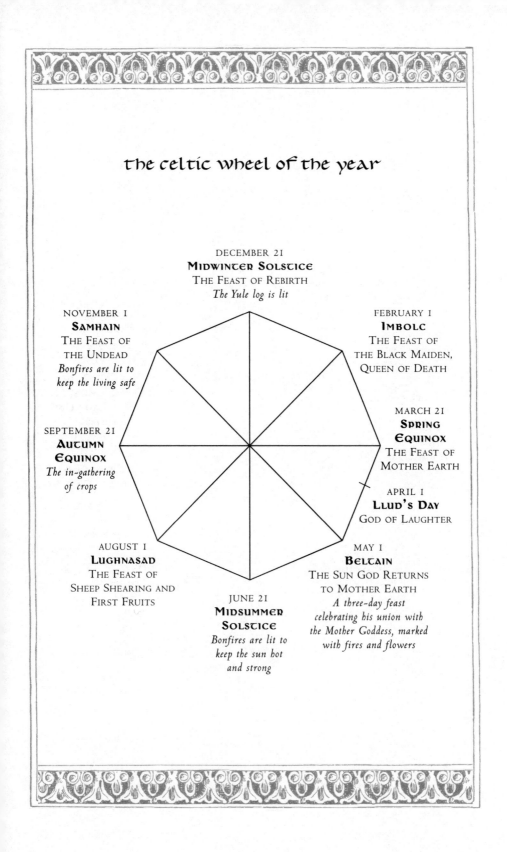

DECEMBER 21
MIDWINTER SOLSTICE
THE FEAST OF REBIRTH
The Yule log is lit

NOVEMBER 1
SAMHAIN
THE FEAST OF
THE UNDEAD
*Bonfires are lit to
keep the living safe*

FEBRUARY 1
IMBOLC
THE FEAST OF
THE BLACK MAIDEN,
QUEEN OF DEATH

SEPTEMBER 21
**AUTUMN
EQUINOX**
*The in-gathering
of crops*

MARCH 21
**SPRING
EQUINOX**
THE FEAST OF
MOTHER EARTH

APRIL 1
LLUD'S DAY
GOD OF LAUGHTER

AUGUST 1
LUGHNASAD
THE FEAST OF
SHEEP SHEARING AND
FIRST FRUITS

MAY 1
BELTAIN
THE SUN GOD RETURNS
TO MOTHER EARTH
*A three-day feast
celebrating his union with
the Mother Goddess, marked
with fires and flowers*

JUNE 21
**MIDSUMMER
SOLSTICE**
*Bonfires are lit to
keep the sun hot
and strong*

the christian wheel of the year

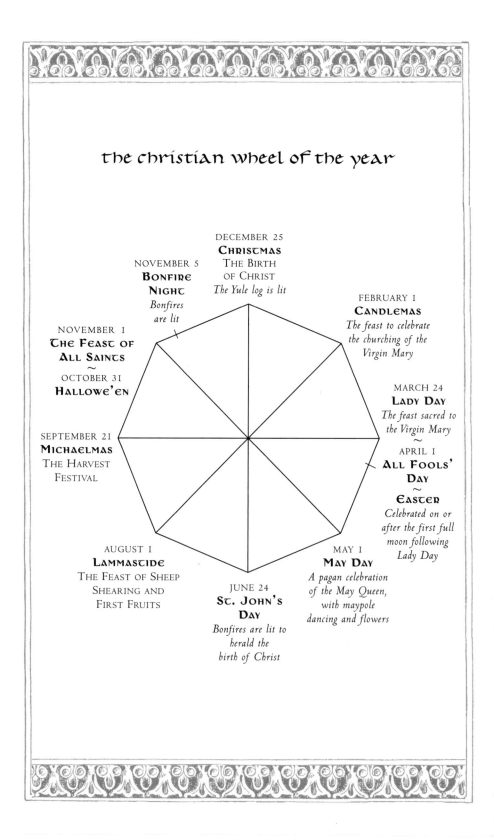

DECEMBER 25
CHRISTMAS
THE BIRTH
OF CHRIST
The Yule log is lit

NOVEMBER 5
**BONFIRE
NIGHT**
*Bonfires
are lit*

FEBRUARY 1
CANDLEMAS
*The feast to celebrate
the churching of the
Virgin Mary*

NOVEMBER 1
**THE FEAST OF
ALL SAINTS**
~
OCTOBER 31
HALLOWE'EN

MARCH 24
LADY DAY
*The feast sacred to
the Virgin Mary*
~
APRIL 1
**ALL FOOLS'
DAY**
~
EASTER
*Celebrated on or
after the first full
moon following
Lady Day*

SEPTEMBER 21
MICHAELMAS
THE HARVEST
FESTIVAL

AUGUST 1
LAMMASTIDE
THE FEAST OF SHEEP
SHEARING AND
FIRST FRUITS

JUNE 24
**ST. JOHN'S
DAY**
*Bonfires are lit to
herald the
birth of Christ*

MAY 1
MAY DAY
*A pagan celebration
of the May Queen,
with maypole
dancing and flowers*

about the author

ROSALIND MILES is the author of the bestselling Guenevere trilogy, as well as *Isolde, Queen of the Western Isle,* the first book of the Tristan and Isolde trilogy. A well-known and critically acclaimed novelist, essayist, and broadcaster, she divides her time between homes in England and California.

FIC MILES
Miles, Rosalind.
The maid of the white hands

DATE DUE